Before the
Sun Falls

Before the Sun Falls

William James

ORBIT

An *Orbit* Book

First published in Great Britain in 1993 by Orbit

Copyright © William James 1993

The moral right of the author has been asserted.

A CIP catalogue record for this book is
available from the British Library.

ISBN 1 85723 130 9

Typeset by Solidus (Bristol) England
Printed and bound in Great Britain by
Clays Ltd, St Ives plc

Orbit
A Division of
Little, Brown and Company (UK) Limited
165 Great Dover Street
London SE1 4YA

CONTENTS

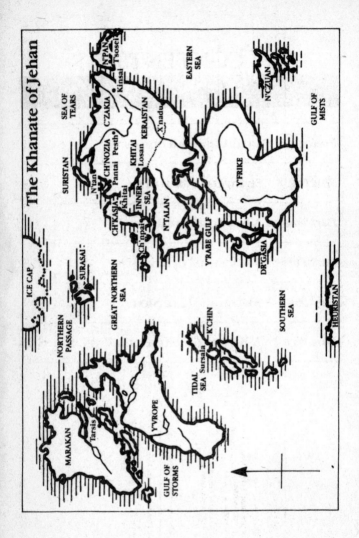

The Khanate of Jehan

The Khanate of the Golden Clan of the Altun

Chart showing principal bloodlines and family relationships.

The names of characters appearing in the books of the SUNFALL trilogy are indicated by capital letters.

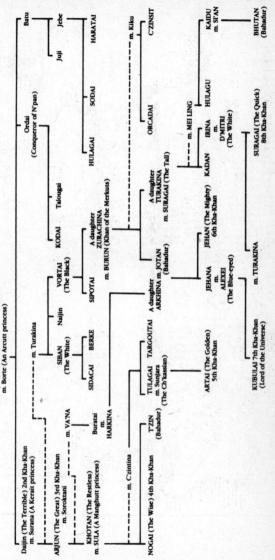

Note: Broken lines indicate second marriages and subsequent step-relationships.

Landscape with Dragon

It was in the last moments before the start of the engagement that Kubulai realised that his breeches were falling down. The fact that they were really someone else's breeches was neither here nor there - like every other man on board, Kubulai was wearing borrowed clothing because his own had been soaked by the heavy seas they had encountered all the way to K'chin. What mattered at the moment was the knowledge that as master of the trireme he was standing in full view of practically every member of the crew. The rowing benches were open to the air, and if there was a man whose eyes were not fixed on him at this crucial moment Kubulai was not aware of it. He twisted his left hand into his waistband, and then spat expressively over the side.

The trireme was the largest unpowered vessel in the world. It dwarfed even sailing ships, and the pirate galleys coming out from behind the headland to the west were only a third of its size.

'Lord, they are coming about,' the comite said.

'I see them.'

The K'chin galleys were two-masted, having both sails and oars. Kubulai wondered if their captains thought that the trireme had been rowed all the way from the Marakan coast. If they did they were fools. He hawked and spat again. The red sun which hung in the sky over the mainmast was brooding and angry, and there were no clouds. An intermittent breeze

3

blew, and the canvas of the great single sail flapped and rippled as air currents rising up off the water disturbed it. Kubulai was stripped to the waist, but it was because he had been unable to find a tunic to fit across his broad shoulders, not as a result of the heat. No Yek was affected by extremes of temperature. He twitched his loosely bound topknot back off his bare shoulder and narrowed his eyes to watch the gradually altering silhouettes of the three ships which were moving to intercept. He had darkened the gold clan tattoo on his eyelids with kohl to ward off the worst of the sun's glare. The red light bounced off the deep green of the water, and he put up his right hand to block the reflection.

'A point to port.'

The comite stirred as if he was about to disagree, and glanced towards the steersmen. Kubulai's principal officer was a Ch'kasian - which was to say he had no talons - a small olive-skinned man whose appointment to the rank of master's mate had been unusual enough to arouse comment in the court at Kinsai. Non-humans quite commonly captained commercial vessels, but there were still few officers of any seniority in either the land or the sea forces who were not of the races of the True People.

Kubulai flexed his free hand deliberately. His talons were sheathed in gold as befitted someone of Altun descent, and they glittered as they extended. The comite became still, and then he looked quickly away. There was little doubt that he had been placed on board as a precaution - because someone was wary of Kubulai's lack of sea experience - but it was to be hoped that he knew his place well enough to avoid offering deliberate offence. If he did not, then the flash of talons was a warning. Kubulai frowned, aware that he had allowed himself to become distracted. He gestured to the captain of the rowers. 'Increase speed.'

The drumbeat picked up steadily. If the pirates were watching, and probably they were, they would think that the master of the trireme was attempting to take his ship out of danger. It was unlikely that they realised they were chasing a military vessel. Triremes looked awkward and out of place away from the coastal waters of the mainland, and even if the K'chin had seen one before, they would think it easy prey. They were in for a surprise.

'Deck there! Two more ships on the starboard quarter!'

A lookout hung over the side of the cage which was at the head of the mainmast. He pointed.

The comite shaded his eyes with his hand. He stared at the new threat. 'Carracks or caravels maybe,' he observed calmly. 'They have us to windward.'

A light wind came off the islands in these parts. Kubulai could see that it was filling the sails of the oncoming ships. He waved to the captain of the rowers. 'Speed maximum.'

Each oar was manned by two men. None of them were slaves. The rowers braced their feet against the rests and heaved. The sweeps descended like a wave washing along both sides of the ship. The water hissed and frothed as it was stirred by the blades, and the trireme leapt forward.

Kubulai squinted at the sailing ships. They were almost certainly caravels - high at the prow, but with a relatively narrow beam - and they looked as if they would be uncomfortable in a really heavy sea. Even if

5

the pirates were berthed in one of the inlets which bordered the channel, they had emerged so quickly that it was as if they had come out of nowhere. Kubulai guessed that there were watch towers on the headlands. Nearly every civilian craft venturing within fifty verst of the K'chin group was being raided, and it followed that the pirates were getting a fair amount of advance warning that a vessel was approaching.

The trireme's sudden increase in speed seemed to take the captains of the attacking ships by surprise. The galleys fell to the rear, and even the caravels approaching to windward were forced to beat round onto a new course. Kubulai watched them critically. 'Ease to half speed.' He turned. 'Let the rowers have water. We have time before they come at us again.'

Orderlies carrying buckets ran down the staging between the rowing platforms. The rowers were a mixture of races – broad Dr'gasians, and here and there a Suristani with a body tattoo like a cloak across his shoulders and down his back. The only crew members who had talons were N'pani or Ch'noze. They contrasted wildly where they sat together, for the latter were big coarse-looking men with clan markings on their cheeks and foreheads, while the N'pani were pale-skinned, with eyes which folded up at the corners.

'Lord, do you want a drink?'

Kubulai's orderly held out a leather bottle.

'Orta, thank you.' Kubulai took the bottle and extracted the stopper. The spirit was k'miss, which was distilled from fermented st'lyan milk. He allowed a little of it to trickle across his tongue, savouring the sharp taste.

The comite grinned. 'Lord, we'll make a sailor of you yet.'

Kubulai made a face at him. He corked the flask and gave it back. 'I didn't know the ability to drink was a prerequisite.'

'It helps,' the comite said. He laughed softly, then turned and spoke in his own dialect to one of the steersmen. The man nodded and smiled.

'Indeed.' Kubulai wrinkled his nose. The moment he had let go of his waistband to uncork the k'miss bottle his breeches had started to slip again. He hitched at them, and remembered that they belonged to Kadan, who was almost twice the size of any other man in the Khanate. 'Jubal, find me a piece of rope. My pants are falling down.'

The steersmen sniggered, but the comite only raised his eyebrows. 'Lord, we thought you were trying out a new pose,' he said. He cut a length of light line from a coil on the rail and held it out.

Kubulai knotted the rope around his waist. 'That's better.' Now that he had both hands free he felt more poised. He glared at Jubal, damning him silently for his condescension, then glanced around at the enemy ships. 'They have the wind again. Full speed. We will have to make this look convincing, or they will run from us.'

Jubal looked as if he thought that the likelihood was remote. They were running down the wide channel between the principal islands. The K'chin cluster reared up out of the sea along an extent of latitude which stretched from near the equator all the way to the southern tropics. Two of the islands were bigger than Suristan, but the populations were small and seemed to rely upon the sea both for food and for many of the other necessities of life. The coastline was rocky, but there were small sand-filled bays and inlets everywhere. The southernmost islets were volcanic, and the slopes all the way down from the tops of the extinct cones were covered with lush greenery. So far as a Yek reconnaissance had been able to ascertain, they were uninhabited.

'They are gaining,' Jubal announced. He glanced past the steering position at the high platform which overhung the stern. The troopers who were assembled there had concealed themselves behind low bulwarks. To the rear of the platform a catapult had been levered into place, and an under-officer lounged beside a brazier filled with oil-soaked faggots. A lighted slow match smouldered between his fingers. The comite said, 'If we had a gun, there would be no need for this.'

Kubulai stared at him. The Khanate used explosives for a variety of purposes, mostly civil, but firearms were forbidden by the Yasa. He said, 'You've been listening to Kadan.'

There was no law against talking. Kadan's father was an offworlder, as Kubulai's was – in fact they were father and son – and Kadan made no secret of his belief that technology ought to be used, and not simply recorded and studied as the Sechem often seemed to think.

'I saw a gun once.' The comite looked stubborn. 'It was at T'ver, in the Alan country. They had it on wheels, and it threw an iron ball this big.' He spread his hands wide. 'Such a thing would surely sink a ship.'

The Alan campaign had taken place fifteen years before Kubulai's birth. He counted in his head and

8

thought that Jubal must have been little more than a boy at the time. 'We are the Kha-Khan's officers,' he said severely. 'It is our responsibility to uphold the law.'

'I am the Kha-Khan's officer,' Jubal rejoined. 'You are his nephew, Lord. There is a difference.'

Kubulai turned away, grinning. The comite had not been serious about the notion that the ship should be armed with guns. It was one of the drawbacks of being related to the Universal Khan. People often said things just to see what the reaction would be. Kubulai reflected that if the caravels had guns this would be both his first and his last independent sea command. Now that the subject had been raised it irked him. The Alan had employed firearms, but a Yek army equipped with bows and hand weapons had crushed them. No one could withstand the Yek, because they never surrendered. Defeat was not a concept they were brought up to understand. Kubulai watched the oncoming pirate ships. They were much closer now. He saw smoke rising from the forecastle of the leading vessel, and guessed at a catapult similar to the one on the trireme's afterdeck. If the K'chin intended to plunder the ship, they were unlikely to try to set it on fire first. Briefly Kubulai wondered if the enemy engineers were any good. He hoped not.

The distance to the first caravel was closing rapidly. It was a hundred and fifty drem, then a hundred...

Something tore through the sail above Kubulai's head, and a man standing at the starboard rail gave a kind of sigh and collapsed on the deck. Kubulai started. The range was fairly extreme, even in such calm conditions. He gestured to the troopers who were waiting at the rear of the quarterdeck, and they raised their shields. A missile thumped into one of them, and the trooper who was holding it exclaimed in surprise. Kubulai glanced round, and saw that what looked like a short arrow was sticking through the oxhide. It was about the length of a man's forearm, and it had only tiny metal flights.

'Name of God,' Orta said, awed.

'God has nothing to do with it.' Kubulai ducked as another bolt struck the mast and bounced off. He gestured to Jubal. 'Get an extra line of men with shields up here. I want two rows, one behind the other. Brace the shields up with timbers to protect the steersmen.'

It did not matter for the moment how the K'chin were achieving such range and accuracy. Kubulai thought that the first few shots had been fired to test the range, and he waited for a full volley to arrive. Another bolt thumped through the sail, and one struck an upraised shield, but the rate of fire did not increase.

'Lord, we have their range now.' The officer who had come down to report was bent practically double. Kubulai was taller than any of his men, but he forced himself to stand up straight. He nodded, feeling exposed.

'It's time we gave them some of their own poison,' Jubal said. He sounded relieved.

Kubulai ignored him. He moved so that he could see onto the afterdeck.

'Bows!'

Half of the troopers stood up. The rest got onto one knee. They drew and loosed with fluid grace, and the space between the two ships was bridged by arrows which flew like a swarm of hornets towards their target. Kubulai watched their flight critically. One of the caravel's foresails tore, and he swore. He shouted, 'Damn you, select your targets! Aim at the steersmen!'

A tall trooper standing at the stern rail cried out. He clutched at his chest, then pitched over into the water. A man ducked, but most of the others were shooting rhythmically. The leading caravel came abruptly into the wind, as if it was no longer under command. Its sails rippled, and a broad-shouldered Merkut yipped in triumph. Kubulai pursed his lips. It was no great achievement to kill a man on the deck of a ship at this range. He said, 'Keep shooting.'

The faggots in the brazier flared when they were ignited. Two men came struggling up the companionway, a pot of pitch on a pole supported between them. They set it carefully on the brazier. Thick smoke rose, and Kubulai knew that the K'chin would realise that there was a catapult on the high stern of the trireme. One of the caravels veered to port. It heeled, shipping water as a gust of wind filled the sails. A bolt fired from the other ship whipped over Kubulai's head and he flinched instinctively. He watched the steady volleys being fired by the troopers, a frown on his face. Probably Jubal was right. A single gun would enable them to stand off and sink or disable all the oncoming pirates. Kubulai suddenly remembered the galleys, and searched the water for them. They were still some way to the rear.

Kubulai knew that his initial reaction to the subject of guns had been the result more of upbringing than belief. In fact there was nothing in the Yasa which specifically prohibited firearms. The law spoke of combat between men with anything other than hand weapons; thus bows were permissible – just. Men

11

justified catapults with the argument that they were designed for use against fortifications rather than people, and the same excuse was used for military explosives – mines and demolition charges. It was nonsense of course. Kubulai had seen catapults hurling powder shells and naphtha at advancing enemy formations, and knew they were devastating. They were also contrary to the law.

The catapult went off with a crash. Its missile was a ball of rags and old cordage which had been immersed in pitch and set alight. It streamed fire as it arched through the air.

There was no need to achieve a direct hit to do damage. Chunks of burning pitch and cordage were sprayed across a wide area. The sails and rigging of the leading ship burst into flames.

Now the caravel which had moved out to port was angling in towards the trireme's stern. The water boiled past the keel, and Kubulai eyed the bow wave and guessed that there was an iron ram projecting forward below the surface. The pirates on the forecastle were using what appeared to be some kind of bow, but they were firing it from the shoulder. The trajectory of the bolts was flat, and they crossed the space between the ships very fast, although it seemed to take the archers a long time to reload.

'Crossbows.' Jubal came up to Kubulai's side. 'They are made of metal, and the string is woven from wire. There is a delay between shots because they have to be cranked back with a handle.'

'They're damned accurate.' Kubulai did not turn. 'If there were more of them we would be in trouble.'

So long as they kept the high stern towards the attacking ship, the rest of the trireme would be protected. The comite eyed the caravel. 'They are going to try to come alongside. If they attack while we have our oars in the water – '

'I know.' Kubulai watched the prow of the enemy ship. He waited until it was less than ten drem from the oar blades, then turned. 'Ship oars!'

The rowers yanked the sweeps out of the water and pulled them back through the ports. They threw their oar shafts to the men on the opposite benches. The ship was just wide enough to accommodate the oars horizontally across the rests. The trireme lost way.

Kubulai stared at the approaching pirate. The caravel was coming round so that it was edging in parallel to their port side. Men holding grapnel hooks were ranged along the rail.

'Hard a-starboard!'

The trireme stopped as if it had run into a wall. What little forward motion that remained had been converted by the big rudder into a turn. The bow swung away from the caravel, which slipped past their stern, heeling as the helmsman tried vainly to follow them round.

The troopers on the afterdeck were shooting at point-blank range. Pirates in the rigging and exposed on deck fell or toppled into the sea. A single grapnel arched out across the space between the ships, its tines embedding in the bulwark not far from the catapult. The under-officer at the brazier ran across and chopped at the rope.

'Oars! Give way together!'

The oars went back into the water with a splash. The rowers heaved on the shafts and the trireme started to move. Both caravels had turned into the wind. 'They'll have to wear ship before they can follow us,' the comite said. He grinned. 'That was well done, Noyon.'

It was intended as a compliment, but Kubulai looked down his nose. 'Next time remember that I was appointed master, not you.'

Jubal seemed to flinch, as if he had been struck a blow. He nodded shortly. Kubulai glanced back at the K'chin. He cupped his hands to his mouth. 'Port your helm! Increase speed!'

The trireme's head came round until it was moving down the channel again. It drew away from the sailing ships, the troopers on the stern firing steadily until they were out of range.

They were going to draw level with the headland at the southern end of the main island before they were caught again. Kubulai stared at the galleys. They were coming on without hesitation, and the wind off the shore was helping them along. The caravels had beaten around onto a following course and they were gathering way again. Both had suffered damage, and they seemed to handle less well than before. The officer who was commanding the troopers on the stern platform came to the head of the stairway which led to the steering position. He said, 'Lord, we lost eight men.'

Kubulai grimaced. It was a lot to lose in one small engagement. The crossbows had made the difference, allowing the pirates to start shooting sooner. 'Very well.' He nodded dismissal. The steady beat of the rowing master's drum boomed in his ears. Kubulai tried to ignore it, and listened instead for the rush of the water past the keel. He stared along the lines of rowing benches, seeing nothing.

Jubal said, 'Noyon, you did not decide on this plan.'

14

He spoke softly, hardly above a whisper. 'It is not your fault the men died.'

'Hunh.' Kubulai knew that the comite meant well, even though he was wrong, and he swallowed the retort which had risen to his lips. A breath of cold air ran across his back and he shivered. He said, 'You were right about the gun. We could have killed them all.'

The comite spat expressively over the side. 'We are going to kill them anyway,' he said.

The trireme ran at full speed down the channel, the pirates in pursuit. Kubulai watched the caravels positioning themselves, and he guessed that the K'chin intended to delay their escape with a co-ordinated attack so that the slower galleys could catch up. He eyed the headland to starboard. If it hid more enemy vessels they were in trouble. Kubulai hitched at his breeches. 'Treat me with respect in future or you will suffer for it,' he said to Jubal. 'Remember who is my uncle.'

Wind caught the sail above their heads. The corner of Jubal's mouth twitched. 'Noyon, your uncle appointed me,' he replied placidly.

Kubulai clenched his teeth. If Jehan had authorised the comite's commission then Kubulai's father doubtless also knew, and had approved the measure.

'Noyon, I'm only here to advise,' Jubal said. He sounded amused.

They were now five hundred drem or so ahead of the leading pirate ship. Kubulai watched as the headland came level. A signal light flashed. He gestured sharply to the steersmen. 'Ready about!'

The drumbeat paused and the sweeps came swiftly out of the water, the rowers resting across the shafts to hold them level. Kubulai waited, judging the

15

moment. He saw the light beyond the headland flash again.

'Hard a-port!'

The steersmen strained against the tiller bar. At the same moment the port sweeps began to back water, while on the starboard side the oarsmen let their oars dip, then pulled in unison. The combined effect of the three sets of forces pulled the trireme round so hard that the timbers created.

It was probably the last thing the K'chin expected. The caravels veered away, one right and one left. Even the galleys seemed to check.

'Three ships on the port quarter!'

The sighting should have come sooner, Kubulai thought, and he guessed that the lookouts had been concentrating on the pursuit rather than on their proper task. 'Ours,' he said shortly.

'God, I hope so,' Jubal murmured.

Somebody laughed.

Kubulai glanced once towards the headland. The plumes of smoke marking the three vessels coming out into the channel should have been indication enough for anyone who was in doubt. The pinnaces which had towed the trireme from Losan were under full steam. They came up on both sides, paddle wheels churning, their decks packed with men.

'Enemy in front!'

The pirates seemed to realise that they had been lured into an ambush. They turned away. Both caravels were heading into the wind now, and their captains had the unenviable choice of either allowing their ships to be caught aback or tacking across the oncoming trireme's bow. One selected the former course, and the other the latter.

16

'Ramming stations!'

The K'chin captain could not have realised that a military galley was built for this purpose above all. The *Losan* was travelling at almost full speed when it struck the enemy vessel amidships. Kubulai was hanging onto the rail, prepared like everyone else on board for the impact, but still he lost his footing. He slid the length of the steering position before recovering.

The noise of the crash was followed by the sound of rending timbers, and then the beat of the rowing master's drum began an altered cadence. The trireme backed off smoothly, and the sea rushed into the hole the ram had torn in the pirate's side. The caravel started to sink.

Some of the K'chin jumped into the water. They swam to the *Losan* and clung to the oars.

Jubal looked over the side at them. He turned, his face expressionless. 'Noyon?'

Kubulai gave him back the same stare. He said, 'They were warned to stop. You know the Yasa.'

The comite nodded. He gestured to the captain of the ship's guard, and made a cutting motion across his throat. Then he turned away.

It was quick. The archers lining the trireme's side went on shooting until nothing moved. The caravel's bowsprit dipped abruptly beneath the surface. The stern rose in the air, and then the whole vessel went under. An explosion of trapped air brought timbers, oddments and a few bodies to the surface. They drifted away on the current.

Kubulai watched, then made a face. At least at sea there remained little of the carnage which was the usual aftermath of fighting on land. The battlegrounds Kubulai had seen had been littered with the

dead, for while the Yek lifted their own for cremation, the enemy they left to feed the soil. Kubulai
could see the patiently circling predators in his mind's
eye, and he remembered the smell. Long after the
bodies of the dead had rotted away it was easy to
identify the place where a battle had been fought –
everything grew up through a matrix of dry bones.

The pinnaces had ignored the other sailing ship.
They charged after the galleys, pulling up alongside
them, and the noise of the engagement rang out across
the water.

The second caravel was wearing around slowly, for
it had lost rigging and sails to a fire. A crossbow bolt
aimed from the stern thumped into the trireme's
mast. Kubulai judged the distance.

'Starboard your helm!'

To use the catapult he would have to bring the
Losan about, Kubulai thought. He considered the
option, then discarded it.

Jubal said, 'Lord, we are too close to them to ram.'

Probably they were not, but they would be unable
to get up a great deal of speed. Kubulai said, 'We'll
board. Get a demolition charge ready.'

The comite raised his eyebrows. 'Are we trying to
impress someone?'

Kubulai glared. 'Just do it.'

They were coming up on the caravel from astern. It
was only just starting to gather way, and detained by
grapnels it was no match for their bulk.

Boarding was a mad scramble. They thundered over
the rail, yelling and striking out, and Kubulai was
never sure if he had killed or not. Tanned foreign
faces rose up in front of him, then fell away again.
Men screamed. He crossed the deck of the pirate ship

18

in the midst of a horde which seemed to sweep resistance aside as if it did not exist. At the far rail he turned, ready to go again. The maindeck of the caravel was a litter of cordage, broken spars, hatch covers and refuse, and across it lay strewn the dead. Most of them were K'chin.

Kubulai drew a great shuddering breath. He was amazed that he was alive. He looked around to see who else had survived, and found familiar faces – Orta, who must have been at his shoulder during the fight because he was so close; Jubal, whose sword and the hand which held it dripped gore.

Now Kubulai recognised other men who were less well known. He realised suddenly that everybody was watching him, and that they were waiting for his command. Jubal's face held an odd, almost enquiring expression. Then he said, 'Lord, I think we're finished here.'

'Yes.' Kubulai gestured with his sword, and thought that he could not remember drawing it. 'Get everyone back on board.'

A few of the pirates must have survived, but they made no attempt to interfere with the Yek evacuation. Surveyed from the deck of the trireme, the caravel looked like a hulk. Nothing moved on it.

Two engineers carried a mine across to the rail. When Kubulai looked over the side he saw that troopers had already been lowered on ropes to the waterline. They were holding the vessels apart with fenders, and a man stood with one foot on either hull, bridging the gap. He waited until the mine came down on the end of a line and then laid it against the caravel's side. A demolition charge was a hemisphere of metal packed with corned black powder. The design provided that two charges could be bolted together for use as a catapult missile. Now the trooper hammered spikes through the bolt holes so that the flat side of the mine was fastened against the timbers of the pirate's hull. He signalled, and was hauled slowly up again so that he could tack the fuse onto the caravel's side.

'Shove off.'

The grapnels had already been unhooked. Men shoved the caravel away with poles, the last trooper lighting the fuse of the mine before he was pulled inboard.

'Give way together.'

The trireme moved off, and Kubulai gazed back. The fuse was hard to see – a trail of grey smoke trickling down the side of the ship. Suddenly the charge exploded with a flat bang. A fountain of water rose up the caravel's side, and then it began to settle by the stern.

Kubulai looked for the other ships. Pinnaces were not designed for ramming, and so their crews had boarded the K'chin galleys and set fire to them. One galley was sinking. The other two were drifting, belching smoke. The paddle ships were lying three or four lengths away towards the coast of the main island. The haze from their smoke stacks drifted lazily down across the water.

'They could have taken the galleys in tow,' Jubal said. 'Why sink them?'

The K'chin had turned to piracy in defiance of the Kha-Khan's order. Now they were paying the price. 'You know the law,' Kubulai said sourly. He knew that the comite was upset because of the value of the enemy ships. It took months to build a galley or a

20

caravel, and a lot of timber was required. Jubal was scandalised by the waste.

'Damn them.' Jubal gave the burning vessels a last look, and then he turned away.

Kubulai wondered who the comite was cursing – the pirates or the crews of the pinnaces.

A pinnace suddenly belched smoke. Its paddles churned the water and it moved away past the K'chin vessels in a curve, then swung towards the trireme. Behind it the white wake dispersed slowly in the green of the sea. Kubulai watched the ease with which the paddle steamer forged against wind and current, and he frowned. Steamships had been in use for over fifteen years. They were necessary because nothing else was capable of negotiating the seas which effectively isolated the continent of Marakan. Steam power ensured that communication across the sea was as rapid as it was on land. It was also strange and outlandish, an offence to civilised eyes.

The problem lay in the Yek approach to the employment of technology, Kubulai thought. A scientific advance could never be used for its own sake, or because it improved upon existing technique. There had to be more justification – the need of the people – and even then application was not necessarily universal, but tended instead to be specific to the circumstance which required it.

Thus the navy employed steam, for it was justified; thus also there were no steam engines in use among manufacturers, or for civil purposes. Commerce was never a justification.

Jubal came to Kubulai's side. He eyed the approaching pinnace, then spat into the water.

Kubulai grinned. The men who were appointed to

21

the few steamships thought that they were a kind of elite in the navy of the Khanate. Traditional sailors like the comite thought otherwise, and the dispute regarding the opposing points of view had existed as long as powered vessels had been in use.

'That's Kadan.' Kubulai pointed. His uncle's towering figure was unmistakable, for the commander of the Kha-Khan's navy stood full head and shoulders taller than anyone else. His girth was in proportion to his height, and he wore his Altun red hair unbound, like a mane, so that he looked more like a p'ntar standing erect than a man.

The comite squinted against the glare of the sun on the water. 'He looks pleased with himself.'

'He usually does,' Kubulai responded.

Kadan's manner was a mask which deceived most people. Men who witnessed his cheerful and often innocent reaction to suddenly changing circumstances made the mistake of assuming that the Kha-Khan's naval commander was too direct and honest to be capable of intrigue or deceit. That was what they were supposed to think.

Probably Kadan was pleased at the way events had turned out, Kubulai thought. He watched as his uncle's arms moved in a kind of abbreviated semaphore – a signalling system not long adopted.

'Lord, we are ordered to follow the pinnace to land,' the lookout at the head of the quarterdeck reported.

Kubulai had already deciphered Kadan's signal. He nodded, and then turned and waved to Kadan as the paddle steamer churned past a few drem from the ends of the sweeps. Kadan was trying to shout something, but his words were lost – drowned by the thunder of the pinnace's engines. A cloud of smoke drifted across the rail, and Kubulai held his breath until it had been blown away on the wind.

The largest K'chin seaport was called Sursala. It was constructed along a rocky promontory which stuck out into the sea about two thirds of the way down the coast of the northernmost island. The south side of the headland was protected from the current, and it was this which was lined with wharves and warehouses. There was a small shipyard.

Behind the stone seafront lay the town – rows of oddly shaped houses with walls which seemed to swell out around a structure of heavy timbers. The roofs were steep, and were covered with either wooden shingles or reed thatch.

Kubulai stared. The external surfaces of the buildings glistened, although it was clear that they were not solid stone. Kubulai guessed at mortar applied roughly around the available materials – maybe timbers washed ashore or cannibalised from beached ships.

People lined the quays along the approaches to the main harbour. They stared in silence at the trireme and its escort of pinnaces.

'See how they hate us,' Jubal said.

If there were lookout posts on the headlands overlooking the channel, then the people knew the fate of their ships. Kubulai looked around the harbour and saw that there were few other vessels of any size. He said, 'They should not have defied the law.'

The K'chin were isolated from the rest of the world by great expanses of sea, and so they thought they could ignore the rule of the Kha-Khan.

Jubal looked as if he thought there was another

issue. 'They were given independence,' he observed.

'They were permitted to govern themselves,' Kubulai corrected. 'Everyone is subject to the Yasa. There are no exceptions.'

It had been Jehan's decision not to impose conquest upon Y'vrope or Marakan, and K'chin had received the same consideration. From one point of view it demonstrated that it was unnecessary to use force of arms to implement the Will of Heaven – that there were other ways to rule. At the same time there were khans who thought that the slow progress of world domination showed an element of weakness on the Kha-Khan's part. Only time would tell which approach reflected the greater truth. If Jehan was completely right, it ought to be possible to disband the armies. In fact they were still required to maintain order. If the dissenting khans were justified in their belief that their ruler was weak, the Khanate ought not to be flourishing. It was stronger than ever.

Kubulai believed that Jehan's attitude to conquest was right. He also thought that there should be no compromise with the Yasa. In any case it did not make sense to try to invade continents which were so far from the centre of power that more time and effort would be spent in transporting men and supplies than would be required for fighting.

Even if Jehan was right, the world probably would not know it until long after he was dead. Men who made changes were seldom honoured for them during their lifetimes.

The *Losan* was being warped into the wharf by troopers landed from one of the pinnaces. The K'chin stood by in surly silence, as if they did not know what was required.

'Don't they understand what is happening?' Jubal asked.

The K'chin had no excuse for pretending that they did not know the law. Kubulai said, 'If there are any doubts, they will soon be resolved.'

All three pinnaces had berthed now, and the men on them were moving onto the quayside in orderly files. They were fully armed. The watching people stirred nervously. More troopers trotted down the gangways of the *Losan*. They formed up, facing the crowd, and were reinforced almost at once by the trireme's rowers, who collected their arms from the racks at the end of the stagings as they ran.

They were expecting one ship – fifty men maybe – Kubulai thought. The K'chin could not have realised that a fully armed trireme carried closer to three hundred. The pinnaces which had circled the island under cover of darkness after separating from the tow each had a complement of around eighty.

'If they fight, we are still outnumbered,' Jubal said quietly. He was watching the K'chin as he spoke.

'They won't,' Kubulai responded, pretending confidence. He saw the comite make a face.

'Noyon, if you say it, it must be so,' he said.

Kubulai ignored the sarcasm. 'Kadan is disembarking.' He pointed. 'Let's go and listen.'

The K'chin were being given no reason to think that this was anything other than an official occasion. Kadan had now changed his clothes, and he moved onto the quayside clad in the splendour of the gold coat of the Altun. His loose silk breeches were stuffed into soft boots. Kubulai was already descending the gangway. He paused in mid-stride, aware that his own appearance in no way reflected his rank, then

25

tramped on. The K'chin were not here to be impressed; only to receive a lesson in the true meaning of power.

Troopers had cleared a space in the centre of the quay. Kadan walked into it, his attendants and officers in cavalcade behind him. The tassels of the banners were caught by the breeze, and the gold embroidery glittered in the afternoon sun. A sound like the buzz of insects rose from the crowd, and Kubulai realised that he was hearing the noise of a thousand awed whispers. Kadan stopped. He gave the K'chin who were crowded in behind the trooper's lances a long, cool stare. The murmur of comment died.

The guard commander's order rang out across the wharf. The troopers saluted and the officers bowed towards Kadan. He turned and nodded acknowledgement. A hawser looped around a bollard on the quay creaked.

Kadan said, 'Where are the aldermen of Sursala? Let them come forward.'

The summons was in Anglic, which was the language common to many of the races which were to be found on this side of the Great Sea. Kadan had not raised his voice, and it was apparent that his words were being transmitted through the crowd to a point in the rear. People began to move aside, creating a pathway. The men who walked down it were all robed. They came up to the troopers and then stopped, staring at Kadan. If they knew that it was customary to bow, they appeared not to care. An officer at Kadan's shoulder made an angry comment, but Kadan seemed not to hear.

The K'chin were thin – the flesh which covered their bones seemed not to run to fat even in old age, but instead became pouched and seamed as if the skin had lost all its elasticity – and their colouring was dark. Kubulai had thought that they were tanned. Now he saw that even the young children were brown. The faces of the men appeared to remain smooth into middle age, and where he could see people's eyes they were huge and liquid. The women were clad in flowing gowns, and covered their faces, but most men wore thigh-length tunics over white trousers which were like two tubes. The feet of many of them were bare.

'Are you the governors of this town?' Kadan had one hand on the hilt of his sword. He gave the aldermen an encouraging stare.

One of the gowned elders nodded. 'We are,' he said.

If Kadan was aware of an absence of respect, it did not show in his demeanour. 'Then approach.' He gestured to an officer.

The lances of the troopers moved just enough to allow the K'chin to file past. There were four of them, and Kubulai guessed that they were merchants or men of business, not nobles.

Kadan waited until they had advanced to within four or five drem. Then he said, 'You are the subjects of the Kha-Khan, and I am his representative. Bow to me.'

The aldermen stopped in their tracks. The face of one of them darkened, and his mouth opened as if to make a retort. Then he glanced uncertainly at the man beside him, who was clearly older. Nothing was said that Kubulai could see, but it was as if a warning had been transmitted. All four men produced bows of varying quality. When they straightened they were unable to hide the expression in their eyes.

'Now you may sit,' Kadan said. He showed his teeth.

There were no chairs. The K'chin looked around, and then it was clear that they realised that they were being humiliated. They squatted reluctantly in the dust.

The murmur of anger which rose from the crowd was the signal for a sharp command from an officer of the guard. The rattle of the troopers' weapons was counterpointed by abrupt silence.

The oldest of the four men had shoulder-length grey hair. He gave Kadan a wary look, then said, 'Lord, you have no right to treat us this way. We have the Kha-Khan's charter, and so we are not subject to your will.'

'Oh?' Kadan opened his eyes wide. He said, 'If you can prove your privilege, do so.' He turned his back on the sitting men, saw Kubulai, and grinned at him.

Kubulai walked quietly up between the ranks of the officers. Behind Kadan the aldermen had their heads together. One of them called out, 'Lord, the charter document can be brought ...'

Kadan did not even glance round. He waved an arm. 'By all means.'

An alderman in a light-blue robe got awkwardly to his feet. He bowed hesitantly in Kadan's direction, backed several paces, and then trotted away towards the edge of the crowd. It parted for him. A man shouted something in a dialect which was strange to Kubulai's ear, and the cry was repeated several times.

A smell of smoke invaded the quayside. Kubulai turned and glanced at the smoke stack of the nearest pinnace, and he saw that a grey haze was being picked up by the breeze. He wrinkled his nose.

The crowd was shifting impatiently, and the noise

of muted conversation was starting up again. Kadan began to unfasten his coat. Beneath it his chest was bare. He gestured to an orderly, and the man brought wine in a flask, and cups. After Kadan had been served, the flask was circulated to his officers. Kubulai accepted a cup. He sipped at the cool wine, appreciating its sweetness.

Kadan walked across. He said, 'Name of God, you look like a beggar. At least you could have changed your clothes.'

Kubulai scowled. 'What clothes? If I have any left that are fit to wear, I'll be surprised.'

'Oh, well.' Kadan gestured airily. 'You can have more made while you are here. You can afford it.'

What remained of Kubulai's wardrobe was sodden and salt-stained, and when he had last seen them the garments had been in a heap on the floor of his cabin, abandoned by his orderly. He said, 'If you had waited another month we would have sailed in fine weather. A trireme ships a lot of water in a heavy sea.'

The K'chin did not know it yet, but the galley was to be the principal unit of a permanent naval patrol around their coastline. 'A month's wait and more ships lost,' Kadan said. Then he grinned. 'You could have had a berth on one of the pinnaces.'

Every member of the Altun knew how Kubulai felt about steam. He gave Kadan a flat stare. A movement in the crowd made him look away. He said, 'They don't understand why we are here.'

'Then they are fools,' Kadan observed calmly.

K'chin piracy had been conducted on such a scale that it had been clear that even if the whole populace was not involved directly, they knew and profited from the crimes. The warning which had been sent

29

some months earlier had been couched in terms which had been designed to allow the men who governed the towns to pretend that they were not responsible. Probably that had been a mistake, even though they had been left in no doubt that they were to be held to account if the raids did not cease.

'We need more men,' Kubulai said. He watched the faces of the people and saw the hatred and defiance which was clearly displayed.

'We will have more men,' Kadan responded equably. 'The troop carriers are slow, but they will be here in less than a week. In the meantime I could hold this place with three troopers and a shaman's cart.'

Many of the men who would have been prepared to fight had probably died when their ships went down. Kubulai gave Kadan a haughty stare. 'I'm pleased you're so confident.'

Kadan laughed. Someone in the crowd behind him shouted something – a command or maybe a warning – and the people at the front pressed to the sides to create a path. The blue-robed alderman had been running. He jogged the last few drem to join the others, a wooden scroll case clasped to his chest. When he reached them he subsided, panting.

'Fasten your coat,' Kubulai said.

'If I do, I'll make you look like a pauper.' The wine cup in Kadan's hand was still half full. He drained it, and at once an orderly ran to take it from him.

Kubulai reflected that it did not really matter what the K'chin thought, and none of the troopers would dare to laugh. He went past Kadan and stood with his feet apart, watching the aldermen. The man with the grey hair got to his feet. He eyed Kubulai doubtfully, and then looked towards Kadan. 'Lord, examine our charter,' he said.

Kadan turned slowly. He had only partially re-fastened his coat. 'Bring it here.'

The charter was a single sheet of parchment. It was plastered with seals. Kubulai glanced at it as Kadan took it into his hands. The writing was Uighur script, which was the only accurate means of setting the Yek language down so that it could be interpreted. 'One of you knows our tongue,' he said to the alderman.

'Lord, yes.' The alderman nodded. 'Or we would not know what our charter contains.'

The language of the world's conquerors was supposed to be universal. In fact it was commonly spoken only in the Khanate, and even official documents were often supplied with a translation. Kubulai was fluent in not only Yek and Anglic but also five or six other dialects. It was a skill which was essential to anyone who hoped to rule, or to command men.

Kadan scarcely glanced at the scroll in his hand. He snapped his fingers in a prearranged signal, and at once an officer came through the ranks. He was holding a lit torch. Kadan applied it to the edge of the parchment, waited until it flared, and then let the burning paper float to the ground.

The grey-haired man looked outraged. 'Lord –' he began.

In front of Kubulai the other aldermen were scrambling to their feet. Kadan gestured economically, and a file of troopers came out from the side of the guard so that the three could neither come forward nor retreat to join the rest of the crowd. They drew into a knot, showing their fear.

'Once you had a charter.' Kadan's voice cut clearly across the protests which were rising. 'It is no more.'

The alderman tried an objection. 'This is not law-ful...'

Kadan gave him a hard stare. 'Do you speak to me of the law?' His voice rose in an anger which was real enough to deceive the K'chin into silence. The crowd had started to surge. Now the people fell back.

Kubulai eased his sword in its scabbard. Few of the K'chin appeared to be armed, but even rocks or stones torn from a wall could become weapons in a riot.

'Listen to me!' Kadan threw both arms up in the air. He took a pace into the open space the troopers had created. 'I speak for the Kha-Khan, whose servant I am. Those rights which were granted to you were at the Kha-Khan's pleasure, and you have forfeited them. Yesterday K'chin was a haven for pirates. Now you will live according to the law.'

The sound of his voice echoed off the walls of the houses which lined the quay. Gradually the people fell silent.

Grey Hair opened his mouth to speak, then closed it again. Kadan was watching the reaction of the crowd to his words. He turned. 'Deny that you received the Kha-Khan's order,' he said.

The alderman licked his lips. 'Lord,' he said, 'it is true that we were ordered to prevent further raids. Are we to be held responsible for our failure?'

'You were told you would be,' Kadan commented. He gave the alderman an expressionless stare.

'Lord, it is not just,' the alderman complained.

Kubulai scanned the crowd and saw that they were straining to hear what was being said. The heat of the sun fell warm on Kubulai's shoulders, and he began to feel more at ease. The surface of the quayside was earth which had been pounded flat, and where it had been disturbed by the movement of the people a red haze hung in the air.

Kadan seemed to be considering the alderman's appeal. Then he said, 'This morning we sank five ships. From which port came they?'

The grey-haired man hesitated. 'Lord,' he said at last, 'they were not all Sursala men.'

'Indeed.' Kadan showed his teeth in the grim pretence of a smile. 'I am glad that some of you are honest.'

The alderman flushed. 'Lord, we have always taken what we need from the sea.'

For a moment there was silence. Kadan was a full drem taller than the alderman and gazed down at him, a gleam of anticipation in his eyes. Kubulai was reminded of the manner of a cat forced to consider a very small mouse.

Abruptly Kadan turned so that he was facing the crowd once more. He said, 'I call those present to witness. In the name of the Universal Khan I take possession of this land. K'chin is fief to the Lord of the Earth.'

Some of the people cried out. The troopers stirred watchfully.

'Lord –' Grey Hair took a pace forward. 'How are we to be governed?'

Kadan gave him a glance. He said, 'K'chin will be a khanate. Your khan will demand of you a tribute – one half of your goods now, and every year one tenth. A third of your young men will be conscripted to serve the Kha-Khan on land or at sea. The people will be as slaves.'

It was a figure of speech. The Yasa permitted only races which had been conquered in war to be enslaved.

33

The alderman paled visibly beneath the tan of his colouring. He said, 'Lord, it is very harsh.'

'Oh?' Kadan showed his teeth. 'I could have ordered your towns burned and your people slaughtered. It was you who spoke first of the law. Do you not know the Yasa?'

It had happened at Surasai, on the islands far to the north. There the pirates had resisted to the last. The harbours had been put to the torch, and the few survivors had been transported. Kubulai remembered the carnage, and he was glad that it had not been necessary here.

Kadan started to unfasten his coat again. He eyed the alderman, then said, 'Tell the people to disperse. The town will be patrolled, and there will be a curfew. If you obey your khan and serve him, in time you will prosper.'

There was something in Kadan's manner as he spoke which made the alderman realise that his new overlord was present. His eyes strayed towards the officers in their finery. Some of them were of noble birth, and they bore their arms on the facings of their coats. 'Is one of them to be our lord?' the alderman asked.

The rope holding up Kubulai's breeches suddenly slipped. He untied it and hitched at his waistband, aware that Kadan had seen and was trying not to laugh. Kadan looked back at the alderman, and followed the direction of his eyes. He shook his head. 'Those men are my officers,' he said. 'It is not customary for the name of a khan to be proclaimed until a khanate is chartered, but if you wish you may greet him.' His eyes moved on past the alderman towards Kubulai clutching at his breeches, and it was clear that it was becoming hard for him to keep his face straight.

Probably the alderman thought to curry favour with his new lord, but his features displayed the suspicion that he was being mocked. He looked towards Kubulai for assistance. 'Lord, tell me his name.'

'I am called Kubulai,' the Kha-Khan's nephew said, and smiled as his breeches finally surrendered to the force of gravity and descended to his ankles.

Jehangir said, 'Khan, this is the largest house in town.'

The building was built only partially from stone, but it was one of the few which had a tiled roof. 'It will do,' Kubulai said. He had caught the hesitation in the guard commander's voice as he used the new title, and it amused him. Word of Kubulai's ennoblement had been kept secret prior to the arrival of the task force in Sursala, and the way in which different men were adjusting to the notion was interesting to watch.

'The chief man is called Sinkur.' Jehangir pushed the door open. A hinge creaked.

'I know. Thank you.'

The hall was filled with furniture. Kubulai eyed it, and wondered if whoever the house had belonged to had now discharged his obligation to tribute.

The guard commander was a Merkut. His eye-shading was silver, and he had jet-black hair which was secured with a gold clasp. His sword was very fine.

'You served my father when I was a boy.' Kubulai remembered the decoration on the hilt of the sword.

'Lord, it was your mother I served,' Jehangir said. He blushed under his tan.

Kubulai grinned. His mother was the Kha-Khan's sister, a grand-daughter of Burun, Khan of the

35

Merkuts. Before marrying Kubulai's father she had kept the kind of household usually only maintained by single men, and her conduct had been the scandal of Kinsai. Kubulai opened the door of one of the rooms and looked inside. 'Are there any servants?'

'Khan, there are a few. The master of your household –'

' – is on a transport in the middle of the Great Sea.' Kubulai looked round. 'Jehangir, this place is filthy. I don't expect luxury, but I do intend to be comfortable. Send somebody to find Orta, my orderly. He can show the servants what to do. Get rid of the furniture first. Burn it or sell it – I don't care. I want the rooms to look as if they belong in Pesth or Kinsai.'

The guard commander flushed at the reprimand in Kubulai's tone. He saluted, and then went out through the door in a hurry, bumping into Kadan who was coming the other way.

Kadan was gorgeous in crimson satin. His hair was freshly combed, and he had bathed. Kubulai could smell the soap. Kadan gazed after Jehangir. 'Trouble?'

'Not really.' Kubulai opened another door. The stale smell made his nose wrinkle. Too much furniture, he thought, and because it was upholstered it was almost impossible to keep clean. He propped the door open with a chair to allow the air to enter, then turned. 'I should have heeded your advice when we discussed this at Kinsai. I need attendants. The men who serve me now are soldiers. If it's warm and dry, they are happy.'

'I'll lend you some people until yours arrive.' Kadan grinned. 'How long will it take you to master all this?'

Kadan was talking about K'chin, and not about the house or the town. Kubulai shrugged. 'A month maybe.'

'Hunh.' Kadan nodded. 'I thought you'd say that. Do you want a slave so that you can learn the language?'

'Yes.' Kubulai considered. 'A man about my own age if possible – fairly intelligent, and co-operative.'

'Why not a woman?' Kadan asked. 'They're comforting.'

A woman would be a distraction. Kubulai said, 'I don't want comfort. I want to learn to speak K'chin.'

Kadan's brow furrowed. 'I forget how young you are. If you don't divert some of your energy, you're going to run your men into the ground.'

'From what I've seen, they are in need of some hard work,' Kubulai observed drily. 'They are very slack.' He walked past Kadan out of the door. A string of the long-eared equines the K'chin used as pack animals were toiling up the hill from the direction of the harbour. A file of troopers escorted them. They saluted Kubulai as they passed.

'It should not take long to bend the people to our will.' Kadan came out and stood in the shade of the doorway at Kubulai's shoulder. 'They are not warlike.'

Probably Kadan was only interested because he wanted to know how soon he could take back the steamships and the extra men. The pinnaces had left on a patrol around the bays and inlets which indented the coastline. Any interdiction of the other K'chin towns was going to have to wait until the arrival of the transports – Kubulai intended to place a garrison on each island. It was possible that further pirate havens remained to be located. Kubulai said, 'When I am satisfied, I will tell you.'

'Hunh.' Kadan laughed softly. 'I can't argue with that. It's your patrimony, not mine.'

'I'm pleased you remember.' Kubulai did not turn.

Kadan thought he could interfere because K'chin was surrounded by the sea. To govern it ships would always be necessary. 'It won't be a rich land at first,' Kubulai said.

'You haven't seen what the people have been bringing in as tribute,' Kadan commented cheerfully.

'Oh?'

'Gold and jewels,' Kadan said. 'Furs and ivory. Scented oils. They are pirates, after all.'

'They were pirates.'

Kadan snorted. 'Whatever you say.'

Kubulai was surprised that the K'chin were surrendering so much of value. Even if they wanted his favour it was strange. Then it occurred to him that whatever the people were giving up, it was probably nothing like the amount they were attempting to conceal. He frowned. There was always hoarding, but the bailiffs and stewards eventually caught up with it, or the system did. He eyed Kadan. 'So maybe it will be rich this year. The people don't farm, or not to speak of. We will have to teach them to support themselves without robbing others.'

It seemed likely that the K'chin had been raiding the sea lanes for years, even though their activities had not attracted the Khanate's attention. A ship which failed to return to its home port was usually judged to have been lost in a storm. It had never occurred to anyone that a human agency might be at work.

'You are young,' Kadan said. 'In ten years this will look like Suristan.'

'God, I hope not.'

There were resources on the islands, of course. The land was thick with timber, although there were laws

38

governing the amount of forest which could be cut down in relation to the size of the population. Basically K'chin would have to become self-supporting simply because it was so far from everywhere. It could not rely on trade.

Kadan walked out onto the path which led down to the gate. Suddenly he said, 'I am going up to Tarsis in a few days. When I return I will take you back to X'nadu.'

Tarsis was the harbour which the Yek were constructing on the east coast of Marakan. Ten verst of sheer cliffs had been blasted into the sea to provide an artificial platform which the current would not erode, and a generation of engineers had been employed on the project.

Kubulai was not sure why Kadan thought that the journey was worth mentioning. He produced an innocent stare. 'I have no business in X'nadu.'

'Huh.' Kadan raised his eyebrows. 'You can't stay here for the rest of your life.'

Now that K'chin was occupied there was no need for Kubulai to be present for more than a small part of each year. Every khan employed a bailiff and stewards to carry out the tasks of year-round administration, for even though it was an overlord's prerogative to decide how a fief was to be ruled, it was for others to concern themselves with the execution. Kubulai said, 'I thought I might stay until the end of summer.'

'What for?' Kadan looked impatient. 'The Kha-Khan needs you.'

'That's a matter of opinion.' Kubulai stared back stubbornly. 'I thought I was given K'chin so that I could prove that I am able.'

'Did you?' Kadan pursed his lips. 'You were given it

because you are Jehan's blood. Your ability has never been in question.'

Kubulai had already been told by Jehan that his role in K'chin was primarily as a military commander. He did not have to be present to be created khan. He said, 'Nothing has changed then.'

'Did you expect it to?' Kadan ran a hand through his beard, his expression pensive. He stared at Kubulai, then said, 'It's hard to be Altun. You are expected to be the best at everything you do, but no one wants to apply the discipline which you have to learn before you can excel. Don't resent your elders because they seek to make you act according to their will.'

'Hah.' Kubulai made a face. 'An occasional explanation would be nice.'

Birds wheeled and swooped over the rooftops of the houses further down the hill. Kadan watched them, then turned. 'That's part of the training,' he said. 'You are expected to work out the reasons for yourself.'

Kubulai wrinkled his nose. 'You make me sound like a petulant child.'

Kadan avoided his eyes. At last he said, 'It was never my intent.'

Whether it was or not, the result was the same. Kubulai said, 'I still don't see why I'm needed. The Khanate is at peace.'

Kadan gave him a long stare. He said, 'If that's what you really believe, then maybe you should stay here.'

The transports were bulky, broad-beamed vessels, only one of which was powered by steam. They crowded the anchorage, and barges and longboats ran busily back and forward between the wharves laden with men and supplies.

When the K'chin saw the st'lyan they were amazed. There were only small equines on the islands, and they were used more often as pack animals than for riding. By comparison the st'lyan were enormous. They danced and screamed as they were brought ashore, and their hooves struck sparks off the paving and cobbles of the street leading to the centre of the town.

The hall of the shipmasters' guild was situated at the end of the quay, and Kubulai stood on its steps to watch the progress of the unloading with Sinkur, the chief of the aldermen. The K'chin was clearly unsure of his exact status now that self-government had been revoked, and he had shed his robes and was dressed like most of the other men in a thigh-length tunic. His feet were bare. He stared at the gilded horns of the first mares as they were led past, then turned. 'Lord, what are these?'

People were hanging out of the windows to see the beasts as they passed. Kubulai said, 'We call them st'lyan.' He stared towards the place where they were being unloaded from the boats. There had been no room for anything other than the basic essentials aboard the trireme. A st'lyan required a stall and fodder, and it was not practicable to transport even the most docile of them in a galley.

Troopers coming up onto the quay were leading a single bay mare on long head-ropes attached to the animal's bridle. The st'lyan danced and sidestepped, and the men on the ends of the ropes looked nervous. The great horn tossed and dipped, and sunlight caught the gilding.

Sinkur said, 'Can such a creature be ridden by a man?'

41

'Oh.' Kubulai laughed. 'Most of them can.' He had been waiting for the bay to be ferried ashore. He walked down the steps.

Orta was following the men leading the st'lyan. He ran up. 'Khan, be careful. She's upset.'

'Indeed.' Kubulai snorted. He ducked in under the head-ropes. The bay reared up, hooves lashing.

Kubulai caught hold of the bridle. 'Easy!' The bay tossed its head and he was lifted off his feet. Orta cried out in alarm. The st'lyan screamed.

The mare was Jehan's gift, intended for breeding, and had never been ridden. Kubulai waited until the head dipped again, and then he sprang clear. A trooper walking behind came too close. The bay kicked out, and the man gave a cry and sat down hard on the ground.

Kubulai caught at the bridle again. He swatted the mare lightly across the nose. She snorted, then whickered and nudged at his shoulder. He laughed. 'Bring a saddle.'

'Khan, she's not ready,' Orta protested.

'She has bad manners, that's all.' Kubulai gave Orta a look. 'Five Merkuts, and you can't handle one lousy Altun st'lyan. Get the saddle.'

Orta threw up his hands in exasperation. He gestured to one of the troopers, and the man saluted. 'The Khan wishes.'

'Khan, if you're thrown ...' Orta started.

'If I am, you can catch me.' Kubulai looked over his shoulder and saw that a small crowd was gathering. He smiled grimly. The bay nudged at him again, and he held his hand to her muzzle. Her rough tongue scrubbed at his palm.

Jehangir came through the crowd with a saddle in

42

his arms. He dropped it on the ground. 'It's for this beast? Khan, you're mad.'

'I never saw the animal I couldn't ride,' Kubulai said.

Somebody in the screen of troopers offered a wager. The men on the head-ropes were straining back to keep the mare's head still. 'I'm a Mordvin, not a Merkut,' Orta said to no one in particular. 'And I've got more sense than to try this.'

A trooper said, 'Khan, she tried to kick the boat to pieces when we were bringing her ashore.'

Kubulai ignored them. He blew gently into the bay's nostrils, and felt her tremble. 'You perverted dragon's dropping,' he said to her. He rubbed the ridges between her eyes, then looked over his shoulder at Jehangir. 'Put the saddle on.'

Jehangir pursed his lips, then shrugged. 'Yes, Khan.' He picked up the saddle by the cantle and went up to the st'lyan's left side. Gingerly he settled the saddle on the animal's back and then bent to tighten the girths. The bay sidestepped in an attempt to trample him, but Jehangir simply moved back out of the way. He stood impassively until the bay was quiet again, and then stooped quickly and finished the task. He nodded to Kubulai.

'Give me the head-ropes.' Kubulai looped them over the mare's head.

Orta came up and took hold of the bridle. He said, 'Khan, if you are thrown off in front of all these people it will look bad.'

'Then I'd better stay on.' Jehangir was cupping his hands to boost Kubulai onto the bay's back. Kubulai grabbed the high cantle with the hand which was holding the ropes. He gave Jehangir a nod. 'Ready.'

The weight of a man on her back did not seem to

annoy the st'lyan at first. Her hooves rattled, but she did not try to lose her burden. Kubulai settled himself in the saddle, waiting. Jehangir had stepped back out of the way. He was watching critically. A murmur of comment ran through the crowd.

'Let her go.'

Jehangir touched Orta's arm. He said, 'The rest of you, stand clear.'

Orta let go of the bridle.

For a moment nothing happened. Then the bay seemed to jump stiff-legged straight up into the air. Kubulai clenched his teeth. When the st'lyan came down again the jolt went right up his spine. He held onto the cantle as the bay went round in a complete circle – a succession of ten or more jumps – while the troopers pressed back out of the way and people in the crowd whooped or cried out.

Kubulai reined in hard. The mare screamed and stopped dead in her tracks. She tossed her head, pulling the ropes through his fingers, and then turned and tried to bite him. Kubulai kicked her sharply in the barrel, tightening his grip on the ropes once more. The st'lyan started to buck, moving across the open quay so that the people watching were forced to jump back out of the way.

They were heading for the wharfside and the water. Kubulai tried to rein the mare around, but she did not respond. Orta and Jehangir ran in and jumped as one man for the st'lyan's head. They each got a hand to the bridle and swung on it, forcing the animal to a standstill. The bay snorted, her eyes wide.

'I've got her.' Kubulai wrapped the ropes twice around his right hand.

Jehangir looked at Orta, his eyebrows raised in an

44

unspoken question. Orta nodded, and they both let go. The st'lyan reared and screamed again. Now she was travelling back towards the front of the guild hall. The cantle of the saddle caught Kubulai in the pit of the stomach, and he gasped and hung on. Suddenly he was being thrown sideways. Either the bay was falling or it was trying to roll on him. He kicked his feet out of the stirrups and stepped clear.

The mare got up almost at once. Kubulai waited until she was on the rise, and then he hopped back into the saddle. By the time the st'lyan was upright his feet were deep in the stirrups again. The bay bucked half-heartedly, then stopped. She looked back over her shoulder at him, blowing through her nostrils.

Kubulai waited. The st'lyan tossed her head, but her feet did not move and it became clear that she had finished. Kubulai tapped her in the side with his toe. At first she did not move. She shook her head as if she was being bothered by flies. Kubulai nudged her again, and she walked sedately forward. A man in the crowd cheered.

Kadan came suddenly out of the crowd to the st'lyan's head. He caught at the bridle. 'I don't know who you are trying to impress, but I should think you've succeeded.'

'Uncle, thank you.' Kubulai dismounted stiffly. Now that the thing was done, he could not imagine a reason.

People were starting to applaud, and Orta and Jehangir were standing side by side, looking pleased with themselves. Kubulai turned and looked towards the guild hall steps. Sinkur's features were expressionless; then it was as if he had only just become aware that Kubulai was staring at him. He touched the

45

fingertips of both hands to his forehead, to his lips, and then to his chest, and he bowed.

Kadan said, 'Tell me what you are thinking about.'

'What?' Kubulai swung round.

'You have that slack-jawed look you get when you are thinking.' Kadan was watching Kubulai intently as he spoke.

It was the tenth day since their arrival at Sursala. The new khanate had been proclaimed with much ceremony at midday, and because it was the custom Kubulai had decreed a festival. Both he and Kadan had given a tun of wine, and the townspeople were just tapping into the second one. 'I won't tell you if you insult me,' Kubulai said.

Kadan laughed.

Nearly everybody on the island was in town. Shepherds and woodcutters had come down from the hills; even the charcoal-burners Kubulai had known existed but had never seen had left their kilns. The meadow to the west of the town was swarming with people. They caroused drunkenly in the streets, and Kubulai had ordered a boat to patrol so that anyone who fell off the quay could be pulled out of the water.

'Well?' Kadan was sitting beside Kubulai on a bench which had been placed against the wall of his house. He stretched his legs.

Kubulai said, 'I was thinking of offering to build a house for the Sechem in one of the valleys south-west of here.'

'The land would suit them, it's true.' Kadan nodded thoughtfully. 'Also the K'chin are unused to the law. The presence of Sechem here would help to spread understanding of the Yasa.'

Kubulai wrinkled his nose. 'I would be happy if they would train clerks for my chancery,' he commented. 'Yek boys won't want to come here.'

'Ah.' Kadan smiled. 'I thought it was something of the kind. You've never been altruistic before.'

Behind the wine wagons there was an expanse of beaten grass. A group of men were staggering across it with something heavy. Kubulai watched them and then looked back at Kadan. 'If I can get my administration running smoothly I can forget about everything else,' he said. 'These people don't really care who governs them so long as there is no oppression.'

Orta came across to the wall. He said, 'Khan, come and see.'

Kubulai stood. 'What is it?' He followed Orta past the wine carts and saw that the men were standing around a double ox yoke which was wound around and around with chains. Kubulai walked up to it.

Jehangir was in the process of stripping to the waist. He grasped the yoke at the centre and heaved. It rose about a hand's-breadth off the ground. 'Name of God,' Jehangir gasped. He let go and stepped back. Troopers slapped him on the shoulder. A jug of wine was circulating. Jehangir drank from it, then grinned at Kubulai. 'See what you can do with it, Khan.'

There were both Yek and K'chin in the small crowd. They shouted cheerfully, challenging him to it. Kubulai walked around the yoke. He pushed at it with his foot, but it did not move.

Kadan was coming across the grass. Kubulai took off his shirt and dropped it on the ground. A young woman loitering nearby lowered her veil and gave him a look charged with feigned longing, but he ignored her. He bent and gave the yoke an exploratory heave. Nothing happened.

'Lord, you could try breathing on it,' a man shouted. Everyone laughed.

'God's Name.' Kubulai wrapped his hands around the wood. He straightened slowly, feeling the pull on the muscles of his back. The chains clinked and the men yelled as the yoke rose. Kubulai got it waist high. He thought about trying to yank the huge weight up to shoulder level, and knew that it was barely within his ability. He dropped the yoke and stepped back, then slapped Kadan on the chest. 'You do it.'

Kadan did not even bother to take off his shirt. He went up to the yoke, a smile on his face, and reached down and lifted it smoothly to his shoulders. Then he grinned at Kubulai, strained, and straightened his arms above his head. The crowd cheered. Kadan turned around once under the yoke, then set it down. At once the other men rushed to try.

Kubulai applauded. He bent down and picked up his shirt. Kadan was drinking from the wine jug. His skin glowed golden in the afternoon sun. Kubulai pulled on his shirt and waited until Kadan was ready to leave. As many K'chin as Yek were crowded around, cheering him.

They walked together back across the grass towards the wall. Kadan said, 'I did not believe it, but you are right.' He shook his head, amazed. 'These people do not care who rules them. I think they have already forgotten they used to be allowed to govern themselves.'

There were three or four places across the meadow where great circles of women were dancing, chanting tunefully and swaying their bodies in time. They were colourfully gowned. Kubulai watched them, but he was thinking about what Kadan had just said. 'They're not very warlike,' he observed at last.

It was hard for Kadan to understand the people's lack of animosity towards their masters. Most men of Kadan's generation would have reacted the same towards a creature which demonstrated a preference for servitude over freedom, because they would have failed to appreciate that for most of the K'chin the establishment of a khanate meant simply a change from one form of government to another. Many thought there was no difference. Probably some of the K'chin did hate the Yek, Kubulai thought, but they knew better than to show it. The rest only wanted to live in peace.

The chancery occupied a large room at the back of Kubulai's house. The room was timbered from floor to ceiling, so it was easy to keep clean. All the furniture had been removed, and now there were only long tables and a few chairs. The bailiff was a Yek called Ordai. He was in late middle age – a well-dressed man with a rotund physique and a pale moon face. His normally slightly bemused expression hid the presence of an astute mind. He had eye tattoos which showed that he was a member of the Seijin Clan.

Kubulai already knew that his presence was unnecessary. The process of accounting for the tribute which had been collected had been proceeding without any kind of a hitch for some time. The bailiff and his stewards deferred to him for form's sake, but everyone knew that he could as well be absent. Sinkur was there to represent the interests of the K'chin, but even he had adopted the traditional manner of the bureaucrat – harried and abstracted – and paid attention to Kubulai only when he was addressed directly.

The corner of the room which Kubulai had chosen to occupy had been laid by the servants with three chairs and a low table. To occupy himself when he was not examining documents or ledgers Kubulai had summoned Ramanur, the man he had engaged so that he could learn the language. K'chin was not difficult, but it was full of labials and too many vowels, and Kubulai spent the time repeating sentences. Ramanur had been some kind of priest – the Yasa forbade organised religion, and so his employment was no more – and appeared to take great pleasure in his new task. He was steadily adopting the behaviour patterns Kubulai supposed were acquired by all teachers. When Kubulai failed to discern the difference between two forms of pronunciation Ramanur pursed his lips and tutted. If there had been space he would have paced up and down – clearly he wanted to – but instead he assumed on each occasion an exaggerated air of patience, then repeated the lesson.

'The man is under the tree,' Kubulai said. 'The man was under the tree. The man will be under the – yes, what is it?'

The orderly bowed. 'The k'miss, Khan.'

'Put it on the table.'

'The man ...' Ramanur prompted.

'The man will be under the tree.' The orderly brought the k'miss flask to the table, then found cups. Kubulai gestured to Ramanur so that he would know that he was expected to play the part of servant, and Ramanur filled a cup from the flask. 'The man is at the door. The man was at the door.' Kubulai accepted the cup and emptied it. 'The man will be at the door.'

50

Ramanur muttered something in K'chin, and Sinkur smiled grimly.

Kubulai said, 'What did you say?'

Sinkur had turned away to answer a question from Ordai. Now he looked quickly back at Ramanur.

'I said, God help us all against men who learn so fast,' Ramanur answered.

Kubulai wrinkled his nose. 'We don't believe that God has anything to do with the affairs of the earth. If he cared about the behaviour of men he would be here, and not in Heaven.' He saw a flash of something – disagreement, or even offence, maybe – in Ramanur's eyes.

'Khan, if we dispute you we are breaking the Yasa,' Sinkur said mildly.

'Hunh.' Kubulai shrugged. 'Argue it if you will. I give you leave.'

The glance which Sinkur gave Ramanur was charged with warning.

Ramanur said, 'Khan, we believe that God is everywhere – He is in the rocks and trees, and in every living creature.'

It was a concept which was not entirely new to Kubulai. Strange beliefs and superstitions occurred in a number of places around the world. On no occasion had the Yek encountered an approach which was capable of withstanding rational argument.

He said, 'You mean the existence of God is proved by the fact of creation. Maybe it is. It doesn't follow that God cares what man does.'

'If God cared enough to create,' Ramanur observed placidly, 'then surely his interest continues.'

Kubulai made a face. 'That's a matter of opinion. You can believe it if you wish. There is no proof.'

Sinkur said, 'Khan, all men believe God exists. No one has ever seen his face.'

They were missing the point, Kubulai thought. He said, 'Whether a man believes in the existence of God is not the issue. It's only important when he allows his belief to affect his conduct.'

Ramanur sat back. 'Khan, surely a belief in God should promote only right acts.'

It was a nice idea in theory. Kubulai reached for the k'miss flask and refilled his cup. Then he looked up. 'The Yasa encourages men to reason what is right for themselves. How can they know what is God's will? He does not speak to men.'

Sinkur looked as if his sense of proprieties was being offended. 'The priests interpret God's will,' he said.

'Oh?' Kubulai raised his eyebrows. 'Does God appoint the priests?'

Ramanur said, 'A man becomes a priest through long contemplation of God's creation, and through subordination of his own will to the will of God.'

'Which will is only made apparent through the voices of other men,' Kubulai observed, and knew that his tone sounded impatient. He drank some k'miss. 'Can a right act exist independent of God?'

It was clear that Ramanur saw the trap. 'Belief in God sanctifies right acts,' he responded. 'They are God's will.'

Kubulai was amused, and allowed the fact to show on his face. 'And thus a man acts according to God's will even though he does not know it. That's a clever argument.' He put down the cup. 'It seems to me that you admit that a man can reason for himself and be right, and so surely it does not matter if it is God's will or not.'

'And if he is wrong?' Ramanur asked gently.

'If he is wrong, then let it be because his reasoning is false,' Kubulai said, 'and not because he listened to some other man.' He gave Ramanur a hard stare. 'A priest interprets God's will, you say, and yet because he is only a man he may be mistaken. God does not speak to men.'

Ramanur pursed his lips. 'Interpretation is not an absolute,' he said slowly.

'But it will be slow to change,' Kubulai observed. 'It must be hard for a priest to admit that his under-standing of God's will is imperfect. Men on the other hand reason for themselves, and they know they can be wrong – indeed there is virtue in the admission of error, for by it a man shows that his understanding has improved.' He sat back in his chair, and saw that Ordai and the others had stopped work to listen.

The expression on Ramanur's face remained un-troubled. He said, 'And if your reasoning here is in error?'

Kubulai met his eyes. 'Then my conduct is accord-ing to the will of God,' he said, 'and it does not matter if I know it.'

Kadan left next day for Tarsis. Two of the transports had already taken men to occupy the three other inhabited islands of the K'chin group, and smaller ships had been sent to carry out a comprehensive survey of the coastlines. If there were still pirates, they were in hiding or had given up their trade.

Kubulai by now felt confident that Sursala could be left to Ordai's management. On the far side of the channel which separated the principal islands lay Murmara, which he ought to visit. The choice was to travel by galley – the *Losan* had been towed to K'chin for precisely the reason that it was suited to patrolling these waters – or by steamship.

'Khan, I will warn Jubal,' Jehangir said at once.

Jubal's promotion from comite to master was yet to be approved, but it was not that which made Kubulai hesitate. Any journey by trireme required a full crew – over two hundred men – whereas a pinnace could be sailed in theory with only the hands needed to steer, stoke the boiler, and run the engines. Kubulai frowned, aware that in the past he had allowed himself to be governed by prejudice. He shook his head. 'No. I'll go by pinnace. It will be quicker.'

Jehangir looked surprised. He opened his mouth as if to comment, and then encountered Kubulai's cold stare. Hastily he bowed. 'The Khan wishes.'

In fact they reached their destination no sooner. A trireme was ready for sea the moment its crew went aboard. A pinnace on the other hand had to raise steam – a process which Kubulai observed took not only an interminable amount of time but was also accompanied by a series of interesting altercations between the N'czuani stokers and the Ch'kasian engineers. As a result it was late in the afternoon before the steamship ran between the headlands which protected the bay of Murmara from the sea. Sunlight reflected off an expanse of tiny wavelets so that it looked as if flames were dancing across the water.

They were hailed at once by a picket.

'Boat there! Declare yourself!'

Kubulai went to the rail so that he could be seen. A trooper saluted. 'Khan, we did not expect you.'

Jehangir said something quietly to the steersman, who jerked the rope which provided communication with the men in the engine space. The beat of the paddles picked up, and they moved past the picket boat towards the quay which extended out into the water.

'They should have recognised us,' Jehangir said sourly.

Kubulai glanced at him. 'They did, eventually.'

At least they had challenged, which was reassuring. Probably they should have known that the pinnace would contain someone of rank, but that was another matter.

A reception party of some kind was assembling on the quay. Kubulai eyed the fluttering banners and the glittering lance points, and he adjusted the hang of his coat and brushed at the facings. Murmara was a town of tidy white houses edged with red stone. The windows were faced with wooden shutters painted in bright colours. Large buildings were topped with towers.

The pinnace had side paddles with high covered arches. When the vessel was warped into the quayside there was a gap which had to be bridged with long planks which bounced and vibrated as Kubulai walked across them. The men who advanced to greet him were officers he knew only vaguely. He made a mental note to find out more about them. It was one of the problems of receiving a khanate while still comparatively young. There had been no time to collect a circle of men whose loyalty he knew he could trust. He had not even assembled his own household. Nearly everyone who served him now had been appointed at Kadan's suggestion, or they were on loan from the Kha-Khan's staff.

'Khan, you are most welcome.' The black-haired

man who was bowing was the senior officer of the force occupying Murmara. He was a Merkut, and Kubulai searched his memory for a name.

'Ogodai, thank you.'

Under normal circumstances Ogodai was a thousand commander – not a particularly senior rank. Here he was virtual military governor. He looked pleased to have been acknowledged, and began to introduce the other men one by one. First there were the officers – young men, most of whom had received their commissions because they were of minor nobility. After them came what Kubulai supposed were the local equivalent of civic dignitaries. Like the Sursala aldermen they were gowned and looked prosperous.

Ogodai said, 'Khan, there are quarters if you intend to stay.'

If it was meant to be an invitation it was poorly phrased. Kubulai gave the thousand commander a cool stare, and saw him flush. If a visit was so unexpected, then maybe there were tasks which had been left undone. Kubulai remembered the promptness of the harbour picket's challenge and he guessed that whatever he was not supposed to find, it was related to a matter other than military administration. He said, 'I'll inspect your guard posts first. Find me something to ride.'

'Yes, Khan.' Ogodai bowed. The shadow of something like relief had passed across his eyes, but Kubulai pretended not to notice. He saw that the aldermen and some of the officers were already vanishing off the quay.

The st'lyan was a spirited chestnut with a white mane. Kubulai waited while Jehangir and the men of his personal guard were provided with suitable mounts, and then he allowed himself to be guided on what was clearly a hastily arranged tour of tidy sentry points and pickets. Dust still hung in the air above the guard quarters, indicating that they had only just been swept, and a cart departing around a corner was half full of sweepings and refuse. Kubulai smiled grimly. It was roughly what he had expected, and indicated if nothing else that his officers were concerned to make a good impression.

Something was still not quite right. The awareness of it worried Kubulai as he rode along the street from the barracks.

'Lord, it's very quiet,' Jehangir said at his side.

That was it. There were almost no people – a few men working in a carpenter's yard, and occasional female faces at open windows, but none of the crowd which might have been expected to assemble now that the news of their khan's arrival had been spread.

Kubulai reined in. Assassination was unlikely, and there were no signs of civil disorder. He recalled the faces of the aldermen. Their expressions had been polite but distracted – as if they had something to worry about other than their new overlord's unexpected arrival.

Ogodai rode back. 'Khan, is something wrong?'

'Where is everyone? I've never seen streets so quiet.'

The thousand commander looked flustered. 'Khan, today is a kind of festival for them. Most are in the next bay.'

Probably the aldermen had been about to leave when he had arrived, Kubulai mused. The thought that both Yek and K'chin had conspired to divert his attention was an unwelcome one. 'What kind of festival?'

'Not religious,' Ogodai said quickly. 'It's the custom each year, Khan. I just wasn't sure you would approve. They are taking gifts to the dragons.'

'What?' Kubulai gaped at him. 'I never heard of dragons on Murmara. Are they real?' It seemed unlikely now that he considered it. Dragons were mythical creatures, the stuff of tales and fables. Songs were sung about them, for the True People were said to have originated from their eggs.

'Whatever they are, it should have been reported,' Jehangir said severely.

Ogodai looked embarrassed. He said, 'Khan, they are dragons of a kind. I remembered the legend, and thought it best to say nothing.'

It had once before occurred to Kubulai that if dragons were mentioned in tales, then probably they had existed. If these on Murmara were dragons in fact, then it was likely that they were the artificial creation of the men who had long ago inhabited Marakan. Kubulai recalled what he had been told by Jehan and by his father about the real origins of the True People – that they had been designed by men, like the st'lyan and the catpeople – and a shiver of unease ran up his spine. If what he had been told was true, the knowledge was a heavy burden, for it was passed on to only a few. Now he was not sure he wanted more confirmation.

Jehangir said, 'Is it far?'

Their journey across the southern headland was completed in almost total silence. Groups of people were coming back along the path towards the town, and when they saw the st'lyan they made way politely and bowed. None of them appeared to find it remarkable that armed men were riding in the other

58

direction. 'A few of my officers went with the aldermen to watch,' Ogodai said apologetically.

Kubulai saw no point in commenting. He guided his st'lyan past rocky outcrops onto the steep slope down into the next bay. Few people remained below, and all of them seemed to be coming away from the shore. The bay was small – a brief strip of sand and shingle which was bordered by cliffs so that the exit to the sea was like a narrow doorway in a high wall. Kubulai searched for movement on the sand or in the water, but he could see nothing. He let the chestnut find its own way down the last stretch of path. The aldermen of Murmara were moving up from the beach, and they stopped when they saw him, looking nervous.

'There,' Ogodai said, and pointed.

At first Kubulai thought they were boulders. Then one of them moved, and he realised that the shapes were beasts which were lying on the shingle above the high-tide mark.

There were seven of them. They were the size of a ship's boat, and were coloured slate grey or reddish brown. One of them reared up as Kubulai watched, and he saw withered brachs – all that remained of forelegs. The hindquarters were massive by comparison, and a scaly tail extended beyond them. The back feet were webbed.

Kubulai dismounted slowly. Whatever else they were, they were nothing like the legend. Kubulai wondered if they could be mutated lizards. He looked for vestigial winglets – for the dragons of the fables could fly – but could see none.

Jehangir said, 'I wonder what they eat.'

It was apparent that they were vegetarian, for the piles of offerings left by the Murmarans consisted of vegetables and fruits. A pile of sea kelp lying to one side must have been gathered specially. Probably it was the creatures' natural food.

'Not meat, anyway.' Kubulai did not turn. Two grey shapes were working their way towards the sea, and he thought that they were better adapted for life in the water than on land. The motion was a slither rather than a walk. Both creatures splashed into the shallows and submerged. They were amphibians, Kubulai realised. A reddish-brown slab on the shingle was rearing around towards him, and he stared at the head. The eyes were recessed, protected by bony ridges, and in place of nostrils there was a blowhole situated in the centre of the forehead. There was no discernible neck. The beast produced a sound which was halfway between a howl and a roar, and then it slithered off into the water. The others were munching noisily at the piled offerings, but it was as if the cry was a signal. One by one they turned and began to leave the beach. Kubulai stared back at Ogodai. 'Are they dangerous to man?'

It was an alderman who spoke. He said, 'Lord, they have never been known to attack, and anyway they are very old.'

Kubulai could not remember the man's name. He looked back at the dragons. Clearly they were one of the artificial species which had failed to flourish. Kubulai was already certain that they had been bred originally by man, but could think of no good reason. Maybe they had been intended to provide meat. He strode down the beach and intercepted the last of the creatures. Jehangir and the alderman followed quickly. The beast's hide was dark grey, and had the texture of weathered rock. Kubulai stood in its path, and at once it stopped. It pushed itself up awkwardly off the soft sand, and opened its mouth and roared.

'Why, it has no teeth,' Jehangir said, disappointed.

The cry was not a threat, only a protest. Kubulai moved out of the way. He had hoped for a kind of grandeur, but if this was a dragon at all it was a sad shadow which mocked the legend. Suddenly he knew why Ogodai had chosen not to make a report.

The alderman was white-haired, and his skin was seamed with age. He said, 'Once there were many. These are the last.'

'How long do they live?' Kubulai turned.

'Lord, no one knows.' The alderman gestured emptily with one hand. 'Only these seven have ever come to our bay.'

'They're too old to breed then,' Jehangir observed. He stared after the departing grey shape. 'We could catch one of them if we had nets.'

Kubulai snorted. 'To what purpose?' He walked back up onto the shingle. Now that the sun was setting the bay was deep in shadow, and the air felt cold. He looked up at the deep blue of the sky and saw the trail of something – a comet, maybe – which passed like the flight of an arrow from south to north.

Ogodai said, 'Khan, I'm sorry I didn't tell you.'

'It doesn't matter.' Kubulai looped his st'lyan's reins over its neck. When he looked round he saw that everyone was still gazing towards the sea and the departing amphibians. The Murmarans watched impassively, but the expressions on the faces of the Yek were subdued.

PART ONE

Strangers at the Gates

Turakina picked up a walnut and threw it so that it bounced off Suragai's bare chest. 'Take me riding,' she said.

He looked across at her. 'That's no way to ask.'

'Take me anyway.' She scrambled to her feet, and at once a maidservant came to smooth the heavy fabric of her skirt. Turakina ignored the attention. She tossed her head, disarraying the careful styling of her Altun red hair. The maid fussed anxiously, and Suragai laughed.

'Sister, you're scarcely dressed for it,' he observed.

It was mid-afternoon. The place chosen by their parents for the picnic was a pleasant meadow from which the walls of Pesth were only just visible. Around it were groves of trees – tall trunks of almost black wood from which sprouted a fuzz of light-green leaves like needles. Suragai uncrossed his legs, and stretched out across the rug which had been laid on the short grass. He had ridden from the city with his father, but his mother and sister had travelled in the carts with the provisions and the servants. Now Turakina wanted to ride. He made a face. 'We didn't bring your mare.'

Her eyes opened wide. 'What does that matter? I can ride Jehu's.'

If she fell off he would be blamed, Suragai thought. 'You can't sit a st'lyan in that skirt,' he objected.

The skirt was heavy brocade, a deep shade of brown

which was embroidered in black. Turakina should not have been allowed to wear it on an occasion such as this, but she was going through a stage of wanting to be considered adult, and the skirt made her look quite grown up, so eventually she had got her way.

'I'll take it off,' Turakina said quickly, as if she sensed that he was running out of arguments.

Suragai gave her a sharp look. 'In front of everyone?' She was only fourteen, but the troopers of the escort were still men enough to enjoy the spectacle.

'We can use the rugs for a screen. I'll change with Shara.' Turakina watched him as she spoke.

Shara was the maid. She gave Suragai a worried look. Suragai glanced towards the copse into which his parents had disappeared some time before, and he guessed that it would be unwise to go after them. He flushed, embarrassed at the thought of what they were probably doing in the shade of the trees. Then he gave Turakina a stare. 'I'll walk with you.'

'I want to ride. If you won't take me I'll find Jehu. He will do whatever I ask.'

Jehu was a slave, and had no choice. Suragai frowned at Turakina. 'And if something happens it is he who will be punished. I thought you liked him better than that.'

It was apparent that the argument was effective. Turakina wrinkled her nose. Her skin was pale, but it was covered in freckles so that her face looked tanned. She glanced at Suragai from under long eyelashes, her expression thoughtful. Finally she said, 'My father would take me.'

Suragai laughed softly. 'You mean that because he gives you your way, so should I.' He shook his head.

Her lips compressed. Her hair had been in heavy

66

plaits during the previous night, and the ends were crinkled as if they had been waved with an iron. She coiled a tress around a finger. 'I'll tell you where Bhutan hid your sword,' she said suddenly.

Suragai sat up abruptly. 'Damn him,' he swore. 'He promised me he did not.'

'Oh, well.' Turakina touched her cheek with a forefinger. 'You were holding him over the well at the time, if you recall.'

Bhutan was the son of Suragai's mother's half-brother – a kind of cousin. He was nine, precocious, and a complete pest. Suragai got to his feet. 'I told him I would not harm him if he told me,' he said. 'Where did he hide it?'

'You'll take me riding?'

'Yes, of course.'

Turakina looked satisfied. 'It's in the big oil jar beside the storehouse door,' she said.

At least it had not come to harm. Suragai nodded slowly. The sword had gone missing ten days earlier. Turakina had probably known where it was all that time, but she had been saving the knowledge until she needed something in return. Suragai decided that he would simply appear with the sword in his sash, and savoured Bhutan's reaction. He would suffer agony waiting to find out if his lie had been discovered. Suragai gave the edge of the rug a tug. 'Move.'

Turakina skipped nimbly onto the grass. 'There's another one over there.' She pointed.

'I know.' Suragai gestured at a pair of lounging troopers. 'You two, come here.'

The men came over, looking puzzled. 'Yes, Noyon?'

He gave the rug to one of them. 'We're going to make a screen so that my sister can change. Ordai, stretch

out your arms. Hold the rug between them. That's it.'
Suddenly Suragai realised that if they stood facing
inwards, they would be able to see Turakina when she
undressed. He gestured. 'No. Hold the rug across your
back instead. Now, Kalai, you do the same with that
one. Stand back to back.'

The troopers obeyed clumsily. Now that the rugs
were stretched out they formed a kind of double
barrier. Four or five other men were loitering in the
shade of a nearby grove of trees. Suragai saw them and
cursed under his breath. Turakina was already going
behind the screen. Shara looked reluctant and had to
be summoned. The troopers under the trees nudged
one another slyly.

Suragai shouted, 'Any man whose face I see will do
double duty for a month.' He saw the men turn their
backs, and produced a grim smile.

The two men holding up the rugs were red-faced
with embarrassment. Between them Turakina and the
maid wriggled and made bumps in the heavy woven
fabric, nudging the troopers as they took off their
clothes.

'You only need to change skirts,' Suragai said to the
back of Turakina's head.

She turned round. 'Brother, which of us are you
watching?'

He felt himself go crimson. 'Hurry up.'

Shara's head came up level with the edge of the rug.
She was pulling her blouse over her head, and when
she noticed Suragai she flushed and ducked down
again. He grinned, and walked off a few paces, whistling softly. Servants were packing a box with cups
and plates. A slave came past with a bucket full of
fodder in his hand. He was staring away from the

screen so carefully that he could not see where he was going. He tripped, recovered, and then moved on. Suragai scowled at his departing back.

Turakina emerged suddenly from the makeshift screen. She was wearing Shara's cream blouse, and her loose knee-length red skirt. Both were on the large side. When Shara came out she was holding Turakina's skirt closed with one hand. The blouse barely covered her. Suragai smiled and he picked up a shawl from the ground and gave it to her. She returned his smile uncertainly.

Suragai grinned at Turakina. 'Sister, that might fit you in a few years.'

She made a face at him. Then she held the material of the shoulders out from her and looked down inside the neck of the blouse. 'You're much bigger than me,' she said to Shara.

Shara was still watching Suragai. 'Mistress, I'm much older,' she said. She gave Suragai a sudden bold stare.

'That's true.' Suragai pretended not to notice the invitation in the maidservant's eyes. He raised his eyebrows at Turakina. 'Keep the skirt but change blouses again,' he suggested.

Turakina was glancing pensively towards her maid. Abruptly she grabbed her hand and pulled her back between the screens. This time the exchange of garments was effected quickly, but it was accompanied by whispers and muffled laughter. Suragai pursed his lips, knowing that he had been teased.

'There.' Turakina came out again. She tossed her head from side to side, and her hair fell into place at once.

The maidservant was still holding Turakina's skirt closed at the waist when she emerged into the open.

69

Suragai nodded curtly to the two troopers. 'Thank you.' They let the rugs fall to the ground and trotted away.

The best course was to ignore the maid, Suragai thought. He walked past her towards the lines where the st'lyan were tethered. Turakina came up quickly beside him. Suddenly she looked back, and then said, 'She is afraid to sit down. I should have thought of that.'

The material of the skirt was probably worth more than the price paid to the maid's parents for her hire. Suragai said, 'Was it your idea to have her tease me?'

Turakina looked innocent. 'Don't you want her?'

Suragai glared. 'Behave yourself.' He snatched his shirt from the tree where he had left it and pulled it on, aware that Turakina was laughing. The lines were guarded by a young Merkut. He saluted Suragai. 'Noyon, your mare is at the far end.'

'Thank you.' Suragai nodded. 'Saddle the grey for my sister.'

The trooper leapt to obey. Turakina followed him, and Suragai heard her trying to start a conversation. The Merkut produced only shy monosyllables in response to her questions, and Suragai grinned.

The st'lyan at the end of the tether line was a dun mare a hand taller than any of its neighbours. Her horn was gilded with silver. When Suragai went up to her she nudged at him and whickered. He gave her oats in a canvas bucket, and then bent and examined each of her hooves in turn. The forehooves were clogged with compressed earth and small stones, and he cleaned them carefully. The st'lyan turned her head back over her shoulder and butted him. He ignored her. When he was done he saddled her, and then picked up his bow case from the base of the tree and lashed it to the cantle of his saddle.

Probably there was no need to go armed, Suragai thought. The land was at peace, and had been settled for years. They were no more than five verst from the city...

He frowned, knowing how his father and stepfather would have reacted to that. 'Vortai!'

The trooper's head popped up halfway along the tether line. 'Noyon?'

'As soon as you have saddled the grey, go and find two men for escort. Tell them to hurry.'

'The Noyon wishes.'

The reply made Suragai smile sourly. A noyon was not acknowledged to have a will which required to be satisfied. Noyons did the bidding of the khans.

Turakina walked along the tether line towards him. 'Can't you guard me yourself?'

'Probably.' Suragai straightened. He unfastened the st'lyan's tether. 'Sister, if you want to go riding, we take an escort.'

She frowned, and then shrugged and walked back to the place where the young trooper was leading out the grey. Suragai stared after her, and then mounted quickly. He had inherited Altun colouring from his mother, but his stature from his father, who was an Alan prince. To gain the saddle it was necessary to vault from a standing position, one hand grasping the dun's mane at the base, for the stirrup irons were too high off the ground for him to use one as a step.

The mare backed several paces, dancing lightly. Suragai drew in on the reins and watched while a trooper boosted Turakina up onto the grey's back. She reined around and rode across, her hands moving economically. A pair of troopers on piebald cavalry st'lyan came riding up through the trees. They saluted Suragai, and he nodded acknowledgement. 'Follow us.'

The far side of the meadow dipped and then rose again to join a rolling plain which was covered with long grass and dotted with occasional trees. Suragai eased his st'lyan up into a trot, but Turakina took one mischievous look over her shoulder at the escorting troopers and then yelled and lashed the grey with the ends of her reins. It bolted like an arrow through the screen of trees. Suragai snorted in exasperation. He turned in the saddle and gestured to one of the two men. 'Stay with her.'

'Yes, Noyon.' The trooper spurred after Turakina.

Suragai edged the dun up into a canter. He saw that the grey was already wheeling around in a wide arc, and he rode across it to intercept. When he came up to her, Turakina was smiling delightedly.

'If you do that again, I'll have to take you back.' Suragai reined in beside her.

'You'll have to catch me first.' Turakina brought her hands down on the reins, but Suragai reached swiftly across. He grasped the grey's bridle.

'I thought you wanted to be treated like an adult,' he said.

It seemed to give her pause. Turakina let her reins fall slack on her st'lyan's neck again, and they rode for a distance in companionable silence. The troopers pulled in a few lengths to the rear.

Clouds passing across the sun threw dark patches onto the plain. No wind was blowing, but the passage of the shadows made the long grass seem to ripple as if it was being stirred by a stiff breeze. Suragai amused himself trying to predict where the clouds would darken the grassland next, and he rode to avoid them. Suddenly they were shrouded in deep shadow. He looked up at the sky. A shape like the hulls of two ships joined together was passing across the face of the sun. At first Suragai thought that it must be enormous, but then he realised that it was dropping rapidly towards the earth.

If they stayed where they were it was going to land on top of them. Suragai grabbed Turakina's reins and spurred hard. He heard the troopers cry out in alarm, and then they were all riding at breakneck speed for the nearest defile. When they reached it Suragai reined in so hard that the dun sat down on her haunches. He looked back.

The dark shape was hovering a hundred drem or so above the plain. There was no noise, and Suragai wondered how it was powered. He watched as it settled slowly. A blast of hot air washed overhead, and the st'lyan reared and screamed.

'What is it?' Turakina did not sound afraid.

'It's a vessel of some kind.' Suragai uncased his bow. When he glanced round he saw that the troopers were doing the same. He ransacked his memory for names – Osep and Mago – and caught the older man's eye. 'If we can, we will ride around.'

The troopers nodded understanding. Their first duty in any case was to preserve Turakina.

Suragai remembered that his grandfather had spoken once of the possibility of something like this happening one day – and that his grandsire had come to this world in fact from a vessel which travelled in the void beyond the sky. It had seemed incredible to Suragai at the time. Now he was suddenly not so sure.

He stood in the stirrups and took a long hard look at the now stationary craft.

There were no windows – no openings at all. Suragai's first impression was of a perfect ovoid, featureless and also colourless. Its curved surface seemed to reflect the sky above and the plain around.

Turakina said, 'Aren't we going to see who they are?'

'Someone else will do that.' Suragai leaned out of the saddle and scooped up her reins. He tapped his st'lyan gently with his toe, so that it picked its way carefully along the depression.

The defile was a crease in the ground which rose at both ends to rejoin the flat land of the plain. Emerging from it they were five hundred drem or so from the ship. Suragai stared ahead, hoping to see his father's men coming up from the camp, but there was no sign of them.

'Noyon, they're moving again.' Osep spoke urgently.

Suragai turned. The ship had lifted without a sound, and it was coming towards them. It descended less than fifty drem away. An opening appeared in one side.

If he sent Turakina off with one or both of the troopers the vessel might follow her. Suragai said, 'I think they want to talk to us.'

'As long as that's all they want,' Mago observed.

Both troopers laughed nervously. Suragai nocked an arrow to his bow. He said, 'We'll ride forward slowly. Sister, stay behind us. If I tell you to ride away, then go as fast as you can for the defile and stay there.'

For the first time Turakina seemed to understand that they might be in danger. She nodded, subdued.

Men were coming out of the side of the ship. Suragai watched them, and guessed that the five who were dressed all alike were soldiers. A sixth man was much older than the rest, and he wore a knee-length coat instead of coveralls. The other men seemed to defer to him.

Suragai walked the dun mare steadily forward. The soldiers were carrying weapons, he saw – firearms of a sort – and he growled softly. They were lining up at the side of the ship, but it was hard to tell if their manner was particularly defensive or threatening. Another figure filled the doorway. This time it was a younger man, but he was dressed like the leader in a coat, and there were designs of some kind embossed onto the material of the facings.

'Noyon, they are armed.' Mago sounded outraged.

'I know. Don't kill them yet.'

If the strangers did not know the Yasa, they could not be blamed for a breach of the law. Excusing such a serious offence made Suragai feel uncomfortable. He drew in the dun's reins, and she danced sideways and then stopped.

The aliens were conversing together in low tones. They seemed at first more interested in the st'lyan than in their riders. One of the soldiers pointed. He said something, laughing, and the oldest of the men in coveralls responded sharply, silencing him.

Suragai glanced to the side, and saw that the troopers had drawn up level. Both had arrows nocked to their bows, but held them so that the threat was not too apparent. Suragai said, 'If the soldiers raise their guns to shoot, kill them all.' He did not look to see if he had been heard.

The soldiers had their weapons across their chests. The leader looked around and said something quietly. Hesitantly they lowered the guns, holding them by what Suragai thought was the barrel at their sides. They looked unhappy. The leader took a single pace forward. He raised his hands, palms outward as if to demonstrate that he was unarmed, and then spoke.

'The highest wisdom has but one science – the science of the whole – the science of explaining the whole creation and man's place in it.'

The language was Anglic of a kind, but the speech made no sense. Suragai wondered if either of the troopers understood. He glanced quickly at them and saw that they did not. Softly, Turakina said, 'That's the Foreigners' Tongue.'

'I know.' Suragai did not look at her. 'Don't let them see you understand,' he said in Yek.

It was clear that the speech was part of a process. The leader did not seem to be concerned at the lack of response. He said something low-voiced to the younger man, who summoned two of the soldiers forward. Suragai observed that they left their weapons on the ground.

The four men stood in a line facing Suragai. The leader touched himself on the chest and said, 'Me.' then he touched the younger man. 'You.'

'Me.' The younger man touched his chest. 'You.' He tapped the chest of the soldier at his side.

They are demonstrating that they have a language, Suragai thought, and he could not help smiling at the cleverness of the idea. The leader's first speech had been intended to show that the aliens used language, and that it was different. Now they were communicating the words for self. He glanced at Osep. 'It's a language lesson,' he said. 'They want to talk.'

Osep nodded. Suragai took his right hand off his bow string, concealing his relief. The pantomime on the ground was coming to an end now. The fourth soldier touched his chest. 'Me.' Then he went and tapped the leader on the shoulder. 'You.'

The leader was staring up at Suragai. I have done all the talking, Suragai thought, and so he knows that I am in command.

'Me.' The older man touched his chest again. Then he pointed at Suragai. 'You.'

The situation appealed to Suragai's sense of humour, and anyway he thought that it was important to make the exercise last as long as possible. He touched his chest with his free hand. 'Me.' Then he pointed at the leader. 'You,' he said in Anglic.

'He understands!' the younger man exclaimed. The leader did not look round. 'Yes,' he said. He touched himself again. 'Me, Valeri Borocheff. Valeri Borocheff, *name*,' he said. Then he pointed at Suragai again. 'You, *name*?'

Mounted men were coming up onto the plain. Suragai detected the movement out of the corner of his eye. He gave the alien leader a level stare. 'Suragai,' he said.

The leader looked pleased. He nodded and smiled. 'Valeri Borocheff.' He tapped his chest again, then pointed. 'Suragai.'

Suragai nodded, but did not smile back.

'Are they men?' Turakina asked in Yek.

'Men like our grandfather.' Suragai nodded.

The younger man had suddenly noticed Turakina. He gave her a smile. 'Constantin.' He touched his chest. 'You?'

They have no manners, Suragai thought. He scowled at the younger man. Osep and Mago observed the reaction, and their hands went quickly back to their

77

bows. The leader saw, and he gave the younger man an angry look. 'Fool,' he said. 'You have offended them.'

Suragai glanced at Turakina and saw that she was ignoring the younger man. He turned and stared at the aliens. 'Whatever happens,' he said in Yek, 'the young one is mine.'

Osep laughed softly. 'Noyon, isn't that Anglic they're speaking?'

'I didn't know you understood,' Suragai said. He kept his eyes on the men standing beside the ship.

'A few words, that's all.' Osep walked his st'lyan up to Suragai's right side. 'They're breaking the Yasa,' he observed.

'I know it. Don't look, but my father's men are coming.'

If there was anyone else in the ship, they must have seen. Suragai could not imagine how they could see through what looked like solid metal, but they had to be able to, or they could not steer.

The younger man was trying to catch Suragai's attention. He held up his hands, an apologetic expression on his face. Suragai grunted as if he understood. 'Ride off a little,' he said to Osep. 'I want them to keep looking at us.'

Osep nodded. He reined around, walking the piebald four or five paces to the side. Suragai flexed his free hand so that his talons glittered in the sun. The younger man saw and exclaimed. 'They are not human,' he said.

Suragai gave him a hard stare, only just remembering that he was not supposed to be able to understand. The older man muttered a reply. He looked back at Suragai and opened his mouth to speak.

A screen of troopers from his father's personal

guard were coming very fast across the plain. Suragai turned in the saddle to watch. They swung round in an arc and reined in, weapons ready. Only at the last could the aliens have heard the thunder of hooves on the hard ground. A soldier cried out in alarm. He pointed and then began to lift his gun. The leader spun round. He shouted, 'No!' Then he looked back at Suragai and spread his arms out carefully with his palms open.

Suragai showed his teeth. 'My name is Suragai Noyon,' he said in precise Anglic. 'I bid you welcome to my land.'

His father's initial reaction was annoyance. 'Turakina should not be here,' he said, and gave Suragai a frown.

Suragai shrugged. 'Father, I know it. We tried to ride off, but they came after us.'

'Lord, that's true,' Osep said quickly.

Suragai saw his father purse his lips. His name was D'mitri, and once he had been an Alan princeling. Now he was castellan of Pesth, which he held of Burun, Suragai's great-grandfather. His fair hair was still cut in the Alan style, like a cap which ended above his ears. He said, 'I suppose you did your best.' He turned in the saddle and stared at Turakina, sitting the grey quietly in the midst of an escort of armed men. 'As for you, lady, we will talk later.' He gestured at the trooper in charge. 'Get her out of here.'

The aliens beside the ship had not moved. The five soldiers looked apprehensive, but the older man was watching calmly. He had not spoken since the troopers' arrival. Suragai saw his father glance at them.

'They only want to talk,' Suragai said.

D'mitri made a face. 'That's how the trouble starts,'

he said. He was riding a bay st'lyan with brilliant black points. Its horn was decorated with gold. He reined over so that he was looking down at the leader of the aliens. Suddenly he turned back towards Suragai. 'Anglic?'

Suragai nodded. His father swung round in the saddle. He let his reins fall slack across the bay's neck, and then he rested one hand on his thigh. He stared down. 'My name is D'mitri S'zltan,' he said in perfect Anglic, 'and I hold the city yonder in the name of the Universal Khan. Who are you, and what is your business here?'

The older man raised his eyebrows. 'Lord D'mitri,' he said, 'I am Valeri Borocheff, an ambassador of His Exalted Highness Priam the Second, Emperor of the Known Universe. My business is with the ruler of this land.'

'Indeed.' Suragai's father produced a flat stare. 'Before you can speak to anyone, you have to satisfy me. Are your intentions peaceful?'

Borocheff raised his hands quickly. 'Very peaceful, my lord.'

'And yet your emperor claims to rule the universe.' D'mitri wrinkled his nose. 'That means he claims this land also.'

The alien expressions were difficult to read. Suragai remembered that his grandfather was of the same species, but thought that he must have become Yek over a period of years.

'That remains to be seen, my lord,' the alien ambassador said smoothly. A flash of something passed across his eyes. 'There are independent worlds in the Empire.'

The offworlders were unprepared, Suragai thought,

because they came expecting language to be a barrier. In Yek he said, 'Because we can talk to them, they cannot hide anything from us unless they lie.'

His father did not turn. To Borocheff he said, 'That's an evasive answer, but as you are an ambassador I expect nothing else. Are you surprised we speak your tongue?'

'My lord, I am, very.' The ambassador spoke with a disarming honesty.

Suragai edged his st'lyan up to his father's side. He said, 'What was that nonsense you spoke when first you greeted me?' His father glanced round.

'This is my son,' he commented drily.

The ambassador was of middle years, Suragai supposed. He was quite tall – taller than most Yek – and he had iron-grey hair and a deeply lined face. He gave Suragai a rueful glance. 'Lord,' he said to D'mitri, 'he does you credit.'

'The speech,' Suragai said. 'What was it?'

Borocheff gestured. 'Words from a book. The man who wrote them is long dead,' he responded. 'I could have recited anything. The idea was to let you know that we use language. But you know that.'

Suragai smiled innocently. 'I did not mean to mock you. It was necessary until we found out your intent.'

'Which is my concern,' his father said. He gave the offworlder a stare. 'If I send you to the Kha-Khan, my master, what will you say to him?'

The alien's head went back. 'Lord, surely that would be for your master to tell you.'

D'mitri showed his teeth. 'And yet you will tell me,' he said.

There was a moment when Suragai was sure the ambassador was going to refuse. Then it was as if he realised his situation. He shrugged. 'My lord, I am here to establish a relationship between this world and the Empire.' He waved a hand. 'We can trade, we think, and there may be things we can teach one another –'

' – the nature of the relationship to be a matter for further discussion,' Suragai's father said. 'I understand. You will find that we are not ready to become subjects of the Empire. In any case it would be contrary to our law.'

The younger man had not moved or spoken, but now he stirred. 'Laws can be altered,' he said very quietly.

Suragai guessed that only the ambassador was meant to hear. Our ears are sharper than theirs, he thought.

Borocheff's face had become still. He glanced quickly up. Suragai saw that his father was pretending that he had heard nothing. 'Speaking of the law …' he said.

His father's head came round. 'What of the law?'

'Their weapons,' Suragai nodded towards the soldiers. 'They are carrying firearms,' he said in Anglic.

The ambassador was listening intently. He said, 'My lord, these are my escort. They intend you no harm.'

D'mitri stood in the stirrups, and then sat down again. 'That does not concern me,' he said. 'But in this land there is a law prohibiting weapons such as your escort carry. The penalty is death.'

The offworlder looked shaken. 'My lord, you cannot mean to kill my men.'

Suragai said, 'Until now they did not know our law, and so they could not be held to blame.'

'Ah.' The ambassador nodded. 'But now that they are aware of it …'

'They risk the penalty if they continue,' D'mitri said.

It occurred to Suragai suddenly to wonder why the offworlders had chosen to land here, and not at Pesth itself. Probably they had been scouting, or they had intended to obtain information. They didn't expect us to be organised to deal with them, he thought.

'My lord,' the ambassador said, 'of course we will respect your laws. But remember I am the representative of my emperor. I should have an escort.'

D'mitri chuckled. 'By all means,' he observed blandly. 'Although you are in no danger. But if these are to be your guard, then let them be armed as ours are, with lance or sword. The guns remain here.'

The offworlders looked unhappy. Their leader pursed his lips. 'My lord,' he said, 'they will put their guns in the ship.'

'Oh?' Suragai's father opened his eyes wide. 'Will you leave that here also?'

Borocheff looked dismayed. 'We had intended to travel in it, my lord ...'

'Then the guns must be destroyed,' D'mitri said. He gave the ambassador a hard stare. 'It is our law. If you will not obey it, then I give you leave to depart. But in that case you will not return.'

The aliens looked as if they had just swallowed bad meat. The ambassador opened his mouth as if to object, and then closed it again. He stared around at the troopers, taking in their readiness to fight. 'My lord,' he said ungraciously, 'you have us at a disadvantage.'

'I'm pleased you appreciate that.' D'mitri grinned cheerfully. 'Will you surrender your arms?'

If they intended conquest, then this would be the

point at which they would choose to depart. Suragai wondered if the offworlders knew how much they were revealing by the pattern of their reactions.

'My lord, we will, but under protest.' The leader of the aliens turned and addressed the soldiers. 'Lay down your weapons.'

The oldest of the men in coveralls looked ready to argue. 'Sir -'

'Do it.'

They had orders to negotiate, and they were prepared to compromise their honour in the process. Suragai said, 'They are metal. Will they burn?'

Borocheff looked back quickly. 'My lord,' he said to D'mitri, 'these are not guns as you would understand them. They fire heat in the form of a beam. If you will let my officer disarm them -'

'- then they could be buried maybe, and recovered later so that you can take them away when you depart.' Suragai's father rubbed the back of his neck with his hand. 'In fact we know about weapons like that. I'm not sure that what you propose satisfies the Yasa, but since you are to be our guests for a time, maybe some allowance can be made.'

The disarming of the weapons was quickly achieved. Suragai dismounted and examined the crystals the younger man was putting to one side. 'These catch light and turn it into heat,' he said in Anglic.

The young officer's head came round. 'That's right. If you understand that, then you must possess technical knowledge. Don't you use it?'

Suragai thought of explaining that the law relating to weapons was formulated so that men would never be too far removed from the act of killing, and so would never take it lightly. Instead he said, 'We use

84

what is needful.' He hefted one of the disabled weapons. 'How far will this shoot?'

The offworlder looked around the plain. He pointed. 'As far as that tree with accuracy. Beyond that …' He shrugged.

The tree was five or six hundred drem away, much further than the range of the strongest bow. Suragai was careful not to look impressed. 'If you are with us long enough,' he said, 'I will teach you to shoot as we do.'

'Oh.' The young man smiled. 'I think I could manage that.'

Suragai doubted it, but he said nothing. He pulled his bow from the case on his saddle and nocked an arrow. He drew as far as he could, lifting the arrow until the point lay against the sun. Men turned to watch. Suragai loosed. The arrow whistled straight up. At the top of its trajectory it stood like a hawk in the air. Against the bright redness of the sun Suragai could see it turn and fall. The offworlders sighed. The arrow fell some way off in the long grass. Suragai looked up at his father's face, but his father only pursed his lips, and then he turned away.

'Somebody has to ride with them,' D'mitri said.

'I know that.' Suragai looked back over his shoulder at the ship. 'I'm not sure why it has to be me.'

It was by now approaching evening. Couriers had been riding back and forth between the ship, the camp, and the city, and Suragai knew that his mother and sister were already on their way back to Pesth under strong guard. Now the aliens were ready to move.

'I'll give you Osep,' D'mitri said. 'They aren't armed, remember.'

Suragai snorted. 'That ship is a weapon,' he commented sourly.

His father nodded. 'And it may contain other weapons we know nothing about. Would you rather let them fly without our supervision?'

'No.'

'I thought not.' His father raised an eyebrow. 'If I want you to go with them, it's because I trust you.'

It was a statement of fact rather than a compliment, but Suragai flushed. His father was about fifty, he thought, and so there was a gap of more than thirty years between them. He stared at his father's face. Apart from a few lines it was like looking into a mirror. 'I'll go.'

D'mitri nodded. 'Good. I've sent to everybody I can think of, but if you get to Pesth before we do, don't let them talk to anyone.'

Suragai nodded. 'Have you told my grandfather?'

His father frowned. 'He's at Kinsai. You know that. He'll hear as soon as Burun does.'

'As soon as the Kha-Khan.'

'Yes. I've sent to your uncle at Khitai.'

Alexei was not really his uncle, Suragai knew. In fact he was the offworlder son of Suragai, his grandfather, for whom he had been named. He said, 'Do you suppose the offworlders know about Alexei?'

'I shouldn't think so.' D'mitri shook his head. 'And not about your grandfather or the others either, so don't tell them.'

Suragai remembered that his grandfather and uncle had both been marooned on the world many years before. The story was a vague recollection, for he had been told it as a child. No one thought of them as aliens any more.

'I wonder why they have really come.' Suragai looked towards the offworlders. The soldiers were climbing into the ship. Suragai guessed that it was ready to leave, and he started to walk towards the open doorway.

D'mitri matched his son's pace. 'Your uncle may be able to tell us that. That's why I've sent for him.'

'Hunh.' Suragai nodded. He put a hand on the edge of the metal surrounding the door and pulled himself up. Then he looked back. His father waved once and turned away towards the st'lyan. Inside the ship the wall was lined with couches made from a material which looked like leather but was not. Everyone was sitting down except Osep and the ambassador. Osep was standing in the middle of the floor, watching the soldiers with a mistrustful expression. The ambassador was waiting near the door. He bowed to Suragai and smiled. 'Noyon, if you are ready, we can leave now.'

The offworlders looked relaxed and confident once more. Suragai guessed that they were reassured by the familiar surroundings of the ship. Here at least they were able to convince themselves that they were superior.

He nodded. 'Osep, sit down.'

The only helm Suragai could see was a kind of yoke which stuck up out of the floor in front of a double couch which faced a blank section of wall. The young officer was apparently the steersman. He sat down on one side of the couch and touched the yoke. At once the solid wall in front of him became transparent. Suragai found that he could see the ground outside. The ambassador indicated the half of the couch which was unoccupied. 'Noyon, if you wish you can sit here.'

87

'Thank you.' Suragai sat gingerly.

The ambassador sat on the nearest wall couch to the side of the helm position which Suragai was occupying. He said, 'We will try to keep pace with your father's men, but it may be difficult. We don't usually travel so slowly.'

It was unlikely that they knew how fast a st'lyan was capable of travelling. Suragai shrugged. 'Go as fast as you like,' he said. 'But if we reach Pesth too soon nothing will be ready for us.'

'Is Pesth the principal city of this land?' the young officer asked politely.

Suragai smiled. 'Our capital city is Kinsai,' he said. 'Pesth is a way-station compared to it.'

The offworlders looked quickly at one another. 'We could have gone there had we known,' the younger man said.

Suragai looked down his nose. 'When the Kha-Khan wants to see you he will send for you,' he said. 'He will know of your presence tonight.'

'So soon?' The ambassador looked surprised. 'Kinsai cannot be far.'

They were using the journey to try to extract information. It was what Suragai had expected. 'Far enough,' he said.

His father and the troopers of his escort were streaming away across the plain. Suragai watched them for a moment. The first courier would already have reached Pesth. Heliograph posts spanned the continent, and so the news would even now be on its way to Kinsai. Arrow messengers would follow – couriers riding hundreds of verst a day, changing st'lyan at way-stations, carrying the privileged communications of the Khanate from one place to another.

The aliens seemed to sense Suragai's reticence. For a time the officer concentrated on raising and steering the craft. They moved with increasing speed in the direction of Pesth, and the ground unreeled below them in a way that filled Suragai with amazement. He did his best to hide his awe, but knew that his expression was betraying his feelings.

'This must be a remarkable experience for you,' the ambassador said quietly. He gestured around the craft. 'What is commonplace to us must appear strange and even frightening to you.'

Suragai hesitated. Finally he said, 'Your machines don't astound us. Even though we use few, our knowledge of science is advanced.'

Both offworlders looked politely disbelieving. 'That is ... surprising,' the older man said.

It was not hard to understand why they doubted what they were being told. Suragai gave him a cold stare. 'You think us primitive,' he said.

The ambassador looked as if he was trying to formulate a believable denial. He smiled politely. 'Appearances are deceptive. You don't seem to employ machines for transport; your weapons, or those we have seen, are not advanced by our standards; you must pardon us if we judge by our experience of such matters.'

Eventually it would occur to them to wonder why he was not more curious about the other inhabited worlds. Suragai caught the younger man's eye. 'My talons surprised you.' He flexed his right hand.

The officer went crimson. 'I did not mean to offend you,' he said after a moment. 'We thought you were of our species.'

Suragai showed his teeth. 'So far as we are concerned,

it is you who are not human.' He watched their reaction, and saw them stiffen. It struck him that they probably equated being civilised with being not only human but also technologically advanced – by their standards. If that was the case, then it was possible that they would underestimate Yek abilities in the event of a confrontation.

Pesth was much closer now. Suragai looked for the clear area near the west gate and pointed to it. 'Land there.'

A company of troopers lined the flat expanse. A few of the st'lyan reared as the ship descended, and Suragai remembered the blast of hot air. 'This could not travel to another world,' he said, suddenly quite sure.

The ambassador and the younger man exchanged a glance. 'This is as one of your small boats to a ship that sails across the sea,' the ambassador said.

Which meant that they had been watching long enough to know that there were ships. Suragai wondered how large the vessel was that could journey between stars.

They had grounded now. The young officer touched something on the control yoke, and the transparent wall became once more opaque. The door sighed open. Suragai stood up. Osep was first out through the door, and Suragai grinned at his obvious haste. The soldiers and the ambassador began to follow. As they went towards the opening the officer said, 'Pardon me, for I do not wish to offend you. The lady who was with you when we landed first – who is she?'

Suragai gave him a cold stare. 'She is my sister,' he said. 'Stay away from her.'

They lodged the offworlders in one of the houses

owned by Burun. It had three floors, and Suragai was interested to see that the soldiers were allocated the rooms at the top. The servants his father offered were politely refused, and so the embassy was not impressive, although it was guarded outside by troopers of D'mitri's own tuman.

'Maybe they think we will spy on them,' Suragai said.

His father snorted. 'The kind of information we need cannot be got that way,' he said. 'Or not at the moment.'

The street where the embassy house was situated was full of tall grey buildings with closed yards. The roofs were tiled, and archways crossed between them at intervals. The cobbles were cool where the shadows were deepest. Suragai rested his back against the wall beside the ring to which his st'lyan was tied. 'If they try to leave, we should kill them,' he said.

D'mitri was tightening his st'lyan's girth. His head came up sharply. 'Why?'

Suragai was not sure how to answer. Part of the feeling was instinct, and defied explanation. 'Whatever they learn about us, it is too much,' he said at last.

'Hunh.' His father nodded slowly. 'But they are few and we are many. How do they threaten us?'

It was not like his father to be so short-sighted. Even if he could not see where the threat lay, he knew better than to be so trusting.

A line of p'tar ambled past. The pack beasts were like st'lyan, but lacked a horn. One of them brayed, revealing a mouthful of ugly yellow teeth. Suragai waited until the pack train had passed, and then he said, 'They have another, bigger vessel somewhere.'

He saw that his father was digesting the information

without apparent surprise. 'Ambassadors are always followed by armies,' D'mitri observed. 'If we kill these, then we will be giving their emperor an excuse to attack us.'

The post of ambassador to the Khanate was by tradition filled with risk. Embassies were sent to deliver demands for submission which were often couched in such terms that the death of the members was practically guaranteed, the point being that the killing of an ambassador was all the Yek needed to justify a war.

'You don't like them,' D'mitri said.

Suragai examined his emotions. He looked up. 'They think we are barbarians.'

D'mitri grinned. 'I'm Alan,' he observed blandly. 'I thought the Yek were barbarians once.'

The racial characteristics of the True People were always dominant, and so they were carried through to the children of mixed marriages. Suragai glanced at his father's fingers, which ended in nails like plates of horn and not with talons. D'mitri was only being flippant, of course. Suragai said, 'Father, be serious.'

'When you say something sensible, I will be,' D'mitri said. He untied his st'lyan's reins from the ring on the wall, looped them over her head, and got up into the saddle. He looked down. 'Are you coming?'

Suragai slid his sword out of his sash and thrust it between the bindings of his saddle. 'I might as well.' He loosened the dun mare's reins and vaulted onto her back. They rode together down the street.

'I have placed a guard on their ship,' D'mitri said.

'Oh?'

A maniple of his father's tuman was riding along the street towards them. The trooper in charge was a C'zak, and he saluted as they rode past.

'If we let them go to Kinsai, they ought to ride.' D'mitri nodded to the trooper.

'Do you think we ought to let them go to Kinsai?'

His father made a face. 'It's true we don't know what they're capable of.' He reined over closer to Suragai. 'If there is another ship, then probably it's above us.'

'Watching.'

'Maybe.'

The aliens did not need to be watching, Suragai thought. He remembered hearing a Sechem talk about invisible waves which carried sound through the air. According to the theory there was a way of sending messages long distances by machines which employed the waves. He frowned. 'You think others will come no matter what we do.'

'Don't you?'

The likelihood that the Khanate might be forced to deal with offworld civilisations had never been considered seriously until Jehan had come to the throne. Then contingency plans had been made, and they had been revised from time to time during the twenty years of his reign. 'We need Alexei,' Suragai said thoughtfully.

'He'll be here tomorrow.'

All they had to do until then was to find reasons not to allow the aliens near their ship. 'They could have an accident,' Suragai said.

'That would be too easy,' his father replied.

When Bhutan saw that Suragai was wearing his own sword, his face went pale. Bhutan's father Kaidu was not Altun – he was the son of Suragai's grandfather by his N'pani second wife – and so he was dark-haired with fair clear skin and eyes which folded up at the corners. His head swivelled so that he could watch as Suragai crossed the garden to the place where Turakina was sitting with her maid.

Suragai rested his hand on the hilt of his sword and smiled. The sword was made to the pattern of the *jusei*, the Manchu great-sword which one of his grandfather's offworlder officers had introduced many years before. Traditional Yek cavalry swords were short and straight with two sharp edges. A *jusei* was curved, and only the leading edge was honed. It was intended for cutting rather than for stabbing, but the point was very sharp and would penetrate anything it touched.

It was likely that Bhutan was wondering if his lie – that he had nothing to do with the sword's disappearance – had been found out and was going to return to him. Suragai was not concerned to be vindictive, but he thought that it was important to teach Bhutan a lesson. Mischief was to be expected from any child. Bhutan's behaviour on the other hand was self-willed, directed at anyone he disliked or who tried to exert discipline, and it required to be checked. Suragai looked quickly round, and he smiled grimly when Bhutan started and dropped his eyes.

The tree under which Turakina sat had branches which curved over and trailed down onto the grass so that it looked for all the world like a green tent. Turakina was sewing pearls onto a blouse while her maid watched. She looked up and saw Suragai, and said something to the maid. The maid got up and walked past Suragai towards the back door of the house. It was the girl with whom Turakina had changed clothes at the picnic. Suragai stared at her, and then turned to watch as she walked on.

She knew he was watching, Suragai thought. He remembered the bold look and the invitation in her eyes. If he showed interest he would be acting predictably. Resolutely he turned his back on her. Turakina was watching, and he glared.

Turakina said, 'If you want her, go after her.'

Suragai looked down his nose. 'She doesn't belong to me.'

If Shara was a member of his household it would be quite permissible to take her if she consented. She was not, and so his behaviour had to be subject to custom.

Suragai slipped the scabbard of his sword out of his sash and propped it carefully against the trunk of the tree. He squatted on his heels at Turakina's side. 'I don't like to be made a game of,' he said.

She was pushing the needle through a layer of material. Her hands stilled. 'I thought she would please you.'

Suragai closed his eyes and then opened them again. 'When you are older, you will understand.'

Turakina frowned. 'Everybody says that to me.'

'It's part of growing up.' Suragai smiled.

The pearls for her blouse were in a shallow dish at her side. Turakina threaded one onto her needle and then ran the needle through the fabric. The sun shining through the leaves made patterns on the skin of her hands and arms. After a moment she looked up. 'Have you been to see the aliens?'

Bhutan was still sitting beside the wall. Suragai glanced in his direction, then turned back and gave Turakina a suspicious stare. 'You have nothing to do with them,' he said. He thought about the young officer's obvious interest in her, and anger burned in his chest.

It was as if she sensed his emotion. She looked away. Suragai stirred the pearls in the dish with a forefinger. The grass beneath the tree was short, and grew like the pile of a carpet in dense tufts which hid the soil.

Suragai said, 'Tell me what to do about Bhutan.'

Her head came round abruptly. 'Don't involve me in your feuds.'

A feud could only be conducted properly between persons of equivalent status. Bhutan was only a child. Suragai showed his teeth. 'It is all your fault. Your desire to go riding has been your undoing.'

Turakina's eyes flashed. 'Don't remind me.'

Nobody had been allowed to hear what D'mitri had said to her about the escapade. Suragai opened his eyes wide. 'You knew Bhutan took my sword. If you had told me sooner, maybe everything would have turned out differently.'

She glared at him. He met her stare steadily, and finally her eyes slid away. She said, 'Whatever you do to Bhutan, he will not learn from it.'

Bhutan's behaviour was not strictly Suragai's concern, although his father Kaidu was in Marakan keeping order among the catpeople. Bhutan was a guest in their house – at the same time he could not be allowed to conduct himself in a manner which was so careless of the convenience of others. Suragai frowned. 'Every boy gets at least one good beating in his life.'

'Some people are not to be disciplined,' Turakina said.

It was what a long-ago Kha-Khan had once said about their grandfather Burun. Suragai eyed her. 'There's no comparison.'

Turakina shrugged. 'Punishment will not change Bhutan.'

It was probably true. Suragai got to his feet with a single elastic stretch of the legs. He picked up his sword and then looked down. 'Stay away from the aliens.' He brushed through the overhang of green boughs and strode across the garden. Bhutan was loitering on the path, and he started guiltily. Obviously he expected to be punished. Suragai stopped in front of him. Bhutan's eyes were extraordinary, like deep black pools, and showed no expression. It was his face that gave him away, for he had not yet learned to control it.

Suragai said, 'I should punish you.'

'Cousin, what for?' Bhutan's voice was thick with innocence. Anyone who did not know him would have been fooled.

'For this.' Suragai brandished his sword. Even now he was tempted to turn Bhutan over his knee. He imagined thrashing him with the flat of the blade, and knew that Turakina was right. It would have no lasting effect.

Bhutan looked nervous. 'You asked me if I stole it,' he said quickly. 'I did not.'

Strictly speaking that was true. Theft implied the intent to deprive the owner permanently. Suragai showed his teeth in appreciation of the cleverness of the lie. Now that he had decided what to do, he could afford to be amused. 'Little boys deny their misdeeds,' he said. 'Men admit it when they have done wrong, even though they are afraid. Get out of my way, boy.'

The knowledge that he had escaped a beating showed for only a moment on Bhutan's face. Then he went very red. 'I am your cousin,' he protested. 'You can't speak to me that way.'

'Oh.' Suragai laughed at him. 'Normally I could not,

for you are a guest in this house. But good manners are only custom; they are not law. If you want my respect you will have to earn it. Now get out of my way.'

An older Bhutan would have struck out. Suragai saw his talons flash as they were extended and then retracted, and he produced an evil smile. Bhutan jumped, and he sidled hastily off the path.

Suragai took a pace past him, then stopped and looked back down over his shoulder. 'Little boy,' he said again.

Bhutan flinched. He turned and ran towards the garden gate. Suragai laughed harshly, satisfied, and then turned and walked on into the house.

Alexei arrived in the middle of the night. It was an indication, Suragai supposed later, of the importance he attached to the aliens' visit. Khitai was over a thousand verst to the south. To reach Pesth so quickly Alexei must have ridden nonstop. Probably he had not even paused for refreshment.

An honour guard of Merkuts lit Alexei's party through the streets from the city gate. The echoes of the sentries' challenges and the shouted countersigns woke Suragai some time before the cavalcade entered the street on which the castellan's house stood. Suragai sat up in bed. He threw the coverlet aside and stood up, then went to the open window and looked out. Between the houses three lines of roofs away the torches were flaring.

Suragai padded naked to the door. When he opened it the guard outside came quickly off the wall to attention. 'Noyon, is something the matter?'

'My uncle is coming.' No one else would have been admitted in such haste in the middle of the night,

Suragai knew. He looked along the darkened passage-way. 'Is my father awake?'

The sentry nodded. 'Lord, he is in the solar.'

'Good.' Suragai went back into the room. He left the door ajar, and a moment later Jehu came through it. He was carrying an armful of clothes. Suragai splashed water from the bowl on the chest over his face and dried himself. He took the hose and breeches Jehu held out and put them on. 'Bring me something to drink.'

Jehu was a Dosani from the far south of Y'frike. His skin was as dark as a moonless night. He nodded silently and left the room.

Suragai wound himself into his sash. He selected a waist-length tunic and put it on. It had no fastenings, and it gaped because of the breadth of his chest.

The slave came back into the chamber with a k'miss jug and a cup. He said, 'Lord, don't you want something to eat?'

'No.' Suragai took the cup out of Jehu's hand. He held it out, and Jehu poured k'miss into it. There was a disapproving look on his face. Suragai drank. The spirit burned its way down into his chest, banishing tiredness. He poked his feet into his boots and pulled them on with his free hand.

'It's not good for you to drink on an empty stomach,' Jehu said. He took the cup from Suragai's hand.

Suragai glowered at him. 'You sound like my mother.' He stalked past Jehu. The house was already beginning to stir. A pair of servants hastened past the open door; they bowed in mid-stride and then raced on. Suragai unhooked a lamp from the wall. He went along the passage and down the stairs. The solar was in the centre of the building – a large chamber with a

99

domed roof of clear glass. The room was very unusual in a land where glazing was seldom transparent, for good reason. Occupying it during the day was like being out of doors, only much warmer.

D'mitri was reading when Suragai entered. The parchment in his hand was decorated with gold seals, indicating that it had been sent from the court of the Kha-Khan. It was much too soon for it to be an order about the aliens – heliographed acknowledgement of the report of their arrival had been received only the evening before – and Suragai realised that his father must be reading the most recent instruction relating to the contingency of offworlder contact.

Suragai said, 'Alexei is here.'

'I know.' His father laid the document aside. St'lyan hooves rattled suddenly in the courtyard outside, and he stood up. Suragai followed him towards the door. The door opened abruptly in front of them, and Alexei came through it. He stared at them, and then turned and nodded to someone standing outside. The door closed.

'Brother, I am pleased to see you,' D'mitri said.

It was really only a courtesy. In fact Alexei was the alien half-brother of D'mitri's wife.

'Thank you.' Alexei was holding his gloves in one hand. He looked at them as if he wondered how they had got there, and then tossed them onto the low table in the centre of the room. He said, 'Is my sister well?'

'Very well.' Suragai's father gestured towards a chest against the wall. On it there was a tray loaded with wine flagons and cups. 'Do you want something to drink?'

Alexei nodded shortly. He walked past them. Suragai saw that his father was turning to follow, and he knew that he was expected to play the servant. He poured wine into three of the cups. Alexei was wearing the sable hat of a khan. He took it off and ran a hand through his yellow hair. Then he laid the hat aside. The jewel pinned to it sparkled in the light of the lamps, and Suragai estimated that it must have cost thousands of koban. He stared in awe.

When Suragai held out the first cup, Alexei took it and drank deeply. 'I did not expect to see you so soon,' D'mitri said. He took the second cup from Suragai's hand and sipped from it.

'I was riding before I got your message,' Alexei said. He drained his cup and set it on the table. 'I saw the ship your visitors came in when it passed over Khitai.'

And knew what it was, Suragai thought. He drank some wine, hiding his realisation.

After the Kha-Khan, and the Kha-Khan's grandfather Burun, this offworlder was probably the most powerful and influential man in the world. Apart from being Khan of Khitai, he was the commander of the armies of the Khanate.

D'mitri said, 'I have sent to Kinsai, of course.'

'Of course.' Alexei gestured negligently.

'Your father will hear as soon as Burun does.' D'mitri rolled his cup between his palms.

'As soon as the Kha-Khan hears.' Alexei nodded. 'But now you want me to tell you what to do.' The corner of his mouth twitched. 'I am sure you have some ideas of your own.'

Suragai saw his father frown. 'They are an embassy,' he said. 'We have no choice but to respect that.'

Alexei laughed harshly. 'That's a matter of opinion. Where have you put them?'

'In Burun's house.'

'Hunh.' Alexei nodded approval. 'And you have their ship under guard. I saw it as I rode in. Good.'

Someone had placed a brazier in a tray of silver sand near the wall. Suragai went to it and stirred the burning coals so that they flared. Above the domed roof the twin moons shone brightly, and through the glass Suragai could see the stars. The coals had been mixed with incense, and the sweet scent of it rose on the air.

'You always said they would come.' D'mitri looked into his cup. He drank from it and then set it aside.

'It seemed likely,' Alexei said. He touched the gold caste mark on his cheek. 'If they are from the Empire I once knew, then maybe they will obey me.'

The mark was supposed to mean that Alexei was of the Blood Imperial, Suragai recalled. For a moment he wondered if that might mean that Alexei's loyalties would be divided, and then he dismissed the notion. Alexei was Jehan's brother-in-law, and his son Kubulai was a khan in his own right. His old allegiance to the Empire could be of no significance compared with that.

'They say they want to discuss trade, and some kind of relationship, but I do not believe them,' D'mitri said.

Alexei produced a grim smile. 'The fact that they have come at all means that we have something they want.'

Suragai wondered if anyone was aware of his presence in the room. Neither Alexei nor his father looked in his direction, even when he moved. D'mitri nodded. 'They mean to try negotiation first,' he said. 'They had guns, but they gave them up in deference to the law.'

'A few guns mean nothing to them.' Alexei moved a

102

stool with his foot and sat down on it. 'It does mean that they are anxious to avoid giving offence,' he said thoughtfully. 'Maybe we can use that against them.'

If Alexei knew what the offworlders wanted, then he had just decided to keep the information to himself. Suragai saw that his father had anticipated a more positive reaction, and was hiding his disappointment. What Alexei knew, the Kha-Khan knew also. The realisation made Suragai feel happier. He poured more wine into Alexei's cup.

'I will talk to them tomorrow,' Alexei said. He picked up the cup and drank from it. Suddenly he seemed to notice Suragai, and he smiled.

It was difficult to assess an offworlder's true age, Suragai decided. He had always supposed that his father and Alexei were of similar years. Alexei's features were unlined, however, and his skin still possessed the suppleness which might be expected to have been lost by a man in middle years.

They are not like us.

The thought struck Suragai with such force that it brushed every other consideration aside, and he was sure it showed on his face. If there was a doubt about Alexei's loyalty, then it centred upon the fact that he was an alien. Suddenly Suragai remembered his own alien blood. He flushed, and avoided Alexei's amused gaze.

A room in Alexei's own house was being prepared for the day's audience with the offworld ambassador. The room's windows looked out onto the main square of Pesth, and through them Suragai could see the troopers of a Merkut tuman who were diverting away non-essential traffic.

The room was about fifty drem in length. A dais had been constructed at one end, and a single carved chair had been placed on it. In front of the dais the floor had been sanded and polished with wax until it reflected the colours of the hangings across the ceiling and down the walls. The Yek had once been nomads, and it was still not unusual to find interior decoration that made a room look like the inside of a tent. A cream C'zak rug had been laid on the polished floor. Its fringes had been teased out so that every strand was visible. Towards the back of the rug there were two plain wooden stools.

Suragai smiled grimly. The arrangement of the audience chamber was a clear message to the alien ambassador that his status was very minor compared with that of a khan speaking for the Dragon Throne. The spaces on the two long sides of the room were already filling with the men of rank who were available. They jostled for position and argued about precedence. Suragai saw Orcadai, one of Burun's sons, in the midst of a crowd of his retainers near the front on the right.

Horns were sounding somewhere on the other side of the square. Suragai glanced out of the window again, but at first he could see nothing. The square was paved with grey granite, and the lighter crystals in the stone reflected the morning sun. Troopers had formed up in a double line across the square. Suragai narrowed his eyes against the glare. A small crowd of onlookers was gathering, but they were not being permitted to approach closer than the fronts of the houses facing onto the open area. A faint cheer rose and died away again. Somebody had seen the embassy's escort, and had mistaken them for persons of rank. The standard of the castellan of Pesth was coming down between the rows of troopers. Behind it rode Suragai's father, and following him came the ambassador and his officer. They had been given st'lyan to ride, and they looked uncomfortable.

Everyone dismounted in front of the house. D'mitri was wearing the silver-faced coat of a s'zltan, and his sword hilts were adjusted in his sash at precisely the correct angle. By comparison the offworlders looked plain. Their coats were a kind of blue-green buckram. A sunburst in yellow was embossed on the left breast of each, and the older man wore a gold chain about his neck – a mark of his office, Suragai supposed. They looked about at the troopers with their glittering weapons, then followed D'mitri inside.

Alexei was entering the room. He was wearing a court dress coat of midnight blue. The facings of the coat were embroidered with his arms, and beneath it Suragai saw the high-necked silk tunic of an officer of the Kha-Khan's household. Alexei was carrying his sword – it would not have been practical to wear it. The scabbard was chased with gold and the hilt was bound with silk and gold wire.

The whole room bowed. Alexei's hair had been dressed Yek style – pulled into a queue which had been folded forward over the top of his scalp and bound with black and gold cords as befitted his rank. His complexion was high, and the caste mark on his cheek seemed to glow luminously. He acknowledged the bows with a nod, and then sat carefully in the carved chair. Attendants and officers rushed to arrange the skirts of his coat, then disposed themselves behind and to the sides of the chair, looking solemn. Alexei placed the tip of the scabbard of his sword against the instep of one foot, then propped the sword so that it was between his legs, the hilt resting on the opposite thigh. His expression was remote, as if he was unimpressed by his surroundings.

Suragai was one of only two men in the room entitled to wear the fancy gold coat of the Altun. The other was T'zin, the last surviving member of the male line of Arjun the Great, and he was sitting on a chair which had been placed for him at the front of the crowd on the left. The collar of Suragai's coat was uncomfortable – it scratched. He ran a finger around the neck band, and then began to make his way towards the dais. Men who turned to find out who was pushing past them nodded respectfully or bowed when they saw him. Suragai ignored them. When he reached the front he bowed towards Alexei. Alexei's head came round. He smiled thinly and nodded.

The doors were opening. D'mitri came into the room, and the two aliens followed, walking side by side. Suragai watched as his father walked onto the front of the rug and bowed low to Alexei. The ambassador and his officer stopped. They both stared at Alexei.

D'mitri said, 'Lord Khan, I present the ambassador of the foreigners and his officer.'

It was not a flattering introduction. Suragai grinned. Alexei nodded and waved a hand dismissively. At once D'mitri bowed again. Then he moved off to the side.

Alexei gave the aliens a calm stare. 'I am Alexei Khan, Lord of the province of Khitai and the representative here of Jehan Kha-Khan, the Lord of the Earth,' he said. 'You should bow to me.'

The offworlders were still staring. They appeared to be transfixed by the sight of Alexei on the dais. After a moment both bowed. The bows were followed by some kind of obeisance, a gesture in which both hands were spread wide. Suragai saw Alexei smile distantly.

'My lord,' the older man said, 'we were unprepared to encounter you here.'

Alexei touched the mark on his cheek. 'You recognise this,' he said.

'My lord, we do.' The ambassador bowed again. 'And we revere it. Had we known your presence on this world we would have presented our credentials to you.'

It was apparent that Alexei was amused by the reply. 'I think you are doing that now.' He gestured at the stools. 'Sit, if you will.'

The offworlders looked at the stools and then at one another. They seated themselves awkwardly. Men in the crowd stirred impatiently. Few of them had understood the significance of what had passed.

'You are as I understand it an embassy for the purpose of arranging trade?' Alexei gave the ambassador an encouraging smile.

The alien seemed to hesitate. Then he said, 'My lord, that is part of our function.'

Suragai supposed that he was not the only man listening who detected an equivocation. Alexei for his part was pursing his lips. 'Your discretion does you credit,' he commented drily. Suddenly he sat forward. 'What trade, specifically?'

It should not have been important, Suragai thought. Trade was a matter for men of business, and not for khans. He watched the offworlders' faces. The ambassador licked his lips. 'Lord,' he appealed, 'you cannot expect us to define our interest so soon.'

The expression on Alexei's face became coldly remote. 'And yet I think you have answered me,' he said. He turned and spoke over his shoulder to one of his officers. The man nodded. He crossed behind Alexei's chair and left the room. Suragai wondered about Alexei's reaction to the ambassador's reply. Nothing of great importance seemed to have been said, and yet it was clear that a critical question had been asked and answered.

Alexei gestured to an attendant, a N'pani, and the man came forward with a cup of wine, kneeling to offer it. The aliens were watching with worried frowns on their faces. Alexei drank, then handed back the cup. His head came round. He said, 'As you have answered, so shall I advise the Kha-Khan. Your answers to the questions he may ask, you should be aware, will require to be particular.'

The ambassador appeared to draw a breath. He nodded and smiled. 'My lord, I thank you.'

'And now tell us if you will of the Empire,' Alexei continued smoothly. 'Of what house are you?'

The new line of enquiry took the offworlders by surprise. They exchanged glances. 'House Nicoleyev, my lord.' The older man bowed awkwardly from his stool.

'Indeed.' Alexei seemed to be inspecting the toe of his boot. Suddenly he looked up. 'And does House Andreeyev prosper still?'

'My lord?' The ambassador's brow furrowed.

Alexei gave him a flat stare. 'I spoke clearly enough, I think,' he said. 'You intend trade with this world. That implies a franchise, or you would not be here. I asked about the house you represent because I would assure myself that the Andreeyev are not involved.'

'They are not, my lord,' the alien responded quickly. He glanced sideways at his companion, and then seemed to gather himself. 'Lord,' he said, 'tell us how you came here. The Empire will rejoice at news of you.'

'That I doubt,' Alexei said, his tone caustic. 'As to the manner of my being here, it may be told simply. I was abandoned by a survey vessel years ago.'

The ambassador's expression mirrored a polite concern. 'My lord, I am sorry to hear it. And yet you are of rank, as you would be in the Empire.'

Alexei had not mentioned his father or the others, and seemed not to intend to. Suragai had expected the audience to take an altogether different course, and thought that too much time was being spent on matters of no importance.

'It is true that I have been honoured by the Kha-Khan for my service to him,' Alexei said. He gave the ambassador a hard look. 'For my imperial rank you should offer me respect and should be open with me. As the representative of the Kha-Khan you must know that I expect no less. Speak to me once more about your purpose here.'

Some of the men standing around the hall were beginning to lose interest in the audience. Whispered conversations were underway. Now suddenly there was an abrupt silence. Everyone waited intently to hear what the alien would say.

If the ambassador was dismayed by the unlooked-for return to the subject, he did not let it show on his face. His expression became resolute. 'My lord,' he said stoutly, 'it is as I have told you our mission to arrange for trade. We have as you may imagine credentials to deliver to the ruler you now serve –' He returned

Alexei's stare impassively. '– and what may follow from that I cannot say.'

It was no answer at all. Suragai waited for Alexei to press the matter, but he did not. After a moment he nodded as if satisfied, and sat back in his chair. 'You have answered me as the Kha-Khan's envoy, and you pay only lip service to my imperial blood,' he commented. 'Well enough.'

'My lord, I meant no disrespect.' The ambassador produced a travesty of a smile.

Alexei showed his teeth. 'Did you not?' He gestured one-handed. 'Ambassador as you are, you are welcome in our land. Accept our hospitality here in Pesth, and in due time you will be the Kha-Khan's guest also.'

The ambassador stood up quickly. He bowed. 'My lord, we are grateful. We ask only that we may be at liberty to travel.'

There was no mention of the ship which must be waiting in the sky above Pesth. Either the ambassador was somehow in communication with it, and did not think that the Yek could interfere, or he was so confident about the outcome of his embassy that he was willing to wait. Suragai kept his eyes on Alexei's face, and saw that he was pretending to consider the request.

'Travel you may,' Alexei said after a moment. 'You will however respect our laws and customs. Your ship for example –'

'– will remain sealed for the duration of our visit here, my lord,' the ambassador said quickly. He did not seem to be perturbed by the fact that restrictions were to be imposed. He went on, 'My lord, we understand now the attitude of the people here to technology. We will try not to offend.'

'In that case you will understand also that I think it would be unwise for you to travel unescorted,' Alexei said. 'I will appoint some person of rank, and he will be your guide.'

The emotion which passed across the ambassador's face was not one which Suragai was capable of recognising. The younger man had risen belatedly to his feet. The older man glanced back at him, and they both bowed. 'We thank you, my lord,' the ambassador said, 'and hope by our conduct to assure you that contact with the Empire represents no kind of threat.'

Alexei sat forward. 'I am pleased to hear it,' he said.

'We learned nothing,' D'mitri said.

It was the afternoon of the same day. Alexei was no longer in court dress, but wore instead the ordinary tunic and breeches of a soldier. He looked up from the document he was studying. 'You did not.'

Suragai felt as if he was being excluded again. He said, 'We have never assigned much importance to trade. Whatever the Empire wants from us, the restrictions of the Yasa will apply, and that will protect us.'

Alexei gave him a stare. 'Trade will be followed by conquest of a kind,' he said. 'There are many ways to conquer.'

'In that case we should tell them to go,' D'mitri said. 'If we refuse to trade with them, they will leave us alone.'

The Merkut tuman had taken over the inner bailey which was the key to the fortifications guarding the city. The bailey was a massive square tower, and the only light which penetrated its interior came through the arrow slits. Lamps and cressets were supported on brackets and in holders from the walls and roof beams. The flames wavered with every air current.

Alexei was sitting at a long table. He turned halfway round in his chair. 'Refusal is the one course we cannot elect,' he responded. 'For force of arms would follow.'

Suragai laid his scabbarded sword on top of a pile of papers. 'Can trade with us be so important?'

'If they want what I think, then probably the answer to that is yes,' Alexei said.

D'mitri stirred. 'You still haven't told us what they want.'

A shadow passed across Alexei's features. He seemed to consider how to answer, and then drew a deep breath. 'Do you remember seeing the poppies that grow in places near the edge of the G'bai?'

There were great expanses of them, Suragai remembered – tall plants with enormous blue seed pods. He nodded.

'They grow in Marakan,' D'mitri said.

Alexei nodded. 'The catpeople used to grow them.'

Suragai could not imagine the catpeople cultivating anything. They were only barely civilised – a protected species because they possessed talons.

'Flowers.' D'mitri looked amused. 'Is that what the Empire wants?'

It seemed unlikely. Alexei was not smiling. 'They are found on only a few worlds,' he said. 'The sap is very valuable.'

'So valuable they would go to war over it?' D'mitri snorted. 'I don't believe it.'

A flash of annoyance appeared on Alexei's face, and was gone again. He touched the papers on the table, arranging them, then suddenly he looked up. 'How old is my father?' he asked D'mitri.

D'mitri frowned. 'I've never asked,' he said at last.

'Sixty or seventy maybe. What has that to do with anything?'

'He's nearly a hundred,' Alexei said quietly.

It was nonsense of course. 'Older than Burun?' Suragai laughed. 'He can't be.'

'He was over sixty when we came to this land.' Alexei looked perfectly serious.

Suragai supposed it could be true. Aliens are not like us, he thought.

The same notion had clearly occurred to D'mitri. 'You age differently,' he observed.

'Some men are prevented from growing old.' Alexei made the statement baldly. He waited while they adjusted to the idea, then he gestured. 'Collect the sap from the seed pods of the poppy and dissolve it in hot water, then add lime. Filter the precipitate and allow it to dry. Take it every two years as a thirty per cent solution and it will prolong life almost indefinitely.'

The idea was unattractive in the extreme. 'No one in the Empire grows old?' Suragai made a face. 'How can that be?'

Alexei produced a flat stare. 'I said the poppy is found on only a few worlds,' he said. 'There is enough for the people of rank - the privileged.'

'And always more is needed.' D'mitri nodded. 'Now I understand.'

The flickering lamplight cast strange shadows across Alexei's features. He laid his hands flat on the table. 'Jehan knows the secret,' he said. 'Burun also - and now you.'

Suragai saw his father raise his eyebrows. 'You feared we would desire immortality,' D'mitri said.

It was a ridiculous notion. Suragai smiled at the look on Alexei's face. He said, 'Alexei, consider how we are made. We don't get sick. We heal very fast. The same things kill us as kill other men, but we live long anyway.'

Alexei had not been worried that the True People would be tempted, Suragai realised suddenly. Other races in the world were less immune to disease. Men grew old, and fell ill. Sometimes dying was not easy. There would always be a few who would see the advantage in staying the hand of God.

'Some men are always afraid to die,' D'mitri said. He inclined his head towards Alexei. 'Khan, we're honoured you trust us with this.'

'It isn't all advantage,' Alexei commented. 'But maybe the Empire doesn't know that yet. The men who ruled Marakan in Artai's time were hundreds of years old. After a while their bones dissolved because they took the drug.'

D'mitri wrinkled his nose in distaste. 'To live like that would be a curse,' he said. 'Your father took it once – you also?'

'Yes.' Alexei nodded. 'I was Blood Imperial and so ...' He gestured. 'The effect of the drug wears off after a time if the treatment is not renewed. Both of us are ageing normally now.'

Or nearly so. Suragai guessed that there was a permanent effect on characteristics like skin texture. He tried to remember if Alexei ever got sick, and thought not. He said, 'If the Empire learns the price of taking it, maybe they will not desire it so greatly.'

'Probably they would not believe me if I told them,' Alexei said. 'The Marakani are long dead.'

The Marakani had been allowed to die. Suragai recalled the rumours, and knew the truth they concealed. Alexei had never been tempted to renew the treatment, even though the poppy was available, because of what he had seen in Marakan.

'Which leaves us where?' D'mitri looked unhappy. 'If we trade with the Empire, conquest will follow, you say. Refuse to trade, and the result will be the same.'

'Negotiations can take a long time.' Alexei stood up. He gave them an oblique stare. 'A lot can happen.'

None of which would make any difference at all if the Empire was powerful enough, Suragai thought. He wondered why Alexei was pretending that they could delay the inevitable.

'And in the end we will still have to fight,' D'mitri said.

Alexei shrugged. 'Maybe. The Empire must believe they can win if it comes to that. Probably they can, but I don't imagine they realise that they will have to kill us all.'

'Maybe we should explain the Yasa,' Suragai said.

'I doubt if it would make a difference.' Alexei smiled sourly. 'Even if we tell them we will never surrender because it is the law, they won't believe it. Remember I know them. There are no absolute laws in their eyes. They live by compromise.'

Suragai thought that it must be very confusing never to be certain exactly what was right. He picked up his sword from the table. 'How can they have order if they compromise their laws?'

'It's what happens when trade becomes more important than everything else,' Alexei said. 'People start to believe that everything is for sale – even right and wrong.'

'You think we can beat them,' D'mitri said, 'or we would not be talking about it.'

'Hunh.' Alexei showed his teeth. 'It's clear they don't

want to fight if they can avoid it. Maybe they can't afford to.'

'A man who attempts conquest and is not prepared to fight to win is a fool,' D'mitri said brusquely.

Suragai could not imagine the circumstances in which anyone would allow themselves to be so circumscribed that they would be prevented from doing whatever was necessary to win. He hoped Alexei would explain, but he did not. Instead he said, 'Are they eating our food yet?'

'They did not at first.' D'mitri frowned. 'They brought food from their ship, but they did not have much. Now they have accepted meat –' He sniffed. '– though what they will do with it without servants is beyond my comprehension.'

Alexei said, 'If they have eaten our food, they are going to get sick.'

'They are?' Suragai could not imagine how Alexei knew. 'Maybe we ought to warn them.'

'And maybe not,' D'mitri said. He gave Alexei a look. 'Are they going to recover?'

'In a day or two.' Alexei nodded. 'You can reorganise their household while they are incapable of arguing about it.'

'You want to know what they are going to do before they do it,' Suragai said.

Alexei turned to stare at D'mitri. 'You haven't told him yet.'

'Told me what?' Suragai glanced from his father to Alexei and back again.

'You are going to look after the aliens until they are ready to leave,' Alexei said.

'Am I?' Suragai took a deep breath. 'Well now.'

*

116

The ambassador fell sick in the early hours of the morning. By the time Suragai got to the house the other aliens were also in distress. The young officer was sitting at the foot of the stairs. Suragai placed a hand on his forehead. 'Name of God, you're on fire.'

'I can't breathe,' the offworlder said. 'Ambassador Borocheff is the same.'

'And your men?' Suragai gestured to one of the troopers. 'Go find a Sechem.' He turned back to look at the offworlder.

'They have fever.' The alien tried to get to his feet. 'You ought not to come so close to me. Either we have no immunity against a sickness which is native to this world, or we have brought something with us, and because the air is different it has altered. Are any of the men who guard us sick?'

'Oh.' Suragai smiled at him. 'We never get sick.' He remembered what Alexei had said. 'Probably it's something you ate.'

The offworlder laughed weakly. He folded over on his side. More troopers were coming through the door. Suragai gestured to them and indicated the alien. 'Look after him.' He went up the stairs. An offworlder soldier was sitting against the wall beside one of the doors. When he saw Suragai he tried to stand. Suragai looked over the side of the staircase at the hall below. It was filling with servants. He entered the ambassador's room. The ambassador was lying over the bed. He had been sick.

D'mitri came into the room at Suragai's back. He looked at the alien. 'God, what a mess.'

Two Y'frike servants came through the door. Suragai pointed at the ambassador. 'Take him down. Clean him up. Wash his face and keep him cool.'

'Yes, Noyon.' The Y'frike bowed.

Suragai went out onto the landing, and his father followed. Men were carrying unconscious aliens down from the upper floor. One of the troopers said, 'Lord, it's like a pigsty up there.'

Suragai wrinkled his nose. 'See to the aliens first. Tomorrow you can strip the house. Burn everything you can't clean.'

D'mitri stared. 'Isn't that a bit drastic?'

It was Burun's house, but now it smelled like a too long-occupied barrack room. Suragai said, 'If I am arranging their household, then they will live like civilised men.'

'I see.' D'mitri looked amused. 'We were right to appoint you to this. Master of the Household of the Foreigners could become one of your hereditary titles.'

Suragai gave his father a cool glance. 'I think not.'

Troopers were hauling pallets in from the cart outside in the street, taking them into the downstairs rooms. 'It's as well we were prepared,' D'mitri said. He gestured around. 'What do you think caused this?'

If Alexei had arranged for the offworlders to be poisoned, there would be no evidence. Suragai shrugged. 'Maybe it's as Alexei said.' Poison was not a Yek weapon, and suddenly Suragai was glad of it. He glanced up the stairs, thinking that he ought to inspect the upper floor, but the stale odour deterred him. Suragai wondered if the aliens were aware of it, or if their sense of smell, like their hearing, was less acute. He caught his father's eye. 'They think they are civilised,' he said, 'but really they are not.'

D'mitri seemed to consider. He said, 'Maybe they will learn from us.' He gave Suragai an odd look – as if what he had said had nothing to do with what he was thinking, and then he went down the stairs and out of the front door.

'This is very fine,' Suragai's mother said. 'Where was it made?'

'It was sent from Alexei's fief in Y'vrope,' Suragai said. 'He gave it to me to give to you.'

Irina ran her hand across the inlays of the chest. 'I don't think I've ever seen anything like it before.'

Suragai shrugged. The Y'vrope were a strange race, completely individualistic in their attitude to everything. Only by settling Yek on their unused land had it been possible to bring them gradually into the Khanate, for most of them had no sense of order at all. Governing them was a lesson in patience. Suragai said, 'Probably you won't see its like again.' Y'vrope craftsmen seldom made anything the same way twice.

The chest opened by sliding the lid to the right. The lid was on an extending hinge, and moving it across unlocked a hook which caught a recess in the main frame. Irina opened it. A scent of herbs rose from the interior of the box, and Suragai thought that the wood must have been smoked or oiled to produce the effect. Turakina was folding sheets, laying each one out on the floor to examine it for wear, and she turned her head and breathed in deeply, smiling.

Bhutan came suddenly into the room. He hesitated when he saw Suragai, and then edged up to Irina, pushing his head up into the curve of her arm so that she was forced to stop what she was doing to give him attention. She rapped him on the top of the head with her knuckles, but there was no severity in her expression and he giggled and pressed against her.

119

There was a mirror at Suragai's side, and in its reflection he saw Turakina's mouth turn down. He grinned, and she scowled at him.

'Brother, you are so ugly, I don't know how I can bear your presence,' she said haughtily.

His mother's head came round. 'He looks like his father,' she said. 'Ugly men are always interesting.'

Suragai frowned. 'I wish women wouldn't discuss a man in his presence as if he were a piece of meat,' he commented. He knelt on the floor beside the low polished table. A pot of ch'ban was simmering on a tiny stove set in a tray of sand. He poured some into a cup and sipped at it.

Turakina folded a sheet lengthwise, and then signed to the maid who was kneeling in the far corner of the room to come and take it. She looked round. 'Handsome men are vain,' she observed.

'Then that's a flaw I must be free of,' Suragai said equably. He emptied the cup. Fine grains of ch'ban had gathered in the bottom, and he pursed his lips at the bitter taste.

'I did not marry your father for his looks.' His mother closed the chest gently. She looked straight at Suragai. 'But because he was strong, but also gentle, brave and yet kind.'

It was as if she was remembering a young girl's emotions, and Suragai flushed. Turakina stirred. 'How old were you when you fell in love?'

Irina looked round. 'Your age or a little older,' she said. 'I married the day I was sixteen. Your father was only a thousand commander then, and because I was a khan's daughter there were men coming from every part of the land to court me.'

Probably they had been courting her less for her

father's rank than for the fact that she was Altun, the grand-daughter of Burun and the cousin of the Kha-Khan, Suragai thought, but he said nothing.

Turakina spread her slim hands. Her extended talons flashed. 'It did not matter to you that the man you loved was not human,' she said.

'Humanity is a matter of degree,' Irina responded, looking at Suragai as she spoke.

'My name is Constantin Zarubin,' the young man said.

Suragai thought that alien names were awkward and ugly, but he did not allow it to show in his expression. The members of the embassy had recovered the day before. Suragai still thought they had been poisoned, although he could not work out the point of only incapacitating a victim. If it had been done so that the Yek could introduce agents into the embassy household, it had been a great deal of effort for no appreciable result.

The garden was a flat expanse of grass dotted with carefully tended flowering trees. Stone benches were set at intervals along a winding path, and close to the house a fountain tinkled. Suragai rolled onto his side. 'You have two names,' he said. 'Most of us have only one.'

The offworlder was sitting with his back to a tree which bore tiny yellow flowers. He was wearing a tunic and trousers of silk like a civilised man, but his hair was still too short to be cut Yek style, and he had refused to permit Suragai to shade his eyelids as protection against the glare of the sun. He shifted. 'In fact we have three. I am really Constantin Sergeivitch - Constantin son of Sergei. Zarubin is my family name.'

It seemed like a lot of trouble to go to simply to identify a man. Suragai wrinkled his nose. 'I suppose I could say I am Suragai son of D'mitri,' he said, 'but it would be of no significance. A man is himself. He is not his father or his family.'

'And yet I remember you used two names when first you spoke to us,' Constantin said.

Suragai frowned, trying to recall what he had said. 'I called myself Suragai Noyon,' he said after a moment. 'That is my rank. I am of noble birth.'

'Ah.' The offworlder nodded. Then he seemed to hesitate. 'There is much I want to ask, but I am afraid of offending you ...'

'Hunh.' Suragai grinned. He had already marked how wary the aliens were about what they said to Yek, and guessed that they had been warned in the strictest terms. He said, 'Ask what you will. Only remember that if your customs are different from ours you should not comment on it as if it is ours that are wrong.'

Constantin smiled nervously. He said, 'Then pardon me, but if you are as you are, how can it be that the castellan calls you his son? You are of different species.'

The question was of a far more personal nature than Suragai had anticipated. He pursed his lips. 'I am Altun,' he said coldly, 'of the Golden Clan, which is to say that I am a descendant of the Ancestor, the first Kha-Khan.' It should have been answer enough, but it was clear from the lack of understanding on the alien's face that it was not. Suragai gestured one-handed so that his talons glittered. He said, 'The blood of the races of the True People is dominant. My mother is human, and her mother. We are Altun

122

through the female line.' In time he restrained himself from observing that his grandfather was alien. The offworlders were not supposed to know that yet.

The young officer licked his lips. 'I had thought at first that talons were a mutation,' he said. 'But too many people have them.'

Suragai raised his eyebrows. The Yasa permitted the mutations which survived to become adults to live in peace, but they were not allowed to breed to produce more of their kind. He gave the alien a flat stare. 'We are a race apart,' he said.

A st'lyan screamed in the street which passed the end of the garden. Constantin's head came up, then he looked back to Suragai. 'So much of what I have seen on this world already is strange to my eyes,' he said.

It was an odd remark. Suragai thought that he would have been surprised to find much which was familiar on another world. He stared at Constantin. 'What did you expect?'

The alien seemed to be considering how to answer. At last he said, 'For one thing we did not anticipate such order - a whole world under a single rule.' He hesitated. 'We expected more chaos.'

'Oh. Why?'

'Well.' Constantin grimaced. 'It's the pattern we have come to expect on worlds like this.' He gave Suragai a swift glance to see if he understood. 'Looking at this land from space we can tell that it was once covered by radiation. We have found that where species survive radiation at all, they are altered. The results can be terrible.'

'Mutations.' Suragai nodded. 'Some still occur, but we have laws which help to control their occurrence.'

The offworlder looked uncomfortable. 'The beasts

you ride are unusual,' he said, 'and I have seen other species I would have thought mutated if they did not breed true.'

He means the races which possess talons, Suragai thought. He gave Constantin a thoughtful stare. The offworlder flushed and looked away. Suragai smiled grimly. 'If you judge by what you have seen elsewhere, it is no wonder you are amazed.' A movement at the edge of his vision made him turn. D'mitri was coming out into the garden with the ambassador. Alexei followed, and Irina and Turakina were hanging onto his arms. They walked across the grass.

Suragai got onto his knees, then stood up. He saw that the offworlder was getting to his feet. Suragai nodded politely to Alexei, but Constantin bowed. 'Khan, good morning.'

Alexei was wearing a loose linen shirt, and he did not appear to be armed. Troopers of his personal guard hovered in the doorway of the house, watching as if they expected him to be attacked. Suragai grinned. Nobody trusted the aliens.

D'mitri said, 'Ambassador, you have met my son.'

The ambassador nodded and smiled. He looked weak from the effects of sickness, and his complexion was pale. 'My lord, yes.' He looked back at Suragai. 'Noyon, good day.'

The nod Alexei gave Constantin was distant. He said something in a low voice to Turakina, and she laughed.

Suragai saw Constantin flush. The alien bowed again. 'Lady, good morning.'

The young offworlder was not of noble birth, or he would have said so. Turakina gave him a single, amused stare. She said nothing. Irina said, 'Let's sit over

124

there.' She pointed to one of the stone benches, and Alexei nodded. They went past D'mitri and the ambassador across the grass. Constantin followed them with his eyes. Suragai saw him frown.

The ambassador said, 'Noyon, I have to thank you for our care these past days.'

'We could not let you die,' Suragai responded lightly. In fact the aliens had required almost no attention. The fever they had suffered had abated in every case after a day or so. They had slept a day beyond that, and then had awakened apparently little the worse. A Sechem had prescribed only sponging to reduce the fever. No other treatment had been necessary.

Borocheff smiled as if he realised that Suragai was not serious. Then he bowed to D'mitri and took Constantin by the arm and led him out onto the grass on the other side of the tree. He started to speak in very fast Anglic. Suragai strained to listen, and heard the ambassador ask the younger man about an earlier conversation. He glanced at his father. 'They are trying to find out how strong we really are,' D'mitri said, 'and if the Khanate is settled and at peace. What did the young one want to know?'

Suragai shrugged. 'We talked about mutations.'

'Oh?' D'mitri raised his eyebrows. The ambassador was walking towards the bench on which Alexei was sitting. When he reached it he bowed and sat down. Suragai saw Constantin watching. There was an odd expression on his face. After a moment the young offworlder turned and started off towards the house. 'The ambassador is minor nobility,' D'mitri said. 'But that one is what they call a kulak – provincial farming stock.'

Constantin was skirting the fountain. 'I don't like his

125

interest in Turakina,' Suragai said.

D'mitri looked thoughtful. 'Don't discourage him too much. He could be useful to us.'

'Indeed.' Suragai made a face. 'I can't think how.' The thought that Turakina might have to put up with alien attentions was so offensive that he dug his talons into the palms of his hands as he considered it. He looked across at Turakina. Her eyes were on Constantin.

'If the Empire wants to trade for the poppy, the people who know they will be excluded from treatment may be our friends,' D'mitri said.

It made a kind of sense, but Suragai was unconvinced. 'A man who is a member of an embassy must be of merit, even if he is not noble.'

D'mitri looked disapproving. 'Alexei says that only the Imperial family and their chief men are assured the drug,' he said. 'After that it goes to those who can pay.'

Suragai had already discovered that much of the nobility of the Empire was based on the ownership of trading cartels. It was inconceivable that anyone could be concerned with acquiring wealth, and still discharge his duty to uphold the law. He remembered what Alexei had said about people believing that right and wrong could be for sale, and suddenly he understood. They have no honour, he thought.

The alien soldiers had been billeted in a small building which adjoined the main Merkut barracks. When the ambassador did not require them they were free to wander the streets and marketplaces of Pesth. None of them so far as Suragai could tell was clever enough to insinuate himself into the confidence of anyone of

126

consequence, and it was without much hesitation therefore that he had relaxed the watch which was kept on them. One of the men was of a rank which Suragai judged to be equivalent to centurion. The rest were common soldiers – very little different in character from the conscripts who filled the ranks of any army.

Alexei appeared unconcerned when he was told. He said, 'It is not the aliens we can see we have to worry about.'

At first Suragai did not understand. Then he realised that offworlders were quite capable of merging with the populace. Physically they were similar to C'zaki – in fact Anglic and C'zak were basically the same tongue. He gave Alexei a stare. 'You think they have placed spies.'

'If they haven't, then I think we can expect them to.' Alexei looked as if he thought the conclusion ought to be obvious. 'It doesn't matter whether the Empire wants to trade or to conquer, they will need information – more than they are getting from us. I think we are supposed to congratulate ourselves on how clever we have been. We have restricted the embassy's ability to travel, its members are watched constantly, and all the time we should be looking elsewhere. In fact I'm not particularly concerned about them spying on us. They'll only discover how strong we are. What worries me is the thought that their agents may try to cause unrest at some point – among the Ch'noze say, or the Y'frike, or maybe the Alan.'

The Ch'noze in particular needed no encouragement to rise in revolt. Ch'nozia was under garrison occupation – and had been since its conquest eighty years before – because the warlike tribes could be relied upon to go to war not only with the Yek but also with each other the moment they sensed any relaxation in control. Suragai frowned. 'It will take more than a few uprisings to trouble us.'

'That's true.' Alexei nodded. 'But the kind of thing I am talking about would only be the start.' He grimaced. 'The Empire is very good at destabilisation.'

Sand had been scattered across the cobbles outside Alexei's house to deaden the noise of passing cart wheels. Suragai glanced out of the open window and saw that a line of st'lyan remounts were being led past the gate by troopers on foot. The hooves of the st'lyan kicked sand high into the air, and the crystalline grains sparkled in the light of the late afternoon sun. Suragai looked back into the room. He was still not sure he trusted Alexei. 'To know what the Empire intends is one thing, Khan. It's another matter to prevent it,' he said austerely.

A corner of Alexei's mouth twitched. 'I'm already doing something about that,' he responded drily. 'We can identify the aliens because they will all fall sick after two or three days. It's not the kind of thing they are going to be able to hide. I'm sending orders to all constabulars and bailiffs to report on anyone who becomes incapacitated.'

'You haven't ordered detention?' Suragai asked.

Alexei wrinkled his nose. 'Once we know who they are, maybe we can use them,' he said.

Suragai could not imagine how. He drew the shutter of the window across. 'And in the end we will still have to fight,' he said.

Eleven more days passed before the Kha-Khan's summons arrived. During that time the arrow messengers moved back and forward across the Khanate, and men whose bearing would have identified them as soldiers if they had not been dressed in styles more becoming to pack traders began to frequent the inns and way-stations on the caravan routes which linked the cities. They sat quietly in the public rooms, listening to the conversations of the travellers. Occasionally they were seen speaking to men wearing plain tunics and serviceable riding cloaks. These rode singly or at the most in pairs, and might have been couriers, for they seemed to stop only long enough to grain and water their st'lyan. Other men camped in small groups in the mountains or in the desolate vastness of the empty plains, and watched the sky.

There was no sign meanwhile that the members of the alien embassy were aware that their progress towards Kinsai was being delayed. Ambassador Borocheff met with either Alexei or D'mitri on a more or less daily basis, and while it was to be expected that he would enquire when he would be permitted to present his credentials, no hint of impatience was ever displayed. If he was perturbed by the evasive answers he was careful not to show it. Instead he smiled politely and changed the subject.

Both the ambassador and his officer rode every day in the countryside around Pesth. Suragai was their escort, and he was forced to observe that neither of the offworlders appeared to be very comfortable in the saddle. That they persisted he presumed must be due to the fact that they knew that permission to proceed to Kinsai would mean a journey of several thousand verst. There could be no other reason. At other times the aliens fulfilled minor social engagements, or else they relaxed in the comparative luxury of the accommodation which had been provided for them. Suragai had directed the organisation of the embassy household, and so the offworlders lived in some style. If they were aware that their servants and attendants were also their watchers, they were untroubled by it. They went as guests to banquets hosted by the minor nobility of Pesth, but at no time could they be said to have contact with anyone who was unknown to Alexei's rapidly developing secret service.

It occurred to Suragai that the Empire might have been maintaining agents in the Khanate for some time. He raised the possibility with Alexei, and was puzzled by the reply he received.

'No.' Alexei shook his head. 'The Empire I knew prohibited men from visiting this world, for they feared the contamination which might result. Any change in that policy must be recent. You cannot imagine how they feel about worlds on which the power which causes radiation has been used, or about species unlike themselves. If they have a new policy it is because they are desperate. If they are desperate, then probably there has been little time for them to prepare.'

Suragai guessed that the answer made sense only in terms of alien understanding. He said, 'If they are desperate, they ought to be more impatient.'

'I expect they are,' Alexei observed mildly. 'But they know better than to let it show.'

The situation was very confusing. Suragai could not understand why Alexei was so calm, and said so.

Alexei smiled grimly. He said, 'Whatever the Empire tries, it will be child's play compared with one of Burun's intrigues.'

Burun was Suragai's great-grandfather, and he knew he ought to be offended. He stared coldly at Alexei, but Alexei only laughed.

'There is another yurt frame over there.' Suragai pointed. 'But the timbers for the floor are in the cart we had to leave on the road. Who are we going to put in the yurt with no floor?'

'I don't suppose the aliens will know the difference,' D'mitri said. He stared around the unwinding chaos of the camp, and then looked back again. 'On the other hand they may. You take it.'

Suragai scowled. An embassy with a small escort could have stayed at an inn. There were enough of them on the road between Pesth and Kinsai. He stood in the stirrups and stared back across the plain to see if the main body of the embassy party was in sight yet. A cloud of dust marked its progress. 'All this for two men.' Suragai spat to clear the dust from his throat. Troopers from the vanguard were hauling yurt timbers off the back of a cart which was parked on the level ground nearby. They dumped the timbers on the grass and dropped the rolled-up strips of felt for the cover beside them.

His father's head came round. He eyed Suragai, looking thoughtful. 'There's a bit more to it than that,' he said mildly.

In fact there was a great deal more. Suragai had anticipated command of an escort of no more than twenty men – the status of the alien ambassador did not justify more in his opinion. Instead he found himself attempting to control a cavalcade forty carts long – and that was only the advance party which was required for the construction of a night camp – along with its guard of five hundred men. Suragai said, 'I suppose I understand why Alexei had to come. The rest could have followed later.'

'Your mother and sister for example,' his father said flatly.

Suragai flushed at his father's tone. Alexei had brought his wife Jehana from Khitai a few days earlier, and her presence – and the fact that she was travelling to Kinsai with her husband – had been all the excuse Irina had required. Now both she and Turakina were riding with the main body which was even now approaching the camp. The women had no interest in the embassy's audience with the Kha-Khan. Unlike his predecessors Jehan did not remain all year round in Kinsai, but made regular progress from city to city. At present he was in X'nadu, returning to the seat of his administration a month early because of the necessity of receiving the embassy. The ceremonial entry into the capital was the social event of the year, and was the one occasion when almost the entire court as well as most of the khans could be expected to be present. 'They should have stayed at home,' Suragai said. He was uncomfortably aware of a glint which had appeared in his father's eye, but pressed on. 'You are too easy with them.'

It was clear to Suragai that there was no place for women in these events. The aliens would be accorded only the briefest hearing by the Kha-Khan, he was certain. Then they would be dismissed and war would follow – Suragai could imagine no other proper course. It did not matter what Alexei said. His opinion was suspect in any case; Jehan would see that.

Troopers propped up a yurt frame in a line with the others, and secured the timbers where they inter-

132

sected. The structure was like an upturned bowl. Men clambered across it. The felt was unrolled and stretched over the frame on one side. As soon as a section was in place it was laced to the uprights.

D'mitri said, 'Don't tell me how to manage my house.'

Suragai felt himself going crimson. 'I'm sorry. I didn't mean to –'

'Irina is husband-hunting for your sister.' D'mitri spoke as if he had not heard the apology.

'Eh?' Suragai gaped. 'While all this is going on? That's madness.'

The st'lyan his father was riding was a chestnut with a light mane. It snorted and sidestepped as men began to throw loose flooring planks into the space inside the yurt. D'mitri reined in, and then looked round at Suragai. 'The world will continue to turn, no matter how anxious you become,' he said. 'Did you think we were going to let the alien court her?'

One of the reasons Suragai was unhappy about Turakina's presence was the fact of her proximity to Constantin. He opened his mouth to say something about propriety, and then saw his father's expression and closed it again. His st'lyan was unsettled by the noise of camp construction. He brought her under control, and then turned to look back across the plain. The main part of the column was an indistinct shadow moving between low hills. Dust hung in the air above it, and Suragai observed the glint of lance points. 'Nobody explains anything to me,' he complained without looking round.

D'mitri laughed harshly. 'You think because you're Altun you should be told everything.'

Suragai ignored the mockery in his father's voice.

The accuracy of the observation made him uncomfortable. 'I am the Kha-Khan's cousin,' he said.

His father snorted. 'Your mother is Jehan's cousin. Your relationship is only an accident of blood.'

Trumpets were sounding off in the distance. Suragai reined around. He gave his father a look. 'Blood is the only real security.'

'Indeed?' D'mitri raised his eyebrows. He said, 'I wondered what this was about. You're concerned because Alexei was an offworlder once.'

'He still is.' Suragai stared back stubbornly. 'Even if the Khanate falls, he will not suffer. See how the aliens respect him.'

'I have seen how they try to avoid telling him anything important.' D'mitri looked amused. 'I think you're angry because you haven't the experience yet to be useful to Jehan.'

Frustration boiled up inside Suragai. 'I don't see how we can trust Alexei,' he burst out. 'And yet his will commands us all.'

The last of the yurts was being covered with felt. It was the one without timbers for a floor, and Suragai scowled towards it. D'mitri said, 'I hold fiefs of Alexei, and serve him. Are you criticising my judgement? Maybe you think my loyalty is suspect also. I'm not human by your standards, after all.'

The rawness in his father's tone made Suragai flinch. He said, 'Father, I'm sorry.'

D'mitri's lips compressed. His blue eyes were cold. 'You use that word too often,' he said. He gathered his reins. 'Don't be sorry. Just don't say what you think all the time. It isn't obligatory, and people will start to imagine you mean it.' He lashed the chestnut's flank abruptly with the ends of his reins. The st'lyan screamed and bolted out of the camp across the plain.

'I never knew animals could travel so fast.' Constantin kicked one foot free of the stirrups and worked his leg to ease the muscles.

Suragai shrugged. 'This is slow.' He thought of telling the offworlder that a Yek army often covered two hundred verst in a day's march, but did not, for it could be considered military information. Alexei had said that the Empire used a unit of measurement called the kilometre – about a thousand paces. A verst was roughly twice that.

It was the final day of their journey. Now they were moving in one unbroken column – there was no advance party because there would be no night camp. The carts were somewhere at the back, and Suragai had left them and their guard to ride out of the dust near the front. Not far away was Alexei, riding on a bay st'lyan with a gilded horn. At his side was his wife, unveiled and dressed in trousers like a man. Beyond them rode the alien ambassador. Turakina was keeping him company, practising her Anglic.

Constantin extracted his other foot from the stirrups. He put his hands one in front of the other on his st'lyan's neck and leaned forward, resting his weight on his arms. 'We don't use animals for riding or load-carrying,' he said. He lifted himself clear of the saddle, wincing.

'Not at all?' Suragai stared.

'The primitive worlds use equines, and oxen to pull carts and ploughs,' Constantin said. He stopped as if he had just bitten his tongue. Quickly he glanced at Suragai. 'I beg your pardon,' he said. 'I meant no offence.'

Suragai showed his teeth. 'I can tell you aren't used to riding far,' he observed. 'Alexei said you use machines for everything. I thought he was exaggerating.'

The mention of Alexei's name seemed to make the young alien stiffen. He came back slowly into the saddle. 'Machines are more efficient,' he said after a moment.

'Oh?' Suragai reined over until he was riding at Constantin's side. 'They might be more powerful, but they use up resources. What happens to a machine when it is old or broken?'

Constantin's brow furrowed. 'Sometimes the metal is melted down to make other things,' he said. 'Mostly we throw away what is old or broken - burn or bury it, or dump it in the sea.'

The notion was contrary to both law and reason. Suragai tried to hide his disgust. 'At least when an animal dies its body feeds the soil,' he said. 'Bones can be burned and the ash mixed with clay to make china.'

It was apparent that the offworlder was assembling arguments. He said, 'You must throw something away. When china breaks -'

'When china breaks it is ground up and used in bricks or in a road,' Suragai said.

'Oh.' Constantin's eyes opened wide. 'Well, you're bound to have some waste.'

'Not much.' Suragai shook his head. 'Old wood still burns, so it can be used for fuel if nothing else. We don't use mortar for building except with bricks. Building stone is cut so that it fits together. What crumbles goes into roads, or we use it to fill holes when we want a level surface.' He paused, then gestured. 'We make everything well, so that it will last

136

as long as possible.'

'Clothes?'

'Old clothes become rags,' Suragai pointed out. 'Old rags can be shredded and washed, then turned into paper or even new cloth.'

Constantin opened his mouth to make a point, and then it was as if the counter-argument had occurred to him, and he closed it again. They rode on for a while. Suddenly the offworlder turned. 'One machine can do the work of ten men,' he said.

Suragai laughed. 'And then what are the men to do?'

'Rest. They don't have to work any more.' Constantin looked as if he thought he had produced an irrefutable argument. 'Machines leave people time to enjoy leisure.'

'Do they?' Suragai wrinkled his nose. 'Machines cost money, and have to be paid for. The men they replace still have to live and feed their families. Where lies the benefit?'

Constantin said, 'Say a merchant has a machine which does the work of ten men. Once he has paid for it his profit will be greater, because he won't have to pay the men. The more machines he has, the more goods he can make.'

'To what purpose?' Suragai asked, puzzled.

'So that he can sell more, and make more profit.' The offworlder looked as if he thought the answer ought to be obvious.

Suragai said, 'The only benefit in such a case is to the merchant, who owns the machine.'

Constantin frowned. 'If he can make his goods more cheaply, then he can sell them for less. People can buy more.'

There was a hole in that argument, Suragai saw. 'A

man can sleep in but one bed, and sit in one chair at a time,' he observed.

'Then he can save his money towards a time when he can work no longer,' the offworlder countered.

The Empire must be quite uncivilised, Suragai thought. He said, 'The old are cared for by the young, and they want for nothing. Why do they need riches?' He felt as if he was trying to explain a concept in a language which had no suitable words.

The young offworlder's face mirrored his lack of comprehension. He said, 'A society which uses machines will become powerful because it can trade to advantage. Profit provides for everyone.'

'Hunh.' Suragai nodded slowly, trying not to show his impatience. 'But eventually the resources upon which that profit is based will be exhausted, and then only the rich will be advantaged. Everyone else will have nothing.' It was why the Khanate had laws to prevent a man from selling goods for more than was deemed just, and why no man who was a merchant could ever be a khan.

Constantin made a face. 'It works in the Empire,' he said stubbornly.

'Does it?' Suragai raised his eyebrows. 'Are there no beggars?'

The offworlder pursed his lips. 'There are the poor in any society.'

In the Khanate a man who was unable to work was fed by his family, and the khan made allowance for the fact when he imposed taxation. No one starved.

'It is a man's right to have riches if he can earn them,' Constantin said sententiously.

Suragai glanced sideways. 'Wealth requires a purpose,' he commented. 'The purpose of wealth as you describe it is to provide more wealth for itself. It cares not for people.'

'The Khanate keeps slaves,' Constantin responded frostily. 'In the Empire everyone is free.'

'Free to do what?' Suragai laughed harshly. 'Is a man who cannot earn provided for? And if he is, what will happen to him when wealth has gathered everything to itself?' In fact no one who was a part of the kind of system Constantin used as the basis for his arguments could be entirely free. If a person desired riches, he had to find the way to earn them, so he was at the mercy of the system and was thus still a slave of a kind.

I am not sure that freedom is anything more than a word, Suragai thought. There are only degrees of liberty, levels of privilege.

Constantin was frowning. 'It is your law that teaches the people not to want more than they are allowed,' he said. 'Where is the freedom in that?'

It was only a point of view, Suragai reflected. He said, 'I would rather be the man who advances himself by showing merit, earning respect because he tries to be the best, than the one who lives only to acquire wealth. A man's efforts in the first case are honourable; but the desire for riches engenders only greed, and that can never be satisfied.'

The plain ahead shimmered in the heat of the sun. Out of it the pillar on which Kinsai was constructed was rising.

'We each believe our way is right,' Constantin said. 'And surrender to the opposing point of view would be to forfeit what we think is most to be desired.' He made a face. 'Can two philosophies like ours live peacefully together?'

139

Probably they could not, Suragai thought. He let his reins fall loose on his st'lyan's neck. 'Ours is right for our world,' he said. 'Nobody asked you to come here.'

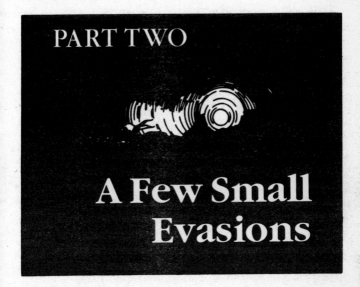

PART TWO

A Few Small Evasions

There was a sheer drop from the top of the watch-tower to the water. Kubulai sat with his legs dangling over the edge of the parapet, staring down. A pebble dropped from this height would create very little disturbance as it broke the stillness of the artificial inlet between the wharves. He found a fragment of rock in a crevice where the masoned grey stones met at the corner of the crenellation, and tried it. The plop as the stone struck the surface of the water was barely audible. Kubulai wondered what kind of splash a man would make. Much larger obviously. The sound of footsteps coming along the parapet made him sit back, but he did not turn.

The footsteps stopped behind him. 'Name of God, Khan,' Jehangir said. 'Come down from there.'

Kubulai stood up. 'I was thinking of it,' he responded lightly.

Jehangir pursed his lips disapprovingly. He said, 'There are easier ways of breaking your neck.'

'That wasn't my intention.' Kubulai grinned. 'Have you never wondered what it would be like to fall and fall - to feel nothing but the sensation of falling?'

The guard commander pursed his lips. 'Falling wouldn't worry me,' he said sourly. 'It's what happens when you stop.'

Kubulai laughed. He recalled that he had once seen his alien grandfather fly in the air - there had been a kind of kite, except that it had not been tethered to the ground. Instead Suragai had lain in a harness beneath it. Flying was different from falling, Kubulai thought, and he wondered how the sensation he had imagined could be achieved without risk. He stared down at the surface of the black water again. It was probably quite deep, but under it there would be waterlogged timbers and a sludge several drem thick.

'Khan, please come down,' Jehangir pleaded.

'Yes, mother.' Kubulai vaulted down onto the parapet. Jehangir assumed an offended expression. He was carrying Kubulai's dress coat over one arm, and now he held it out wordlessly. 'Is it time?' Kubulai asked. He put on the coat. It was deep blue with a high collar. The embroidery on the facings was black.

'Past time,' Jehangir said. He reached inside the collar of the coat to adjust the material of Kubulai's shirt, and then smoothed his hands down Kubulai's shoulders. 'At least you're clean.'

Trumpets were sounding behind the tower somewhere, and Kubulai heard people cheer. He looked back across the roofs. X'nadu was the principal seaport of the Khanate, and it had so expanded that it stretched beyond the bay around which it had first been built. Artificial headlands curved around, enclosing the harbour, and ships of every description were anchored there. The southern part of the city was reserved for trade, and it was at the extremity of this that the watchtower was situated, past the wharves and shipyards. To the north were the lines of tall neat houses roofed with bronze tiles in which the merchants and tradespeople lived. The mansions of the khans and nobles were on higher ground, and many of them were roofed with gold. The morning sun made the metal glow, and the last of the mist rising off the water wreathed them.

'There are letters from your father,' Jehangir said.

Kubulai looked round quickly. 'Oh? Where?'

'The Kha-Khan has them.' Jehangir tried to usher Kubulai towards the doorway which led to the stairs down to the yard. 'Most were for the council, I think, but I saw one for you.'

'Then maybe I'd better go and see,' Kubulai said tartly. He strode along the parapet ahead of Jehangir. Below in the yard waited the troopers of his personal guard. Some of them were already mounted. Everyone else was out watching the start of the ceremonial. At the doorway Kubulai stopped. He gazed back towards the upper part of the city.

'In X'nadu did Kubulai Khan,
  A stately pleasure dome decree –'

The words came from nowhere into his mind. He stopped, realising that he had spoken aloud. Jehangir's expression was puzzled.

'What's that, Khan?'

'Oh.' Kubulai wrinkled his nose. 'Lines from a poem. My father used to speak them to me when I was a child. I have not thought of them for years.'

'They don't make sense,' Jehangir said.

The roof of Kubulai's house was not a dome, that much was true. Kubulai looked for the outline of the house, but the sun's glare was too strong. He turned and went through the door onto the head of the stairs. It came to him that the poem originated from Terra, the lost homeworld of the aliens, and he thought that it was strange that some time in the distant past there had been a place called X'nadu, and a khan called Kubulai.

'Khan, the procession will be starting,' Jehangir

prompted anxiously.

'I know.' Kubulai started down the stairs. It was the least attractive aspect of Jehan's habit of shifting his court around the realm, he thought. The inhabitants of the Khanate's cities were accustomed by now to their ruler's intermittent presence in their midst. It did not stop them treating every occasion like a festival, and they had to be restrained from expensive demonstrations of their loyalty and affection. A few minor events were to have been celebrated over a period of some weeks – opportunities for the burghers and guildsmen to show off seldom-worn finery. Now the Kha-Khan was leaving for Kinsai, and all the small parades and fairs had become one main event which, because it was in Jehan's honour, had been declared a matter of obligatory attendance for the gentlemen of his household.

A groom waited respectfully in the ward, the reins of Kubulai's st'lyan in his hand. It had rained briefly a while earlier, and the animal's back was covered with a blanket. Jehangir whisked it away, and in the same motion boosted Kubulai into the saddle. The st'lyan was a roan with a silver horn. It backed up a pace, tossing its head, and the sweep of the horn made the groom flinch nervously. He waited until Kubulai had gathered in the reins and then backed swiftly out of range.

Kubulai reined around and rode out of the gate into the street. At this end of the city there was relative quiet, but up ahead there were dense crowds.

'They've already started,' Jehangir said. He rode up at Kubulai's side.

'It doesn't matter.' Kubulai concentrated on keeping the st'lyan in check. It danced nervously, and he reined in hard. 'We can wait until most of the procession has passed, and then join on.'

'After the carts.' Jehangir looked mutinous.

'Don't forget the jugglers and clowns.' Kubulai grinned. It offended Jehangir's sense of propriety for a khan to ride behind common men.

The street was overshadowed at one point by the height of an old warehouse which backed onto a wharf. The timbers of the gable were ancient, and were full of holes as the result of removal of fittings and signs. 'I don't know why we had to come down here at all,' Jehangir said disapprovingly.

Kubulai gave Jehangir a cool stare. In fact the guard commander knew perfectly well why they had been to the tower. It would not have been a good idea for the Kha-Khan's nephew to have been seen receiving the report of a spy at his house, where everyone could remark on it. A degree of privacy had been required.

The court was already packed to travel to Kinsai, the capital of the Khanate a thousand verst to the north. Men of every degree – carters, caravan masters, drovers and the like – had been coming and going for days in the square which fronted the houses occupied by Jehan and his household. It was unlikely that one more stranger would have attracted attention, and so perhaps the precaution had been unnecessary. Kubulai thought about that, and reflected on the appearance of the man he had met at the tower. A soldier looked like what he was, and an officer even more so, even when he was not uniformed and equipped. Someone would have noticed. It might not have mattered. 'I don't know why we have to ride in this parade,' Kubulai said. He kicked the roan into a trot.

Loyal to a man – and anxious to show it – the

burghers of X'nadu had laboured in the face of an edict which prohibited the expenditure of more than one koban for every thousand head of its population. Processions were not after all a necessity. Accordingly they had done their best with hangings and tapestries to create a triumph fit for the occasion. Where the decoration had run out they had pinned ivy and ch'in-sei, the silver-leafed creeper which grew on land where nothing else would survive. The Kha-Khan's device – an eagle intertwined with a p'ntar – was still wet on the ends of buildings and on the cloths which had been erected to screen the ends of side streets. It was even in the streets like this which were away from the route of the parade. The people had worked very hard.

Kubulai rode up to the barrier which prevented access to the thoroughfare beyond. He stood in the stirrups and looked over.

The procession was perhaps a third of the way past the spot. A cart which bore a number of smiling men dressed as women was being pushed past by more men – the significance of the tableau was unclear. A company of the Kha-Khan's personal guard rode behind, followed at a careful distance by a group of musicians. The tune they were playing was a matter for conjecture, for they were competing both with the noise of the crowd and with the cartful of bell-ringers who were being pulled by oxen a few drem to their rear. More troopers and several gentlemen of the household followed, and Kubulai grinned. Not only was the Kha-Khan's entourage the audience; it was also expected to form part of the show. A trio of serving women dangled from a balcony across the way. Seeing Kubulai's head above the level of the

148

screen they waved. Kubulai waved back, noting the location of the house for future reference.

'Lord, we should go round,' Jehangir said. He came up to Kubulai's side, stood on his st'lyan's back to look, and then got down into the saddle again.

'Nonsense.' Kubulai gave one end of the screen a tug. It was only tacked to the wooden frames of the houses which were at the corners. The canvas folded obligingly. He tapped the st'lyan with his toe, edging her forward. A few spectators moved smartly out of the way. Kubulai wheeled in behind a pair of Shojin noblemen who had elected for some reason to walk – the better to show off their parti-coloured hose, Kubulai guessed. He crowded them, aware that Jehangir and the troopers were forcing their way into line at his back, and they turned and glared. Kubulai smiled back, and saw the glares falter. The Shojin seemed to become aware that the intruder was wearing court dress, and that he had Altun red hair. They attempted to bow while they backed down the line of the procession. One man tripped, then recovered. Jehangir rode up to Kubulai's side. He treated the Shojin to a stare. 'Popinjays,' he said sourly.

Kubulai frowned him to silence. The cavalcade was already wheeling into the square in which the principal thoroughfares of the city met. A wooden platform had been raised at one side of the square, and on it stood Jehan. Behind him was Burun, Jehan's grandfather, and at Burun's shoulder Kubulai saw his own grandsire, the alien men called Suragai the Tall. At the side of the platform waited the Kha-Khan's pure white st'lyan. The sweating alderman who had been awarded the task of holding the bridle was at the same time awed by the honour and petrified by the side-to-side sweep of the gold-chased horn.

Apparently Jehan had himself ridden in the procession which was in his honour. Kubulai grinned again, and then he bowed in the saddle. Jehan nodded, but there seemed to be no recognition in his eyes.

It was the wrong time of day for a banquet, but that had not deterred the aldermen and guildsmasters of X'nadu. There was the unfortunate fact that the hall owned by the principal guild – the pilots and shipmasters – was insufficiently large to accommodate more than a fraction of those who now sought to be admitted. The lesser merchants and tradespeople who had been invited to watch had already gained entrance, Kubulai saw, and lined the wooden staging which had been erected along the walls. Those who had been invited by the provost to dine – a cold collation only, in view of the hour – now did their best to make sure of their places. Mild chaos reigned.

A fanfare of trumpets heralded the Kha-Khan's entry into the room. This was just as well, for it meant that the people who had seated themselves were required to rise, and so Jehan had room to pass. The nineteen aldermen who were already ensconced at the High Table got up, bowed, and then smiled superior smiles at their less privileged friends on the staging. It was clear where Jehan was expected to sit, and likewise his principal retainers, because three high-backed chairs had been placed on a raised dais. Some of the khans were Altun like Kubulai, but where they were to be seated was for a brief time thereafter a matter of controlled frenzy.

Kubulai walked purposefully towards an empty chair which was immediately below the dais. A lesser khan of the Seijin who reached it first took in his competitor's rank, and the colour of his hair, and yielded with an ill grace. The chair on one side had already been occupied by Kadan, who seemed to have managed to enter the chamber ahead of anyone else. On Kubulai's left sat a man in shipmaster's regalia – a Losani whose expression was clearly designed to intimate to the people around him that he was prepared to fight anybody who disputed his right to be there.

'Try some of the wine,' Kadan said loudly. 'If you're not drunk, you ought to be. This is going to be terrible.'

An alderman at the end of the High Table glowered in their direction.

'Be quiet.' Kubulai kicked Kadan under the table.

Kadan laughed. 'If you want to start a fight with me, do it now so that we can leave.' He poured wine into two cups and gave one to Kubulai. 'Here.'

The steadiness of Kadan's hand suggested that he was only pretending to be drunk. Kubulai took the cup and sipped at the wine. It was tart, and he pursed his lips. 'The people have done their best,' he said quietly in Kadan's ear. 'If you cause trouble I will kick you again.'

'In that case,' Kadan said amiably, 'you will have to carry me away from the table.' He made a face at Kubulai and put his hands over his ears. The noise was deafening. The fumes of food and wine were mixed with the smell of sweating aldermen in clothes which had been preserved with camphor against the moths, and the combination made Kubulai feel dizzy. The doors at the end of the chamber had been closed with difficulty only a moment before. Now they burst open again, and more men started to enter. There was no room for them, of course. Kubulai saw that they were all minor functionaries of the court. Some had been invited, no doubt, but others were simply hangers-on. They crowded towards the benches, and the captain of the guard could be seen to hesitate. The expression on his face said that the task of deciding precedence was now beyond him. Kubulai saw his head come round as if he sought assistance. A loose baulk of timber fell from the end of the staging. It hit the floor with a crash, and for an instant there was silence. Kadan used it to climb ponderously to his feet. 'Gentlemen!' he shouted. 'The gentlemen at the door! The staging is about to fall on you!'

The majority of the incomers departed abruptly. The men on either side of the doors flung themselves against them, forcing them closed. Diners beneath the staging who had risen hastily subsided again.

Kadan gestured to the captain, and said something. Then he turned towards Kubulai. 'I've told him that if he lets anybody else in, I'll shout "Fire". That will be the end of everything.'

The noise of conversation had risen once more to an unbearable level. The men on the other side of the table from Kubulai were screaming cheerfully at one another. The trumpets braying to announce the entry of servants bearing the platters of meats and pies added only slightly to the clamour.

Kadan was yelling something. Kubulai cupped a hand to one ear. 'What?'

'I said that failing all else, I would recommend trumpets for quelling a riot,' Kadan bellowed. 'But not here!' He started to turn away, and then leaned across the table without warning and wrenched from a startled mercer's grasp the silver cup from which he was drinking. Wine splashed everywhere. The merchant started to his feet, protesting. His voice was drowned by the commotion around him.

'Whatever rights you may have in X'nadu,' Kadan roared, 'the right of stealing my silver is not one of them!' He brandished the cup.

The mercer's face went as crimson as the wine stains on his linen. 'My lord,' he cried, 'you insult me, and you insult the city that does you honour!'

Kadan's head went forward. 'Honour? What honour?' he demanded. He stared suddenly at the man on the mercer's right, and then looked round. 'Kubulai, your cups are here also.'

'So they are.' Kubulai eyed the cup in the merchant's hand, and smiled. The merchant put the cup down hastily. 'I don't think I object,' Kubulai said. 'I believe the idea is to make us feel at home.' He pointed at a gold tray on which a cold joint of meat had been laid. 'Look, there's another of yours.' Kadan lunged for it.

Instead of protesting, the men on the other side of the table were falling silent. Somebody bowed. Kubulai looked round, and saw that Jehan was striding around the end of the High Table. Kadan was still on his feet. The Kha-Khan seized a handful of the cloth between the shoulders of Kadan's coat and hauled. Kadan fell over.

In fact it was more of a gradual collapse than a fall. Kadan was big – head and shoulders taller than anybody else in the room – and it was only surprise and a loss of balance that brought him down. He subsided, catching at the arm of his chair. It went over with a crash. The tray in Kadan's other hand went up, and the joint of meat slid greasily into his lap. Somebody laughed nervously.

Kubulai looked across the fallen chair at Jehan. 'You borrowed the silver,' he said.

The Kha-Khan wrinkled his nose. 'Somebody had to help,' he responded. He pulled Kadan to his feet again, and then looked back at Kubulai. 'I thought you might have realised,' he said. 'They had four days to prepare once they knew that we were going back to the capital. The silversmiths couldn't supply everything they needed, and there was no time for them to send to Kinsai. They trusted me with their honour.'

It was a clear reprimand. Kubulai flinched. Kadan looked cheerfully unrepentant. He had known about the silver all the time.

'We are chastised,' Kadan said to Kubulai.

'You will be,' Jehan said shortly, 'unless you apologise to these gentlemen for the affront you have offered them.'

They did their best to salvage the occasion. The soothed merchants seated themselves, and more food was brought to the table. A minstrel began a lyric which had been composed in the Kha-Khan's honour, and there was enough of a reduction in the noise level for most of it to be heard. But Jehan's disregard for protocol had unsettled the commons, and the indifferent management began to find its way to the surface. All the pies arrived at one table, and the sauces at another. A line of Keraistani, who had no talons, had no knives – indeed they had no cutlery at all. Guests near the door captured the best wine as it was brought in, refusing to let anguished servants carry it further. The Kha-Khan smiled patiently through it all, showing no awareness of the embarrassment of his hosts.

'I said it was going to be terrible.' Kadan had now

assembled his borrowed silver under the table – a problem for the diners from whom it had been recovered, for they were forced either to drink from the flasks or to share the cups which remained.

Kubulai gave Kadan a hard stare. There were times when it seemed as if the Kha-Khan's admiral did not know that there were qualities which were laudable other than a sense of humour. He said, 'Why did you do it?'

Kadan opened his eyes wide. 'At least this way it was amusing,' he observed. 'If the people can laugh, they can salvage their pride. The whole thing would only be sad otherwise.'

He was at least partly right, Kubulai could tell. The servitors were clearing the tables at last, and the people – aldermen and nobles alike – were waiting for Jehan to decide to leave. Most of the guests looked subdued, but it was apparent from the expressions on the faces of the burghers that they did not feel that they were entirely to blame for what had occurred. Everyone – even the Kha-Khan – had been involved in the disaster.

'Your father says the embassy will negotiate with us if they can,' Jehan said.

His father's letter lay open on the table. Another scroll, still sealed, lay beside it. Kubulai said, 'It's no surprise, surely.'

The Kha-Khan was in his late forties, a man of middle height with a lanky muscular frame and aquiline features. His hair was a rusty red-gold colour, and highlights in it glinted in the late afternoon sun. 'We could not predict how they would behave,' Jehan said. 'Now they are here, we have to find a way to deal with them.'

There was more to it than that, of course, Kubulai thought. Everyone knew that there were contingency plans for dealing with an alien embassy. Probably there were plans within plans as well. Jehan would know them, and Burun maybe. Everyone else would be told only what was necessary for them to play their part.

Jehan picked up the unopened letter. 'This is yours.'

Kubulai took the scroll. His father's seal was imprinted on the wax which held the ribbons together. He broke it with the tip of a talon, scanned the contents without surprise, and looked up. 'He wants me to agree to a betrothal.'

There had been hints in earlier letters. A khan could expect offers. As nephew of the occupant of the Dragon Throne they were inevitable.

A shadow of something passed across Jehan's eyes. 'To whom?' he asked.

'It doesn't say.' Kubulai held out the letter for Jehan to see. There was nothing really private in it.

'Oh, well.' The Kha-Khan took the letter one-handed. 'You can't be betrothed without your consent.'

Kubulai showed his teeth. 'I would expect to be asked for my opinion, certainly.'

'And in any case I have to give my consent,' Jehan said smoothly. There was an odd unreadable expression on his face.

There had been a time when the Khanate's ruler had kept himself more apart – when he had been less approachable – and so had commanded not perhaps a greater but rather a different kind of respect. Now Kubulai wondered if the progression had not gone too far. He said, 'Lord, I doubt if the choice will be contrary to your will.'

'That wasn't what I meant.' Jehan frowned. He looked out of the window. The horizon to the west was filled by the setting sun. 'If I could avoid burdening you with this, I would,' Jehan said. He glanced back at Kubulai. 'But these are uncertain times. I am going to nominate you as my heir.'

The announcement struck Kubulai like a blow. He stared at Jehan. 'When?' He could think of nothing else to say.

'When I return to Kinsai,' Jehan said. He was watching Kubulai's expression.

There was a tightness in Kubulai's chest as if a weight was pressing on it, and suddenly he knew that he was afraid. 'I don't want it.'

The Kha-Khan raised his eyebrows. After a moment he went to the table. On it there was a tray which was stacked with cups and flasks of wine and k'miss. He took two cups and filled them, then gave one to Kubulai. 'Drink,' he said.

Kubulai looked at the cup in his hand, not sure how it had got there. He lifted it to his mouth and drank. The sharp taste of the k'miss revived him. He drank again, and then put the cup down on the table.

Jehan said, 'I always thought there would be time to bring you to it gently, by degree, so that you would learn to accept it. Only a man who is insane would want to rule.'

A long line of carts was moving slowly along the street outside with its escort. Most of the Kha-Khan's movable household was already on the road. To-morrow Jehan himself intended to leave.

'I will refuse it.' Kubulai did not look towards Jehan

as he spoke. There was no immediate response, and at last he turned to see the effect of his words.

'If you are elected, you have no choice,' Jehan said gently. 'You know the Yasa.'

The highest duty was to the people – the whole Khanate – after which came the clan, then family, and finally oneself. Kubulai frowned. 'There are better men.'

'Oh?' Jehan's head came round. He stared at Kubulai, and then drank. The cup in his hand was a fragile bowl of crystal which was enclosed in a tracery of gold wire. It looked too delicate to resist the pressure of a hand around it. Jehan said, 'Consider the line of the Ancestor. Of the children of Arjun only T'zin survives.'

The Kha-Khan before the one before Jehan had been T'zin's brother Nogai. Kubulai pursed his lips. 'I know about his vice. Go on.'

Sentries passed the open window. The eyes of the young officer in command flickered when he saw Jehan and Kubulai standing together. He saluted, then strode after his men. The Kha-Khan did not react. He said, 'Ordai's sons are old men; Batu's also.'

'Which leaves the second marriages.' Kubulai nodded. 'What about Sidacai?'

The Kha-Khan smiled. 'You're clutching at straws. The whole world knows why Sidacai will never be Kha-Khan, even though he is probably worthy.'

Sidacai was away ruling Y'vrope, hating every minute of it because there was no fighting involved. Kubulai had no difficulty in remembering the stories – how Sidacai had sought to impose a military dictatorship on the realms, had been condemned for it, and had redeemed himself by service to Jehan in the days before he became Kha-Khan.

'That leaves the Merkuts.' Jehan's lips twitched. 'I know that's what men call us, though we are Altun.'

Burun was Khan of the Merkuts, and he had married a great-grand-daughter of Daijin, son of the Ancestor. His son Jotan had also married into the Altun line. Kubulai was Jotan's grandson, and so he was twice related to the Ancestor's line. He grimaced. 'I'm the son of an alien,' he protested. 'The khans will never elect me.'

'They elected me,' Jehan said. 'They will acclaim you.' He looked amused.

Kubulai summoned the confused family tree of the ruling families of the Khanate into the forefront of his mind and scanned it. 'There is Kadan,' he said.

Kadan was also Burun's grandson, and thus Altun by blood. Jehan wrinkled his nose. 'Kadan is my cousin, and he serves me well,' he said. 'Ask him why he will never reign, if you do not already know.'

The tone of Jehan's voice made Kubulai blink. 'He's not a drunk,' he said. 'But sometimes he reminds me of T'zin.'

The Kha-Khan nodded. 'Exactly.'

It was unnecessary to mention Jehan's father. Jotan was the provincial governor of the Alan country, but no one named Burun's sons in the Kha-Khan's hearing if they were wise. Too many old conflicts and betrayals lay buried in the past. In any case there was no provision for the nomination to move back up a line.

In X'nadu the horns were sounding for the closing of the city gates. The echo of one was picked up by another, and then was carried away on the air. Kubulai stared at his hands. He extended his talons, then retracted them. 'I cannot,' he said. 'Do not ask it of me.'

159

'We are the Altun,' Jehan responded soberly. 'It is our duty.'

The statement contained a kind of appalling finality. Kubulai found it difficult to meet Jehan's eyes. 'Who else knows about this?' he asked.

A servant came suddenly into the room. He bowed to Jehan, but Jehan ignored him. He met Kubulai's stare, pursing his lips. 'It is my decision.'

He had not answered the question, Kubulai thought, but he knew better than to ask it again. He watched the servant lifting a cup which had been laid on the table. Jehan seemed to become aware of the man's presence. He glanced back over his shoulder. 'Get out of here,' he said coldly.

The servant flinched. He bowed hastily to Jehan, and left the room.

Jehan stared after him. Suddenly he turned. 'You should prepare yourself,' he said in Kubulai. 'Once you are the Successor, every man will seek your favour.'

There seemed to be no point in arguing the matter to a conclusion. Kubulai nodded shortly. He went towards the door, and then a sudden thought struck him. He looked back at Jehan. 'You will reign for years yet. I could die before you.'

The Kha-Khan's eyes opened wide. After a moment he nodded. 'It's possible.'

'In that case everything we do will be for nothing,' Kubulai said. 'Our line will cease.' He waited for what he had said to register, but Jehan shook his head.

'No,' he said. He gave Kubulai a flat stare. 'If you die, there is one other.'

They left X'nadu before sunrise the next day, but still

the people came out onto the streets to cheer Jehan. Kubulai was riding behind with Jehangir and the troopers of his personal guard. Watching the faces of the men and women at the roadside he was amazed by their enthusiasm. It seemed to Kubulai that it mattered little who occupied the throne. The Yasa was the constant upon which men relied – the basis of everything – and that being so, the character of the Kha-Khan was surely of no consequence.

'Bow to your left, Khan,' Jehangir said.

A group of merchants stood on the corner of a side street. They were bowing to Kubulai. He inclined his head towards them, and then looked up the line to the place at the front where Jehan was riding. The column was really quite small, consisting of the Kha-Khan and the principal gentlemen of his household with their escorts. The baggage which had not yet been sent to Kinsai would follow in a few days.

People lined up outside a row of tall houses were cheering and waving. The more noise they made, the more people came out from the houses ahead to swell the throng. Jehan nodded and waved as he rode, and every time he did so the crowd cheered louder.

'It will be good to get out into open country again.' Jehangir reined over to avoid a wagon which had been left at the kerb. 'I've never liked the city.'

A Kha-Khan spent much of his time being nothing more nor less than an object for men's respect, Kubulai thought. Jehan had made himself more visible – accessible to ordinary men. He had less privacy than his predecessors as a result, and although he was treated with awe, it was his office which men accorded reverence, and not the authority of his person.

Kubulai frowned. He had never considered what it

was to rule before. Now he could think of little else. He glanced sideways at Jehangir. 'Five days or less and we will be at Kinsai,' he said. 'That's the biggest city of all.'

Jehangir made a face. 'Kinsai is different,' he said finally.

'Indeed?' Kubulai managed a grin. 'You would not think so if you had to live there.'

The pace increased as soon as they were out of X'nadu. The road followed the coast for only a short distance, and then it veered inland through gently rolling hills and across flat plains. A small vanguard rode ahead, and screens of troopers moved parallel to the line of march on both flanks; the dust which hung in the air above them marked their position.

Kubulai extracted first one and then the other foot from the stirrups, flexing his legs to ease the stiffness. The first time the column halted he stepped out of the saddle onto the top of a flat rock. He did a deep knee bend to undo the kinks in his spine, then turned. A lot of other men were doing the same thing. Kubulai smiled sourly. Yek troopers were capable of riding enormous distances, but most of them were out of practice. 'We need a war,' he muttered to himself.

Jehangir had dismounted only a short distance away. He gave Kubulai an enquiring stare. Kubulai met his eyes innocently, then looked away.

The Kha-Khan called a halt shortly before nightfall. There were no servants, and so they made a military camp - small fires around which groups of men gathered, but no tents. The night was warm, and most were happy to sleep out under the stars.

Kubulai sat down at a fire around which Jehan, Burun, Suragai - Kubulai's grandfather - and a few of the older officers were gathered. Burun was old, but seemed not to show his age. There were only a few strands of silver in his black hair, although his moustache was sparse. He was muscular like Jehan, but his waist had thickened now that he was past middle age. When darkness fell he put on a fur-lined cloak, grumbling about the cold.

'A woman is better than a fire for keeping a man warm,' one of the officers said.

Several men laughed, but Burun sniffed. 'I have wives,' he said. 'I don't need any more.'

Jehan was kneeling at the fire. He propped a pan of stew on the coals, and then looked round. 'Too old to deal with a new woman, Grandfather?'

'Old enough to know better,' Burun responded shortly.

The subject of wives touched Kubulai on the raw. He said, 'No one suggested you should marry, Khan.'

His great-grandfather's eyes were dark, like the eyes of the meerkat from which the clan took its name. Burun gave Kubulai an amused stare. 'I think I see a man about to be betrothed,' he said, and showed his teeth.

Kubulai felt himself flush. Either his father had told Suragai, who had told Burun, or else Jehan had mentioned the contents of the letter.

'Take a young wife, Khan,' an officer said. 'A pretty one with an empty head, full of nonsense.'

Burun glanced round. 'The women who can convince men that they are empty-headed are the ones to watch,' he said.

Men laughed, but Jehan frowned. 'Kubulai must marry well,' he said quietly, so that only Burun and Suragai seemed to hear.

Burun raised his eyebrows at Kubulai. Kubulai flushed. 'Khan, who I marry is my business,' he said.

The pan on the fire was giving off steam now. Jehan wrapped the hem of his cloak around his hand and lifted it off. He ladled the stew in the pan into bowls, and gave one to Burun and another to Suragai. The third bowl he offered to Kubulai. 'I haven't done this since I was a boy,' Jehan said.

'I remember.' Burun forked a piece of meat out of his bowl with his talons and popped it into his mouth. 'You used to light a fire and camp before you were old enough to go to war.'

Jehan nodded. 'Good times.'

A boy who was not old enough to go to war usually remained with the clan. Learning to ride and shoot a bow were part of growing up.

Suragai made a face. 'I don't suppose it's the same,' he said, 'but I hated my time as a cadet.'

Yek boys of noble blood became ensigns – officers in training. It was for the individual to decide the age at which he became a man. Probably there were similarities, Kubulai thought. He forked meat from his bowl and swallowed it. It burned going down.

'Being a boy but not a boy.' Jehan nodded. 'Learning to command men, but being treated like a slave.'

Ensigns were given every lowly task, and there was always somebody bigger and more experienced to point out any fault. Kubulai remembered the first time he had served with a Merkut tuman. He had been Altun, but still he had been roughly treated. Ensigns were always the last to be fed – they were supposed to see that the troopers had been fed first – and the younger boys usually had to fight for whatever food was left at the end. Kubulai recalled being beaten and

164

robbed, and reflected that as soon as he was older he had done the same to every boy who was weaker than he was.

'Training doesn't last long.' Burun was watching Jehan's face as he spoke. 'And it teaches a boy to stand up for himself.'

The officer who had offered Kubulai advice about taking a wife nodded. 'Lord, that's true,' he said. 'It isn't such a bad time.'

'Parts of it are not so bad.' Jehan laid a line of bowls out on the grass beside the fire so that men could come and take them. 'Working with the st'lyan; learning to fight.'

Suragai nodded slowly. 'Simple choices,' he said.

Burun laughed softly. 'All life is simple when you are young.'

He was speaking generally, Kubulai thought, but the officer nodded again. 'I served under Arjun,' he said. 'It was a good time. Everybody speaks well of it.'

Yek arms had started to conquer the world during Arjun's time. Before that there had been occasional reverses. All at once Kubulai wondered if men a hundred years hence would talk about Jehan's reign, and long to be there.

'Memory plays tricks on old men,' Suragai said quietly. He looked across the fire at Jehan as he spoke. 'Maybe it is only youth we wish for, and not the times.'

On the fourth day they came within sight of Kinsai. From the plain the pillar of red rock on which the city was built rose like a huge tower out of the haze, and at its base a camp had been set up to accommodate the Kha-Khan and his gentlemen until his ceremonial entry into his capital should be achieved.

It was nonsense, of course. Jehan did stop, it was true, at the camp, and took up residence in the huge yurt which had been prepared for him. Burun and Suragai rode straight on into Kinsai, and a steady flow of couriers and functionaries at once began to move between the ruler below and his administration above, while Kinsai went happily about its preparations to receive him.

Kubulai was one of those who remained for the moment with Jehan. There was little for him to do – the Kha-Khan did not follow the ritual of the days made traditional by his predecessors; the ceremonial which had lasted from late morning and languid attention to the business of state, through afternoon rest and into evening amusement or diversion. Instead Jehan rose early – often he was up before sunrise. His toilet was attended by a single valet, then he threw himself energetically into a work schedule which would have crippled any other man, and this continued generally until late afternoon. If he had leisure at all, Jehan spent it in the company of the men who served him most closely in his council, or if they were not available then with the captains of his guard, the men who attended the Kha-Khan discreetly throughout both day and night, whose role it was to exercise with him if such was his will. The evening might include a formal banquet, but it was just as likely to entail a late conference with advisers. If Jehan retired it was to study the transcripts of the cases sent to him for appeal, and the lamps in his chambers burned late into the night. His gentlemen – the young noblemen who were appointed because of their rank to add their wit and athletic prowess to their sovereign's glittering presence – were little more than decoration. What duties they were assigned could have been as easily performed – and were on occasion – by clerks or common soldiers. At all other times it was the two men who served the Kha-Khan as second selves – his grandfather Burun and the alien known as Suragai – who poured his wine or held his st'lyan's head when he chose to ride abroad.

Kadan rode in after another day. The Kha-Khan's naval commander had remained behind in X'nadu to superintend among other matters the removal of the remaining baggage. What else he had engaged in was capable of conjecture, but he burst like explosive upon the order of the camp, shaking the young men out of their torpor.

'An entry means entertainment,' Kadan said about the approaching ceremonial. 'What have you planned?'

There were at the time only a few men in the antechamber outside Jehan's apartments, and these were noyons and lesser khans for the most part, all of them young and ready for an escapade. Kubulai looked around and saw that he was the senior, at least in rank. 'We're not obliged to plan anything,' he said. 'What did you have in mind?'

It was hard as always to remember that Kadan was now in his mid-thirties, for his energy was boundless and his air of cheerful enthusiasm was suited more to a person with no responsibilities of state. He treated the occupants of the chamber to a stare which was filled with amused disbelief. 'The good burghers of Kinsai are to offer their respectful homage to the Kha-Khan,' he said, 'and they are spending koban by the fistful to do it. Are you telling me you intend to offer them nothing in return? At least you could amuse them.'

'What do you suggest we do?' Kubulai enquired rudely. 'Dance?'

Somebody tittered. Kadan's head came round. 'You could do that. But I thought a race would be a better idea.'

'A race,' Kubulai said flatly. 'What's entertaining about that?'

'Oh well.' Kadan smiled. 'I think it depends where you hold it.'

The following day promised to be fine – light showers were to be expected at this time of year – and it was apparent that once the mist had been burned off by the sun it would be bright and clear. Kinsai was several hundred drem above the level of the plain, and although the heat made the gold-covered roofs shimmer, yet there was not the unpleasant heaviness of atmosphere which persisted on the land below.

Weather regardless, the people of Kinsai were in any case on the streets. The Kha-Khan's ceremonial entry was an occasion no one cared to miss. As inhabitants of the capital of the Khanate they were used to pageant, but this was the city which bore each newly enthroned ruler around the Grand Parade on men's shoulders. Universal Khan he was without a doubt, but also he was their own lord, an office far more personal.

The main streets radiated out from the Golden Yurt like the spokes of a wheel. The palace itself was in the exact centre of the city, and was surrounded by a river of golden water which flowed between the banks of a canal incised into the bedrock. The water was not gold, of course - only coloured to appear so - but the effect was spectacular. Four bridges crossed the canal, and beyond them lay the gardens and wide promenades from which the streets spread. These were packed with people.

It was obvious from the first that the restrictions upon expenditure which Jehan had imposed had been far exceeded. The use of public finance he could and did control. There was nothing however to prevent the populace from demonstrating their loyalty by private contribution. Wooden arches had been erected at intervals across the main thoroughfares, and these were draped with hangings which, if they were not gold or silver in fact, had been dyed or painted appropriately. The Kha-Khan's arms and the devices of the city were prominently displayed, and every building had been festooned with banners and pennants. Cressets and lamp holders were wreathed with ivy. Mythical beasts made from papier mâché adorned every street corner - the dragons Kubulai passed were nothing like the ones he had seen in K'chin - and staging and platforms had been thrown up to supplement those which already ran between some houses, so that everybody could see.

'There's your father,' Kadan said, pointing.

They were in the section of the procession which was directly behind the Kha-Khan and his escort. Kubulai followed the direction of Kadan's eyes. The arms of Khitai were mounted on a frame above the balcony of one of the houses. On the balcony stood Kubulai's mother and father. With them were D'mitri the White, castellan of Pesth, and his family. Two other men watched beside them.

'Those must be the aliens,' Kadan said.

The two men looked so ordinary, like C'zaki, and Kubulai felt somehow disappointed. 'They are plain,' he said.

Kadan snorted, his expression amused. 'What did you expect?' he demanded. 'Horns and tails?'

The crackle of exploding fireworks above their heads announced the fact that the Kha-Khan was riding into the Grand Parade. The burghers of Kinsai were lined up behind a guard which had been positioned more for the purpose of preventing spectators from invading the processional route than from any thought to protect the great and noble from assault. Kubulai dragged his eyes away from the balcony and its contents. 'They are our enemy,' he said. 'I thought to recognise it when I saw them.'

He stood in the stirrups and looked back. Behind them the Household and its escort filled the entire street, and following them were the floats – tableaux intended to represent the power of the Khanate, fantasies to flatter the Kha-Khan – which were carried on carts or even on the shoulders of the men of the Ten Districts. The sun shone down on everything, and an uninformed eye would have missed occasional strained faces, and the too-frequent looks towards the balcony on which the alien embassy stood to watch.

A moulding in the shape of a bear crashed suddenly down from the corner of a building to Kubulai's right. His st'lyan reared and screamed, and he reined in hard to check her. The dun being ridden by Kadan side-stepped towards the crowd, its hooves rattling. Kadan was swearing steadily. A trooper of the guard which lined the roadside lunged for the animal's bridle, and clung to the harness as the dun tossed its head. It screamed, reared, and then stood trembling.

Kadan gave the trooper a nod of acknowledgement. He gathered his reins and urged his st'lyan on up to Kubulai's side. They both looked back. Where the moulding had fallen there was a press of people. The thing was clearly heavy – an invention of paper and plaster applied over a wooden frame – and men were struggling to raise it. Kubulai saw that there were several old men and a single woman below. Somebody's face was streaming blood. A limp figure was lifted on a forest of hands and arms, and was passed over the heads of the crowd towards the quiet of a side street.

In the open parade the Kha-Khan had already dismounted. His head came round, and he said something curtly to one of his officers. The man nodded, and began to walk back down the line towards the scene.

Jehan turned away, as if the incident was of no further interest. The burghers were advancing towards him. One of them bore a black velvet pillow upon which reposed a golden key. He bowed to Jehan and offered it. Jehan touched the key with his fingertips, and said something, a polite smile on his face. The burghers nodded and smiled, looking relieved. Kubulai realised that the gesture was something new – clearly it was symbolic. The gates of the city were closed in fact by a clever series of interlocking levers, and they required no key. The burghers were all bowing now – the deep formal bows which had replaced prostration in all cases save private audience. Jehan inclined his head.

'If that thing had fallen sooner –'

The sound of Kadan's voice in his ear made Kubulai turn. The plaster bear was being hauled away through

171

the crowd. The white underside was stained with fresh blood.

'You mean it could have been intended to harm Jehan.' The idea was preposterous. Kubulai frowned. 'It was too far back from the road for that,' he pointed out.

Kadan made a face. After a moment he nodded. 'That's true,' he said. 'But I still don't trust the co-incidence.'

Jehan was mounting, ready to ride on. Kubulai turned in the saddle, and stared towards the balcony on which his father and the aliens stood. One of the offworlders was older than the other, and he seemed to have lost interest in both the procession and what was happening in the crowd. Instead he was speaking urgently to Alexei. Kubulai saw his father look round after a moment. There was an odd expression on his face. Then he nodded slowly.

'You received my letter,' Alexei said.

It was early evening. The house which his father had chosen to occupy was not far from Burun's mansion, but it was much newer. The stone was light – a shade approaching pink – and had been hauled from some far-distant quarry to Kinsai. The roof was covered with the bronze tiles which were popular in X'nadu.

Kubulai sat back in his chair. There was a raised patio at the back of the house, and if he looked up he could see the edge of the roof where it overhung the gable. He stared past it at the twin moons. One was practically overlapping the other. Finally he looked back at his father. 'You know I did.'

Alexei's lips compressed. 'Don't tilt with me over

172

this,' he said. 'I know you are a khan, and old enough to make your own match. You're also my son. It's your duty to heed my will.'

It would have been too easy to fight. Kubulai bit down on a retort. He took a breath, not looking at Alexei at all while he did so. When he had let it out he said, 'I meant nothing.' He caught his father's eye. 'You have made your choice obviously, or you wouldn't be so troubled about my opposition. Who is she?'

A noise from the direction of the house made his father look away. Two of the upper windows were open. A servant was framed in one of them, pulling the shutters closed. He did not look down at the patio. Kubulai watched his father's face outlined in the bright moonlight. He looked as if he was thinking what to say. When the man who was closing the shutters had gone, Alexei looked back. 'The Kha-Khan has spoken to you.'

Kubulai clenched his teeth. 'Yes.'

'Then you know how important it is for you to make the right marriage.' His father's tone was persuasive.

Kubulai frowned. 'I don't want to talk about it.' He stared at the flagstones between his feet, and then looked up quickly. 'Jehan has never married.'

A shadow crossed Alexei's face. 'Jehan has his reasons,' he said obliquely.

It was no kind of explanation. Kubulai raised his eyebrows. 'And maybe I have mine,' he said. He saw his father frown. It was clear that he did not think that the suggestion was a serious one.

Hooves rattled in the street beyond the front of the house. A sentry shouted a challenge, and was answered. It was a distraction which gave Kubulai time to assemble the line of argument it had suddenly occurred to him to use. He said, 'If we were not on this world, you would not expect to choose a wife for me.'

Alexei started, but recovered quickly. He wrinkled his nose. 'Did you think of that yourself?' he asked. 'It's true that if we lived in the Empire you would be free to marry anyone. It doesn't alter the fact that there are marriages which are suitable, and marriages which are not. Do you think I will match you with someone impossible?'

Kubulai said, 'You seem to want me to agree to accept your choice, but you won't tell me who she is because you know I will object to her.'

His father pursed his lips. He sat back in his chair, watching Kubulai. Suddenly he said, 'What do you think of Turakina?'

She was a cousin of sorts, but the possibility that she might be his father's choice had never crossed Kubulai's mind. 'She's a little girl,' he said.

'She's fourteen.' Alexei sat forward. There was a serious look on his face. 'Her mother was a wife when she was barely older.'

'And for that reason I should accept her?' Kubulai made a face. 'I don't bed children.'

'I don't recall asking about your preferences,' Alexei said calmly. 'In fact I think you will find she is woman enough, but as it happens that is beside the point. What is most important is the fact that she is Altun.'

'The daughter of a non-human and the grand-daughter of an alien,' Kubulai said. He saw a flash of anger appear on his father's face. 'I know, I am of a similar bloodline. The point I am trying to make is that neither of us will be thought suitable by the people of the Khanate.'

174

'Oh?' Alexei stared at him. 'Jehan doesn't agree with you, obviously.'

Someone had left cups and a k'miss flask on the flagstones beside an empty chair. Kubulai picked up a cup, tilting it in the moonlight to see if it was clean, and then he poured some k'miss into it. He drank slowly, ignoring his father's eyes.

Finally Alexei said, 'If you have an alternative preference, then tell me.'

Kubulai could not help laughing. He choked on the k'miss, and spluttered. 'My preference is not to marry at all,' he said when he had recovered. He set the cup aside, and then gestured. 'I'll wait until we're under Imperial law. If the aliens have their way, that will be soon enough.'

His father fingered the gold caste mark on his cheek, his expression thoughtful. Then he shook his head. 'The sun will fall first,' he said soberly.

'Who are you running with?' Kadan asked.

Kubulai was watching Jehan, who was seated at the High Table. He turned. 'I don't know. In fact I'm still not sure it's a good idea.'

A servant laid a platter heaped with slices of roast lamb on the table between them. Kadan speared the lamb with his talons and dropped a slice on Kubulai's plate. 'The clues have nearly all been laid,' he said. 'You can't back out.'

'Can't I?' Kubulai made a face. The race Kadan had proposed was to cover a course which stretched between the great main gate of Kinsai and the tower of the Golden Yurt. Men of the Kha-Khan's personal guard had been allotted the task of deciding the precise route, which was to be determined by a series

175

of written clues. The event was to take place at night – that night in fact – and there was to be a provision disqualifying any contestant whose foot touched the ground between the start and the finish.

The air of suppressed hilarity which hung over the low tables was the product of the return from his errand only a short time earlier of one of the guard captains – marooned on a rooftop by the accidental removal of a ladder, he had fallen and broken his wrist.

'I notice you haven't told Jehan what we intend,' Kubulai said. He knew that his tone sounded frosty, but he could not help it. The Kha-Khan was probably one of the few inhabitants of Kinsai who did not know by now what was going on. News of the race had spread with uncommon speed once the arrangements had been finalised. By late afternoon the troopers of the various guard companies had been discussing it. Now that it was night there were unusually large numbers of people on the streets, and the watch was showing no interest in enforcing the curfew.

'It's an entertainment,' Kadan said cheerfully. 'Of course I haven't told him.'

Probably Jehan was suspicious all the same, Kubulai thought. It would have been remarkable if the Kha-Khan had not noticed the high spirits and the anticipation on the faces of at least the younger men in the chamber. Every time a trooper came in to report to Kadan, the gentlemen who were sitting near enough to him to hear turned to listen. Word of mishaps in laying the trail of clues – another fall, the accidental invasion of somebody's attic, an encounter with one of the apes which occupied the gables of the houses close to the western quadrant of the wall - was greeted with shouts of laughter. Kubulai saw the Kha-Khan glance perplexed in Kadan's direction. Kadan seemed to become aware of it, and he climbed to his feet and toasted Jehan, then sat down again.

The evening wore on. No form of diversion had been provided to amuse the guests - it was well known that the Kha-Khan did not favour them - and so the end of the meal was effectively a signal for people to depart. Jehan left with his escort, and Kubulai saw that he was followed almost at once by not only Burun but also Alexei and the elder Suragai. A late council appeared to have been arranged.

The disappearance of the whole cavalcade down the street was a signal for several of the older men to re-enter the house. Kubulai guessed that some of them had wine to finish, and a game of chess had been commenced. The other guests - nearly all of them members of the court - were starting to move with their torch-bearers and personal guards in the direction of the looming shadow of the bailey which protected the city gate. Kubulai hesitated, and then joined them.

Progress through the streets was not altogether without incident. The night was at least clear - Kinsai was well known for the mists which often clung to its cooling stones - but it was marred by the presence of the revellers who now obstructed free passage. There were exchanges of words, most of them good-natured, and two scuffles which had to be broken up by the guardsmen. Most of the men who had elected to take part in the race had already formed themselves into three-man teams. Kadan had collected a Merkut officer and a lesser khan of the Seijin, and walked arm in arm with them. Three Kerait noblemen who were walking at his heels offered to wager against the chances of his team. All of them had been drinking heavily – so had a lot of the men who had dined at Alexei's house – and Kubulai glanced round quickly and caught Kadan's attention, raising an eyebrow. Kadan saw, and grinned. He looked back at the Kerait and accepted their odds.

It was now that Kubulai noticed that his cousins were in the crowd ahead. Turakina was swathed in a heavy cloak, and the presence of a quartet of Merkut troopers with protective expressions on their faces suggested that she was out with permission, but he frowned disapprovingly. He lengthened his stride, amazed to see her. It would do her reputation no good to be seen in this company.

The younger of the two members of the alien embassy was walking at the younger Suragai's side. Kubulai stared. He nodded abruptly to Turakina, and then caught her brother's eye. 'You shouldn't be here.' He indicated Turakina with a jerk of his head. 'This is no place for her, even if she does have an escort, and as for him –' He paused, unsure how much Yek the alien understood. '– if Jehan gets to hear of it, we will all be in trouble.'

Suragai was very like his father D'mitri in appearance. He was short, but broad-chested and muscular. Only the colour of his hair made him look Altun, although he had talons. He eyed Kubulai for a moment, and then he looked round at the offworlder at his side. In Anglic he said, 'This is my cousin Kubulai, Alexei's son. Address him as Khan when you speak to him.'

The alien smiled and inclined his head, then bowed

in mid-stride. 'Khan, I am happy to meet you,' he said. 'My name is Constantin.'

Kubulai nodded curtly. He put a hand on Suragai's arm. 'Did you hear what I said? None of you should be here.'

'I'm not deaf,' Suragai said calmly.

'Then heed me.' Kubulai knew that his tone sounded querulous. He saw that Turakina was listening, amused, and he flushed. 'You are supposed to be responsible for the aliens until they see the Kha-Khan. You must be mad to bring that one here.'

The massive tower of the bailey filled the end of the street. A crowd was gathered around it, and torches and cressets flared. 'We thought of running in the race,' Suragai said ingenuously. 'But we can't find a third man. Who is in your team?'

'I'm not running,' Kubulai said, making up his mind. 'And neither are you.'

They had arrived at the base of the bailey wall. A tracery of vines ran across the red stone like veins standing out on the back of a hand, and some men were starting up them, ignoring the stairs inside the tower. Suragai said something quietly to Turakina, and she laughed and nodded. The alien was looking appraisingly at the route which was being used by the leading climbers. Kadan came past Kubulai, the Merkut and the Seijin in tow. They started up.

Kubulai tightened his grip on Suragai's arm, restraining him. Suragai wrenched and twisted, and suddenly there was only an empty tunic in Kubulai's hand. Five or six drem up the wall Suragai crowed and swung on a stretcher of vine. He held out a hand. 'Cousin, come on. We need a partner.'

The alien was already on the lowest offshoot of

another vine. Kubulai dropped the tunic on the cobbles and went after him. The alien scrambled out of reach, laughing.

Kubulai stared up. 'Damn you, come down.'

'Come up and look after us,' Suragai called.

There would be trouble if either of them fell. Kubulai glanced back at Turakina. The Merkuts were closed in around her like a fence, and she was smiling up at her brother and the alien. She saw Kubulai watching, and made a face at him. Kubulai clenched his teeth, then set his face to the wall and started to climb.

There was a broad parapet along the top of the wall, but the wall itself was not particularly high – it had no need to be, for there was a sheer drop of several hundred drem on the other side. It was not a difficult climb, and even as Kubulai arrived at the top Kadan was leaning out through a crenellation to yell down for torches and the first packet of clues.

The torches rose in the air like fireflies. Sparks showered down on the people who were standing immediately below, and someone cried out in alarm. The men on the wall caught the torches and held them aloft, laughing and waving them so that they flared. Kubulai snatched the last one as it came up, and then he turned. Suragai and the alien were standing side by side, watching. Kubulai glowered at them. He said, 'I should stop you here. There are stairs at the end of the parapet.'

Suragai nudged the offworlder. 'He doesn't look like an old man,' he said. He grinned at Kubulai. 'Even if he sounds like one.'

Kubulai ignored the insult. He glanced past them to

the other men, counting heads. There were thirty-three – eleven teams.

Kadan was passing out the clues. A clue consisted of two things – a verse which directed contestants to a location, and a word which required to be memorised. The team to arrive first at the Golden Yurt – with the final message assembled from the words – would win the race.

The numbers were going to be the problem to begin with, Kubulai realised. More than thirty men would crowd one another across the rooftops – at least until the field thinned out. He took the piece of paper Kadan held out and glanced at it, uncaring. Some men were already starting away along the parapet. Suragai grabbed at the clue and scanned it. 'The house of T'su Tse the bowmaker,' he said. 'Come on.' He hauled at the alien's arm, and together they pulled at Kubulai.

If they were going to compete, they might as well try to win. Kubulai raced with them in the wake of the others. Two hundred drem from the bailey there was a place where a line of houses had been built quite close to the wall. The leading team leapt across the gap and ran along the coping to the next roof. Everyone followed. For a distance of four houses the contestants ran in column, for there was no room for anyone to gain an advantage. Then they came to a place where a building had been raised at right angles to the others. It was much taller.

The men at the front were already beginning to climb. Kubulai could see no way to pass them. He waited until all the other competitors had started up the gable, and then he caught at Suragai's arm. 'Not that way.' He extinguished his torch against the chimney head at his side, and then clambered back across the coping to the centre of the roof. Another line of houses ran parallel to the first, the rows separated by a gap of several drem. Kubulai ran down the slope of the tiles and launched himself, arms outflung. He smashed into the roof on the other side, slid, and stopped with his feet in the gutter. He was still clawing his way up to the crest when Suragai thundered onto the tiles beside him. The alien followed, crying out as he banged into the surface of the roof between them. He started to slide towards the gutter. They grabbed at his arms and pulled him up. A loose tile dropped over the edge and struck the cobbles below. Kubulai glanced down, and saw the people who were crowding the streets to watch. Deliberately he kicked more tiles loose, showering them.

Suragai was already up on top of the coping. He ran lightly along to the next house and disappeared around the chimney. The offworlder was swearing softly in Anglic. Kubulai grinned at him and they hauled each other hand over hand up the roof to the top, scrambled to their feet, and ran in pursuit. They recrossed the gap at the end of the line of houses, and when Kubulai looked back he saw the bobbing torches of the other runners a clear two rooftops behind. A leap onto the staging which crossed the street below, and suddenly they were beneath the face of the house of the bowmaker.

The house was very old, and it had small windows like a ladder up the front wall. Kubulai found it easy to pull himself up from one to another. An open window at the top indicated that the clues were in the attic. He climbed through. A packet was hanging from a book above a workbench. Kubulai rifled it, then climbed back out of the window and hauled himself onto the roof where Suragai was waiting. Suragai read the verse and grinned. 'The bathhouse in the next square,' he said.

A Kerait who was the leader of the first of the other teams was already climbing up to the window below the eaves. He stared at them, dismayed to find them there, and then he disappeared inside.

The bathhouse was an easy run along the staging which passed across the streets and yards in this part of the city. Here was a merchants' quarter, and building space was at a premium. Shops which had started as stalls in alleys off a main thoroughfare had become in time permanent structures, and wooden bridges had been erected to carry goods and passers-by in the space between the buildings above. The stagings were supported for the most part on props which were fastened to walls. Occasionally a gap had been cut through a warehouse or even between the walls of a house, and here the passageways were like tunnels, narrow and ill-lit.

Their lead was now much reduced. The Keraits were but a short distance behind, and hot on their heels ran Kadan's team, their leader easily identifiable because of his size. All of them, like Kubulai, had abandoned their torches. Flares which bobbed in the darkness to the rear showed where the rest of the pack still came on. None of them were close enough to offer serious competition.

Down below the audience was also running. People packed the streets and yards, and some of them had made their way up onto the staging to obstruct the contestants. Lamps swung, torches flickered, and voices shouted insults or encouragement. Kubulai paid little attention, but Suragai and Constantin pelted them occasionally with refuse or loose tiles, and crowed or catcalled when they had the breath.

The bathhouse was a long, low structure of pale stone. It had a dark tiled roof with wide overhangs. The clues hung from the eaves, and it was the alien who crawled to the edge to get at them, leaning out and down while Kubulai and Suragai held his legs. They were only moments ahead of the others now. Both Kadan and the Keraits reached the clues before they had clambered back up onto the staging.

'Name of God, there isn't time to spit,' Suragai said in Anglic, and the alien laughed.

Kubulai tore the clue out of Constantin's hand. There were four lines of verse, an acrostic in Yek, and they were followed by a single word.

Suragai peered past Kubulai's shoulder. 'What does it say?'

> 'Joden sings,
> But has no mouth;
> Seek him high,
> Against the south.'

It was simple enough. Joden was the great tenor bell of the peal which hung in the south watchtower. Kubulai pointed to the place where the tower loomed against the skyline. 'There,' he said.

'And the word?'

Kubulai glanced at the paper again, and then screwed it up and let it flutter away. '*Honour.*'

They were only a house-width ahead of their closest rivals, the Keraits, when they came to the pinnacle of some Yek merchant's workrooms. Across from them, separated from them by a four-drem gap, was the roof of the hall from which they could gain access to the tower. The roof on which they stood was steep, and covered in slates. Below them there was a drop of four floors to the street. It looked impossible.

Kubulai flexed his talons, and started to lower himself over the gable. Suragai's hand descended on his arm, detaining him. Kubulai looked up.

'If you take your boots off, it will be easier,' Suragai said.

It had not occurred to him. Kubulai nodded. He let himself be pulled back up onto the chimney head, then kicked off his boots and swung over once more. Suragai was taking his own boots off. He shied them at the lamplit faces of the people in the street below. Kubulai hung by his hands, feeling with his toes for crevices in the gable wall. He glanced up at the alien. 'You have no talons,' he said. 'Wait here until we find a way to bring you across.'

The offworlder craned out to look at the drop. Quickly he nodded.

There was a wall connecting the two buildings, but it was ten drem below. To reach it Kubulai had to work his way down the face of the gable. He sensed that Suragai was above, but did not look up. Reaching the wall he ran across the gap. The tower entrance was open, and he raced up the stairs. The clues were hanging from the clapper of the tenor bell. It stirred and hummed as he undid the packet. Suragai was at his side. His d'jaga flashed, and then he began to coil up a length of bellrope. They charged back down the stairs, knocking one of the Keraits aside as he tried to enter the tower. This time it was Suragai who took the lead. He swung down onto the connecting wall, ran across it, and threw one end of the rope to the alien, who looped it round the chimney head. Moments later he had descended, then he and Suragai ran back to Kubulai's side.

Kubulai looked at the clue word. 'That gives us *Justice, Energy, Honour* and *Agility* so far,' he said.

Suragai laughed. He said, 'In that case I nominate *Nausea* for the next.'

In fact it was *Nobility,* and they found it in the carving above the upper window of the house of the Khan of the Keraits. Kubulai hung over the eaves to get at it, and was pulled back again by the alien. He caught Suragai by the arm. 'Where is Kadan?'

'On the next roof,' Suragai said. He looked back. 'He has a rope now. The Keraits have one as well.'

Kubulai wrinkled his nose. There was very little to choose between the three leading teams. 'We must try to lose them,' he said, and saw Suragai smile.

Possession of the ropes made all the difference. Now that they all had one, there was little advantage to be gained. None of the other teams were close enough for their efforts to matter.

The next destination was an eating house which was situated on the other side of one of the main thoroughfares. To reach it they had to go across the roofs until they came to one of the wooden archways which had been constructed for the Kha-Khan's entry.

At a sheer wall, the difference in height between one building and the next, they were once more slowed by the offworlder's lack of talons. Kubulai and Suragai climbed the face of the building, and then let down the rope so that Constantin could join them. The Keraits passed them while they were pulling him up onto the coping.

One of the triumphal arches bridged the street only a house-length ahead. The Keraits crossed, and the last man kicked part of the framework away from its supports, jeered at them, and ran on. Kubulai got down into the gutter and put one foot on the timber. It rocked, and he made a face.

'There is another one a hundred drem further down,' Suragai said.

Kubulai glanced along the street. Kadan and his team were already crossing – they had gone up the street. Kubulai let his full weight down onto the archway. It swayed alarmingly, but it did not fall. He swarmed across it, and then turned to steady it so that Suragai and the alien could follow.

The eating house was overhung by another building which loomed above. The Keraits had let down their rope from the eaves, and one of them had already descended. He tugged at the skylight in the roof on which he had landed and leaned through.

On the far side of the building there was a storehouse. Kubulai worked his way hurriedly around to it. He pointed to the overhang and its suspended rope. 'It would be a pity if they were to be allowed to profit from what they tried to do to us,' he said to Suragai.

Suragai glanced up, and then he nodded, showing his teeth. He scrambled away.

Kubulai climbed through a window. Inside the storehouse there were racks and heaped-up barrels. He moved across them towards the open doorway, perched on a ladder, and looked through.

Probably it was not all that unusual for the cooks to be working at this time of night. A number of spits were in use, and a man was pulling loaves from an oven. The place reeked of hot fat and old bread. A shelf ran round the wall. Joints of meat hung from it, and it was on this that one of the Keraits was standing. His hair had come loose from the cords which bound it and was plastered across his face. He glared down at the men working in the shop below, and utensils scattered around showed where he had searched without success for the next clue. 'There should be some papers,' he said. 'Where are they?'

The head roaster was a huge Keraistani with a shining red face. He turned as if he had only just become aware of the intruder. 'Lord?'

'The papers.' The Kerait gestured impatiently from his perch. 'A guardsman was here today with papers. Where did he put them?'

'Oh.' The Keraistani shrugged. 'They were burned. An accident.'

'Burned!' The Kerait glanced back at the open skylight above his head. The other members of his team were framed in the space. They shouted advice. Several more sets of feet pounded across the roof. Hastily the Kerait waved to attract the roaster's attention. 'Can you remember what the papers said? What was the word?'

'Oh.' The Keraistani glanced casually at his workmates. They grinned at one another slyly, and then the roaster shrugged again. 'I have a bad memory.'

Kadan's face appeared at the open window above. He leaned through. 'Offer him something, you fool,' he said.

The Kerait fumbled in the purse at his waist. Gold gleamed in his hand. He tossed a coin to the Keraistani, who smiled. 'The word was *Trust*,' he said.

'And the verse?'

The Keraistani weighed the coin in his hand. There

was a knowing expression on his face. 'Lord?'

'I have no more money.' The Kerait looked back at his companions.

'But I have.' Kadan climbed through the skylight. He got onto the shelf at one end, and it creaked.

The purse Kadan dropped into the roaster's hands was bulging. He bowed amiably. 'Lord,' he said, 'the word was as I told you. As for the verse, it went like this –

> For the next,
> Turn to the east;
> Seek out the Bear,
> A noble beast.'

The bear was the totem of Siban the White, Sidacai's father, and his empty house was on the other side of the city. The words were barely out of the roaster's mouth when the Kerait sprang for the opening above his head. Kadan was ready for him. He put one hand on the other man's face and pushed. In the open skylight the remaining members of the two teams were struggling.

The Kerait went headlong. He clutched desperately at one of the shelf supports, cursing Kadan, but the shelf was designed to take the weight of carcases, and not men. It collapsed with a crash, and the spectators who came through the eating-house door were in time to witness the Kerait's disqualification as he hit the floor amid the debris.

Kadan was already hauling himself back through the window space. Kubulai clambered back across the storeroom, opened the window, and climbed out onto the roof to join the alien. They looked up. One of Kadan's team was already starting up the rope which

189

hung from the overhang. Suddenly he dropped back onto the eating-house roof. The rope fell in a cascade on top of him. A man's voice called angrily.

Kubulai chuckled. He tapped the offworlder on the arm, and they worked their way back across to the buildings on the eastern side of the square. Suragai was descending a staircase towards them, a broad smile on his face. 'You should have pulled up the rope,' Kubulai said.

'I thought of it,' Suragai said. He looked towards the eating house. 'There will be time, I think.'

They used staging where they could, running hard across the city. All the main streets had been bridged at one point or another by decorative arches, or by cables from which flags were suspended, and so there was very little to delay them. Siban's house was a tall mansion of dark stone. The roof was sheathed with gold, and even in their bare feet they made marks on it where they crossed.

'There is a bear carved above the door.' Suragai pointed.

Kubulai nodded. 'I see it.' He looked back over his shoulder, but there was no sign of Kadan and his team, although they could not be far behind.

The rope was only just long enough. Suragai looped it round a spire which projected up from the front of the roof and lowered himself. He seemed to be feeling in the crevices around the carving, and then suddenly he started back up again. He waved a sheet of paper. 'I have it.'

This time the word was *Hope*. It was not until they were slipping and sliding back across the roof that Kubulai saw that the members of Kadan's team were lurking in the deep shadows of the tall chimney head.

He opened his mouth to shout a warning, and in the same moment the alien was tripped, and tumbled towards the gutter.

The intent was brutal in the extreme. Kubulai threw himself headlong, catching the offworlder's wrist as he went over the edge. Constantin swung dizzily. Kubulai felt himself being pulled into the wide gutter. Metal groaned.

Kubulai dug his talons into the roof. Suragai was making his way carefully down the long curve to the edge. He leaned out over the guttering, catching the alien's free hand, and together they drew him back up. Kubulai got to his feet. He saw that Kadan was perched on the crown of the roof watching. His face was expressionless. He said something to the Merkut who was working his way along to the spire above the doorway, and the Merkut laughed. Kubulai clenched his teeth. He felt Suragai's hand on his arm. 'Come on,' Suragai said. 'This is no place to fight.'

The two teams covered the next five clues with seldom more than the width of a roof to separate them. Twice Kadan was in front, and then there was some rough horseplay. Suragai was pelted with eggs taken from an abandoned bird's nest. The rope was slashed while Kubulai was halfway down it, and he fell ten drem into a hay cart.

The race was now more a test of agility and stamina than a challenge to the intellect. The interpretation of the clues indeed required limited ability, and only once did the acrostic give them pause for thought. There was now little sign of the other contestants. Kubulai saw a torch waver on a rooftop several streets away, and then it was gone again. The crowd moving below was only barely in touch with their progress, and every change of direction was greeted with shouts of discovery.

'*Tolerance*,' Suragai said, reading the thirteenth clue. 'We could do with some of that.'

Kubulai pursed his lips. Suragai was only two or three years younger, but his approach to everything was far more light-hearted. 'Where now?'

'The tower of the Guards Barracks.'

'Which has to be the last,' Kubulai said.

'Yes.' Suragai nodded. 'The only way to get from the barracks to the Golden Yurt is by the cable they were stringing across the Grand Parade this afternoon. Whoever gets to the top of the tower first is certain to win.' He turned away and started to follow the line of the wall on top of which they had halted to examine the clue.

The presence of the cable had not been explained to anyone. Maybe there was no good reason for it to have been put in place other than to provide contestants with a means of crossing the divide between the barracks and the palace, but Kubulai wondered what Jehan had been told. He looked down and saw that the alien was sitting on the wall. 'Come on,' Kubulai said. He pulled the offworlder to his feet.

No one was by now either fresh or sure-footed. The crowd in the streets seemed to sense that the race was drawing to a close, and they were streaming towards the Grand Parade. Few even looked up at the figures trotting along the wall. A movement at the corner of Kubulai's field of vision made him glance to the left, and he saw that Kadan's team were running across a line of flat roofs on the opposite side of the street. They were neck and neck, but the wall on which Suragai had set their feet led directly to the barracks. Kadan was going to have to cross the street at the next staging to reach it.

Somebody in the crowd of spectators had thrown up a flask of wine. Suragai drank from it, and then tossed it back over his shoulder. Kubulai caught it one-handed. Wine splashed over his wrist, and he tried to snatch a mouthful at the same time as watching where he placed his feet. Constantin stumbled, and they both fell, clutching the top of the wall. The wine flask fell to the cobbles.

'Name of God, look at you.' Suragai had backtracked. He looked down at them, hands on hips.

The expression on Suragai's face was so disapproving that Kubulai felt compelled to laugh. He clung to the alien, who was laughing too. Suddenly the whole escapade struck Kubulai as ridiculously funny. He brayed helplessly. Suragai hauled them to their feet, then ran on.

Kadan was faring no better on the other side of the street. The Seijin and the Merkut were both quite clearly exhausted. They were staggering as they jogged across the rooftops, and Kadan was between them, hauling them along by the arms. The staging which crossed the wall ahead joined two buildings, both of them storehouses. Suragai reached it, and pulled himself up. On the other side there was a single length of wall which ran all the way to the barracks.

'Give me your arm.' Suragai reached over the rail of the staging. He pulled Kubulai up first, then Constantin.

Kubulai stared back across the street. Kadan was up on the staging too, and he was dragging the Merkut over the rail. 'We're going to be first,' Kubulai said breathlessly.

'So we are.' Suragai sounded thoughtful. He gave the alien a push towards the far side of the staging. 'Both of you go on. I'll catch up.'

There was a lot of light now. The twin moons were both bright in the sky, and torches and cressets lit not only the street but also the staging. Kubulai got down onto the wall with Constantin. They walked along it for a distance of several drem, and then stopped and looked back. Suragai was busy beside one of the storehouses. He trotted back along the staging, and a moment later he was following them onto the wall. Kadan charged over the bridge, his companions hurrying behind. Suddenly he seemed to stumble. There was a yell of alarm, and then the thud of bodies colliding with timber. A string of curses issued out across the night air.

Suragai looked satisfied. 'There were some old oil jars,' he said to Kubulai. 'I greased the staging.'

There were sentries on the wall of the barracks, but no challenges were issued. Instead the troopers grinned. The door of the tower was locked.

Kubulai stared up at the dark face of the tower, then turned. 'A man with talons could climb it,' he said. 'But the rope isn't long enough.'

'Then be damned to it.' Suragai looked displeased. 'We have come this far. There must be a way.'

They could try forcing the door. Kubulai glanced at the amused expressions on the troopers' faces, and guessed that there would be no assistance from that quarter. Below the barracks wall a crowd was gathering. Lamps were bobbing and swaying. Somebody called out a wager.

Suragai had moved back to get a better view. He pointed. 'There is a window.'

There was. It was tiny, like an arrow slit, and would not admit them to the tower stairs.

'One of us could climb up there,' Suragai said. 'Then he could lower the rope –'

'– and the other two could pull themselves up,' Kubulai finished. He nodded. 'Yes. Constantin could use the window for a perch while we climb the rest of the way to the top.' He looked back the way they had come. Kadan was leading his team along the top of the wall from the staging. They were moving slowly. The Merkut was limping.

'If we hurry, we'll be up the first stretch before Kadan gets here,' Suragai said.

He spoke Anglic so that the alien would understand. Kubulai laughed at the phrasing, and shook his head. 'In that case we should both go.'

The side of the tower was a sheer face sixty drem high. One stone was slotted into the next without the benefit of mortar, and the crevices between them were minute. Kubulai used his talons and kept his hands low. Across the Grand Parade loomed the sculptured shape of the Golden Yurt. Lights were blooming on the open balconies. Above the heads of the crowd in the concourse stretched the thin black line of the cable. Halfway up, Kubulai paused to catch his breath. Every sinew was aching. Suragai was crawling up the wall like a spider. He got an arm into the window, wedged the knotted end of the rope, and then let it unwind. Constantin came up in a hurry. Below them was Kadan, just passing the sentries on the barracks wall. Kubulai reached across and jerked the rope out of his reach. The alien hung from the window slit and wound up the coils one-handed.

Kadan started to climb. He looked up at Kubulai,

but there was no hint of recognition in his eyes. If he reached the window before they could pull the off-worlder to the top, he stood a chance of winning – all he had to do was capture the rope. Below Kadan the Merkut and the Seijin were arriving at the base of the tower. Kubulai glanced upwards. Suragai was halfway up the second stretch, an end of the rope looped through his belt.

Kubulai worked his way past the window. Constantin was staring upward, his pale features illuminated by the moonlight. If he realised that he was in danger, it did not show. Below was Kadan, moving steadily.

Whatever happened, they were going to be the first to cross. Suragai hauled himself onto the top of the tower. He tied the rope, then waved. Constantin understood that the rope represented a chance for Kadan. He tied the lower end to his belt before he started to climb, and it rose with him. Kubulai had found a section where a few of the stones had moved by a fraction. There were tiny ledges, enough to provide purchase, and he used them thankfully.

The summit of the tower was partially enclosed. Four square stone pillars supported a bronze roof. The cable running from the top of the palace had been secured around two of them. It stretched off into the darkness. The sheet of paper on which the final keyword was written was pinned to a beam. Kubulai glanced at it. Constantin hauled himself over the edge of the tower at almost the same moment. They cast the rope loose, and it slithered down past the heads of Kadan and his team. Someone called out angrily. Kubulai ignored the shout. He put a hand on the secured end of the cable, feeling the vibration, and looked towards the palace. Two thirds along was Suragai, arms scissoring, legs crossed over the line. Kubulai nudged Constantin. They pulled themselves up onto the cable and began to work their way painfully across. They were a little more than fifty drem from the tower when an increase in the tension on the rope announced the fact that Kadan was also on his way.

The summit of the Golden Yurt held among other things an open area which contained the ceremonial cremation bowl. There was a guard post to one side of it, and the space was crowded with people.

Kubulai craned his head to stare back along the line. Kadan could not hope to win now, and yet he was still moving with speed and determination. A core of disquiet grew inside Kubulai's chest as he pictured the kind of accident which might occur if Kadan caught up while they were crossing. He pulled himself more swiftly along the thickness of the heavy plaited ropes, dropping onto the roof of the palace as soon as he was across the balcony wall.

Most of the court appeared to have assembled. Some of them were men who had started in the race, and who must have dropped out or been disqualified. There were a few women. All of them were parting to let Suragai through to the guard post. He tacked a sheet of parchment onto the door frame. On it were written the words taken from the clues - a column in careful Uighur script. The first letter of each word had been underlined. A junior officer of the Household peered past Suragai to read them aloud.

'*Justice, Energy, Honour, Agility, Nobility, Trust -*' he started.

'Just the first letters,' one of the guard captains said.

'*Jehan the Mighty*,' the young man said.

People cheered, and one or two slapped Suragai and Kubulai on the back, ignoring the alien. The Kha-Khan came suddenly through the arcade with his retinue. He congratulated them, smiling thinly. When he saw the alien, he stared. Then he raised his eyebrows at Suragai, although he said nothing.

An ironic cheer from the edge of the assembly heralded Kadan's arrival. Kubulai turned, his jaw tightening. He began to push towards Kadan, but Suragai caught quickly at his arm. He said, 'I don't know what you intend, but I think the honours are even.'

Kubulai did not agree, but this was not the place to argue it. Above all he wanted to know why Kadan had attempted the offworlder's death. He shrugged as if he did not care, turning away. At Suragai's shoulder stood the alien, filthy, stinking, and exhausted. Kubulai showed his teeth and clapped him on the shoulder. 'You ran well,' he said in Anglic.

The offworlder produced a tired smile. 'Khan, if this is what you do for amusement ...' he started.

The ambassador came abruptly through the crowd. He bowed very low to Jehan, and then took Constantin by the arm and drew him aside. The language he used when he spoke was not Anglic, but his meaning was clear. He gestured angrily, and Constantin flushed. He responded with a single word – a negative, it seemed to Kubulai – and then strode away towards the guard post. The ambassador compressed his lips. He started after the younger man, but was restrained by Alexei, who placed a hand on his shoulder, talking and smiling genially so that the ambassador was forced to reply politely.

Kubulai pursed his lips. He was appalled by the ambassador's bad manners. He glanced at Suragai. 'I meant what I said. The alien ran well.'

'And now you are wondering if you should not have done more to prevent it,' Suragai said. He sounded amused. The young offworlder was standing in the door of the guard post. One of the captains was giving him his cloak. Suragai eyed him, then grinned at Kubulai. 'I doubt if you could have deterred him,' he said. 'He is in love with Turakina, and he desired to impress her.'

'Oh,' Kubulai said. He looked at his hands and saw that they were covered in tar from the cable. Kubulai scrubbed at it, adjusting his expression. When he raised his eyes he gave Suragai a wide-eyed stare. 'Is he indeed? That is unfortunate.'

'If I have offended you,' Constantin said, 'then I apologise.'

The alien embassy was housed in a quiet street not far from the Grand Parade. The sentries guarding it had orders to admit only those who were authorised, and the gate at the end of the yard was closed and barred.

Kubulai scraped the toe of his boot across a cobble. He looked up. 'I don't know what you mean,' he said.

The offworlder's eyes were pale grey. They widened, as if he sensed an evasion. After a moment he looked away. 'You are to be betrothed to Turakina,' he said.

Troopers were crossing the yard. They waved to Constantin, their expressions friendly. Kubulai glared at them. Then he stared at the alien. 'Who told you that?'

'Oh.' Constantin gestured with both hands. 'D'mitri and Suragai have both mentioned it.'

The initial negotiations always took place between the heads of the families, and the male relatives tended to be involved at an early stage. Kubulai felt annoyed that he had not been consulted, but he knew that he could not object in fact. He had not said that he would refuse the match.

He said, 'Probably nothing will come of it.'

The alien smiled sourly. 'That's not what Suragai seems to think.'

It was not a subject Kubulai thought he wanted to discuss. He frowned, and then glanced at Constantin. 'I am not courting Turakina,' he said flatly. 'And you have not offended me.'

The ambassador came out of the door of the house into the yard. He saw Kubulai, and bowed. 'Good morning, Khan.'

Kubulai nodded. He did not like the ambassador, and sensed that the politeness of his manner hid contempt. The expressions in alien eyes were so difficult to read that it was impossible to be certain. There was a bench under the tree which grew in the centre of the yard. The ambassador went to it, and sat down. He did not look back towards Kubulai, but appeared engrossed in the activities of the sentries. A cart loaded with sacks and barrels was being admitted. The driver was a thin Ch'kasian. Kubulai knew that he was one of Alexei's junior officers, and he smiled grimly.

'I may be on this world for some time,' Constantin said. 'I hope we can be friends.'

The duration of the embassy's stay would be determined by the outcome of their audience with the

Kha-Khan. It had been postponed several times, and was now scheduled to take place the following day.

Kubulai digested the words, eyeing the alien. He said, 'You are an enemy of this land. How can there be friendship between us?'

Jehan was judging a series of appeals. The hall which was being used for the purpose was long, with white walls and a light timber floor which had been sanded and polished. A dais had been constructed at one end of the chamber, and Jehan was sitting on a carved wooden chair near the front of it, leaning forward. A clerk who was acting as his recorder sat on a low stool behind the Kha-Khan and to his left. Everyone else was standing.

The first two cases had been matters of quite complex litigation – claims and counterclaims between merchants – which had depended on the testimony of witnesses about the nature of the agreements which had been entered into by the various parties. Kubulai lounged against the wall to the rear of Jehan's chair, unsure why he had been commanded to be present. Gentlemen of the Household were not usually required to attend the Kha-Khan on such occasions, for they were fairly informal.

People were packed into the other half of the hall. It was the right of any subject of the Khanate to appeal a judgement to his overlord, although few in fact went so far. Often Jehan gave his opinion in writing – a matter of the confirmation of a penalty, or the interpretation of a point of law – but there were times when he sent for the litigants, the better to judge the truth of an offence, or when the plaintiff or defendant felt strongly enough to travel to Kinsai.

201

A chamberlain paced the open floor in front of the dais. He bowed to Jehan. 'Lord, the next case is the one I told you of.'

'Indeed.' Jehan had a hand on one knee. He waved the free hand. 'Then let the people approach.'

'The Khan wishes.' The chamberlain was a N'pani, gorgeous in a long gown of black silk. He bowed again, and his single oiled black scalp lock dangled, and then was tossed to the side.

A large group of men and women waited nervously near the front of the crowd. The chamberlain gestured imperiously to them. They edged forward, eyes downcast.

Jehan was craning round the side of the chair. He waved to Kubulai. 'Come and listen to this.'

Kubulai had unfastened the top three or four catches of his coat for the sake of comfort. He pushed the uppermost hastily into place, then went up to the side of Jehan's chair.

The open space in front of the dais was by now occupied by what appeared to be several different small groups. All the people seemed to be N'czuani – the inhabitants of the islands beyond the Gulf of Mists – and Kubulai guessed that the case was both complex and important for them to have come so far to obtain justice. On the extreme left there were five men – merchants or tradesmen by their garb. Their coats were good but not gaudy. The upcurved toes of their slippers were decorated with silver.

To the right of the men were five women. They were gowned but not veiled, and so were matrons. The offended stares on their faces were directed at one moment at the men, and at the next towards another woman, more richly gowned, who stood

202

apart. To her right stood a man on his own. He looked nervous, and was licking his lips as he eyed first the dais and then the other litigants.

'Lord,' the chamberlain said, 'this case has been submitted to you for judgement by Kadan Khan.'

Kadan was lord of N'czuan. Any case he felt unqualified to judge would have to be interesting indeed.

Jehan nodded. 'Continue,' he said.

The chamberlain appeared to draw a breath, gathering himself. He gestured towards the man who stood alone. 'Lord, this is T'sun Cha, who brings a case for compensation against these men, whom he found in adultery with his wife.'

The Kha-Khan's head went back. 'All of them together?' he enquired.

The plaintiff had on a brown coat over a white gown, and the toes of his slippers were decorated with gold. He shifted from one foot to the other, opened his mouth, and then closed it again.

'Lord,' the chamberlain said, 'there are in all five claims, one against each of these men, for five cases of adultery.' He indicated the men on the left. All the men had their eyes cast down.

The Kha-Khan wrinkled his nose. 'Very well. You need not name the defendants for the moment.'

The chamberlain looked relieved. He inclined his head. 'Lord, thank you.' Then it was as if he sought to compose himself again, gathering the facts in his mind. He pointed to the lone woman. 'Khan, this woman is T'sun Lin, the wife of the plaintiff. It is she who was taken in infidelity.'

The woman was slender, olive-skinned, with bold dark eyes. Her stare was unrepentant, and Kubulai saw Jehan frown. 'I am surprised she is still his wife,' Jehan said. He nodded to the chamberlain. 'Go on.'

'Lord, these are the wives of the men against whom T'sun Cha makes claim.' The chamberlain indicated the five matrons with a wave of his hand. Then he looked back at them. 'They are claiming compensation from T'sun Lin for her adultery with their husbands.'

The people filling the end of the hall stirred, and a mutter of comment started up. The Kha-Khan held up a hand, and after a moment there was silence. 'Five claims and five counterclaims,' Jehan said. 'That's certainly unusual. Is there anything else?'

An inscrutable expression appeared on the chamberlain's face. He said, 'Lord, there is a summary from Kadan Khan in which he says that T'sun Cha is the richest man on the main island of N'czuan, his wife having been found in adultery a number of times in the past. He says that while there is no precedent to allow the counterclaims of the wives, yet he was not disposed to dismiss them.'

Jehan sat back in his chair. He caught Kubulai's eye. 'Kadan could not tell me about this case for laughing,' he said. 'See what you can do with it.'

Kubulai said, 'The people want your judgement, not mine.'

'In that case you had better decide well,' the Kha-Khan observed equably. He looked at the litigants. 'Kubulai Khan will decide this case.'

The women all looked at Kubulai. The matrons watched him with wary eyes, but the adultress stared openly, so that he flushed. He moved to the side of the dais in front of the five men. 'Do any of you deny your adultery?' he asked.

All the men looked startled. They met one another's

eyes. One of them seemed to hesitate. He turned back to his co-defendants, seeking support, and another man made a gesture of encouragement.

The N'czuani said, 'Khan, we did not encourage her to come to us.'

It was a neat point. Fines in cases of adultery were quite common in both Y'frike and N'czuan, but payment rested upon the principle that a husband required to be compensated for the alienation of his wife's affections, and a divorce usually followed.

'And is that the defence of you all?' Kubulai scanned the faces of the men. Eventually they all nodded. Kubulai crossed to the other side of the dais. He gave the adultress a hard stare. 'You, T'sun Lin, do you admit that you went with the men?'

Her eyelashes fluttered, and she nodded. 'Lord, they tempted me,' she said plaintively.

One of the matrons took an angry pace forward. 'Lord,' she said, 'that is a lie. I saw her place herself in the way of my man.'

'Oh?' Kubulai frowned. 'Was that on the occasion of the adultery?'

The woman was plump, and very plain. She went crimson. 'No, Lord,' she admitted. Then she gave the adultress a venomous glance. 'It is her custom to walk abroad every day. All the men watch her, and the women who can, watch their men.'

'Knowing the woman to be unfaithful by habit.' Kubulai nodded. 'I see.' He looked at the expressions on the faces of the other women. They were angry with their husbands, but it was more for the ease with which they had been snared by the wiles of the temptress than for any performance of an unfaithful act.

The plaintiff had assumed a virtuous face. He bowed carefully to Kubulai. 'Lord, I witnessed the men encouraging my wife,' he said. 'They do not deny they went with her. I ask you for justice.'

Kubulai stared coldly. 'Justice you will have in due course of time,' he said. He caught the chamberlain's eye. 'Are there any witnesses?'

The chamberlain shook his head regretfully. 'No, Khan.'

It was one of those unusual cases where judgement ought to rest more upon what was right than upon the law, Kubulai thought. He paced towards Jehan's chair, then stopped and stared over the heads of the N'czuani at the people who were standing behind them in the hall. Everyone was straining, waiting to hear what he had decided. He said, 'The claim of the husband against the men with whom his wife was unfaithful depends upon whose will it was that led to her infidelity.' He glanced once towards the defendants. 'These men say that the woman came to them without their encouragement. The woman is supported by her husband, and says that she was lured.'

The five men looked worried, but the plaintiff's head came up abruptly. Anticipation showed on his features.

Kubulai ignored the reaction. 'Under the law I should accept the word of two against the word of one.' Kubulai pitched his voice so that it carried to the back of the hall. The murmur which had greeted his summary of the essential facts of the case died promptly. 'The circumstances are unusual, however,' Kubulai said. He caught the plaintiff's eye, and the N'czuani looked hastily away. Guilty, Kubulai thought. He waited until the five men were looking up, and then he said, 'One case of adultery I would have to believe. Five, with more attested by your khan, are more than simple coincidence, I think.'

The defendants produced embarrassed smiles. Their wives glowered, and the adultress bridled, an angry frown on her face.

'The claims of the wives of the men against the woman with whom all their husbands were unfaithful is a somewhat different matter,' Kubulai continued. He paused, as if in thought. 'There is no provision in the law for compensation in such a case, and yet it seems to me that there should be, for surely a wife is just as injured by her husband's lack of fidelity as a husband whose wife is stolen by another man.'

The tradition of the Yasa was based on the fact that a woman was expected to return to her family. Every marriage contract allowed for the refund of a portion of the dowry in the event of a divorce.

'I do not hold that this should become a precedent in all instances of infidelity,' Kubulai said, 'for the events in this case are surely remarkable, but I award compensation to the wives.'

The announcement evoked a cry of protest from the plaintiff. He said, 'Lord, why should I pay these women because their men seduced my wife? It is not just.'

Kubulai wrinkled his nose. He met the man's eyes. 'I said you would have justice by and by,' he said. 'So you shall. It seems to me that you have grown rich on the fruits of your wife's infidelity. Had you put her away the second or even the third time, I might have been disposed to believe that you were innocent. Instead you sought to profit from her conduct. Maybe you even encouraged her.' He saw the plaintiff start, and knew that he had hit the mark. 'For attempting to use a good law for a bad purpose, I fine you one koban,' Kubulai said. 'One that is for every claim made, and you will pay the wives and not their husbands – for it is clear that they have already enjoyed some benefit.'

The observation produced appreciative laughter. The five men blushed.

'For seeking to take advantage of your wife's habit of infidelity I likewise fine you.' Kubulai spoke across the disturbance. 'Again you will pay every wife one koban; and as compensation for your wife's conduct in causing their husbands to be unfaithful, one koban more.'

'Making fifteen in all,' Jehan said softly.

The N'czuani went white. 'Lord, such a penalty will beggar me,' he protested. 'I do not possess it.'

'Then maybe you can come to some arrangement with the women you owe, or with their husbands,' Kubulai responded coldly. He gave the adultress a disdainful stare. 'Let us see how you like it when your wife is committing infidelities to the advantage of others.'

The Kha-Khan laughed, delighted. 'Yes.' He nodded. 'That would be justice indeed.'

Kubulai turned his back. The people standing at the end of the hall were applauding the judgement, but for himself he felt only anger. When he looked round he saw that the litigants were being ushered away.

'Your approach is original,' Jehan said. He leaned back in his chair, then grinned at Kubulai. 'I particularly liked the way you fined the plaintiff for two matters which had not been laid against him.'

'I should have ordered the woman whipped,' Kubu-

208

lai said austerely. He looked down his nose.

'In which case she would be unable to discharge her husband's debts,' the Kha-Khan observed smoothly. 'Do you think that is how they will resolve it?'

Kubulai thought that it would be a fitting end to the matter, but he snorted and shook his head. 'Probably not,' he said.

'I think you are supposed to court me,' Turakina said. She smoothed her hand down the embroidered brocade of her long skirt, and her talons flashed.

Kubulai paced from one side of the open window to the other. The view down into the garden was obstructed by the tops of the trees. He stared at the shadows, trying to decipher shapes in them, and then turned abruptly to look at her. 'Why do you think that?' he demanded.

There was a hint of pink beneath Turakina's freckles. She rearranged her skirts again. 'We are to be betrothed,' she said simply. 'It is expected.'

A sentry passed along the path between the trees. Kubulai watched him out of sight. The night was still, and the only sound came from within the house. D'mitri was entertaining several of the khans, and Kubulai could hear the rumble of their conversation from the floor below. He smoothed his hand down inside the facing of his coat, trying to find the words to express what was in his mind without offending her. Finally he turned. She was watching him solemnly. 'I wouldn't make a good husband,' Kubulai said.

The remark appeared to amuse her. 'That's what my mother says of you,' she commented.

Kubulai pursed his lips. A lamp on the wall wavered, and he smelled the incense which had been mixed with the oil. 'She is right,' he said. 'You should marry another.'

Turakina's overgown was too old for her. It was fine lace, and her breasts looked like two buds beneath it. She did not look at him, but seemed instead to be concentrating on a point beside the door. A frown creased her forehead. 'You don't want to marry me.'

He breathed in. 'I don't want to marry anyone right now.'

'You wouldn't be marrying me now,' Turakina said. 'In a year or two maybe.'

The response made the corner of Kubulai's mouth twitch. He said, 'I was under the impression your affections were engaged.'

There was a moment of silence which seemed to stretch into infinity. Then Turakina's head came round. The irises of her eyes were amber, and caught the light. 'You mean Constantin,' she said calmly. 'He makes me laugh.'

'Something I shall probably never do,' Kubulai said flatly. He crossed the room and sat down beside her. 'Turakina, this match is our parents' idea, because we are Altun.'

'Oh,' Turakina said, 'I know that.'

Her hair had been combed out, but because it had been in plaits the whole length of every strand was kinked. Threads of gold glinted in it. Kubulai pressed his hands against his thighs. 'I am to be named Successor,' he said. 'Has anyone told you?'

Turakina shook her head. She gave him a sharp glance. 'It troubles you,' she observed.

Her sensitivity took him by surprise. 'I fear it,' he said.

The warmth of her body was magnifying her per-

210

fume. She stirred, and the scent overpowered him. He held his breath. He would not court her.

'Your wife will be Khatun,' Turakina said.

'Eventually.' Kubulai nodded. 'Jehan will live for years. I could die first.'

'Then she will be the wife of a Khan,' Turakina observed prosaically.

It was as if she was aware that he did not know how to put her off. Kubulai wrinkled his nose. He caught her eye. 'Do you want to be my wife?' he asked. 'You scarcely know me.'

It was quite often the case in an arranged marriage, but probably she did not know that.

Turakina's hands stirred in her lap. She said, 'It is much easier for a woman than a man. No man is born to be a husband. I have always known that I would be a wife someday.'

She had not answered the question, Kubulai thought. He frowned, and said, 'If I refuse this match, it will shame you. You have to do it.'

If she would not, then probably he could not. It was a realisation which created a strange sensation inside his chest – as if there was no air in his lungs.

Suddenly Turakina stood up. She moved round to face him, standing inside the reach of his arms so that he could feel the warmth coming from her, her body like a furnace. 'Don't you want me?' she asked softly.

Kubulai knew that he could put his hands on her, and she would not flinch away. Briefly he wondered who had persuaded her to behave like this. Her behaviour was surely not natural to a girl of her years. Her parents probably desired the match, Kubulai thought, and they might be willing for her to go to considerable lengths to ensure it.

His first instinct was to thrust her away, but when it came to it he could not use violence against her. Instead he put his hands on her arms below her shoulders, lifted her, and set her to one side like a chair which was in the way. Then he got up and went out through the door without looking at her again.

The Kha-Khan's audience chamber was an octagonal room with a floor which had been covered with gold foil so that every knot and irregularity of the grain of the timbers showed like a ripple in an iridescent golden pool. In the centre of the room there was a roofed dais of carved ivory. The Dragon Throne was in the middle of it. There was no other furniture.

When Kubulai had completed the prostration he sat back on his heels. To his left in a line knelt his father Alexei, Alexei's father Suragai, and Jehan's grandfather Burun. On the right and slightly in front were the alien ambassador and his officer. They had prostrated themselves awkwardly, and both were climbing to their feet.

Kubulai stared at his reflection, distorted by the way the gold surface flowed in uneven expanses. Burun was still kneeling, and Suragai, but Alexei was standing up – an elastic movement of sinew and muscle which must have been the result of years of practice. He said, 'Magnificence, I present the ambassador of the aliens and his officer.'

Jehan was wearing a long open coat of gold silk. The fabric was stiff with pearls and embroidery. He moved one hand fractionally. His extended talons glittered. 'Let them approach and name themselves,' he said.

The ambassador had been coached by Burun. The

ritual was the old one which was intended to be used by the embassy of a conquered nation – three paces, kneel, and bow – and Kubulai smiled grimly as he watched it being performed.

'Lord Khan,' the ambassador said, 'my name is Valeri Borocheff. I am the ambassador to this world of an Empire which rules the known worlds of the Universe. This is my officer, Constantin Zarubin.'

The Kha-Khan looked down his nose. 'We desired only your names,' he said haughtily.

Kubulai saw the ambassador flush, and then it was as if he realised that he was being tested. He seemed to gather himself, and bowed silently.

Burun stood up, his face expressionless. Jehan glanced towards him, and then he addressed the ambassador again. 'This world is known to the Empire. Do you claim to rule us also?'

'Lord, no,' the ambassador said quickly. 'Indeed the Empire has known of this world for many years, and has protected it from interference.'

It was one way of phrasing it, Kubulai thought. He recalled his father's description of the manner in which their world was kept apart from contact with the rest of the Universe – of weapons floating in the void of space which would destroy anything that approached.

Jehan said, 'We know, as you may imagine, much of the Empire. Speak to us of your purpose in coming to our land. Our counsellors have spoken to us of trade.'

The ambassador inclined his head. He had shed the Yek tunic which he had worn since Pesth, and was now dressed in what Kubulai thought must be the formal clothing of his rank – a coat and trousers of blue-grey buckram. A gold sunburst decorated the

213

breast of the coat of both the ambassador and his officer, but Borocheff also wore a gold chain around his neck. 'Lord Khan,' he said, 'I would offer you the credentials of my embassy.' He glanced quickly round at Burun, who signalled to one of the chamberlains who waited in a row beside the door. The man was another N'pani. He came forward, an oblong case in his arms, and offered it up to Jehan.

The Kha-Khan touched the case fleetingly with the tips of his fingers. 'We receive them,' he said.

It was clear that the ambassador had expected Jehan to examine the contents of the case. His mouth opened, and then closed again. The chamberlain was bowing once more. He took the credential case to Burun, and knelt in front of him. Burun opened the case, lifted out the document inside, and scanned it. 'Authority to arrange trade,' he said. 'Also mention of a formal diplomatic relationship – a request for facilities for a full embassy, the provision of land, buildings and so forth.' He passed the credentials to Suragai, who began to read them with care.

If the ambassador had not looked closely at Suragai before, he did so now. They did not expect to find men like themselves in the Khanate's service, Kubulai thought, pleased.

Suragai rose to his feet. Standing, he was the tallest man in the chamber. He bowed to Jehan. 'Lord,' he said, 'these are in order, though they are not signed by the Emperor.'

'Oh?' The Kha-Khan's head went back, as if he had been offered an affront. 'Are we then not worthy to be addressed by him?'

The purpose of the whole audience was to place the aliens off guard – to ascertain their true intent without them realising that they had revealed it. Borocheff was still eyeing Kubulai's grandfather. The awareness that he was being spoken to by Jehan seemed to strike him suddenly. His head went round. 'Lord, the matter of accrediting an embassy such as ours rests in the hands of those who are authorised to deal with the matter of trade.'

'The Nicoleyev,' Suragai said.

The ambassador glanced back. 'Sir, I do not know you,' he said, 'but it is clear to me that you know much of the Empire.'

An acid smile appeared on Suragai's face. 'Once I was its servant,' he responded. 'As Sergei Rostov I was an Admiral of the White.'

The abrupt comprehension on the ambassador's face was quite interesting. His eyes moved towards Alexei. 'Then this is –'

'– my father.' Alexei nodded.

'Ah.' Borocheff's tone was thoughtful, but the look in his eyes was suddenly wary. 'I did not understand,' he said, but it was not to Alexei that he spoke. Abruptly he turned back towards Jehan and bowed formally again. 'Lord Khan,' he said, 'I ask your pardon. These who serve you will be of interest to my own lord.'

'Of that we have little doubt,' the Kha-Khan commented drily. 'Your interest in them will wait, however. We will now discuss the matter of the commodity for which you wish to trade with us.'

It was apparent that the ambassador was taken by surprise by the directness of the approach. He seemed to hesitate, and then said, 'Lord Khan, surely that would be a matter to be arranged between one merchant and another.'

215

The phrasing was intended to imply that the details themselves would be beneath the Kha-Khan's notice, and Kubulai smiled wryly at the deftness of the response.

Jehan touched his cheek with a taloned forefinger. He said, 'That might be so, were we not aware of the nature of your trading interest.'

Borocheff shot a single glance in Alexei's direction. The expression on his face suggested that he thought he had been betrayed. Quickly he adjusted his features. He looked up at Jehan. 'Lord, there are many commodities which are likely to be of interest to us.'

'But only one which would cause you to alter the Quarantine Laws,' Suragai said, his tone harsh. 'You want the poppy.'

The ambassador did not look round, but his shoulders stiffened. Constantin was standing a little off to Borocheff's right. He stared back towards the place where Alexei and Suragai stood together, his expression unhappy.

There was a moment when Kubulai thought that they were going to offer a denial. Borocheff appeared to draw in a deep breath, and then to let it out again. 'Lord Khan, it is true that there is a plant which grows on this world which interests us...'

'The Imperial Poppy,' Jehan said austerely, 'the sap of which you use to prolong life.'

A sound like a wave washing gently against a sandy shore disturbed the silence. Alexei glanced up, and he saw that the broad mats of the fans were moving gracefully back and forward, stirring the still air.

'If you know of its properties, then you must use it yourselves,' Borocheff said. He sounded resigned.

Jehan snorted. 'Are we mad?'

Borocheff looked confused. 'Lord?'

Suragai said, 'The poppy prolongs life, but over long periods of time its effects are also lethal. It dissolves bones, and tissue becomes transparent.'

Kubulai saw the ambassador blink. 'That is an effect I am not aware of,' he said carefully.

Even if they knew of it, they would deny it, his father had said. Kubulai watched the alien's face and saw the truth in his eyes. It was the first time he had been sure that he had correctly interpreted an offworlder's emotions.

The ambassador turned to address Jehan. 'Lord,' he said, 'the juice of the poppy not only prolongs life. It also prevents the onset of disease and accelerates healing in men of my species. The True People are well endowed in that respect, and have no need for its assistance.'

He had used the Yek name for their race. Kubulai saw the grim smiles on the faces of his grandfather and the other men as they contemplated the irony.

There was a look in Jehan's eyes which suggested that he was ready to reveal his knowledge of the truth about the origin of the races which possessed talons. Abruptly he sat back on the throne. 'As you have seen, you can conceal nothing from us,' he said. 'You should speak to us therefore without evasion about your intentions. You desire trade, you say. To what extent?'

Borocheff appeared to swallow. He avoided Jehan's eyes for a moment, then he looked up. 'Lord Khan,' he said candidly, 'the poppy grows in abundance on this world. We will purchase it all –'

'Paying with what?' Burun spoke suddenly.

'As to that –' The ambassador spread his hands. '– I am empowered to offer anything within reason. Your

217

knowledge of technology is advanced, even if you have no use for it. Certain military items are restricted, I regret. As for the rest ...'

Burun laughed. 'Machines,' he said. 'Is that what you are offering us?'

'Or gold,' Borocheff said quickly. 'Goods of value to you. We understand your laws concerning machines, and respect them.' He looked from Burun to Jehan, and back again.

Jehan wrinkled his nose. 'What need have we of greater riches?' he asked. It was a rhetorical question.

The ambassador pursed his lips. 'Lord Khan, there may be articles or even creatures from other worlds which would be of interest to you. Surely that would be a matter for further discussion once we have agreed the principle of a trade between this world and the Empire.'

A rejection was the one response they could not afford to give, Kubulai knew, although he did not understand why. He saw his father stir. 'You would expect us to harvest the poppy, of course,' Alexei said.

Something flashed across the ambassador's eyes. He said, 'If the areas in which it grows are restricted, and you do not desire to use them for other purposes, then we would be happy to undertake that ourselves.'

'It is a process which does not employ machines,' Suragai said.

There was something here which was of crucial importance, Kubulai guessed, though he could not imagine what it was. He watched his father's face, and saw the careful control of expression which indicated a restraint of temper.

Borocheff's head had gone back. 'That is so,' he said.

'Then would you bring labour in to carry out your

218

harvest?' Alexei enquired politely. 'Our law would restrict such a practice, I fear.'

A look of polite amusement passed across the ambassador's face, and it was as if he knew that he had been invited to step into a snare. He smiled at Alexei. 'We would prefer to employ people from this world, if you would permit it,' he responded. 'Of course we would pay you for their hire, just as we would pay for the poppy.'

The idea of hire and reward was not entirely foreign. It was in use in Y'vrope. Kubulai saw the Kha-Khan exchange glances with Burun.

Jehan said, 'The poppy grows wild in a number of places. Would it interest you if we were to cultivate it?'

'Indeed yes, Lord.' Borocheff nodded hastily.

'The quantity would be a matter for future discussion,' Burun rumbled. 'And likewise the matter of payment.'

It sounded as if they were preparing to agree. Kubulai stared.

Jehan was gazing into the middle distance. Suddenly he looked straight at the aliens. 'In that case we give our agreement in principle to the arrangement of trade between the Khanate and the Empire,' he said. 'On the condition that our sovereignty is not to be infringed upon, or our law disobeyed.'

The ambassador looked pleased. It was clearly more than he had expected at this stage. 'Lord Khan, we thank you,' he said. He seemed to hesitate, and then continued. 'Lord, the nature of our agreement ought to be negotiated by the others of my species who wait word of my audience with you –'

'You mean you would like to expand your embassy,'

the Kha-Khan said drily.

The alien appeared to be only a little embarrassed. 'With your permission, Lord, yes.'

The Kha-Khan did not attempt to hide his look of enquiry in Alexei's direction. Kubulai saw his father nod. 'Subject to restrictions,' he said.

Jehan's head turned. He raised an eyebrow in the ambassador's direction. 'Well?'

Borocheff bowed. 'Lord Khan, we will comply with any reasonable requirement which will enable us to trade in friendship with one another.'

Kubulai wondered if Jehan was going to comment upon the alternative had an agreement not been reached, but the Kha-Khan only gestured to indicate that the audience was at an end. The aliens were led gently through the ritual of retiring from the chamber, and the chamberlains filed out after them.

When the doors were closed Jehan stood up. He shrugged one arm out of his coat, and then slipped it off. Suragai still had the embassy credentials in his hand. He walked to the dais and offered them up to Jehan. The Kha-Khan gave the document a single disinterested glance, and then let it fall on the seat of the throne. He said, 'Did they believe it?'

It was Alexei who responded. He moved to the front of the dais and sat down on the edge. 'I think they did,' he said. 'Once they became aware that we knew what they wanted, it was reasonable for them to assume that we would agree to trade to avoid the alternative.'

'They expect you to have told me that they will employ conquest to get the poppy if they have to.' Jehan nodded. He glanced towards Kubulai. 'Did you understand everything?'

'Nearly everything.' Kubulai pursed his lips. He

caught his father's eye. 'What was that about harvesting?'

Suragai chuckled. 'I told you he would spot that,' he said to Alexei.

Jehan said, 'If we allow them to take over the land on which the poppy grows, they will use it as a base from which to start to overcome us.'

'And if we give them people to harvest the poppies, they will turn them into slaves,' Suragai said soberly.

There was more than one way to bring about a conquest. Kubulai remembered his father saying it. Now the words took on a fresh meaning.

'The way I asked it,' Alexei said, 'they are not sure we have told Jehan everything. On another world where the poppy grows, the people are slaves, but it was not the Empire that enslaved them. The rulers of the land did it themselves, so that they could remain the overlords.'

Kubulai could not believe that the aliens understood so little about the Yasa that they imagined that such a thing would ever happen in the Khanate. He thought about what his father had said. Suddenly the reasoning became clear. 'You are of their species,' he said, and looked from his father to his grandfather. 'You mean them to think that if they offer you enough, you will betray Jehan.'

The idea was disgusting, but it made a kind of sense from an offworlder point of view.

Jehan nodded. 'If that is all they try,' he said, 'we will easily overcome them.'

PART THREE

A Room Full of Strangers

The Imperial lander was huge, three times the length of the largest trireme, and it rested on the ground between patches of dense forest. The grass of the plain was tall, spiky and sharp-edged. The paths used regularly by the aliens were trodden flat, and broken stalks lay strewn everywhere, dried like straw by the heat of the red sun. Suragai walked his st'lyan along one of them, his reins gathered in one hand. Close to the lander there was permanent deep shadow, and the smell of rotting undried grass made his nostrils twitch.

A solitary guard was perched on a box at the foot of the main ramp. The box was painted grey, and words in some language Suragai did not know had been stamped or embossed in black across one side. When the alien saw Suragai he stood up quickly and bowed. He was wearing offworlder coveralls, but somebody had given him one of the wide conical hats which N'pani coolies used to protect their heads so that they could labour in the worst heat of summer. The combination looked ridiculous, and Suragai tried not to smile. He nodded acknowledgement of the bow, and then dismounted. His st'lyan was a red roan. Fine white hairs were sprinkled through its coat, and it had a pure white mane. When it lowered its head to graze, the alien eyed the gilded horn nervously.

Suragai said, 'I want to speak to *Shen* Constantin.'

Shen was a courtesy title, a form of address employed towards non-human minor nobility. The offworlders were not noble of course, but the officers had rank of a kind, and so it had been decided that it would be a politeness to use the word – even though it gave them a dignity they did not deserve.

The guard seemed not to understand at first.

'*Shen* Constantin,' Suragai repeated slowly in Anglic. Few of the offworlders appeared to speak their own language with the same accent – something Suragai thought was strange. It was as if they were all foreigners, even to one another.

'Oh.' The alien had understood this time. He nodded quickly. 'Lord, I will summon him for you.'

There was a talker – Suragai could think of no other word to describe the small black box the aliens used for communicating with each other – lying in the grass beside the foot of the ramp. The guard lifted it. Suragai held up a hand. 'There is no need,' he said. 'I will go to him.'

Probably it was the fact that he was prepared to enter the vessel at all which startled the guard. The alien's mouth opened, but no sound issued. He seemed to hesitate, then he bowed once more. He said, 'As you wish, Lord. I will tell him you are coming.'

Alien manners were very odd, and it was difficult to know when they were being deliberately rude. Suragai wrinkled his nose, then nodded curtly and strode up the incline of the ramp into the lander. Inside there was a long passageway lined with metal – the way the aliens employed metal was profligate in the extreme – which led left and right. Doors were let into it at intervals. Suragai turned right, and kept walking until he saw a door with a red panel on the face. A

226

clear plate had been let into the wall at one side of the door. Suragai pressed the palm of his hand against it, and it hissed open.

The strangeness of the vessel was part of its attraction, Suragai reflected. The aliens were so wasteful – their possessions were designed to wear out after a time, so that the owners would have an excuse to buy new – and at the same time so ingenious. They were always trying different methods, and if there was a flaw in that aspect of their nature it lay in the fact that they seldom preserved old ways, even when they worked.

Through the open door there was a room which was illuminated by panels in the ceiling which glowed white. Constantin had told Suragai that the light came from the sun, but Suragai could not see how that could be. Sunlight would have been red – a colour which apparently the aliens found uncomfortable to the eye until they became accustomed to it – and in any case there was no way for sunlight to travel through the outer skin of the vessel to so many different places. Probably the white glow came from heated elements, Suragai thought, and he wondered how the heat was produced, and if it was that which came from the sun. These were Constantin's quarters – cramped chambers which he now occupied in preference to the spaciousness of the embassy house at Kinsai. The air smelled strange, and Suragai wrinkled his nose. He had not noticed it so much when there were only a few of them, but all aliens smelled different. Even when they kept themselves clean like civilised men there was an odour which lingered around any place they occupied for a length of time. Constantin was sitting at a table which projected out from the wall. When he saw Suragai he stood up, looking pleased. 'The ramp watch said only that Suragai was coming to see me,' he said. 'I did not know whether to expect you, or maybe your grandfather.'

Suragai's grandfather was so far managing to ignore the offworlders' attempts to persuade him to visit their vessel, but Suragai saw no point in commenting on the fact. 'You find the similarity of our names confusing,' he said.

'I do.' Constantin nodded. 'How does anyone know the difference?'

'Oh well.' Suragai gestured. 'My grandfather is Suragai Khan, or Suragai the Tall. I am only Suragai Noyon.'

The alien registered the explanation. Then he frowned. 'But what if you become a khan?' he asked. 'How will men identify you then?'

It was clear that the offworlder did not understand the importance of his question. Suragai gave him a stare. 'The Kha-Khan decides which men are to rule,' he said. 'A khanate is not passed from father to son. It goes to he who most merits it. Maybe I will always be a noyon.'

Outside the lander beyond the forest a number of tents had been set up. The alien tents were made from a greenish-coloured material which was not quite transparent, and the Yek had learned not to touch it with their talons, because it tore if it was pierced by anything sharp. There were no poles or timbers in an offworlder tent. Instead sections were made rigid by pumping in air. When they leaked the whole structure sagged.

The men of the guard company assigned to watch

the ship were Merkuts. Their yurts were constructed on platforms to lift them clear of the long grass. Suragai thought the alien encampment looked untidy by comparison, for their tents were dotted everywhere. Beyond the yurts there were covered tether lines for the st'lyan, and on the far side of those was the archery range. Suragai pulled Constantin up behind him on the roan's back, and rode around the camp towards it.

Another offworlder came out of one of the tents. He waved to Constantin.

Suragai said, 'Surely he is not a soldier.' The man was old, with narrow shoulders and a pot belly, and his beard was nearly white.

Constantin laughed. 'That's Professor Karpov.'

'A scientist?' Suragai wrinkled his nose. The watch had not said that men other than soldiers occupied the tents, and he had assumed that their presence was nothing more than an attempt by the aliens to provide a balance to counter the numbers placed to guard them.

'He intends no harm,' Constantin said quickly. 'He only wants to find out why coming here makes us ill.'

All the aliens had been sick, even those who had stayed in the lander. Some had been restricted to a diet of offworlder food – cakes of something that looked and smelled like ground and compressed cooked meat, but was not – but after two days they had fallen ill just like the rest.

Suragai raised his eyebrows. 'Why does it matter? You always get better, and you don't sicken again. Why should it trouble you?'

'Anything we don't understand troubles us,' Constantin responded.

That was certainly true. Alien curiosity was insatiable. They wanted to know everything. Their motivation was something Suragai neither trusted nor understood, and he wondered if Constantin suspected that his behaviour was the subject of constant analysis by the men whose task it was to watch him. He believes that I am his friend, Suragai thought, and felt momentarily guilty about the deception.

At the end of the range they dismounted. Around twenty men, a few of them offworlders, occupied the flat open ground between the marker posts. Targets had been set up at various distances, but for the moment nobody was shooting at them. When the officers at the back saw Suragai they made way for him. Osep was one of the troopers who were marking. He picked up Suragai's bow case from the grass at his feet and came over with it.

'Osep, thank you.' Suragai took the case and opened it. The bow was a double reflex curve made of layers of wood and horn which had been glued together, compressed, and then cured. The finish on either side of the guard was so finely sanded and polished that it was impossible to tell where one layer ended and another began. Suragai strung the bow, resting one tip against his instep so that he could push the loop up into the groove. The strung bow vibrated musically when he lifted it.

D'mitri walked up through the gathering crowd. 'I didn't see you arrive,' he said. 'Now we can start.'

Suragai gave his father a wide-eyed stare, then turned towards Constantin. 'I said I would teach you to shoot as we do,' he said. 'Do you think you can draw my bow?'

Constantin took the bow. He hooked two fingers of

his right hand around the string and pulled it back. He made a face. 'Maybe.'

The arrows in Suragai's case were fletched with peacock. He took the bow back from Constantin and nocked one. Then he drew back and loosed at the nearest target.

'Gold in the first,' Osep announced.

When Suragai turned he saw that Alexei and Kubulai were coming to the front of the crowd. 'You should have specified your point of aim,' Alexei said, and smiled.

When Constantin saw Alexei he bowed. His hands moved out from his sides in the odd formal gesture all the aliens seemed to employ when they saluted Alexei. Suragai remembered that it was something to do with Imperial rank. He said, 'Khan, I'll match you shot for shot if you care to compete against me.'

Kubulai showed his teeth. 'I think I hear a challenge.'

Alexei pursed his lips. He gave Suragai a superior stare, but said nothing. D'mitri stirred. 'Maybe we should teach these youngsters a lesson,' he said to Alexei.

A few of the watching Merkuts grinned. One of the officers said, 'A koban the khan wins.'

'Which one?' Kubulai asked. He looked round. 'If you mean my father, I'll take some of that.'

Most of the guard were wearing old campaign tunics - short sleeveless waistcoats which were open down the front to reveal their bare chests. Alexei took off his riding coat and rolled up the sleeves of his shirt. He said, 'Somebody give me a wrist guard.'

Kubulai laughed harshly. He pulled off his coat and dropped it on the grass. Then he took off his shirt. The tall officer who captained his guard was holding a bow. Its guard was wound with gold wire. Kubulai took it out of his hands. He plucked an arrow from Suragai's case, and fired it into the hard ground at the foot of the marker post. The arrow shattered length-wise.

Suragai stared. He held out his hand for the bow. 'Let me see that.'

The bow was half as thick again as Suragai's. He squinted at the chop imprinted at one end of the upper binding. 'It's one of T'zun tu's,' Kubulai said. 'I have four of his.'

The master bowmaker of Kinsai was famous throughout the land. Suragai handed back the bow. 'You are a khan, and can afford them,' he said. 'No wonder my arrow shattered.'

'Mine have more spline.' Kubulai nodded. He turned towards his officer. 'Jehangir, send someone for my arrow case.'

The Merkut nodded. Men in the crowd were laying wagers. A tall elderly man with nearly white hair was uncasing Alexei's bow. Suragai saw that it was another of T'zun tu's. He took another arrow and stepped up to the mark. 'Fourth target,' he said.

The arrow whipped across the range and struck the target on the outer edge of the gold. D'mitri said, 'If you can score gold in the fourth, then the targets are too close. Osep, send some men to move the last two another fifty paces.'

'Yes, lord.' Osep trotted away up the range. The third target was carried fifty paces beyond the one Suragai's arrow had scored in, and another one was set up fifty paces beyond that.

Alexei came up to the mark. He peered downrange.

232

'The light is very bad,' he said. 'I'll try the fourth.' He nocked an arrow, and then drew and loosed in a single fluid movement.

'Gold!' Osep's voice carried the length of the range.

Kubulai came up to Suragai's side. 'Use my bow,' he said. 'Yours will barely carry that far.'

'I'm used to it.' Suragai brought the arrow head down onto the target, and then let it come up a hand's-breadth. He let fly. The arrow hit the very edge of the gold.

D'mitri's first arrow struck the centre of the fourth target just short of Alexei's, and Kubulai's went between them. He looked at his father. 'Your turn.'

This time Alexei nominated the fifth and furthest rondel. The fluting at the tail of the arrow caused it to whistle as it went down the range.

'Solid hit!' Osep called.

'You must use my bow this time,' Kubulai said. He held it out.

Suragai tested the pull and grimaced. 'Give me an arrow.'

The flights of Kubulai's arrows had been stained in his colours. Suragai ranged on one of the middle marker posts and loosed. The arrow whipped across the top of the post, and the trooper standing beyond it moved back hastily.

'Was that a competition shot?' D'mitri asked, laughing.

Suragai glared. He tested the bow again. The heaviness of the pull was causing his arm to come up fractionally when he let go of the string, he decided. He took another arrow from Kubulai and nocked it. 'Fifth target.'

A thin streamer of cloud was passing across the face

233

of the sun. The line of shadow creased the ground, darkening the straw barricade behind the rondel. Suragai waited until it had passed, and then he drew and fired.

'Gold!' Osep shouted.

Some of the Merkuts cheered. An officer slapped Suragai on the shoulder. D'mitri ignored the commotion. He stepped up to the mark and let fly. His arrow struck beside Suragai's. Kubulai's also hit gold.

'This is getting us nowhere,' Kubulai said. 'We're only going to miss when we go beyond the range of our bows.'

Alexei was pulling off his shirt. His skin was tanned light gold, and there were lines of tiny fair hairs across his chest. He took his bow from his officer and nocked an arrow. Then he went up to the mark and stood with his back to the range. He looked at Kubulai. 'Go up and move the last target. Put it anywhere you like.'

Kubulai opened his eyes wide. He nodded, grinning, and trotted away up the side of the marker posts.

'Do you know the game the children play with walnut shells?' Alexei caught D'mitri's eye. 'They throw one up in the air, and they have to pick up all the others and then catch it before it hits the ground.'

D'mitri nodded. 'I don't see the connection,' he said. He stared uprange, frowning. then his expression cleared. 'Yes I do.' He turned. 'Somebody give me a coin.'

The officer who had offered to wager on Alexei had a gold koban in his hand. He flipped it to D'mitri, who caught it. 'Lord, remember where you got it,' the officer said.

Men chuckled. Suragai looked up the range. Kubulai

had collected two troopers and he was moving the fifth target so that it was well to the left and turned at an angle. Only a narrow oval of the face was visible. After a moment he stepped back and waved. 'Ready!'

Suragai saw his father walk up to the mark at Alexei's side. Alexei was still facing towards the crowd. He glanced at D'mitri. 'Throw.'

The coin went up into the air, turning over and over. Alexei turned, raising his bow. He drew and loosed, then caught the coin as it fell.

'Red!' Osep shouted.

Alexei looked satisfied. He glanced towards Suragai. 'You try it.'

Kubulai was coming back down the side of the range. Suragai went up to the mark. He nocked an arrow and stood facing towards the watching men, breathing slowly. Alexei said something in a low voice. D'mitri nodded, and strode away.

The trick of shooting well was to ignore the coin, Suragai thought. He saw Alexei toss it to Kubulai.

Moments passed. Kubulai was flipping the coin up and catching it. He stared up the range past Suragai, and a tight little smile appeared on his face.

'Ready!'

Suragai took a breath. He nodded to Kubulai, and saw the coin start to rise. Without haste he turned.

The target had been moved back to more or less its original position, and its full face was exposed. It was an insult, and Suragai swore angrily. He fired, and put out his right hand. The coin fell into it. Suragai tossed the coin to Kubulai. He snatched another arrow out of the case in the hand of Kubulai's officer, nocked it, and loosed again. The shaft flew past D'mitri's head.

He ducked and gestured rudely. When he came back to the firing point he was grinning broadly. He said, 'Your first shot hit gold, but your second was a clear miss.'

Suragai glared at him. Then he stared round at Alexei. 'Khan, if that was your idea, you owe me an apology.'

Alexei showed his teeth. 'You hit it, didn't you?' He looked back over his shoulder at the owner of the gold coin. 'Jenjin, I think you owe my son money.'

Kubulai tossed the coin in the air, laughing. He said, 'If we set up some more targets, everybody can try.'

'Yes.' Alexei nodded. 'It isn't a game after all.'

'Don't move your left arm.' Suragai tapped Constantin on the arm just below the shoulder.

Constantin lowered the bow. He said, 'I'm getting tired.'

A line of troopers stood to Suragai's right, shooting at the other targets. Suragai glanced past them towards the place where Alexei and Kubulai were talking to the guard commander, then looked back. 'I thought you could shoot.'

'I said I knew how,' Constantin replied in a patient tone.

Suragai found it hard to believe, but did not let his feelings show on his face. He said, 'Try it again.'

The bow was one Suragai had used before he had come into his full strength, and the pull was fairly light. The target was only a hundred paces away. Constantin nocked an arrow.

'Draw to your cheek,' Suragai said. 'That's it. Aim up.

Now bring the point down slowly. Yes.'

This time the offworlder's left hand jerked only slightly. The arrow struck the outer circle. Constantin looked pleased with himself.

It was the fifth time he had managed to hit the target. Suragai took the bow out of Constantin's hands. He slid it into its case. 'That was better.'

'But now you think I should stop while I'm ahead.' The alien produced a dry smile.

Only three other aliens were still watching the shooting. All of them were standing behind Constantin. Suragai glanced at them. Two of them had tried the bow he was casing now, but neither of them had hit anything. Suragai met Constantin's eyes. 'If you are really tired, then you ought to stop.'

'I'd like one more try,' the offworlder said.

Suragai wrinkled his nose. 'All right, but use the other bow.' He set the light bow aside, and picked up the one he had used at the start of the competition.

'It's much harder to pull,' Constantin said doubtfully.

'Maybe you can design a machine that will pull it for you,' Suragai said tartly. 'I never said it would be easy.'

An offended look appeared on Constantin's face. He pursed his lips, and then took the bow when Suragai held it out. He nocked, drew and fired in one continuous succession of movement. The arrow clipped the outer edge of the red.

'I should have insulted you sooner,' Suragai observed. 'You shoot better when you're annoyed.'

It was now close to midday, and the sun was almost directly overhead. A heat haze made the far end of the range look as if the ground was vibrating. Beyond it in the distance the red pillar of Kinsai was barely visible.

Suragai said, 'Tell me again how you learned to use a bow.'

Constantin began to case Suragai's bow. 'The same way all officers learn,' he said. 'It's all done by machine.'

'The machine imagines it for you,' Suragai said flatly. He still did not see how it could be possible.

'That's right.' The offworlder nodded. 'When you are connected to the machine, the situations it places you in seem real. You kill men, but they are only ghosts created by the system.'

'And to join you with the machine they have to shave every hair from your body.' Suragai gave the alien a disbelieving stare.

'Yes.' Constantin gestured. 'You mustn't feel anything other than the input from the machine, and so you are immersed in liquid. The messages – the sensations your brain thinks it is experiencing – are passed through your skin.'

Suragai tried to imagine it, but could not. The notion of a man breathing liquid was inconceivable. 'Kubulai says his father spoke of learning to shoot that way,' he observed. 'He didn't believe it either.'

A corner of Constantin's mouth twitched. He propped the bow case carefully against a marker post, then milled his arms around in a circle as if to ease a stiffness in them. 'I know how to shoot, although I never handled a bow before today,' he said. 'I learned to ride and to use a sword and spear the same way. My brain remembers, even if my hands do not.'

If every alien's remembered abilities were of the same quality, then probably the experience was of little value, Suragai thought, and knew in the same instant that he was being blinded by his prejudice.

He picked up the bow case. 'Next time I come I will take you hunting.'

Two more aliens were crossing the grass from the direction of the lander. Suragai realised that one of them was a woman, and for a moment he stared at her. No one had said that the embassy contained women. She was dressed in the light tunic and breeches which all military members of the contingent now wore, and the insignia of her collar showed that she was the same rank as Constantin.

When she saw Suragai she bowed like a man.

Constantin said, 'Noyon, allow me to present Lieutenant Natalia Tereshkeva.'

Suragai frowned. 'You have women in your army?' She was quite beautiful, and so he did not look at her or acknowledge her bow.

'Men and women are equal in the Empire,' Constantin said. 'We have women scientists and engineers too.'

'Indeed?' Suragai attempted to adjust to the idea. He said, 'Men and women are different. How can they be treated the same?'

Among the offworlders the faces of the men exhibited wry smiles, but the woman's head went back. 'You think women are inferior to men,' she said in precise Anglic.

The observation made no sense. Suragai eyed her. 'I said that they are different,' he responded coolly. 'A comparison only works when it is made between things which have the same nature. A woman's nature is different from a man's.'

'And so she should be treated as an inferior,' she said tartly.

Her attitude was so aggressive that Suragai was amused. 'Lady,' he said, 'don't put words into my mouth. In my land men and women have different rights because we hold that they are different species. Both have freedom and self-determination of a kind, and each is protected by the law.'

The alien woman was slim, and she had very fair skin. Her hair was light brown, cut quite short, and Suragai was fascinated to see that there were Altun red-gold highlights through it. He saw her flush as she became aware of his scrutiny. Abruptly she said, 'Women are always treated as inferiors by primitive cultures.'

There was a moment of embarrassed silence. Suragai raised his eyebrows. 'You mean to imply that your level of civilisation is greater than ours,' he said. 'I disagree with you, as it happens, but I don't know that you are capable of appreciating a reasoned argument about the subject. In our culture it is considered bad manners to give offence to someone when you are enjoying his hospitality.'

The young woman went bright red. Quickly Constantin said, 'Noyon, I apologise for the lieutenant's rudeness. She does not yet understand your customs.'

'Then she should remain silent until she does,' Suragai said coldly, and saw the men flinch.

The woman's mouth opened. It was clear that she wanted to make an angry retort, but no sound came. Suragai picked up his bow case. He stalked past the aliens towards the rear of the firing position. As he walked away he heard the woman say, 'Constantin, I don't need you to apologise for me.'

Suragai thought the offworlders were fools to dispute in the open where people would listen. It was obvious that they did not realise that he could still hear what was being said. He slowed his pace by a fraction.

Constantin said, 'He is related to the Kha-Khan, and we need his co-operation.' The alien was trying to speak in a low voice, but his tone was irritated and so probably it was difficult. One of the other men said, 'Natalia, it doesn't matter if he tells you that black is white, agree with him.'

Natalia's reply was inaudible. Suragai grinned. His pretence at anger had been a ruse to end the conversation. Now he felt a surge of satisfaction at the way events had turned out. Because the woman had spoken out of turn, she was being blamed by the others for the offence they suspected she had given. It was a situation which placed the embassy at a disadvantage. Suragai wondered how he could exploit it, and how the woman would behave next time he spoke to her.

'We are running out of ways to put the aliens off,' Alexei said. He rolled his empty wine cup between his palms, and then set it down on a low table.

It was old news. 'So I have heard,' Suragai said. He refilled the cup.

The lamps which lit the inside of the yurt were the old kind – a long wick which trailed in an open bowl of scented oil was held in a clasp – and their flames dipped and wavered when the air was disturbed by movement. Pools of yellow light were reflected off the timbers of the floor where it was not covered by the big circular carpet. Odd shadows crossed Alexei's face, and when he looked up it was difficult to read his expression. 'Soon we are going to have to pretend to give them what they want,' he said.

Suragai made a face. 'Khan, I wish I didn't suspect

241

you mean to involve me. I'm tired of nursing aliens.'

Kubulai was sitting off to the side. He laughed softly. 'But you're so good at it.'

Alexei picked up the filled cup. 'You're a great help,' he said to Kubulai. He drank, then put the cup down with a bang. 'Listen to me, both of you. I want the alien trade commissioners kept busy. Suragai, you are going to take them to see the poppies.'

'Am I indeed?' Suragai produced a stare which he hoped displayed his lack of interest in the notion. The trade commissioners were presently at Kinsai, where they had been negotiating with Burun the rate of exchange of poppy gum for gold. So far the question of quantity had been skirted around. The commissioners wanted as much as they could get. The main problem was the fact that nobody could say how much was available.

'We have given them permission to use one of their ships,' Alexei said. 'You will travel with them to Marakan. They also want to look at the northern G'bai.'

Suragai was pouring wine into an empty cup. He looked round so sharply that the wine splashed. 'They must be mad.'

The part of the G'bai where the poppies grew was also an area of persisting radiation. The Yek avoided it.

Alexei shrugged. 'They only want to fly over it. I don't think they believe it is particularly dangerous.'

'Or they don't care,' Kubulai said. 'They must be quite desperate.'

The spilled wine looked like a pool of blood. Suragai touched it with his fingertips. 'I hope the offworlders know how to test for radiation,' he said.

'Better than the Sechem,' Alexei responded. 'At Marakan they will probably want to try to arrange for a harvest. I've sent a letter to Kaidu about that.'

Bhutan's father was still keeping order among the catpeople. If there was to be a harvest at all, they would have to carry it out.

'You want the aliens to believe we are starting to be reconciled to their presence,' Suragai observed, 'or you would not be allowing them to use one of their ships.'

The nails at the ends of Alexei's fingers had been permitted to grow, and they had been filed and lacquered with gold. They still did not look like talons. 'It's only a small vessel,' Alexei said, 'like the one the embassy came in. But you're right. One of our aims at present is to avoid giving them any reason to suspect our motives – so that they will not look past the surface of how we behave. The trade commissioners still think we are negotiating trade with them because we believe that the alternative will be conquest. The whole process will be easier for them if they can gain our co-operation, so while they imagine that we can be flattered or persuaded into working with them they will do their best not to offend us.'

'Which will give us opportunities we will not have if they are scrutinising our every move.' Kubulai stood up suddenly. He walked over to the table, poured wine into a cup, and stood drinking it.

Suragai was not sure what kind of opportunities they were talking about. All that concerned him was the prospect of being in close and continuous contact with the aliens as a group. He said, 'My father told me nothing about this. Is it a command?'

'You can take it that way if you want to.' Alexei picked up his cup. It was made of dark-red gold, and it glowed in his hand as he drank from it. He treated Suragai to an expressionless stare.

There was nothing to be gained by arguing, Suragai thought. He glanced towards Kubulai. 'Is he coming too?'

'Yes.' Alexei nodded.

It was obvious that Kubulai had been given separate instructions. Briefly Suragai wondered what they were. Outside somewhere a sentry was shouting a challenge. Suragai heard the countersign being given. 'This is why we were summoned here,' he said. He was annoyed that it had not occurred to him before. 'Why didn't you warn us?'

Alexei looked down at his hands, spreading his fingers so that the lacquered nails glittered in the lamplight. 'It wasn't necessary for you to know,' he said. 'A man who knows a thing can betray his awareness of it by accident.'

Suragai thought about it. He wrinkled his nose. 'You have only just told the commissioners you are letting them go to Marakan.'

A flash of something close to respect crossed Alexei's features. 'They are being told about now. Probably they will be ready to leave tomorrow.'

The reason for such secrecy escaped Suragai. 'Is it such an important concession?' he demanded.

'It is what they desire above all else,' Alexei said. 'Freedom to travel and access to the poppy. Burun is making it look as if we are yielding to their demands because we have run out of arguments – the aliens think I have advised it. You have been back and forward between Kinsai and the lander all the time since it arrived. Constantin is here, and you are supposed to be his friend. You are the natural choice to guide them.'

244

'They think I am an innocent,' Suragai concluded drily. He saw Kubulai grin.

'Say rather that we haven't involved you enough in what has been going on for them to suspect that your presence may be important,' Alexei said. 'If it offends you, I am sorry. This is the way it has to be done. You don't have to know why. Just do it. Go with the aliens and keep them happy.'

His mistrust of offworlders as a species was blinding him. Suragai tried to see beyond the task to its meaning, but could not. He produced an ironic bow. 'The Khan wishes.'

Kubulai appeared to be inspecting the contents of his wine cup. 'Eventually we will have to fight them,' he said quietly.

The expression on Alexei's face did not vary. 'Yes,' he said after a moment. 'But when we do it has to be on our terms, and not on theirs.'

'I am leaving for Pesth,' D'mitri said. 'Your mother and sister are staying at Kinsai in your grandfather's care.'

Suragai nodded absently. A long caravan of carts and pack beasts was winding its way across the plain towards the camp from the direction of Kinsai. He narrowed his eyes to see it better.

'You are upset because I knew what was planned and did not tell you,' his father said.

'Am I?' Suragai looked round. 'My part in this has been explained to me, also why I was chosen.'

D'mitri pursed his lips. A hint of a smile appeared on his face. 'You do have a tendency to say exactly what you are thinking,' he pointed out. 'You don't pretend to like alien behaviour and attitudes, but you can get on with them. You fit the pattern of behaviour they expect from us, that's all. If we have not given you information, it was so that you would never have to pretend to know less than you did.'

'I still don't know anything,' Suragai said petulantly. He turned to watch as the head of the caravan entered the camp. There were men riding st'lyan at the front, and with them were both of the commissioners.

'In that case you will be able to play your part to perfection,' D'mitri said equably. He nodded abruptly to the captain of his escort, and the waiting troopers stirred expectantly. A few got into the saddle. 'If you mistrust Alexei's intent in all this, you are mistaken,' D'mitri said.

Suragai avoided his father's eyes. 'Have I said that I do?'

D'mitri frowned. 'You scarcely have to.' He scraped at a tuft of coarse grass with the heel of his boot. 'Some of Alexei's behaviour is going to suggest that his sympathies lie with the aliens,' he said. 'It has been planned that way.'

One of the commissioners was trying to dismount. He got one foot out of the stirrups, but when he attempted to swing his free leg across the saddle he lost his balance. He clung to the st'lyan's mane, and men rushed to his aid.

'How are we to know which of Alexei's actions reflect his true loyalty?' Suragai asked. He glanced back over his shoulder. 'The more he has to pretend, the more confused he may become.'

'Oh.' D'mitri snorted. 'If that is what you really think, then we have cast you well.' A groom led up his mare, and he got into the saddle and rode away without another word.

•

The leader of the commission was a large moon-faced man called Fedyev. He was taller than the average Yek, and he had a belly which appeared to be held up by his belt. When he addressed Suragai his manner was polite but condescending. His ready smile never quite reached his eyes.

The vessel in which they were travelling was similar to the one in which the embassy had arrived. The main cabin provided a view forward. Constantin was steering, and there were two other officers. One of them was the woman.

'This landscape is fascinating,' Fedyev said. 'It must be an experience for you to see it thus, Noyon.'

The vessel was moving across a section of the long escarpment which marked the northernmost extremity of the G'bai desert. Suragai looked round. 'I have been here before,' he responded. 'A bird would see the land this way I suppose, but I am not a bird.'

The offworlders were becoming used to his dismissive approach to their technology. Suragai saw the officer who was sitting next to the commissioner nudge the woman at his side, and they both smiled. He pretended not to notice.

'Black sand,' Constantin said. He touched a control on the bar Suragai thought was equivalent to the tiller. 'It looks very strange.'

Suragai supposed that sand would always be the colour of the rocks from which it had weathered. He said nothing.

'The basin must have been basalt, or something like it,' the commissioner said. 'See where there are still some pieces of it.' He pointed.

The area they were approaching was one where great angular segments of the original plain had been folded up on end. Where some of them met there were caves or passages running beneath. It was a landmark Suragai knew well, and he stirred with disquiet. He said, 'This is a bad place. Men die if they stay here too long.'

Fedyev looked unimpressed. He smiled round at some of the other occupants of the cabin, but then touched a panel of small square keys which was at the side of his couch. Numbers and characters in red were projected onto the transparent wall in front. One of the numbers flashed angrily, and Constantin indicated it. 'He is right,' he said.

The alien faces inside the vessel went pale. Only the commissioner looked unworried. 'We are safe enough,' he observed. 'We are not even breathing the outside air.'

Suragai was not sure what that had to do with anything. Inside the facing of his coat he had fastened a disc of white ceramic. His fingers strayed to it, and he drew it into the light, seeking reassurance. Discoloration would indicate radiation danger. The disc was still pristine. Suragai tucked it away again, then glanced across the cabin. Kubulai was on the couch next to the door. His hand was also inside his coat. He looked up, and they exchanged nervous smiles.

'Where are the poppies?' Fedyev asked.

'Three or four verst to the south.' Suragai turned to look ahead. He forced himself to relax back into the couch.

Constantin made a face. He said, 'Too close to the radiation for safe harvesting.'

'Not necessarily.' Fedyev shook his head. His grey eyes held no hint of expression.

The second commissioner was a small man, dumpy and bald as an egg. He said, 'There will be contamination…'

'There are ways of removing contamination,' Fedyev replied. He gave the other man a hard stare. Then his head came round again. He gave Suragai an artificial smile.

The vessel was passing over the outer edge of a rolling plain. The sand ended. At first there was only sparse vegetation, and then suddenly the ground was carpeted with purple flowers. 'There,' Constantin said.

Fedyev came to his feet. He craned forward to see. The other commissioner came up to his side. 'Five or six kilometres of them,' he said. 'I wonder, could we -'

Suragai stared at them. An odd look came onto Fedyev's face, and then it was gone once more. Abruptly he sat down. He said, 'They are too close to the radiation.'

'Of course.' The second commissioner nodded quickly.

The aliens had said one thing, but they had communicated another, Suragai realised. He glanced quickly at Constantin for confirmation, and thought he detected a frown of disapproval.

'And now Marakan,' Fedyev said. He spoke as if nothing had occurred.

'West,' Suragai told Constantin. He sat forward, avoiding the commissioners' eyes, and tried to decide what had passed between them.

Heading out from land the vessel was pursuing the sun. The sea was coloured a deep blue-green, and the light reflecting off the wavelets made a shimmering golden path for Constantin to follow.

If the alien ship was fast enough it could overtake

the sun and pass on into the night. Suragai wondered if it was capable of such speed. If it was, then the experience might be a novelty.

The vessel's speed was certainly increasing. The sparkle of the light on the surface of the sea became a blur, and when Suragai turned away to rest his eyes he saw that the two trade commissioners had their heads together, deep in conversation. Fedyev's hand was up at his mouth as if to hide the fact that he was speaking. He became aware that Suragai was watching, and at once he sat up straight and smiled.

Suragai opened his eyes wide, but he did not return the smile. The commissioners were talking about the poppy. The only poppies they had seen so far were in the northern G'bai, and now Suragai suspected that they did not care that they would be dangerous to harvest. The aliens wanted as much poppy gum as they could get. Probably it did not matter to them how they obtained it.

A ship with sails - a carrack, Suragai thought - appeared in the sea ahead. It flashed beneath them. A sailing ship would take up to thirty days to cross the Great Sea. This alien vessel was completing the journey in a fraction of the time.

'There is land ahead,' Constantin said.

It was not yet Marakan. This was Y'vrope - a land where no settlement was large enough to be called a city, a country where every man believed that he was individually responsible for the conduct of his life and recognised as a result no central authority or government.

'The poppy would flourish here,' Fedyev said. The ship had been slowed at his instigation so that they could see the character of the land.

'I doubt if the people could be persuaded to grow it,' Suragai responded drily.

The natives of Y'vrope approached the issues which affected their lives with mind-stretching simplicity. It would not make sense to them to cultivate anything they had no use for, and they did nothing which did not make sense. It had taken a decade to bring them into the Khanate – staunch iconoclasm resisted even the sensible values of the Yasa – and there was no likelihood that they would be willing to co-operate with the Empire.

The reply did not please Fedyev. He said, 'Surely the Kha-Khan rules here?'

Suragai grinned. 'It is because Jehan rules that the people still have the right to grow what suits them. *Shen* Commissioner, there will be poppy enough for you in Marakan.'

Something flashed in Fedyev's eyes – irritation maybe, or the revelation of an intent – and then he nodded amiably. 'Noyon, forgive me,' he said. 'The land is the Kha-Khan's of course, but we are traders. If we seem to you overeager, it is because of the poppy's value.'

'Indeed.' Suragai produced an innocent stare. 'It prolongs life, I have been told.'

Fedyev nodded. 'That is true, Noyon.'

'But the drug's use is restricted,' Suragai continued. 'Is that not so?'

A cautious expression appeared on the faces of both of the commissioners. Fedyev spread his hands. 'Noyon, the poppy is scarce, and the Empire has a population of many millions.'

'And so the price is high.' Suragai nodded. 'Now I understand.'

The cost of producing the drug made from the poppy did not matter to anyone. It was being sold at many times its true value. It demonstrated how wealth and not the rule of law controlled the Empire, and suddenly Suragai knew that there could be no compromise with these men.

It was as if Constantin had read Suragai's mind. He said, 'In the Khanate you control the price of all goods.'

'We control profit,' Suragai said shortly. 'It is not wrong for a man to make his living selling to others, but it is contrary to the Yasa for someone to make himself rich from needs which are common to all. A khan has the authority to decide what profit is just in relation to the true value of a thing. Thus food and clothing are priced so that everyone can afford them. Merchants who trade in a manner which is a breach of the law are fined twice the sum they are accounted to have gained.'

The commissioner was sitting forward to listen. He said, 'Profit benefits all men.'

'Oh?' Suragai looked round. 'I have heard this argument before, I think. You live by profit. I would expect you to tell me that it is good.'

The expression which reached Fedyev's eyes belied his fixed smile. He said, 'Noyon, this world is ruled under a system of law which accords with nothing I have encountered elsewhere. A subject of the Empire knows that there are other ways to arrange men's lives. Our approach is suitable to us, even though you think it strange.'

The commissioner's words were intended to divert the attention of his listeners away from the comments Suragai had made about controlling profit. The

252

scarcity of the poppy drug probably placed it beyond the access of the officers and the others in the cabin. Suragai had noted thoughtful expressions on the faces of several of them when he had explained the Yasa. Now he looked straight at Fedyev. '*Shen* Commissioner, how old are you?'

Fedyev appeared to hesitate. If he understood the purpose behind the question, then he was seeking for a way to answer as if it was of no moment. After a moment he shrugged. 'I am nearly a hundred.'

'The age of my grandfather.' Suragai opened his eyes wide. 'And still active. You are fortunate indeed.'

There was nothing in Suragai's tone which could have been interpreted to suggest that it was anything other than an observation of fact. Fedyev sat back. 'My life is active,' he said. 'It would be bad for those who rely on me were I to be made incapable by age or sickness.'

Suragai said nothing. In front of the vessel the view was changing once more as they crossed the western coast of Y'vrope. Now the sea was dark, and a strong flow of current carried the waves towards the south. The shore was bleak and rocky, and there were no signs of habitation.

'A little north, and we will cross over Tarsis.' Suragai touched Constantin's arm.

The east coast of Marakan was protected by a line of reefs and islands. Yek engineers had blasted the high cliffs with explosives, and the rock had been deposited in the water to provide a shelf nearly ten verst in length upon which a port could be constructed. The size of the shelf had been determined by the ability of the sea to wash a lesser barrier away. The tides in these parts were so fierce that there was no

253

other harbour or place for a ship to come to land. To the north there was a deep inlet by which access could be gained to the interior of the continent, but it was navigable only by steamship. On the shelf was Tarsis, a port without a city, built for the sole purpose of permitting men and supplies to be brought ashore and moved inland. From the alien vessel it looked barren and desolate. Bare rock held back angry water. Even where soil had been dumped, nothing grew because of the constant passage of carts and st'lyan. A single ship occupied the deep artificial harbour behind the headland.

'That's a paddle steamer,' Constantin said. He sounded surprised.

Suragai nodded. 'The current is too strong for us to use sailing ships.'

'Then you don't altogether prohibit machines,' the offworlder said. He looked as if he was trying to balance what he could see against what he thought he knew.

It was the kind of response Suragai had anticipated. He gave Constantin a stare. 'Where a thing becomes necessary there is an exclusion under the law.'

The expressions on the faces of the aliens suggested that they thought that the Yek had cleverly provided for themselves a means by which they could ignore the law when it became inconvenient. Suragai was tempted to explain further, but did not. Let them believe that we are venial, and that we are willing to compromise our beliefs, he thought. If they think we are weak they will underestimate us. If they underestimate us they will be unwary.

Beyond the coastline the landscape in the south of the continent was like an enormous bowl – high along the circle of cliffs but dropping to a flat plain in the centre. Parts of an old rampart still remained around the top of the cliff boundary, and running towards the plain from various points on the rampart like the spokes of a wheel were the causeways – pathways of artificial stone upon supports which raised them thirty or forty drem above ground level. Below the causeways the slope down to the central plain had been stepped – shelves fifty to a hundred drem wide – and these were covered with dense vegetation.

The aliens crowded to the front of the cabin to see. Suragai had thought that they must have surveyed the whole world from space, and had expected them to know what they would find. He was puzzled by their awe and amazement.

'Second Empire,' someone said.

The covering running along the top of one of the causeways had crumbled or had been eroded down to thin strings of another material. Suragai had seen it all before. Now he wondered if he should have paid more attention.

'We were told that this land is inhabited by a species which occurs nowhere else in the world,' Fedyev said. 'Are there none of our kind here?'

There had been a few, but they had been permitted to die. Suragai shook his head. 'No. This is protected land. Our own people are here only to maintain order. As soon as the Marakani are judged capable of understanding our law, they will be admitted to the Khanate.'

A look of something like amusement passed across Fedyev's features. 'They are primitive then. Are they human?'

Suragai frowned. 'You would not think them

human,' he said. 'They have talons like the True People, but their bodies are covered with fur.'

It would be unfortunate if the aliens wanted to know more. Suragai wondered how they would react if they were to be told that the catpeople belonged to a species of true-breeding mutations which had been genetically engineered and domesticated by the original occupants of the land. Workbeasts, the long-ago men had called them. Suragai recalled that Alexei had spoken of it, for it was he who had first explored Marakan.

'Ah.' The commissioner made a face which suggested that the nature of the origins of the Marakani had suddenly ceased to be a matter of interest. He said, 'Noyon, all this was built by men of an empire earlier than ours. Seeing it made me hope that their descendants might have survived.'

The ramparts and causeways had been built by offworlders who had sought to seal off their domain from the rest of the world at a time when their empire was disintegrating. The commissioner could not imagine the extent of Yek knowledge about the place, but Suragai veiled his eyes and pretended not to be interested. 'Only Yek and catpeople live here now,' he said.

They travelled quite slowly towards the centre of the basin. Beyond the last of the terraces there was a place where a line of buildings had been constructed beside one of the causeways. The structures were like pyramids, and Suragai knew that they had once been occupied by the cloned descendants of the builders. Now they were empty – the contents removed by the Sechem against a time when the technology they had

256

found would be needed – and near them were orderly lines of yurts.

None of the fields around the pyramids appeared to be under cultivation. The grass was bright green, and it waved and rippled as if disturbed by the breeze when the offworlder vessel descended towards the cleared area beyond the causeway. A road ran past the side of the line of pyramids. On it troopers of one of the guard companies were assembling.

'It looks as if they are expecting us,' Fedyev said as the ship grounded.

The tone of the commissioner's voice indicated lack of surprise. Suragai was rising from his couch. He gave Fedyev a sharp stare. Their visit to Marakan had been represented as having been agreed at short notice. Now it seemed probable that Fedyev had guessed that it had been planned ahead. We are not as clever as we thought, Suragai realised, and wondered what other mistakes and miscalculations had been made.

A man on a neat bay st'lyan was riding across the grass from the nearest pyramid. He was helmeted, and his unbound black hair flowed out behind him, blown by the wind. The commissioners moved towards the door. Kubulai came past them to Suragai's side. 'That's Kaidu,' he said.

Suragai looked at him. 'I had forgotten you were with us,' he said. 'You haven't said a word since we left the site near Kinsai.'

Kubulai showed his teeth. 'You were doing so well.' He glanced past Suragai at Constantin. The offworlder did something to the control yoke, and the transparent section of the cabin wall became opaque once more. 'I'm not sure this was such a good idea,' Kubulai said in a low voice. 'That commissioner is a clever man.'

Outside the ship the ground was shimmering in the heat of the sun. The tops of the trees on the nearest terrace were a green blur. Everything further away was invisible in the haze.

The commissioners were standing a few drem away. Kaidu was watching them from the saddle. Not until he saw Suragai and Kubulai did he dismount. 'Nephew, good day.'

'Uncle.' Suragai produced a polite nod. Bhutan's father was a small man with pale skin and looks inherited from his N'pani mother. His moustaches were long, and his eyes folded up at the corners. Suragai waved towards the aliens. 'I present Commissioner Fedyev, leader of the alien trade delegation.'

Kaidu inclined his head. '*Shen* Commissioner,' he said in careful Anglic, 'I am Kaidu Khan.'

Suragai wondered if the commissioners were capable enough at reading Yek facial expression to realise that Kaidu was making no attempt to hide his dislike. Fedyev bowed to Kaidu and smiled. 'Lord, I am pleased to meet you.'

The other aliens were staring at the pyramids. Kaidu gave them a single all-embracing glance, and then eyed Fedyev again. 'You are here to see the poppy fields,' he said haughtily. He rested a hand on his decorated sword hilt and tilted his head back so that he could stare down his nose.

'Lord, we are.' The commissioner nodded. 'When it pleases you to allow us to visit them.'

'Oh.' Kaidu raised his eyebrows. 'You are free to travel where you will. If you intend to ride beyond the grassland you should take an escort. My nephew will arrange it. How long will you remain here?'

Fedyev spread his hands. 'Lord, that depends on

what we find.'

'Indeed.' Kaidu wrinkled his nose. 'I was not told, but yurts have been prepared for your use.'

'You expected us then,' Fedyev observed. His smile was benign.

Kaidu pursed his lips. 'A message was received,' he said.

The offworlders never ceased to enquire about Yek communication methods – they were amazed by the arrow messengers and by the chain of heliograph stations – but the answers they received tended to be evasive in the extreme. Now the commissioner's smile broadened still further. 'Lord,' he said, 'I am very pleased to hear it.'

'I am commanded to provide facilities for you,' Kaidu continued prosaically. 'This I will do of course, but you should remember that this is protected land. The poppy fields are nearby. Elsewhere there are Marakani settlements. You should not enter them unless you receive invitation.'

Something odd registered in Fedyev's eyes, and then he nodded and bowed. 'Lord, I am at your direction with regard to such matters. Will you now greet my deputy?'

'You may introduce him,' Kaidu said.

Fedyev motioned to the other commissioner. The man took a single pace forward, and bowed. 'Lord,' he said, 'my name is Zilitsin.'

Kaidu gave him a distant nod. Then he turned his back the aliens. 'Noyon, my officers will show you the yurts the aliens are to use,' he said in Yek. 'After you have seen them settled I want to talk to you. You as well, Khan.' He looked past Suragai at Kubulai.

Suragai grinned. 'Uncle, I am at your disposal. What

259

shall I tell the commissioners?'

'Oh.' Kaidu did not glance round. 'Tell them anything you like. Tell them I said goodbye.' He looped the bay's reins over the animal's neck, pulled himself into the saddle, and spurred away. Riding past the troopers on the road, he flung up one hand in salute. All along the line the lances came down and then rose again, and at once the captains rode out and came across the grass towards where Suragai stood.

'You brought me some strange guests,' Kaidu said. He paced across the carpeted floor from the hangings on one side of the yurt to the other. Then he turned. 'The land here is protected by edict. How can it be farmed for the benefit of the aliens?'

An orderly came through a gap in the hangings from the back of the yurt. He bore a tray on which were plates of savouries and sweetmeats. Their aroma made Suragai's mouth water. He waited until the tray had been placed on the low table at his side, then nodded to the orderly, dismissing him. 'Thank you.'

Kubulai was sitting cross-legged on a pile of cushions on the other side of the table. Several of Kaidu's cats were playing on the floor. Kubulai pulled one of them into his lap and ruffled its fur. 'Khan, it isn't intended to be a permanent measure,' he said. 'We're keeping them occupied, that's all.'

Kaidu was wearing loose black trousers which were tucked into half-boots. His campaign tunic was sleeveless, and open down the front. He put a hand inside it and scratched at his chest. 'I am to give them facilities,' he said, and produced an irritated frown. 'That could mean anything. Do you know what it means? Tell me if you do.'

Suragai knew the answer to that, but he waited for Kubulai to respond. Kubulai rolled the cat over onto its back. It was a Suristani, black and white, with a long prehensile tail. It yowled and slashed, but Kubulai ignored the distraction. 'You are to let them have anything they want so long as it doesn't break the Yasa,' he said.

One of the plates of savouries held finely sliced slivers of p'tar meat which had been seasoned with ch'min and dry-roasted. Suragai selected a piece and popped it into his mouth. He chewed to soften the meat, and the juices ran across his tongue.

'But the poppies are in full bloom,' Kaidu said. He looked worried. 'What am I supposed to do if they want to arrange to harvest the gum?'

'In that case I think you should let them.' Kubulai let go of the cat. It streaked out of his lap towards the deep shadows in the corner beside the door. 'Of course they will have to do their own agricultural work,' Kubulai said cheerfully. 'You are sorry but you don't have men to spare. What a pity.'

Kubulai had a full tuman – ten thousand men – but they were dispersed around the plain. So far as the offworlders were concerned what was available was what they could see.

'They could have people waiting to be brought down from the ship which is above,' Kaidu said. He gestured upward, and Suragai guessed that his uncle was uncomfortable with the notion of space. He hid a smile.

'Then they are to be permitted to land them,' Kubulai said. 'The numbers to be subject to our approval. Our information suggests that they will prefer to recruit local labour, however. The catpeople could do the work – they used to when the old Keepers ruled here – but the aliens are not to know that.'

Suragai swallowed the chewed meat. 'The people of Y'vrope won't work for them,' he observed. 'Although if the commissioners want to try recruiting them we shouldn't stand in their way –'

'– because it will take up time.' Kaidu nodded. 'I begin to understand.'

Kubulai showed his teeth. 'Khan, I was sure you would. After the aliens try Y'vrope for workers they will be forced to look to the mainland of the Khanate. This is our harvest time too, and so there won't be many men who will be willing to leave the fields, not even for the kind of rewards the commissioners will probably offer. It will take them some time to find the people they need, and more time to bring them here. If they leave it in our hands, we'll use military transports – forty days or more.'

Kaidu sat down abruptly on a stool which was in the centre of the floor. 'I still don't like it,' he said. 'I don't like having them here, and if it was not a command ...' He gestured expressively.

It was clear that this was why Kubulai had been sent. Kaidu would have argued much harder with someone who was not of his own rank, and then he would have done his best to circumvent the orders he had received.

'Whatever happens, the aliens must believe that we are trying to help them,' Kubulai said. He gave Kaidu a flat stare. 'There will be delays of course, but none of them must appear to be our fault. In fact we will be seen to be offering sound advice –'

'– which we hope they will ignore,' Suragai finished. He eyed the tray of savouries. His stomach was growling, and he realised that he had not eaten since early morning.

'Which we will offer in such a way that they will be certain to ignore it,' Kubulai corrected. 'Our function is to buy time – two months at least.'

Time to prepare, Suragai thought. He was still of the opinion that the Kha-Khan's approach was only putting off the moment when there would be no alternative but to fight and die. The Khanate would never surrender, of course, but faced with the weapons the offworlders were said to possess it was unlikely that it would win.

Kaidu still looked unhappy, but after a moment he nodded. He stared down at the carpet between his feet, and then looked up again. 'We have some poppy gum in store,' he said. 'Did you know?'

Kubulai sat up sharply. 'No, I did not. I doubt if anybody else knows either. Where did it come from?'

'Oh.' Kaidu made a face. 'The Keepers trained the catpeople to add it to their food, to pacify them. There was a storehouse full of it – blocks of resin about a drem square – when I came here. We could have burned it, I suppose, but there was always the possibility that we would require it ourselves some day –' He stopped, looking embarrassed.

Jehan's policy of allowing the catpeople to develop in their own way towards civilised patterns of behaviour was one of the more controversial issues of the day, and it was well known that the khans were divided about it. Unpacified, the Marakani were fierce, and family groups fought for the best hunting grounds. Military patrols were maintained to discourage actual warfare. Apart from that there was little interference.

'If the commissioners find out about it, they will know that there are people here who are capable of harvesting,' Suragai said. 'That's the last thing we want.'

'I'm surprised the stuff is still worth having.' Kubulai caught Kaidu's eye. 'Have you looked at it lately?'

'Yes.' Kaidu nodded. 'We moved it yesterday, because it was stored close to the poppy fields. Now it is further away, in barns up on the third terrace. That's Soklosh land, and so probably you can persuade the aliens not to go there.'

The Soklosh were the most savage of the Marakani family groups, Suragai remembered, and silently applauded his uncle's choice of hiding place. 'Is the resin still usable?' he asked. The last Keeper had died more than fifteen years earlier. Suragai was amazed that anything extracted from a plant could last so long without rotting.

'It smells a bit,' Kaidu said. 'But poppy resin does smell. I don't think there is anything wrong with it.'

'The only way to find that out is to offer some to the aliens,' Kubulai observed. He shook his head. 'I wish you had burned it.'

Kaidu produced a grim smile. 'It would have needed a big fire. There were twenty cartloads.'

'I suppose we could let them have it a little at a time,' Suragai said pensively.

'And tell them what?' Kubulai demanded irritably. 'We would have to explain how we came by it. Even if they believed that we harvested it ourselves, they would start to wonder if there was a field they hadn't been told about.'

The aliens still found it hard to believe that the Khanate had no interest in a drug which had the ability to prolong life. Suspicion that another source of the poppy existed would be regarded by them as confirmation that the Yek were misrepresenting their attitude.

'They shouldn't find it, now that it has been hidden,' Kaidu said.

'Who are you trying to convince?' Kubulai asked sardonically.

'Myself, I suppose,' Kaidu answered, and he grinned wryly.

In the morning they rode out to see the poppy fields. The commissioners had been provided with st'lyan which were big but docile. Fedyev looked unsure of his balance. He bounced awkwardly in the saddle, out of time somehow with the motion of his animal. Zilitsin appeared to be much more in control. He managed his reins with careful economy, and there was no sign of discomfort in his bearing.

Around them rode an escort of twenty men. The troopers were all either Yek or Merkut, and so there was no need to direct them. They maintained a sensible screen which was a respectful distance from the path Suragai chose. The two commissioners travelled side by side a length or so behind. None of the other aliens were present, and so Kubulai had stayed in the camp to keep an eye on them.

The poppy fields bordered on the lowest of the terraces, and lay west of the pyramids and Kaidu's base camp. The flowers were large and purple, and where the seed pods were visible they were streaked with blue. A heat haze was already obscuring everything beyond the terraces. Suragai knew that the fields stretched for another ten verst. He watched the expressions on the commissioners' faces as they took in the sea of purple which extended away into the distance. They were unable to conceal their avarice, and Suragai wrinkled his nose.

Fedyev dismounted with difficulty. He took a small folding knife out of his coat pocket and used it to make a number of small cuts down the seed pod of one of the poppies. The cuts began to ooze white sap. The alien nodded approvingly. 'The sap will turn brown when it dries,' he announced. He glanced back at Suragai. 'Gathering it is simply a matter of scraping off the tears. The resin is formed into a ball or a cake.'

'Indeed.' Suragai stared expressionlessly. He wondered how may cuts it would take to produce twenty cartloads of gum, and how Fedyev would react to the news that such a quantity existed. 'Clearly it is a task which requires many hands.'

Zilitsin had remained in the saddle. He nodded quickly. 'A field the size of this would provide employment for several hundred men, Noyon,' he said.

A stirring among the bands of purple blooms made Suragai tense. He stood in the stirrups and put up one hand to blot out the sun. Dark figures were advancing through the poppies. Suragai watched them for a moment, judging the direction they were following, and then he said, '*Shen* Commissioner Fedyev, get back on your st'lyan.'

The troopers of the escort had already observed the movement in the field. Men uncased bows and nocked arrows. Their captain sidestepped his mare up to Suragai's shoulder. 'Lord,' he said, 'we could ride away.'

'No.' Suragai shook his head. He reined around to face the spot where he thought the approaching creatures would emerge from the field, and then glanced back over his shoulder. 'Commissioner, come out of there.'

There was an annoyed expression on Fedyev's face. He said, 'Noyon, I have not yet completed my examination of –'

'Come back here, quickly,' Suragai interrupted him. He gestured to a trooper. 'Get him mounted.'

The figures moving among the poppies were much more distinct now – a hunting party, Suragai guessed. The Marakani did not have tails, but apart from that they looked just like erect p'ntar. Their features were feline, their ears were pointed, and their mouths were full of sharp white teeth.

Two troopers hustled Fedyev towards his mare. They shoved him up on its back. The commissioner said, 'Noyon, I protest –'

'Be quiet.' Suragai looked back over his shoulder at the aliens. 'A Marakani hunting party is coming this way. Whatever happens, you must sit still in the saddle. Do not speak or take your hands off the reins.'

'Oh,' Fedyev said. He stared nervously across the field. 'Where are they? I can't see them.'

Suragai ignored him. He unlocked the catch on the hilt of his sword and loosened it in the scabbard. At this part of the field the poppies were taller than a man. They parted suddenly, and a line of Marakani males stepped out onto the grass. They halted, the expressions on their faces unreadable to human eyes. Suragai saw that they all wore breech cloths and carried weapons. He frowned. The catpeople did not require weapons to hunt game. His mare tossed its head so that its gilded horn caught the sunlight. Suragai reined in without haste. The catpeople had not moved. Seven of them were out on the grass, but it was possible that there were more in the field. Suragai said, 'Brothers, I greet you.'

The black-furred creature in the centre of the line was apparently the leader. He handed his bow to one of the others, then started forward. Muscle rippled carelessly beneath his fur.

Marakani tribal markings were hard to identify. Two parallel lines were just visible on the creature's right shoulder. Suragai searched his memory and decided that these were Barkash. 'Lord,' the escort captain said softly, 'you must dismount.'

The ritual of greeting was simple enough, but Suragai had seen it performed only a few times. Allowing his reins to fall slack across his st'lyan's neck, he got slowly and carefully down out of the saddle. The approaching Barkash was of medium height, but was very broad. His eyes were amber, and they reflected the light. Extended talons glittered.

Suragai flexed his hands so that his talons became visible. He brought them up to shoulder level, palms up, and then retracted them again. At once the Marakani's claws disappeared. He stepped warily inside Suragai's reach. Suragai took a deep breath, then exhaled in the catman's face. 'Brother, I greet you,' he said, speaking slowly and precisely in Anglic.

The Marakani's exhaled breath indicated that he had not yet eaten. 'Brother,' he responded. The word came out as a kind of bark. 'I, Karpak of the Barkash, greet you.'

Good manners now required Suragai to step back. He took a pace to the rear. The Barkash lowered his hands to his sides. 'Brother, do you hunt here?' he demanded.

'No.' Suragai had to restrain the urge to shake his

head – a movement which a Marakani would take to imply aggression. 'The way is yours. Hunt it in peace.'

Now the Barkash backed off. 'Brother, I thank you.' He barked a single word in his family tongue. The members of the hunting party sidled to the right, and then they moved away through the next field.

Suragai took several deep breaths. Marakani did not often attack armed troopers, but it was not unknown. He drew his st'lyan's reins over so that they trailed on the ground. Then he caught Fedyev's eye. 'You can get down now.'

This time Zilitsin dismounted as well. He came and stood beside Suragai on the grass verge. Fedyev was in among the poppies, but he never strayed far from the edge of the field.

'Those were Marakani.' Zilitsin made the observation without expression.

About half of the troopers had moved out so that they were in a line which ranged across the path the Barkash had taken. They were watching the field intently.

'Yes.' Suragai nodded. 'Males of the Barkash clan. They hold terraces west of here. Usually they don't come down onto the plain. If I had said that we were hunting, they would have given way to us. They know that this is our land.'

'Ah.' The commissioner nodded understanding. 'Then we were in no danger after all.'

'Oh well.' Suragai grinned. 'It depended on how hungry they were.'

Zilitsin went white. 'Are they cannibals?'

'Not at all.' Suragai gave him an amused stare. 'They eat meat, but not each other. Anything else appears to be reckoned fair game. They aren't sure about us,

269

because we have talons. I don't know if they are capable of distinguishing between your species and ours, but if they are, then probably they will regard you as meat – just another animal.'

The commissioner looked unhappy. Fedyev was coming out of the field now. He said, 'Noyon, these fields are everything we hoped. We will want to harvest them if it is possible.'

A tiny blue and white bird swooped suddenly out of the sky. It darted across the poppies, hovered at one of the blooms, then flashed away.

Suragai picked up his st'lyan's reins. 'I imagine something can be arranged,' he said. He had expected the commissioner to say something of the kind. 'We ought to speak to the elder of the Barkash –' He nodded his head towards the path taken by the Marakani. '– otherwise they may think you are contesting their right to hunt this land.'

Fedyev's expression indicated his disdain. He said, 'They are animals. They are not civilised.'

A sound like the roar of a p'ntar rang out suddenly across the fields. Suragai glanced in the direction from which it had come, and then stared at the commissioner. 'I think that's a matter of definition,' he said amiably. 'The Marakani aren't civilised in terms of either your understanding or mine. They do use language, however, and they have a culture of sorts. Families will fight to hold onto the best land and hunting grounds, but when two opposing sides are evenly matched so that neither can gain an advantage they arrange a peace. They have learned to compromise in order to preserve their race.'

Several of the mounted troopers were standing in the stirrups, gazing across the field into which the

Barkash had gone. One man turned. He said, 'Lord, they have started a deer.' Another roar, deeper in timbre than the first, came as a counterpoint.

The poppies were so tall that Suragai could see nothing at first. Fedyev and Zilitsin were also looking towards the noise. Suragai said, 'If we get back into the saddle again we can watch.'

It required the combined efforts of Suragai and Zilitsin to boost Fedyev up onto his st'lyan's back. When Suragai had regained the saddle he reined around. The verge was raised above the level of the field at one point. Suragai rode up onto it, and the commissioners followed.

'What is happening?' Fedyev asked. He peered out across a carpet of poppies.

Dark heads bobbed in line about two hundred drem away. Suragai pointed. 'Watch.'

The quarry was invisible at first. The Marakani were moving forward in extended formation, a distance of four or five drem between each. One of them drew back his head and roared. At once the poppies shuddered. A deer charged away, swerving to the right.

'They have bows,' Zilitsin said. 'Why don't they shoot?'

'That isn't how they hunt.' Suragai shaded his eyes with a hand, and then pointed again. 'Look ahead of the deer.'

The pursuing Marakani were bounding forward. The deer continued its run to the right. Suddenly a dark figure popped up in front of its path. It wheeled away, startled, and dashed across the front of the advancing line. Another Barkash jumped up, waving his arms and snarling. The deer swerved and ran away ahead of the hunt.

'Now,' Suragai said. 'Do you see him?'

The leader of the hunting party was waiting motionless in the poppies almost directly in front of the running deer. It veered a little as it came up to him, and he ran beside it for several drem. An arm came out, and Suragai saw talons flash. The deer seemed to stumble. It fell, and the Barkash leapt on it. By the time the other members of the hunt came up, the deer was still.

Suragai reined around, and he rode back down onto the level grass again.

'I said they were animals.' Fedyev came up at Suragai's side.

'So you did.' Suragai gave him an oblique stare. '*Shen* Commissioner, I think you're trying to find a way to tell me that if the Marakani are a threat to the conduct of your harvest, they ought to be removed or killed.'

Fedyev frowned stubbornly. 'We could fence the fields,' he said. 'But it would add greatly to the cost of producing resin, and I don't think it would guarantee the safety of our workers.'

'You don't have any workers yet,' Suragai pointed out. 'But that's beside the point. Commissioner, you were told that this is protected land. That means that we are obliged by the Yasa to permit the catpeople to live according to their customs. The Marakani grow a few crops, but their natural diet is principally meat. Some of it comes from the cattle they herd along the terraces. The rest they get from hunting. That's why it's so important to them to control territory.'

'And if they start hunting us?' Fedyev enquired sarcastically. 'What will you do then?'

'Oh.' Suragai gestured cheerfully. 'In that case we'll

protect you also, of course.'

It was not long before the commissioners were pressing Kaidu politely but firmly for the construction of warehouses and other accommodation closer to the poppy fields. As soon as the required structures had been raised the aliens moved their vessel. Thereafter they were seen infrequently at the camp.

The trade commission had not been large at first, but soon the number of offworlders was seen to have increased.

'They are landing people from space,' Kubulai said when he learned of it. 'They haven't asked for permission, so we can object if we want to.'

Suragai could not see the point. He had been up to the poppy fields; Kubulai had not. He said, 'They're trying to harvest poppy resin. They'll soon get tired of it.'

Probably they were tired of it already. The aliens were all either crewmen or soldiers. None of them seemed to possess agricultural ability, and it was clear that they were unused to field work. Predictably the newly landed men fell sick after the first couple of days. The others were kept so busy looking after them that resin-gathering stopped. Suragai allowed a few more days to pass, and then he rode out for a visit. The aliens were occupying sheds which had been turned into a kind of barracks. Most of them seemed to have recovered from illness, but no one was working in the fields.

Fedyev was sitting at a table which had been placed under an awning. When he saw Suragai he rose and bowed politely. 'Noyon, good day.'

Apparently the commissioner had been recording the weights of resin blocks. Several small blocks were stacked on a kind of sledge at one side of the table. The resin was very dark brown, and a sweet, sickly smell rose from it. Suragai wrinkled his nose. He inclined his head towards Fedyev. '*Shen* Commissioner, I have come to see if there is anything I can do to help,' he said.

It was an approach Kubulai had agreed to with a degree of reluctance. In fact the aliens had refused an early offer of assistance relating to worker recruitment. Perhaps they had understood the delays which were bound to be involved. The fact that they had attempted to do the work themselves was yet another confirmation that they were desperate.

A travesty of a smile appeared on Fedyev's face. 'Noyon, thank you,' he responded. 'We have encountered some difficulty, it is true. I myself am more used to negotiation and to the direction of enterprise than to direct management.'

'Maybe you should have accepted our advice,' Suragai said mildly. 'We understood that a quick harvest was of importance to you. You made that clear.'

'But as you pointed out, we are not field workers, and working through the worst heat of the day is difficult for people who are not of your species.' Fedyev nodded. 'Noyon, you were right, of course. We thought we would become accustomed to the climate.'

'You will, eventually.' Suragai showed his teeth. 'Are any of your people still sick?'

A light breeze carried a current of warm air through the canopy space. The scent of poppy resin enveloped Suragai, and he held his breath until it had cleared again.

'No.' The commissioner shook his head. 'They are

unwilling to continue working in the fields, however. It is not work they are used to.'

Suragai was wearing loose trousers of silk, and his chest beneath his open coat was bare. He eyed Fedyev's buckram coat, and tugged at his scalp lock. 'I thought they would tire of it,' he said.

In the Khanate it was accepted that a farmer might turn to soldiering or to the sea. Likewise it was held that such a man would be unwilling to return to the soil. Conscripts found trades or occupations upon the expiry of their term of service, of course. Suragai thought about the aliens, and he wondered if there was a comparison to be made. Alexei had said there was not. Possibly he was right.

'We need to recruit men to gather the resin,' Fedyev said suddenly. His tone and manner betrayed his concern. He waved a hand. 'Noyon, I am responsible to the Emperor for the success of this venture. It must not fail.'

Something was driving the commissioner which Suragai was unable for the moment to comprehend. Suddenly it came to him that the circumstances of trade in the Empire might have altered drastically since his grandfather's time. A period of close to forty years had elapsed since the first Suragai had come from space. A lot could change in that time.

He said, 'You haven't explained why this particular harvest is so important. Surely there are other sources of supply.'

A flicker of expression appeared in Fedyev's pale eyes, then he gestured airily. 'I forget sometimes that you are related by blood to men who were once servants of the Empire,' he said. 'Yes, as I am sure you know, there are other sources of the poppy. It is to be found on two other groups of worlds. The fact remains that this crop is very valuable. The poppy not only prolongs life; it also prevents sickness and accelerates healing. These are benefits the Emperor is anxious to provide for as many as possible of his subjects. Thus my concern.'

Suragai guessed that there was more to it than that. The commissioner had not mentioned profit, of course, but there was something motivating him, pressing upon him, which was even more urgent.

If I understood, then maybe I would know how they can be conquered, he thought.

Zilitsin emerged suddenly from one of the long sheds nearby. The female officer Suragai had met at the range was with him. When they saw Suragai they both bowed.

'Noyon, good day.' Unlike the other aliens, Zilitsin was wearing Yek silks, and he looked cool and comfortable. 'Are you looking for Lieutenant Zarubin?'

It took Suragai a moment to realise that Zarubin was Constantin's last name. He shook his head. Then he saw that the woman was staring, and he nodded to her. 'Lady.'

The two commissioners exchanged a glance, but Suragai was unable to tell what passed between them. Fedyev said, 'I was in the process of asking the Noyon to help us to recruit workers.'

The woman said nothing. All at once Suragai realised that the aliens expected him to be attracted to her. Maybe it was in their minds to use a relationship to obtain information or advantage. He became aware that both men were waiting for him to say something. Workers, Fedyev had said. Suragai glanced once more at the woman, then turned to answer.

'If you need more men, you will have to travel away from Marakan to find them.'

If the trade commissioners had ever suspected that the Marakani were capable of field work, then probably their brush with the hunting party had persuaded them against the notion. Both Fedyev and Zilitsin nodded. 'Noyon, we understand that,' Zilitsin said. 'We thought of Y'vrope. The countryside there is filled with farms.'

This at least was predictable. Suragai made a face. 'I think we have already discussed Y'vrope,' he said. 'You can try to recruit them if you want to, but they won't be interested.'

They did not believe him, of course. He had intended that they would not.

Fedyev's head went back. 'I thought the people were ruled by the Kha-Khan,' he said haughtily. 'He could command them to work for us.'

'As to that, their right of free choice is guaranteed by our law,' Suragai observed blandly. 'I doubt if we would compromise it for the sake of trade.'

A nerve jumped in Fedyev's cheek. 'Then maybe we can persuade them to work for us by offering high rewards.'

Suragai shrugged. 'Maybe,' he said.

'Maybe we should not talk, in case I offend you again,' the woman said.

They were walking slowly along the edge of the longest of the poppy fields. The poppies were so tall that they cast shadows which moved constantly. Here the seed pods had not yet been cut to obtain sap, and so the only scent was from the blooms. Suragai sniffed at the air. He glanced at her. 'How should I address you?'

'I am called Natalia,' she said.

Suragai knew that. He wrinkled his nose. 'We call your officers *Shen.*'

'That's very formal.' Natalia was carrying a wide-brimmed hat in one hand. She put it on.

'It would not be proper for us to behave informally,' Suragai said lightly.

At first she seemed not to realise that he was teasing her. Then she stared obliquely. 'The first time we spoke, you were very rude to me.'

'Was I?' Suragai produced a wide-eyed stare of innocence.

'I spoke honestly, and you accused me of bad manners,' she said. 'You only wanted an excuse to walk away, but that's beside the point.'

'Oh.' Suragai laughed. 'It was not your honesty that provided the insult. But here we don't disparage the conduct of others by comparing it unfavourably with our own. If we need to show that our ways are better, then we do so by argument.'

'It doesn't alter the fact that you think your approach to everything is right, and that other points of view are wrong,' Natalia objected.

Suragai stopped walking. The grass here was short, grazed by beasts perhaps, and he wondered if she would be offended if he sat down first. 'I'm not sure that's true,' he said. 'It's a matter of being able to defend a point of view with logic. Sometimes we find that the logic no longer fits, and then we know it's time for an adjustment.'

Natalia's overall was light-coloured, the shade of the fine sand which was to be found on the banks of some

278

of the rivers in northern Khitai. The garment was open at the neck, and Suragai could see the slick of perspiration on her skin. She looked around, first at the poppies on one side, then at the high coarse grass on the other. She said, 'Do you want to sit down?'

'I'd like to.' Suragai nodded. He waited until she had seated herself, and then he squatted on his heels. 'I prefer riding to walking,' he said, and smiled wryly. He plucked a short grass stem from the ground at his side and chewed at it. 'Your honesty doesn't offend me, in truth,' he said to her. 'But you can't demonstrate the rightness of a position by showing that the alternative is wrong. One doesn't follow from the other.'

Above the poppies there was a wide expanse of deep-blue sky. The sun was a ball of red brilliance at the edge of Suragai's field of vision. It filtered warmly through the poppy heads, and he luxuriated in the sensation of the heat on his skin.

'I am supposed to make friends with you.' Natalia spoke suddenly.

Suragai plucked another grass stem. He split it lengthwise with the tip of a talon, and then looked up. 'I guessed that.'

She looked startled. 'In that case I am surprised that you are talking to me at all,' she said.

'Oh well.' Suragai smiled. 'If you are as honest as you say you are, you will be incapable of deceiving me.'

Natalia snorted. 'I am too honest for my own good, it seems,' she said. She moved her hands in a half-gesture. 'I would not have told you, only...'

'Only you thought I might work it out for myself,' Suragai said. He watched her face.

She stiffened. 'If that is what you think, there is nothing more to be said,' she responded bleakly. She

279

eyed Suragai. Then she said, 'I told you because you ought to know that we are not all Fedyev's creatures. This is a trade mission now. The Navy should not even be here.'

Apparently the commissioner had offended her somehow. She had some fixed if incompletely reasoned ideas about the status of women. Maybe the fact that she had been told to offer encouragement to a male of a species other than her own was unacceptable to her. Whatever the reason for her reaction, her statement indicated that there were factions among the aliens which might be used to undermine their enterprise. Obviously the soldiers resented being ordered to serve merchants. That was understandable, and it was so in accord with Yek attitudes that Suragai had previously given it no significance. Now he knew that he had been wrong. They are not like us, he thought. There is no comparison which is valid. I must remember that.

Natalia said, 'I have told you the truth because I think you should understand that all of us are not the same. I am still a servant of the Empire. Don't expect me to betray that.'

She would hardly say such a thing unless she was in possession of information which would help to damage the Empire's cause. Suragai settled himself on the grass. He stretched lazily. 'I don't suppose you can tell me anything I care to know,' he said.

When Suragai rode back into the camp he saw that an arrow messenger's st'lyan was being walked in a wide circle by a groom. The places where the harness had rubbed at the animal's coat were caked with dried sweat, and it was clear that it had been ridden hard.

The messenger was coming out of Kaidu's yurt. Suragai went past him through the door. Kaidu had an open letter in his hand. He looked up when Suragai pushed the hangings aside, and he nodded. 'You are here. Good. It saves me the trouble of sending for you.'

The parchment around the letter was covered in official seals. Suragai eyed them and guessed that the letter had been sent from Kinsai. 'Is there trouble?'

'Trouble enough.' Kaidu made a face. 'I've sent to Kubulai. Wait until he gets here, and then I'll tell you both. I don't care to repeat myself.'

A second, much thinner scroll was lying on the table at Kaidu's elbow. Like the first it was decorated with gold seals which bore Jehan's insignia. Suragai waited until Kaidu had bent his head to read again, and then moved unobtrusively around the table so that he could see what was written on the open page. There was a noise outside, and then the hangings parted abruptly and Kubulai entered. It was apparent that he had been sleeping, because he was wearing only silk trousers and his feet were bare. He gave Kaidu a glare. 'Khan, I left my sentry orders that I wasn't to be disturbed. Your orderly woke me anyway. What is so urgent that my authority is ignored?'

'Read this.' Kaidu extended his hand with the letter in it. He stared expressionlessly back at Kubulai.

Kubulai snatched the letter. He scanned it quickly. 'Oh,' he said.

Suragai shifted impatiently. 'Somebody tell me what all this is about,' he said.

The letter was being subjected to a further scrutiny, and Kubulai did not raise his head. Kaidu said, 'There is a revolt in Ch'nozia, and another smaller one has broken out in the Alan country. The Kha-Khan has ordered Kubulai to travel at once to Pesth. He's to pick up the three tumans which are in summer quarters and take them north through the mountains. Kadan is moving west from C'zakia with two more.'

It seemed like a lot of response for one revolt. 'It won't take long to deal with it at that rate,' Suragai said. He raised his eyebrows at Kubulai.

'The whole country has risen.' Kaidu stood up. He took the letter out of Kubulai's hand, but he did not offer it to Suragai. 'N'tan and T'tai are under siege, and what is left of our garrison is walled up inside the towns.'

Ch'nozia was in the north-eastern corner of the land. It was a hilly country inhabited principally by family groups of independent clansmen. A screen of high mountains formed the southern border, and the cities which Kaidu had mentioned were both on the north coast.

'Surely all the clans cannot be in revolt?' Suragai thought of holding out his hand for the letter, but did not. He said, 'They have always been as happy fighting one another as making war on us. It's unheard of for them to co-operate.'

'That's what they are doing nevertheless,' Kubulai observed grimly. He moved a stool with his foot and sat down. 'It isn't coincidence of course. We have been expecting something of the kind, although not so soon.'

'You mean the aliens are at the bottom of it.' The conclusion was obvious. Suragai frowned.

Kubulai shrugged. 'We know that some of the agents they landed last month found their way to Ch'nozia,' he said. 'We thought they would stay their hand until the trade mission was established. Apparently we were wrong.'

'Destabilisation.' Suragai remembered the word Alexei had used. 'The aliens don't care whether or not we are willing to come to terms with them. They intend to overthrow us.'

'Oh well.' Kubulai showed his teeth in the grim pretence of a smile. 'We always knew they had intentions along those lines. In some ways it's a relief to discover that they are behaving as we anticipated.'

It was not hard for Suragai to deduce that there were things he was not being told – which Kubulai had been ordered not to disclose. Probably much of it related to Alexei's plan to deal with the offworlders, but Suragai was irked by his lack of knowledge, and it fed his mistrust. He looked round at Kaidu. 'What has any of this to do with me?' he demanded. 'Am I being sent to the Alan country? Is that it?'

Kaidu was folding the letter carefully. He shook his head. 'I think Jotan can manage well enough without your assistance,' he observed drily. 'No, the Kha-Khan commands you to remain here with the trade mission. He has given you full authority to arrange whatever facilities may be required, and I am to accept your direction in all matters which relate to them.' He gave Suragai a sharp look to see if he understood.

'I am to have the power of a khan, but not the rank.' Suragai wrinkled his nose. 'And after the aliens are settled?'

'After that you are to return to Kinsai,' Kaidu said. 'The timing is to be at your discretion, so long as it is not more than two months hence. The trade commissioners are to be invited to attend the celebrations to mark the anniversary of Jehan's accession – all the aliens are. Maybe they will carry you to Kinsai if you ask them nicely.'

Suragai looked down his nose. He said, 'Uncle, if you are going to be subject to my authority, you had better moderate your tone.'

A sour smile appeared on Kaidu's face. 'Noyon, you may have the authority now, but you should remember that I will be here long after you have gone back to Kinsai, and then everything will be as it was before.'

Kaidu was really talking about the difference in rank which lay between them. Suragai met his uncle's eyes, but said nothing. There was a moment of silence, and then Kaidu snorted softly. He picked up the unopened scroll and held it out to Kubulai. 'This came for you.'

Kubulai's hand went out, and then it was as if he hesitated. The gold seals decorating the document glittered in the light of the oil lamps.

The crease of a frown worked its way across Kaidu's forehead. He gestured impatiently with the hand which held the scroll. 'Take it.'

'I know what is in it,' Kubulai said. His tone was odd. He withdrew his hand. 'Open it if you care to.'

'If that is what you want.' Kaidu assumed a superior expression. He used a talon to split the wafer which secured the tapes. The scroll contained a single sheet of off-white parchment imprinted with Jehan's arms. 'It's a copy of a proclamation,' Kaidu said prosaically. He started to read, and then looked up sharply. 'I had a letter asking for my opinion about this,' he said. 'It names you as Successor.'

The fact that Kaidu had not been called upon to vote did not mean that he had opposed Kubulai's nomination, Suragai realised. Jehan had required the agreement of only a two-thirds majority of the khans, and must have obtained it without much difficulty. Kaidu's stare was impassive. 'I should congratulate you,' he said to Kubulai.

At first Kubulai did not answer. He seemed to look right through Kaidu, and then his head came up. 'I told Jehan I did not want it,' he said. His tone was so intense that Suragai shivered.

Kaidu said nothing. He rolled the parchment and slid it into its container again.

Kubulai stood up abruptly. He went over to the door and pushed the hangings aside. Then he turned and looked back. 'Only a madman would desire the throne,' he said. 'I would rather be a slave than accept it.'

'Let's stop there.' Constantin pointed.

The feature he indicated was a circular knoll which stuck up out of the middle of the flat plain. It was covered with trees – tall spars of black wood from which sprouted whippy branches bearing clusters of pale-green leaves – and it looked like a jagged island in the middle of the sea of waving grass.

'Very well.' Suragai thought that the bump must have been considered too much trouble to clear of timber, even in the days when the fields had been cultivated, for now it was almost completely over-grown. He reined over.

Constantin's st'lyan was a piebald mare with one white foot. It had pale eyes and bad manners, and the offworlder had scarcely dismounted before it backed up, snorting and tossing its head, so that Constantin lost his grip on the reins. They trailed along the ground. The offworlder lunged after them, but the mare kicked up its heels and trotted away into the meadow. Then it lowered its head and started to graze.

Suragai watched the expression on Constantin's face. The offworlder glared after the mare. Then he threw up his arms in a gesture of exasperation and turned away. Suragai slid easily out of the saddle. He led his roan over to a tree and tethered it, looping the reins over a branch. A cloud of insects rose from the ground, and the st'lyan snorted and shied.

'This is a quiet spot,' Constantin said.

'Yes.' Suragai nodded. He rubbed at the bony ridges between the roan's eyes. It whickered and blew through its nostrils, then nudged at him.

Out in the meadow the piebald mare's head came up suddenly. Whatever it had heard or sensed, Suragai could see nothing. He sat down with his back to a tall old tree. Constantin was unfastening his shirt. He pulled the tail out of the waistband of his trousers. Then he sprawled on the grass near Suragai's feet. 'I will never accustom myself to this heat,' he said.

'Hunh.' Suragai grunted noncommittally. He guessed that Constantin had something to say, but did not know how to start. Three days had passed since news of the Ch'noze and Alan uprisings had been received. Suragai had stayed away from the aliens at first, wary in case they should sense the strength of the antagonism he now felt towards them. Constantin had ridden into the camp without warning, and so there had been no way for Suragai to manufacture an excuse not to be in his company. The conversation had been limping along for more than an hour.

Constantin looked away towards the meadow. Then his head came round. 'You have been avoiding me,' he observed. 'How have I offended you?'

Suragai's first reaction was one of amazement. He had known that the offworlders were quite uncivilised. Now it was apparent that they were also incapable of distinguishing between peace and war, and between friendship and enmity. He opened his mouth to speak, and then closed it again. Anger burned in his chest, but it was frustration caused by the fact that he felt that he was constrained by the Kha-Khan's order from expressing his true feelings, and he knew that to expend it on Constantin would be pointless. 'I have been busy,' he said finally.

'Oh?' Constantin opened his eyes wide. He stared at Suragai for a moment, and then he produced a dry smile. 'There is an atmosphere between us I could cut with a knife.'

The piebald mare was moving back towards the knoll now. It broke into a nervous canter, as if it had been startled by something. Suragai watched the waving grass, but there was no sign of unusual movement. Catpeople, he thought.

'Natalia likes you,' Constantin said. He leaned back on his elbows, his eyes on Suragai's face.

'Does she?' Suragai looked down his nose. 'Are you her go-between?' He selected the Anglic word for a person involved in sexual intrigue, implying that Constantin was a procurer.

The offworlder flushed. Then it was as if he realised that Suragai was attempting to pick a quarrel. He sat up. 'You will have to do better than that if you want to start a fight with me,' he responded equably. 'I am Natalia's friend, just as I am yours.'

Either the alien notion of friendship was different from that which was understood by the Yek, or else

287

the statement was a lie. Suragai stared stubbornly, saying nothing.

It was clear that the offworlder had expected a more positive response. He was silent for a time, then he pursed his lips. 'Natalia told me that she had given you cause to mistrust her interest,' he said. 'I can only confirm what she said when she spoke to you. She is not Fedyev's creature. Saving her duty to the Empire, she will be true to you.'

The idea that a friendship might be equated with duty to race – held in equal regard, so that no conflict could be found to exist between the two – was so alien that Suragai was unable at first to accept it. He said, 'You are both servants of the Empire, and have committed acts of war against us. How can I believe that you are my friends?'

'I don't know what you are talking about.' Constantin looked genuinely surprised. 'Noyon, if we have contravened your law in some way, then I promise you it is the result of ignorance, or because your customs are strange to us. As for acts of war –'

'It is contrary to our custom to continue in friendship with those who break agreements or betray our trust,' Suragai said coldly. He was finding it impossible to keep a rein on his tongue. 'Agents of the Empire have incited the people of Ch'nozia to rebellion, and if you belonged to this world you would die for it. Only the Kha-Khan's order saves you.'

'I know nothing of this,' Constantin denied stoutly. He did not look away.

'You are one of them,' Suragai accused. 'You are all forsworn.'

Constantin got to his feet. He said, 'This is not a military expedition. Navy personnel are here only to provide protection for the diplomats and traders. If what you say is true, then it is not only a betrayal of your trust, it is also a breach of our law. Surely the Kha-Khan will protest to our ambassador?'

Suragai did not think Jehan would make any kind of complaint. He said, 'If we had refused to trade with you, you would have attacked us. If we break off relations with you now, you will use it as an excuse to wage war.'

He had expected the offworlder to react with a pretence of outrage. Instead Constantin laughed stupidly. 'I can't imagine why you should think that,' he said. 'It's true that the Empire has pressing reasons for desiring to establish a trading relationship with this world; but if the alternative to an agreement was ever thought to be war, then I would know of it.'

A denial was to be expected, Suragai thought. He was annoyed at himself for revealing so much of what he felt, and now he schooled his features so that it looked as if he was considering what had been said. 'Maybe I have misjudged you,' he said at last. He looked up at the offworlder.

'If someone is causing trouble for you, I ought to report it.' Constantin looked worried. 'My difficulty lies in the fact that I am responsible for most purposes to the ambassador or to the trade commissioner ...' He broke off.

Suragai realised that Constantin was concerned in case the ambassador was involved or had guilty knowledge. It made no sense for men who possessed power or authority to contravene laws which were designed to bring order into their lives. In the same way Suragai did not understand how the military could expect to regulate the conduct of men if they were also subject to their will. He said, 'I think you are saying that if you report it to a civilian, you cannot trust him to act in accordance with your law. But surely the ambassador is like one of our khans. Why should he ignore the law?'

Constantin produced a wry smile. 'The Navy is sworn to uphold Imperial law,' he observed. 'We hold our duty above family, and above personal interest.'

'And so you trust one another.' Suragai nodded. It made an odd kind of sense.

'Diplomats answer to career, and traders to profit,' Constantin continued flatly. 'Even though a man means well, he may be misguided in his actions.'

There was more to causing a rebellion than mere error, Suragai thought, but he did not voice his reaction. He stood up. 'Have you no commander?'

Constantin appeared to hesitate. Then he nodded. 'Of course I have.' He gestured abstractedly with one hand. 'But he is in space. I can talk to him; but everyone who uses the same equipment will be able to listen.'

The alien was saying that not even the highest among them could be trusted to uphold their law. They do not regard law as a shield, Suragai realised suddenly. The few who believe in it – who are sworn to uphold it – have to force the others to live according to its precepts. It seemed inconceivable to Suragai that any group of people would agree laws, and then ignore them as soon as obedience became inconvenient. Obviously the aliens allowed laws to be enacted which they held in no regard. It would be confusing to live inside such a system, Suragai thought. There would be no stability. Probably the lack of a responsible attitude to law and custom was the reason profit

290

was so important to them. The gathering of wealth served personal interest in offworlder society, and so it was regarded as a justification for every aberration of behaviour.

'If you cannot be certain that your report will have a beneficial effect, you should say nothing,' Suragai told Constantin. 'The Ch'noze are not a problem. We have dealt with rebellions before.'

'My only concern is for the relationship which exists between the Khanate and the Empire,' Constantin replied in an austere tone.

Suragai pretended to believe him. 'If you did not cause the trouble, we will not blame you,' he said.

The offworlder looked relieved at first, and then he produced a suspicious stare. 'I can't believe you're so easily satisfied.'

'Oh well.' Suragai turned and jerked his st'lyan's reins free from a branch. 'I never said I was satisfied. You have introduced an element of doubt, that's all.'

A dark figure rose suddenly out of the long grass on the other side of the meadow. Suragai saw feline features and a flash of bared fangs, and then the Marakani sped away – a blur of movement which defied the eye – and disappeared into the haze beyond the grassland. The piebald mare tossed its head and snorted. It trotted up onto the knoll and stood patiently while Constantin retrieved the reins.

The offworlder appeared to be unaware that the catpeople had been watching from the field. He gathered his reins in one hand and reached up to the crupper of his saddle. All at once he looked up. 'Fedyev told me to ask you again about Y'vrope,' he said. 'He still wants to try to recruit workers there.'

Suragai was astounded by alien effrontery. If agents of the Empire were behind the Ch'noze and Alan uprisings, then probably the trade commissioners were involved with them. It seemed unlikely that they imagined that their deceit would not be uncovered, and yet they were behaving as if they had done nothing untoward. Suragai treated Constantin to an expressionless stare.

'If your answer is no, then I ought to explain why,' the offworlder said. He produced a nervous smile. 'Now that you have told me how you feel, I understand. But even if Fedyev is at the bottom of what has happened, he will deny it.'

It made a kind of sense for the trade commissioners to pretend to be ignorant of any cause for animosity. Suragai nodded thoughtfully. He reviewed the things Constantin had said, and tried to decide which of them represented aspects of the truth. Probably all of them did, but only in part. He said, 'Very well. If that is what he wants, then of course I will arrange it.'

'You will?' Constantin looked surprised.

'I just said so, didn't I?' Suragai vaulted into the saddle, pleased that he was being unpredictable. The roan sidestepped, jostling the offworlder's mare so that it reared and screamed. Suragai drew in on his reins. He waited while Constantin regained control of his st'lyan and mounted, then he rode out of the shadow of the trees into the sunlight.

There were no cities in Y'vrope. Where people lived in communities at all, the size of the settlement was determined by the need for self-sufficiency. The economy of the whole land was based on a system of barter, and since the activity of the people was direc-

292

ted principally towards either fishing or farming, they gathered into groups solely for the sake of amenity. Villages tended to be convenient locations for the shops of the tradesmen – the smith, the tailor, the weaver – along with maybe a tavern and an eating house. The fisherfolk lived in groups which were decided by the size of their boats or by the numbers required to manage nets. Elsewhere there were a few places which were capable of being considered towns, and in one of these – a place called Sistos – the Yek had established what little provincial government the continent required.

Viewed from the air Sistos was a disorganised cluster of low white buildings which nestled between rolling hills at a river ford. Most of the houses appeared to be roofed with oat thatch. Beyond the main streets lay what looked like storage barns, and further on more buildings had been raised – structures which were newer, larger, and more uniform in layout and character. Suragai directed Constantin towards a field which was behind them. 'Land there.'

Constantin nodded. The sudden appearance of an alien vessel was exciting only minimal interest on the ground. Suragai could see men working in nearby fields. One or two of them raised their heads and stared incuriously, but no one moved towards the landing place.

Fedyev was already rising. The section of cabin wall in front of the steering couch turned opaque, and Suragai watched as the commissioner went to the door. He posed in the opening as if he expected some kind of reception, but outside there was silence. Suragai stood up. He crossed the cabin and looked past the commissioner at the still-empty field. Fedyev turned. 'No one has come to meet us,' he said accusingly. He sounded offended.

'*Shen* Commissioner, I warned you about this.' Suragai smiled blandly. 'The people here don't accept that one man is any more important than another. It's harvest time, and so you mustn't accept them to pay attention to us without cause.'

Y'vrope philosophy was so remarkable that it had been necessary to explain it at length to the aliens. Now it was clear that they had not believed what they had been told, or maybe they had not understood. Fedyev's brow furrowed. 'You told me that this was the centre of the government,' he said. 'It's very small.'

Suragai glanced out at the field. The ship had been landed so that the door was facing away from the buildings. A man was sauntering past on the other side of a neat hedge which was nearly a hundred drem distant. Suragai leaned through the door and waved, but the Y'vrope did not respond. 'I said that this is where the khan lives.' Suragai gave Fedyev a level stare. 'The guard will have seen us land, so probably somebody will come eventually.'

'It's all very informal.' Fedyev looked unhappy.

'It's the only way we can govern,' Suragai responded cheerfully. 'You were told not to look for the kind of treatment you would receive at Pesth or Kinsai. The khan's secretariat is small. No one in Y'vrope bears arms – the people don't use violence for any reason – and so he doesn't maintain a large guard. Most of the Yek who live here work on the land.'

The explanation was a repetition of part of what had been said earlier, but Suragai guessed that it was probably wasted. Only when the aliens tried to deal with the people who were native to the land would they begin to appreciate the strangeness of their attitudes. Fedyev still looked perturbed. He climbed awkwardly through the door and got down onto the grass, and Suragai followed. He moved to the front of the ship.

A man was walking across the field from the buildings. He was a Yek in his middle years, tall and rangy with loose black hair which was streaked with silver. When he saw Suragai he waved.

Constantin came up to Suragai's side. The commissioner followed more slowly. When he saw that only one man was approaching, his mouth tightened into a thin line.

Suragai was amused by the alien's reaction. He said, 'Both of you should bow.'

It was a moment before Fedyev seemed to adjust to the fact that he was meeting someone of consequence. He produced a hesitant bow.

'Noyon, I am pleased to see you,' Sidacai said. He ignored both aliens.

'Khan, this is the trade commissioner of the off-worlders.' Suragai indicated Fedyev with a wave of his hand. Fedyev's features were frozen with affront, and it was clear that he understood that he was being slighted.

'I had your message.' Sidacai nodded offhandedly. He looked at the commissioner. 'You want to hire men to work in the poppy fields. Surely you have been told that you are wasting your time here?'

The bluntness of the question appeared to take Fedyev by surprise. He flushed, and his head went back. 'Lord, the ways of this land are new to us,' he said. 'On other worlds men can be persuaded by the offer of high rewards. We thought to try that approach here.'

'On Y'vrope?' Sidacai laughed harshly.

The other aliens were descending from the ship. Suragai glanced back at them and saw that the last to come through the door was Natalia. He smiled at her. Then he turned back and looked at Sidacai. 'Khan, we should let them try if they want to.' It was important not to allow Sidacai to indulge his wolfish sense of humour too far.

Sidacai was wearing an old campaign tunic over loose black trousers which were tucked into half-boots. It was possible that his attire was another deliberate slight aimed at the commissioner's rank, or the lack of it. He wrinkled his nose, and then gestured amiably. 'I suppose we can talk about it,' he said.

'First you must understand the conditions under which we govern this land.' Sidacai leaned back in his chair. He hooked one leg over the arm. All the windows were open, and a *khamsama* was operating a fan, pulling with regular strokes at the cord which was attached to a mat of woven straw hinged to the beam above their heads.

'I have been told that the people here live according to a philosophy which does not permit them to be conquered by normal means,' Fedyev said ponderously. 'And yet you claim to rule them in the Kha-Khan's name. I admit I do not understand how one can follow from the other.'

'Maybe it would be more accurate to say that they have learned to accept our presence.' Sidacai smiled sourly. 'The Yek have been in Y'vrope for nearly twenty years. Only they and their descendants address me as Khan, but I govern here nevertheless.'

It was clear that Fedyev did not understand the neat

distinction which had been made. He said, 'How can you rule people who do not acknowledge your authority?'

An orderly came into the room carrying a tray on which there were cups and flasks of wine. He served Sidacai first, and then Suragai, bowing to each of them. Finally he handed a filled cup to Fedyev.

Sidacai drank from his cup, then balanced it precariously on the arm of his chair. He eyed Fedyev. 'How much do you understand about the Y'vrope attitude to government?' he asked.

The commissioner shrugged. Then he gestured towards Suragai. 'The noyon has explained it to me,' he responded. 'The people cannot be conquered because they are non-violent, he says. In my view that is a characteristic which ought to make them easy to overcome.'

'Oh well.' Sidacai chuckled. 'You might think so. I remember that I thought something of the kind the first time I visited this land.'

The first time Sidacai had come to Y'vrope, he had been with Jehan and Alexei. What he had seen here had caused the Kha-Khan to formulate a gradual approach to the government of the continent. Why he had chosen Sidacai to be khan was still a matter for conjecture, for Sidacai had been a soldier of considerable renown.

Sidacai said, 'The best way I can explain it is by offering you an example. Let us suppose that someone has decided to make himself lord of the land hereabouts. A man can install himself wherever he pleases, and no one will argue or offer resistance. The problems don't start until he tries to exercise control.'

Suragai had heard this case before. He drank some

of his wine, and watched the commissioner's expression.

'The new lord waits until the harvest is in,' Sidacai continued, 'and then he demands tribute. It's a demand which is ignored, because the people don't acknowledge that anyone has the right to rule, and they don't render goods to another except in settlement of a debt. The new lord sends his men to take the corn by force.' He paused to allow the picture to register in Fedyev's mind. 'Now the corn has to be milled. The miller is a man of the people, however, and he refuses to work the mill. The new lord throws him into prison. Then he finds that the miller's assistant won't do the job either, and the same applies to the men who are brought to the mill in chains. Soon the would-be lord has a jail full of millers, and the corn still hasn't been ground. He kills the next man who refuses as an example to the others, but to no avail. In the meantime his own men are ready to revolt, because they are starving. They can't get feed for their animals, or ale brewed, or their clothes and gear repaired – they can't even get a load carried from one place to another. Anything they aren't prepared to do themselves doesn't get done. The whole population is either dead or in chains, but in the end the man who seized power is the lord of nothing but a wilderness.'

The notion that men would die before they would submit was so remarkable that it stretched credibility. Suragai had seen civil disobedience applied in practice, and yet he still found it hard to accept that it worked.

Sidacai said, 'The approach relies on the assumption that men who seek to exert their will over others will see that the use of force is futile if there is no way to employ it to achieve their aims.' He picked up his cup.

'I suppose we could have conquered Y'vrope by the kind of means we used elsewhere, but probably we would have had to kill everyone who lived here in the process.'

'I think you are saying that the Yek call themselves the lords of this land,' Fedyev observed in a superior tone, 'but in fact they are nothing of the kind.'

The response made Sidacai smile grimly. He said, 'It's true that Jehan decided he did not want to be the lord of a wilderness. As to whether we rule or not, I think that depends on your interpretation. The people live very much according to their own set of rules – basically a man is free to dress, think and act any way he pleases, so long as he doesn't inconvenience others. An individual can't take his desire to be different too far, because food and shelter, even services, are got by barter. A man who does not like you doesn't have to trade with you. It's a whole culture based on the principle of live and let live.'

Fedyev said, 'Lord, if you don't influence the way the people live, you can't claim to govern them.'

'I said it was a matter of interpretation,' Sidacai said mildly. 'One of the important things we discovered when we came here first was the fact that the land belongs to the man who works it. We have moved our own people in over the years, and they live according to our law. The two cultures trade with one another, and there has been a degree of intermarriage.'

'And so a small proportion of the population recognises the Khanate.' The commissioner looked down at the cup in his hand, then raised his eyes again. 'With respect, I don't think that means you are the masters here.'

'Oh.' Sidacai showed his teeth. 'I hadn't finished

explaining it to you. As I said, we let the people live according to their own rules. The same rules allow us to govern them.'

'I don't see how.' Fedyev frowned.

'Road-menders and stevedores,' Suragai said softly.

Sidacai laughed. 'That's right.' He nodded, and then looked at Fedyev. 'We've never tried to extract tribute,' he said. 'But before we came the roads were maintained on an intermittent basis by the communities they served. Now and again the people would bring in men to carry out repairs, and then they repaid them for the labour by feeding them or giving them goods.'

'But roads are land.' Suragai set his cup carefully on the floor beside his feet. 'And so they belong to whoever works them. We brought in road gangs of C'zaki and Keraistani. Now the Yek control the whole road network, and everyone who uses them has to pay a toll which is calculated according to the value of the goods he is carrying. A farmer who wants to move his corn from the fields to the mill has to pay for the privilege. In fact all the people pay. They need roads, and they hate to be indebted to anyone. They could build and maintain their own roads, of course, but it would be too much trouble, and it wouldn't make sense to build a second road in a place where one already exists.'

'They're a very rational people.' Sidacai nodded again. He gestured to Suragai. 'Explain about the stevedores.'

'Probably I should have told you all this before,' Suragai apologised to Fedyev. 'You might have understood the rest of it if I had. The point about the stevedores is that anything that doesn't move on land is carried by sea. When we came here we extended the

300

ports and improved all the harbours, and that way we established a claim to them. The men who operate them now are all servants of the Khanate. The situation is similar to the one which relates to the roads. It never occurred to the people to claim ownership of places where vessels could be docked or landed. They built wharves when they needed them, of course, but after that it was up to the whole community to arrange for repair and upkeep. They are quite happy for us to do it, and they don't mind paying for the service.'

'It means that we control the roads and the coastline,' Sidacai said. 'Instead of taxes we extract tolls, but the people end up with the same service they would expect from a khan if they paid tribute. Over the years they have found that it's better to come to Yek courts for the settlement of disputes. They still think we're outsiders, so they know the judges can't be biased. A Yek won't take offence at the way a man dresses his hair, and won't be concerned about his relationship with his neighbours so long as he obeys the law, and thus he won't allow his personal feelings to affect his judgement. They have even started coming to me for help in starting farms and other enterprises. A man who wanted to start a farm used to have to put himself heavily in debt. He owed produce to the carpenter for building a barn, and to the smith for implements. I send men to put up his buildings, and I give him tools and equipment, but I don't ask for so much in return.'

Suragai wondered if the aliens were capable of seeing that the control Sidacai exercised was every bit as effective as that which was the result of oppression. The expression on Fedyev's face suggested that he was attempting to come to terms with the idea. Clearly he had not encountered anything like it before.

Fedyev said, 'Khan, I think I understand now. But if as you say the people barter their service, surely they will be receptive to an offer of a reward for their labour. I had thought to pay them like the workers on other worlds, but I could buy goods with gold instead, and then use the goods to repay those I hire.'

The thought had already crossed Suragai's mind. He pursed his lips. 'It's possible, I suppose.'

Sidacai drank his wine. 'If you feel you want to try, I cannot stop you,' he told the alien. 'I think you are ignoring the fact that it is the nature of these people to be independent. They would rather work for themselves than for others. Also it is harvest time. Some men like to move around the country, but even those have employment now. I don't doubt that you can offer more than the farmers, but you may still find that no one wants to work for you. The men of this land don't grow crops they can't eat to turn into things they can use. I don't suppose you intend to offer them the benefit of the drug you make from the poppy – they would not be interested – but even if you explain it, they will not sympathise with your desire to gather the poppy sap. As I told you, they are very rational people.'

'And they mistrust all strangers,' Suragai added.

'Yes.' Sidacai gave Fedyev a sharp stare. 'Really you have wasted your time coming here.'

The farmer Sidacai took them to see was a small man with iron-grey hair and a full beard. He listened while Fedyev outlined what he wanted, and then he frowned. 'Lord, you know I have crops to gather,' he said to Sidacai. 'Why do you bring this to me?'

'Boris Zaitsev, you have eleven sons,' Sidacai said. 'They work your farm, and you hire them out to other men as well. Of all the farmers hereabouts you must be in a position to consider the alien's offer. He will give you maybe twice what you can get from your neighbours for the labour of the sons you do not need.'

A row of neatly painted buildings and a well-tended orchard testified to the farm's prosperity. Two young men were transferring sheaves from a cart into a barn. The farmer indicated them. 'Those are my youngest sons,' he said. 'Yesterday they were stacking corn for my neighbour Irbayev. Today I need them, and he has released them back to me.' He looked at Fedyev. 'But working for you they would be many verst hence. How if the sons who remain to work my farm fall sick?'

'Then you could hire others,' Fedyev pointed out. A patient expression had appeared on his face. 'With what you will be paid for the labour of the sons who work for me, you can employ twice their number.'

'Oh?' The farmer raised his eyebrows. 'I do not know of any men who are free for hire at this time of the year, and if you do maybe you should employ them.'

'You fear for the loss of your crops,' the commissioner said. 'I understand that. What if I were to offer to get corn to replace any which you lost because your sons worked for me?'

The grey-bearded man looked offended. 'And what kind of farmer would that make me?' he demanded. 'I would be a fool to plant corn if I could not harvest it. What is this crop of yours which is so important?'

Fedyev started to explain. The farmer's expression grew steadily more disbelieving, and he glanced at

Sidacai as if he suspected that he was being made fun of. 'Flowers,' he said flatly. 'Can they be eaten?'

'The aliens make a drug from the sap.' Suragai supplied the answer. 'It is said that it prolongs life.'

The farmer sniffed disapprovingly. 'All men die,' he observed, and looked Fedyev up and down. 'It is the natural order of things.'

'Surely a long life is to be desired,' Suragai suggested mildly.

'Longer than what?' the farmer enquired. 'You speak as if the years of men's lives are predetermined. I could fall into the river and drown tomorrow, in truth; and I could live forever. It seems to me that one is as likely as the other.'

The commissioner shifted impatiently, and it was apparent that he thought that they were moving away from the point. He said, 'Surely it does not matter what a man thinks of my wishes, so long as I am prepared to pay him to work for me.'

Sidacai and the farmer exchanged significant glances. 'Every man has the right to please himself,' the farmer replied sententiously. 'You can farm flowers, or not, as it pleases you. Men can work for you, or not, as it pleases them. There are fools in plenty in the world. It stands to reason that they will find one another if they search long enough.'

The implication was clear. Only a fool would work for an alien. Fedyev flushed. 'I see that I cannot persuade you,' he said. 'Will your sons be of the same mind? May I speak to them?'

'Speak to them if you wish,' the farmer responded with perfect amiability. 'I haven't raised any fools that I know of.' He nodded politely to Sidacai and walked away.

Fedyev stared after him. His expression reminded Suragai of the look on the face of a p'tar faced with a thick hedge. He did not know whether to charge it, eat it, or go around it. The alien shook his head angrily. 'Surely he is not typical,' he said.

Sidacai wrinkled his nose. 'Probably he is not,' he said. 'Maybe you didn't notice, but he addressed me as Lord. Also he stood and listened to you far longer than politeness required. Another man would have walked away as soon as he decided he wasn't interested in your proposition. Time is like everything else to these people. They don't waste it without reason.'

Probably the commissioner thought that the farmer had been chosen because he was bound to refuse the alien's offer. Certainly he seemed to be trying to decide what to do next.

'You are wondering if I brought you here because I knew what the farmer would say.' Sidacai gave Fedyev a wide-eyed stare. 'I did know. Every man you speak to will react the same way.'

They visited two more farms – places Fedyev insisted on selecting without reference to Sidacai. At the first the commissioner barely had time to announce that he was looking for field workers, and then he was ignored. The men stacking corn at the second farm did not even pause from their work to listen.

'There must be places where the people gather.' Fedyev still looked as if he did not believe that the lack of interest in his proposition was anything other than misunderstanding. 'Surely you could summon them to listen to what I have to say.'

At least the alien realised that there were no community leaders, and that he was going to have to appeal to individuals, Suragai thought.

'I could summon them,' Sidacai said, amused. 'But there is no way to force them to attend. I thought I had explained that. You could speak to them at the taverns.'

The commissioner's expression indicated what he thought of that idea. His moon face was shining with sweat. The late afternoon sun was huge, and it seemed to fill the sky. Suragai gazed up at it.

'I should have taken your advice,' Fedyev said. He was at Suragai's side. 'But I could not believe that your intent was to help me.'

This was the alien who was probably behind the activities of the Imperial agents in Ch'nozia. Suragai stared at him, unwilling to voice what was now on his mind. Sidacai had provided st'lyan for them to ride. Suragai untied his mare's reins from the fence rail at the end of the path.

'Twice you have given me good counsel.' Fedyev spoke again. 'I should have left it to you to find the workers we need.'

If the alien really believed that the Yek were trying to help, he was a fool. Suragai remembered the approach Alexei had outlined. Its purpose was to persuade the commissioners that they were receiving genuine co-operation, and that the problems and delays they encountered were unavoidable. A man who was deceived by the course of events would not be involved in subversion, Suragai thought. Fedyev was clever, and so he was only pretending to be convinced that the advice he had received had been honest.

Suragai shrugged. '*Shen* Commissioner, the task will be as difficult for me as for you. This is harvest time in many parts of the world.'

'I understand that.' Fedyev nodded. His features shaped the approximation of a smile, but no expression reached his eyes. 'I place myself in your hands nevertheless.'

The commissioner's st'lyan was a tall bay. Suragai saw that the alien was going to have difficulty getting up onto its back. He cupped his hands together, motioning Fedyev to use them to mount. The commissioner climbed up awkwardly. He got his left foot into the stirrup. Then he swung his free leg over the bay's back and settled himself in the saddle. Suragai looked up at him. 'I will do what I can to find men for you,' he said. 'It will be easier in Keraistan than here.'

'In that case I will place one of our ships at your disposal,' Fedyev responded smoothly.

Suragai untethered the bay. He looped the reins over the st'lyan's head and gave them to Fedyev. Sidacai came down the path from the farm they had just visited. He grinned at Suragai, then vaulted onto his st'lyan's back and rode away at a brisk trot.

Fedyev stared after him. He gathered the bay's reins. Suddenly he looked down at Suragai again. 'You are the grandson of Admiral Rostov,' he said.

The st'lyan sidestepped. Suragai had wrapped the reins around his arm so that he could help the alien to mount. He tugged at them, and then he eyed Fedyev. 'My grandfather is Suragai Khan,' he said sourly. 'He would not thank you for using the other name.'

If the commissioner was put out of countenance, it did not show in his manner. 'Noyon, I intended no offence. It's an honoured name in the Empire.'

'Hunh.' Suragai pulled himself into the saddle. He was disturbed by the knowledge he saw in Fedyev's

307

eyes, and he wondered why the subject had been changed so abruptly.

'If you travel to Keraistan, you will see him,' Fedyev said.

'My grandfather?'

'Yes.'

'I suppose I may.' Suragai drew in on his reins. He watched the alien curiously.

'In that case maybe you would give him a message for me,' Fedyev said. 'Tell him that I am in communication with his wife, and that she sends her regards.'

'His wife?' Suragai stared. His grandfather had two wives. Both of them lived at Kinsai, and the commissioner had not met them.

'That's right.' Fedyev nodded, and smiled. 'Will you remember to speak to him?'

Sidacai was already some distance down the road. A cloud of dust hung in the air, darkened by the redness of the sun. 'I will tell him,' Suragai said.

'Good.' The commissioner nodded, a pleased expression on his face. He tapped his st'lyan in the barrel with the toe of his boot and rode sedately away.

PART FOUR

Alarms and Excursions

Kubulai turned right round in the saddle. He had three arrows left, and he fired them one after the other at the oncoming Ch'noze. His men were scattered all along the river bank. The ground across which they were galloping was as rough and broken as the worst stretches of the western G'bai. Behind them was a pursuing army which consisted of the members of five different Ch'noze clans. The leaders screamed insults at the Yek troopers, daring them to turn and fight.

The ground fell away abruptly. Kubulai's st'lyan gathered itself and then leapt. Kubulai grabbed at the mane. The st'lyan landed awkwardly and went down, so that Kubulai was thrown. The depression had been the bank of a small stream and the ground was rock hard. He lay for a moment, his vision blurred, then climbed to his feet. The st'lyan was standing uncertainly in the water, one foreleg lifted as though something was broken or torn.

Ch'noze voices howled nearby. Kubulai had been close to the rear. He climbed the bank onto level ground. His men were pretending to retreat, and the Ch'noze who saw him wheeled and charged.

'Khan!'

Jehangir was urging his st'lyan along the line of the bank, lashing it with the free ends of his reins. A thrown lance landed in the space which separated them. Jehangir flinched and then lashed the st'lyan again. Beyond him the Yek were turning, ready to return to the attack, but they had ridden off a distance of two or three hundred verst. It was too far. Jehangir pulled up hard in front of Kubulai, and Kubulai grabbed the roan's mane with one hand and Jehangir's outstretched arm with the other, then leapt up behind him.

'Help me!' Jehangir shouted. 'Hold them off while we ride away!'

Kubulai looked back. The Ch'noze were galloping flat out across the plain towards them, lances extended. A group of three men raced ahead of the others. The st'lyan ran at breakneck speed towards the safety of the Yek line, but the three Ch'noze were already drawing level. Kubulai snatched Jehangir's bow out of his hand, pulled arrows from the case on the saddlebow, and turning, fired back across the roan's hindquarters. The Ch'noze in front pitched out of the saddle.

'Come on!' Jehangir yelled. He stood in the stirrups and waved to the Yek who were at the head of the new attack.

Arrows whipped past their heads. Kubulai pulled out another arrow. He drew, and brought the head down until it was resting on the space between one of the two remaining Ch'noze and the neck of his st'lyan, then loosed. The man threw up his hands and toppled sideways. The third Ch'noze wheeled away.

The oncoming Yek formed a solid wall which was advancing on the Ch'noze army. Kubulai reached around Jehangir and dragged the reins out of his hands. Then he pulled the roan's head around. Yek troopers swerved past them, and they hurtled towards the Ch'noze, yelling triumphantly.

The Ch'noze faltered. Their insults became cries of alarm, and on the far end of their line men started to desert. Kubulai estimated that they outnumbered the Yek by about two to one. He took a deep breath and added his voice to the howls of victory.

'Yaeeeiyah!'

Yek arrows were sleeting down on the leading Ch'noze formations. Kubulai fired off the last of the arrows he had found in Jehangir's case. The roan bunched and leapt over a man lying in its path. There were dead men and animals everywhere. An equine which had an arrow lodged in its flank galloped straight at them, and Jehangir seized the reins and pulled up. Kubulai looked back over his shoulder. His men were moving forward at the walk, enveloping the Ch'noze, their arrows pouring continuously into their line. Jehangir cheered.

One of the Ch'noze flanks had re-formed. The storm of Yek arrows had decimated them, but now they swung up their shields and spurred forward. A mass of men drove like a battering ram towards Kubulai's place in the advance.

There were no more arrows in Jehangir's case, and the roan was halting again. Troopers swept up on both sides of them, carrying them along. They encountered the stream once more, and the roan was forced down onto the bank. Jehangir yelled, and Kubulai prepared himself to jump clear, but the st'lyan only staggered, then charged on through the shallow water.

Ch'noze were chasing them along the bed of the stream. A st'lyan screamed shrilly. The roan checked and stumbled, and Kubulai slid off the animal's back. Ch'noze equines surged up around him. A sword blade whistled past his ear and water splashed his chest.

Jehangir's roan had collided with a Ch'noze st'lyan. It staggered and Jehangir shouted something. He looked back at Kubulai, and hauled on the reins. Kubulai took several running paces and vaulted back up behind him. A Ch'noze who had facial tattoos indicating that he was a war-leader was leaning out of the saddle to swipe at them with a sword. Jehangir parried awkwardly. Kubulai snatched his d'jaga out of his belt. He reached across and grabbed at their assailant's arm, then plunged the d'jaga deep into his side. They reeled together and fell off into the water. The Ch'noze was on top, kicking and struggling. Kubulai's head went under the surface of the stream.

The water was bitterly cold. Kubulai felt the Ch'noze go limp, and he shoved at the body to free himself of its weight. Water ran into his mouth and down his throat. He felt a surge of panic and pushed with his booted feet, searching for the bottom. When he found it, he kicked hard. He surged up to the surface, gasping.

All the Ch'noze appeared to be dead. Kubulai could hear shouting from the level ground above the bank of the stream. The noise was like the roar of a huge fire. He stood up and found that the water only came up to his chest. Suddenly he started to shiver.

Jehangir rode up. He slid out of the saddle and pulled Kubulai up onto the bank. Somebody threw a cloak around his shoulders, and Kubulai clutched at it with fingers which felt numb. The troopers who were gathering were saying something about a fire and dry clothes.

Kubulai said, 'Where are the Ch'noze?'

'Dead or scattered.' Jehangir started to pull off Kubulai's boots.

They stripped off Kubulai's clothes and rubbed him with cloaks and blankets until he was dry. He saw no point in resisting. He could see across the stream, the grass beside it white with frost because the plateau was so high. Equines and dead men were dotted about the far bank. Kubulai stared at them. Someone thrust a bowl of stew into his hand, and he ate absently. The hot food burned its way down into his chest. A thousand commander brought dry clothes, and orderlies made him stand up so that they could work the tunic over his head.

'Khan, you were lucky,' Jehangir said. 'You could have drowned or frozen.'

Kubulai caught at the shoulder of Jehangir's tunic. 'We mustn't let the Ch'noze re-form,' he said.

The thousand commander was attempting to dry Kubulai's boots. He looked round. 'About half of them got away, but we killed the rest. We'll find them again.'

'We only have to follow the trail of dead equines,' Jehangir observed. Somebody laughed.

Kubulai frowned, displeased. He had given command of the reserve tuman to Orcadai, Burun's son, and a great-uncle of sorts. Orcadai had been out of contact for a day. If he had not, the Ch'noze would never have managed to escape in such numbers. Kubulai gave Jehangir a stare. 'Send some men out to find Orcadai. If he isn't moving north, I want to know why.'

Jehangir hesitated a moment, then he seemed to realise that it was not the time to argue. He nodded. 'Yes, Khan.'

They rode forty verst before nightfall. Most of the

Ch'noze plain was on a plateau which was at an altitude of over fifteen hundred drem. Autumn had come early, and the ground was already frozen hard. The white frost which covered the grass each morning never dispersed before midday, and the branches were bare of leaves.

There were small walled towns at the river crossings and at the places where the principal roads met, but Kubulai ignored them. The Ch'noze were open-country fighters who preferred to strike from ambush. Even if clansmen remained inside the settlements, there would be time enough to deal with them after the main segments of the rebel army had been defeated. In nearly every case the town gates were shut, and people lined the walls. They threw rubbish and shouted insults at the passing troopers, and Kubulai smiled at the angry looks on his troopers' faces. If they caught the Ch'noze army in the open they would charge right through them. There was nothing like a good wholesome anger to make a soldier ignore the odds.

When it was dark they camped. The men searching for Orcadai's tuman had not yet reported back, and irritation burned inside Kubulai's chest and he was short-tempered with everyone. Couriers rode back and forth between the main body and the vanguard, and the men of Kubulai's escort lay unhappily in clearings among stands of pine trees. The st'lyan cropped at the sparse grass, and when that was gone they tore at the bark of the trees. There was no moon, and a rising wind rustled and moaned through the needle-covered branches.

Kadan rode in about the third hour of the night watch. He had only a small escort, and he left them milling about among Kubulai's men and stalked over to the fire around which Kubulai and Jehangir and a few of his officers were huddling. He said, 'You have lost some men.'

Kubulai looked up.

'We found part of the Ch'noze army. They outnumbered us somewhat.'

'More than somewhat, it looks like.' Kadan squatted down beside the fire and held out his hands to the flames. 'I'm camped twenty verst to the east,' he said. 'Did you kill all the Ch'noze?'

'Only about half.' Kubulai shook his head. 'Have you seen Orcadai in your travels?'

'Have you lost him?' Kadan looked amused. 'That was careless.'

Kubulai glared at him. He knew it had been a mistake to award a command to Orcadai, even though he was experienced, because he had shown consistently that he was incapable of accepting the authority of a general who was many years his junior. Kubulai said, 'When I find him again, he will pay for it.'

Kadan laughed softly. 'Maybe you should let me control him,' he said.

Their relationship had been uneasy ever since the night of the roof race at Kinsai. Kubulai looked up slowly. He gave Kadan a level stare. 'You are all under my orders. I thought the Kha-Khan made that clear.'

D'mitri rode up to the fire and dismounted. He said, 'I have posted sentries in rings centred on this camp. The furthest outposts are nearly half a day's ride from here.'

'Good.' Kubulai nodded. He glanced back at Kadan. 'When you ride out, keep your line extended so that you can find the Ch'noze if they are out there. If they attack you, fall back. Send me news so that I can circle around and trap them. If you don't think a courier will reach me soon enough, send him on a straight line, and then retreat along a curve. Don't try to engage the Ch'noze army on your own.'

Kadan cleared his throat. 'Can we stop to piss when we want to?'

One of the officers on the other side of the fire laughed. Kubulai wrinkled his nose. 'You can, if you think you can make such an important decision on your own.'

It was D'mitri who laughed this time. The expression on Kadan's face was calculating. After a moment he shrugged. 'You are in command,' he said.

'I'm glad you accept that.' Kubulai stood up. The night air was cold, and the chill made his bones feel brittle. 'The Ch'noze are between us and the north coast. Part of their army is besieging T'tai. We are going to deal with them first. After that we will move gradually west, sweeping the rest of them before us.'

'They will escape through the western passes towards Pantai,' D'mitri objected.

'I've thought of that.' Kubulai picked up the cloak which was draped across his saddle. 'A half-strength tuman of my father's is camped on the plain south of there. I am sending to the commander to bring up his men to block the roads.'

Kadan's head came up sharply. 'Don't you think you are exceeding your authority?'

'I don't believe so.' Kubulai showed his teeth. 'And if my father objects, we can argue about it later.'

Kadan tapped a smouldering piece of wood with the toe of his boot, pushing it back into the fire. 'Give

Orcadai to me,' he said. 'I can handle him.'

'So can I.' Kubulai looked around the faces illuminated by the firelight. 'If he annoys me again, I'll send him back to Kinsai. I can always use the extra st'lyan.'

They digested the threat. Kadan leaned forward, and his eyes reflected the light from the fire. 'I hear a lot of talk,' he said. 'What else do you have?'

Kubulai saw the men around the fire tense. He caught D'mitri's eye. 'Make sure no one interferes.'

D'mitri nodded

'Come on then,' Kadan said. His tone betrayed his eagerness. 'Come and fight me.'

Kubulai dropped the cloak, and unbuckled his belt. 'I would have thought you would have realised by now. I don't come to you. You come to me.'

Kadan bared his teeth. He jerked out his d'jaga and plunged around the fire. He was a whole head taller than Kubulai, and his arms were longer. He held the d'jaga low, the point aimed at Kubulai's belly, and Kubulai sucked in his stomach. He waited, watching Kadan prowl around the edge of the firelight towards him. The belt dangled from his hand.

'Haaah!'

Kadan's first rush was like the charge of a p'ntar. The d'jaga blade flashed in the yellow light. Kubulai jumped back, and slashed with the belt at Kadan's face. Kadan jerked back out of range, and Kubulai moved in swiftly. He knew he had to end it quickly. The point of the d'jaga came up suddenly towards his chest. He caught it on his forearm, wincing as the tip struck bone, and lashed at Kadan with his belt.

A man shouted. Kubulai charged Kadan and knocked him off his feet, then pursued him. He was holding the buckle of the belt, but the other end had a metal tip fastened over the leather. It opened welts across Kadan's arm, and he rolled, lashing out with one foot. Kubulai dodged out of the way. He flogged Kadan across the arms and shoulders, hearing the flat thud as the leather struck flesh. Kadan kicked out again, and his foot caught Kubulai across the shin. He grunted and sat down hard.

'Stop!' Jehangir shouted.

Kubulai scrambled to his feet and backed off. He pulled his sleeve back so that he could look at the wound on his arm. It was deep, but the cut was clean, and already it was beginning to seal.

'Kadan?' D'mitri was on his feet, his features taut. He went over to Kadan, and put a hand on his shoulder. Kadan had rolled to the edge of the fire. His hands were at his face, and Kubulai could see that they were ridged with welts. A cut on the part of his face which was not covered by his hands oozed blood. D'mitri stooped and whispered something. Then he straightened. 'You have both broken the Yasa,' he said harshly. He pulled Kadan to his feet.

Jehangir looked uncertain. He said, 'The Yasa ...'

'The Yasa says that the blood of no high-born man shall be spilled,' Kadan said. He wiped his face with his hand, and then came past the fire and caught Kubulai by his injured arm and held it towards the light of the fire. The sleeve of Kubulai's tunic was sodden with blood from the d'jaga slash. 'There is no penalty against either of us,' Kadan said. He let go of Kubulai's arm. 'We will settle this another time,' he said more softly. He turned and strode away.

D'mitri walked across the grass. 'You could have blinded him with that belt. Why are you fighting?'

Kubulai shrugged. 'He's been setting himself up

320

against me since Kinsai,' he said. 'Maybe he resents my authority.'

'He's your grandfather's son,' D'mitri pointed out. 'And he is my brother-in-law. Don't ask me to support you if it comes to kanly.'

Kanly was the formal duelling code by which men of the races of the True People were permitted to settle their feuds. Men fought naked with talons, and they had to have the Kha-Khan's permission, because kanly was a contest to the death.

'Oh.' Kubulai grinned sourly. 'It won't come to that. Jehangir, find me something to drink.'

'He'll kill you the first time you're alone with him,' D'mitri said. 'Let me mediate it for you.'

'Don't be stupid.' Kubulai waited until Jehangir had found a flask of k'miss, and then he took it from him and drank. When he lowered the flask he looked at D'mitri again. 'He may try to kill me, but he won't succeed. Go and talk to him.' Kubulai showed his teeth. 'Then come back and tell me what he says.'

The snow came down when they were still a hundred verst south of T'tai. Kubulai was riding beside D'mitri, and he turned up the collar of his cloak and rammed his hat down over his ears. Before he could find his gauntlets the snow was falling like a curtain. D'mitri managed to signal his escort, and then he slowed his st'lyan's pace down to a walk.

'Jehangir.'

Kubulai's guard commander galloped up out of the ranks behind. He saluted D'mitri.

'You know this country. Can you find your way to T'tai in this?'

Kubulai wrenched at the fastening across the

321

mouth of one of his saddlebags, and extracted a length of woollen cloth and wrapped it around his face. Jehangir was frowning at the prospect he had been offered. At last he nodded. 'As you command.'

'Take as many men as you need,' D'mitri said.

Jehangir trotted his st'lyan away. D'mitri pulled out of line, looking for his standard-bearer, shouting for lanterns. Then he turned towards Kubulai and spoke, but the words were lost on the wind which had sprung up. Kubulai shrugged and shook his head to show he did not understand.

The wind screamed past them. D'mitri sidestepped his st'lyan closer, and he leaned across and shouted. 'Turn round.'

Kubulai worked himself around in the saddle. He was able to see only the vague shapes of other men beyond the rumps of the remount st'lyan. The rest of the two tumans strung out behind them were invisible because of the driving snow. Kubulai strained his ears to catch the sounds of movement and realised that he could hear the clink of metal and the screams of st'lyan. D'mitri pulled a rope out of one of his saddlebags. He tied the end to the pommel of his saddle, then tossed the rest to Kubulai. Kubulai wrapped a loop around the saddle tree, then looked for somebody else to link to the line. D'mitri's standard-bearer forged up through the blinding snow. A rope was already fastened to the harness of his st'lyan. He took Kubulai's rope and knotted the two together. D'mitri was yelling for the commander of his escort, but there was no reply. All Kubulai's remounts pulled up at the same time. They turned and stood with their tails to the driving wind. D'mitri bellowed again.

It was only late afternoon, but Kubulai could not

see the sun. Lights moved in the greyness where the army was. At first they were only splashes of colour – reds and greens – then a man with lanterns hanging from his saddle cantered up to them. He passed the lanterns to the standard-bearer, who strung them on his pole.

'I want every hundred commander to make sure that his men are roped together,' D'mitri said. 'And he is to carry a white lantern. Tell everyone to watch for signals.'

Jehangir returned. He said, 'All my scouts and couriers will be carrying green lanterns. I'll string men out as I ride to make sure you are following my trail.'

D'mitri nodded. Jehangir reined around and vanished into the storm. Kubulai narrowed his eyes, trying to follow his progress. A green light flickered, so faint that Kubulai could barely distinguish it. That was Jehangir. The green light bobbed, then disappeared.

'Is everybody ready?' D'mitri called.

Kubulai stood up in his stirrups and peered to the left and right. The vague outlines of riders stretched off into the greyness. D'mitri's standard-bearer was behind, and the rope which ran from his st'lyan's harness to the next man in line stretched off into nothing.

The dun mare Kubulai was riding hated the wet, and when they started off it kept its head down as if it was cropping at pasture. Snow blew into Kubulai's face and plastered the front of his cloak. After a hundred strides he pounded at the stiff material with one hand to loosen it. D'mitri was hunched down on the back of his roan, his face thoughtful. Kubulai reined across so that he was riding beside him.

They were forced to lean towards one another to speak. D'mitri rose in the stirrups, then rested one arm across Kubulai's shoulders. He said, 'I'm not sure we can signal in this light.'

'We can if the hundred commanders do as they have been ordered,' Kubulai yelled.

'This storm is no bad thing.'

'Oh, how?'

'The Ch'noze will think we have been prevented from advancing.'

Kubulai chuckled. He worked himself down in the saddle and thumped at the snow-covered fabric of his cloak. When he looked back he saw that his remounts were in a line behind the dun, following the track she had broken. Every time the wind changed Kubulai could hear the shouts of other men as they attempted to stay in contact with the ranks on either side. Still he could see nothing.

One of the tumans behind had two thousand Alan conscripts. Kubulai wondered how they felt moving up to fight under Yek officers they must know would kill them if they baulked. No news had come in yet about the progress of the Alan rebellion, but Kubulai decided that he would be unhappy to be an Alan conscript in a Yek army if the word was not good.

A green light blinked in the dimness ahead of them. It grew steadily, and then Jehangir galloped suddenly out of the curtain of snow. He waved an arm, gesturing in agitation off to the east.

'Wotai!' D'mitri shouted. 'Signal the turn. Blue lantern.'

The standard-bearer lowered his staff. He closed the shutters of two lanterns, then raised it again. D'mitri held up a hand to stay the men who were coming out of the blizzard. He made everyone continue north for a time so that the commanders on the flanks would have a chance to see the signal and respond to it. Kubulai could see D'mitri counting off the strides of his st'lyan. Suddenly he signalled, and Kubulai reined over. The thicket of thorn bushes was barring his path, and he rode around it.

Abruptly the wind died. Kubulai was able to hear the whistling and yelling of the officers who were directing the individual columns. He glanced back to the place he knew was occupied by the closest formation, but the snow was still falling thickly, and he could see neither man nor animal – only the flicker of lanterns. When he turned to look ahead Kubulai saw Jehangir's green lantern bobbing in the distance. Jehangir had waited to make sure that everyone had turned. Kubulai caught D'mitri's eye, and saw him nod approvingly.

D'mitri shouted, 'How long do you think the storm will last?'

Kubulai frowned. He raised one hand and gestured with it to indicate that he had no idea. D'mitri scowled. He said something, but Kubulai was unable to hear. He let himself relax in the saddle, and knew that he was tired. Hunching himself down inside his cloak he went to sleep.

The snow was still falling steadily when Kubulai awoke. He guessed that it was night, because the grey was much darker, and the wind had risen again. Now he realised that he was covered with snow, encased in it, and he punched at the frozen mass with his gauntleted hand, then brushed the broken chunks aside so that they fell to the ground. The st'lyan's mane was stiff with icicles and crusted snow.

D'mitri was hauling on the rope which connected them. Kubulai realised that it was the jerking of the line which had woken him up. He reined over, tugging aside the cloth which was wound around his face.

'Jehangir thinks we ought to make camp,' D'mitri said.

Kubulai stood in the stirrups. Huge snowflakes were blowing across his field of vision, and he raised a hand to shield his face.

Jehangir rode up. He waved an arm. 'There is a place ahead, Khan,' he called. 'Good pasture for the st'lyan.'

Kubulai hesitated, then nodded. D'mitri was already telling his standard-bearer to signal, and when he turned his back, Kubulai saw that it was solid with driven snow.

After they turned Kubulai counted the paces. At five hundred he reined in. The snow all round was flat, trampled where the men of the first thousand of the left flank had wheeled across it. A gust of icy wind tore at them, and Kubulai flinched. The rope leading to D'mitri's mare was like a rod of ice. A section of the rear thousand of Kubulai's tuman was curving past to the right. He reined around and rode into the middle of the great circle which had been created by the turning tumans. Passing a file of Alan he saw that their faces were sullen, oppressed by cold and misery.

D'mitri said. 'How far have we ridden?'

Jehangir was dismounting. He looked up. 'Sixty verst maybe,' he answered. 'A good day's travel.'

Kubulai got down out of the saddle. He performed a deep knee bend and winced at the soreness in his calves. D'mitri swung one leg over the saddle, and he slid to the ground untidily. 'Name of God,' he said. 'My legs have gone to sleep. Is that the baggage train? I'm going to sleep in one of the carts.'

'It's coming.' Jehangir looked past the hindquarters of his st'lyan and pointed. 'I found a meadow of a kind over there. Fair pasture.'

D'mitri grunted. The two-wheeled wagons of the pack train were already rumbling into the camp. Orderlies were jumping from them while they were still rolling, running to find their officers. A C'zak who was in D'mitri's service came up. He was swathed in blankets and extra layers of clothing. Awkwardly he stripped the saddles from the lead st'lyan, then tied them together by their headropes and led them away.

With the departure of the animals the cold was intense. Kubulai selected a cart, and crawled into it. An orderly was crouching on the wooden floor, tending a brazier which had been set up in a tray of sand. When he saw Kubulai he took a pan from the flames and poured the contents into a bowl. Kubulai accepted it gratefully. D'mitri came to the tailgate of the cart and stood. His face was blue with the cold.

The bowl was filled with a kind of stew. Pieces of meat floated in a thick gravy. Kubulai speared them with his talons, and then tipped up the bowl and drank the hot liquid.

'I thought the Yek were immune to cold,' D'mitri said. He climbed up into the cart beside Kubulai.

'I think my blood has gone thin.' Kubulai frowned. 'I never thought we would see snow so early in the season.'

D'mitri took the bowl the orderly held out. He used his fingers to find a chunk of meat and popped it into his mouth. 'Even if the Ch'noze have placed outposts,' he said, 'they won't see us. If this snow keeps up we will be on them before they have time to prepare.'

Kubulai saw a flask of k'miss on top of a bag by his side. He laid his bowl aside and lifted the flask. 'It gives us an advantage, that's all,' he said.

A courier rode into the cleared circle of snow. He stood in the stirrups, looking about, and D'mitri leaned out of the cart and waved him over. 'Lord,' the courier said, 'I come from Kadan Khan. He is camped fifteen verst to the east.'

'Good.' Kubulai nodded. 'Go and find yourself a place to sleep.'

The man saluted and rode away. 'I wasn't sure Kadan would keep riding,' D'mitri commented.

'It's Orcadai I'm worred about,' Kubulai responded. The scouts who had ridden in just before the start of the storm had reported that Orcadai's tuman was over to the west, following the course of a dried-up river. 'If he won't obey my commands, I'll have to replace him.'

Orcadai thought he should be a khan because he was Burun's son. In fact he had never been more than a fairly mediocre commander, and had made the mistake of siding with his brother Jotan when Jotan had conspired to become the power behind the throne in the days before Jehan had been elected Kha-Khan.

Kubulai unstoppered the k'miss flask and drank from it. Jehangir came up, and climbed over the tail of the cart, dragging a pile of furs with him. 'Eat,' Kubulai said. He took a bowl of stew from the orderly and thrust it into Jehangir's hands. Then he upended the k'miss flask, draining it.

After D'mitri and Jehangir had eaten, the orderly threw sand over the fire and covered it with wet canvas. Kubulai wrapped himself inside his cloak, and then dragged furs up over that. D'mitri was propped against the side of the cart, snoring. The orderly drew furs up from the pile inside the tailgate. He covered D'mitri with them, then lay down and wriggled inside the loose folds.

Kubulai raised his head, and stared over the tail of the cart at the driving snow. The camp was completely quiet, and not a man seemed to be moving. He pulled his cloak up around his shoulders, put his head down, and closed his eyes.

'Wake up,' D'mitri said loudly.

Kubulai sat bolt upright, and D'mitri laughed in his ear. The darkness was smothering, and through the walls of the cart Kubulai could hear the screams of st'lyan and the high voices of men. He threw off the furs and crawled to the tailgate.

The snow outside was up to the bottom of the cart. 'Eat something hot,' D'mitri said.

'Later maybe.' Kubulai kicked at the catches securing the tailgate. The hinges squealed as the flap fell open.

D'mitri was struggling to get his arms into the sleeves of a heavy coat. He shouted past Kubulai at a trooper who was passing, but the man did not appear to hear. A loose st'lyan cantered past. At the head of the cart the orderly was tending a new fire in the tray of sand. The sweet smell of gruel filled the cold air.

'I hate gruel,' D'mitri said. 'Is there nothing else?'

'Lord, I've put honey in it.' The orderly handed him a bowl.

'Here.' D'mitri passed the bowl to Kubulai. 'You have it.' He rummaged under the cloaks and furs and found a bottle of k'miss and drank from it.

Kubulai sipped at the gruel, and swore when the hot rim of the bowl burned his mouth. D'mitri laughed. He climbed over the end of the cart and jumped down into the snow. 'This will slow us down,' he said.

'I can't think why.' Kubulai emptied the bowl. He threw it through the open end of the cart, then bent and dragged his saddle out from between the wheels.

'Somebody catch that brute of a st'lyan!'

The voice was Jehangir's. Kubulai turned and saw that the dun mare was trotting down between the line of carts. Its reins trailed along the ground. A man dashed out in front of the animal, his arms waving. The st'lyan reared, and its hooves lashed out. Kubulai plunged through the men who were rushing up to try to hold the bridle and reins. The mare saw him coming and spun around, legs braced.

'Calm down, damn you. Easy.' Kubulai took the reins out of someone's hand, and then went to the st'lyan's head. 'You perverted pig's dropping.'

The dun licked at his hand. D'mitri was mounting, shouting orders in a ringing voice. Two couriers galloped up, called out their messages, and then rode away.

A drover's whip cracked. Men were backing oxen and p'tar into the yokes. Kubulai forced the bit between the dun's teeth and saddled it. He jerked the girth tight, but the st'lyan would not stand still. When he got up into the saddle it tried to bolt. He reined in hard.

'I'll ride up with the vanguard,' D'mitri said. 'We should meet the Ch'noze today.'

Kubulai nodded. He fought the dun mare over to the side of the nearest wagon and took down a red lantern. The first thousand of the leading tuman was already moving. An orderly ran up, towing Kubulai's remounts. Kubulai hooked the leadline to the traces at the back of his saddle. When he turned he saw that D'mitri was riding away. He reined around and wheeled in a long curve so that he would come up at the side of the moving column of men.

The trees at the far side of the grazing meadow were thick with riders. Each thousand was moving up into position, and the noise they made riding across the hard-packed snow drowned out the wind. Kubulai glanced up at the sky. The sun was a vague crimson splash behind heavy grey clouds. Lanterns flashed everywhere among the moving troopers, and all at once the pace had picked up.

Rocks humped up out of the snow. The dun mare bucked, and Kubulai kicked her hard in the barrel and urged her past. The animal lengthened her stride to pass a line of riding men. Kubulai allowed the reins to lie loose across her neck, and let her have her head.

In the greyness the riding was treacherous. The lines of men were orderly, but the visibility was so poor that if a beast stumbled or a rider fell the men behind would ride right over him before they had a chance to swerve. D'mitri's signals flashed busily ahead, directing the movement of the column away from obstacles. The wind rose steadily, and in the distance a wolf howled.

Suddenly a green lantern flashed in front. It blinked three times, and Kubulai stood in the stirrups and turned. 'Left flank, swing out.' He rode around to the end of the extended wing and galloped the dun forward. The troopers in the leading thousand were urging their st'lyan on, and they hurtled across the snow beside him.

Smoke hung in the air ahead, and Kubulai saw a flicker of light against a stand of trees – a watchfire. Men at the fire were getting to their feet. Ch'noze. He pulled his bow out of its case, dropped his reins, and found an arrow.

The troopers plunged towards the fire. The Ch'noze started to run through the trees. Arrows pursued them, and they fell.

One man was only just getting up when Kubulai reached the treeline. He gave the dun mare her head, and she ran at the Ch'noze and knocked him down. He yelled. When Kubulai reined around he was climbing to his feet again. He had no weapon.

Jehangir rode up at Kubulai's side. The Ch'noze was tall and lanky with long dirty fair hair. He seemed to be readying himself to try to run. Then he looked around and saw the troopers who were riding through the trees, and his shoulders went down. He said something in Ch'noze, and Kubulai frowned, translating the words in his head.

'He's waiting for us to kill him,' Jehangir said. 'Do you want me to do it?'

Any Ch'noze who was taken in rebellion ought to be killed. Kubulai wrinkled his nose. 'Bind his wrists and find him something to ride,' he said. Then he looked at the Ch'noze again. 'It's your lucky day, clansman,' he said in careful dialect. 'What's your name?'

The young man appeared to realise that he was not going to die after all. He stared aggressively. 'I am Han,' he replied. 'My father is war-leader of the Arpid Clan of the northern Ch'noze.'

'Then your father is probably dead.' Kubulai slid his bow back into its case. 'Most of the Ch'noze we killed four days ago were Arpid.'

Jehangir dismounted. He took a length of rope out of one of his saddlebags and tied the captive's wrists with it. A trooper came up leading a loose equine, and Jehangir boosted the Ch'noze up onto its back. 'Don't try to ride off,' he said.

The Ch'noze held onto the pommel of the saddle with his bound hands. He stared past Jehangir at Kubulai. 'Why am I still alive?' he demanded.

'There are things I want to know,' Kubulai told him.

'Then you might as well kill me.' The Arpid's head went back. 'I will tell you nothing.'

Kubulai grinned. 'We'll see about that.' He glanced at Jehangir. 'Put him under guard,' he said in Yek. 'Don't let him harm himself.'

Jehangir nodded. He leaned out of the saddle and caught up the equine's trailing reins. Then he rode away towards the centre of the army, towing the Ch'noze behind him.

Lighter patches were appearing in the sky. Kubulai stood in the stirrups and stared around. Red lantern signals were flashing to the north through the thin screen of trees, and the lines of troopers were straightening once more, moving towards them. The wind shrieked around Kubulai's ears.

'I had a dream last night,' D'mitri said. He sidestepped his roan over until he was riding at Kubulai's side.

'What kind of dream?' Kubulai veered the dun mare around a snow-covered clump of shrubs and let it pick its own way down the steep slope.

'I dreamed that we were on the plain outside Kinsai. It was a battle, and all the peoples of the earth were ranged against us – the Alan, the Ch'noze, the N'pani – men from Y'vrope.'

333

Kubulai drew in on his reins. 'It was only a dream.' The dun wallowed through a deep snowdrift. On the other side there was a ravine. As it started up the side, its hooves skidded on rock and ice, and it stumbled. Kubulai reined in.

'Maybe it was an omen,' D'mitri said. He looked troubled. 'I have had it in my mind since we started this campaign. Maybe the coming of the aliens is to show us that we were never meant to be the masters of this world. We rule, it is true. But how many of the subject races love us?'

D'mitri was talking like a Yek, forgetting that he was Alan. Kubulai kicked his feet free of the stirrups. 'My father says the aliens are here because they have no choice,' he said. 'If that is what has been on your mind, then it is no wonder you dreamed it. Let's stop. I have to clear this rat-eaten nag's hooves again.'

The slopes and the low vegetation were covered with snow which was so white that it hurt Kubulai's eyes to look at it. D'mitri was reining in. Kubulai dismounted and picked up the dun's left forefoot. The ice had balled up in the hoof so that the animal stood on a pad of rock-hard snow.

'No one ever remembers that I am Alan,' D'mitri said. He kicked one foot out of the stirrup and crossed his free leg over the saddle. 'When I heard my people had risen, I reacted like a Yek. I was angry that they had rebelled. We have treated them so well over the years.'

Kubulai knocked the loosened pad of ice out of the dun's hoof. He moved around and raised a hind leg. It was clogged in the same way. When he had cleared it he raised his head. 'I don't think anyone considers that you are Alan now,' he said.

They rode on. Scouts ranged ahead, looking for a

334

sign of the Ch'noze army, and when Kubulai stood in the stirrups and stared back he could see the rest of his own men spread out over the white ground like a huge shadow. Gusts of wind came up and whipped long streamers of snow off the ground across their track. The sun was almost invisible behind a solid grey bank of cloud.

'It's going to snow again,' D'mitri said.

'Maybe.'

Kubulai watched the scudding clouds. If they met up with the Ch'noze during a storm, there would be chaos. He reached into one of his saddlebags and extracted a lump of dried p'tar meat. He carved shavings from it with his d'jaga and chewed them. His stomach growled.

'How far are we from T'tai?'

'I'm not sure.' Kubulai frowned. They should have encountered the Ch'noze by now. The plain ahead dipped and then rose again. One part of it was covered with a series of irregular lumps. He pulled up.

'It looks like a camp,' D'mitri said. He rode up to Kubulai's side. 'But I don't see a fire.'

'Herdsmen maybe,' Kubulai said, but he knew that men would not sit like that – shrouded with snow – not in the hard light of the day. He wrestled his bow out of its case and found an arrow. 'Hold my reins.'

D'mitri reached across. He rode forward, leading the dun mare. At first the st'lyan advanced willingly. Then it stopped, and would not walk on again, even though D'mitri hauled on the bridle. The nearest of the lumps of snow was ten drem or so away. Kubulai grimaced. He dismounted, holding his bow at the ready, and paced forward. He gave the mound a nudge – it was a man. The snow cracked open and a herdsman's frozen

335

corpse fell from the shell in which it had been encased. D'mitri's roan reared and screamed.

The dun was attempting to bolt. D'mitri clung to the reins, but he was hampered by the need to control his own mount. Kubulai snatched at the dun's bridle, grasped the great horn, and hauled downwards. 'These are Gepids,' he said. 'We must be near the Ch'noze army. They were guarding a herd, I think, and froze to death.' He led both st'lyan around the obstacle, then mounted once more and kicked the dun into a canter.

Early in the afternoon they rode up to the walls of T'tai. Ch'noze banners hung from the walls, and the people lining the walls jeered and screamed insults at the troopers as they massed opposite the gates.

'Damn them,' D'mitri said. 'We should have known they would do this.'

In fact it had not been predictable. Kubulai had known that T'tai was under siege, and had expected it to hold out until relief arrived. Briefly he wondered what had happened to the Yek garrison.

More men were riding out from between the hills to the west. 'That's Orcadai.' D'mitri pointed. 'At least he got here when he said he would.'

Kubulai grunted. T'tai was situated on the coast, and the external wall ran right around a small bay which was its main harbour, enclosing it completely. The army washed like a flood past the bases of the buttresses which supported the wall, and the troopers encircled everything – the city, the wall, and the rise on which it was constructed. The main gate was tall, and it was set between two high towers. Flags and pennants flew from the battlements and from the roofs of the buildings near the gate. Just below the causeway lay a cluster of dead and frozen men – most of them Ch'noze. Kubulai realised that the enemy had only just managed to gain entry to the city before the arrival of the Yek, and he cursed himself for not moving the army on at a faster pace.

'Kubulai.' Orcadai jogged up through the ranks of D'mitri's escort. He was riding a bay st'lyan with a silver gilded horn. His face glowed with exertion, and he gave Kubulai a paternal smile. 'Where do you want me to camp my men? I thought you would be inside already.'

If Orcadai had maintained better contact during the move north they might have been able to surprise the Ch'noze. Kubulai stared at him coldly. 'Camp at the western end of the wall.'

'It shouldn't be too hard to storm,' D'mitri said in a placatory tone.

A few hundred Yek had held T'tai for over two months against intermittent siege. Kubulai wondered how hard the Ch'noze had tried to get into the city, and why they had not turned to fight in the open when the Yek had approached. A catapult on the right-hand tower of the gate crashed, and a single stone arched through the air and thumped into the ground near the end of the causeway. Fire arrows popped from the battlements.

'Surely they know snow doesn't burn.' Orcadai stared, his expression amused.

'I think they are frightened,' D'mitri said.

'They have cause to be.' Kubulai allowed his reins to fall loose across his st'lyan's neck. 'When we attack I want you to send the Alan conscripts in first. Give them a choice. They can take T'tai or die.'

Orcadai opened his eyes wide. 'I would hate to share a siege with you,' he said.

'We won't siege it.' Kubulai reined around and walked the dun down the slope in the direction of the main gate. Men were already rigging tents beyond catapult range. A wagon rolled up and an orderly started to throw lengths of treated canvas out onto the snow. D'mitri rode up and dismounted. He threw his reins to a waiting trooper, and then he looked round. 'Are we going to attack straight away?'

Kubulai slid out of the saddle. 'We'll wait until Kadan gets here.'

'Orcadai thinks you blame him because we didn't get here in time to catch the Ch'noze in the open,' D'mitri said.

It was not a question. Kubulai wrinkled his nose. 'I should have given him more specific orders,' he said. 'If he is feeling all that penitent, he can lead the main attack.'

'It's not really a city,' Kadan said. 'Just a large town.'

'It could be troublesome all the same.' Kubulai extended his bare toes towards the fire. 'We need to deal with it before we move on, or else the Ch'noze will use it as a base to attack us from the rear.'

'In that case we had better take it quickly.' Kadan poured k'miss into two cups. He gave one to Kubulai. 'If the rest of the clans come up while we are sitting here at the coast we will be in trouble. Either way it looks as if they are trying to trap us between the two halves of their army. It's a nice strategy.'

'I'm pleased you're impressed.' Kubulai swirled the k'miss in his cup, then drank. Somebody was advising the Ch'noze, and had provided the clans with an

338

incentive to fight together. He sipped at the k'miss. 'Name of God, you've put honey in it. How can you ruin good k'miss like that?'

'I'm getting old.' Kadan grinned.

'Tell me when you have saddle sores.'

Kadan laughed softly. 'I think we should call a truce while we are fighting this war,' he said. 'I'm not sure why we're feuding anyway.'

'I thought you started it because you were bored,' Kubulai said. He tensed himself, ready to leap if Kadan attacked. Kadan raised his cup and drank, watching Kubulai over the rim. Simultaneously they looked away. 'All right,' Kubulai said. 'Truce.'

'Good.' Kadan leaned forward. 'Now tell me how you want to carry out the attack. The wall is made of stone, so we can't burn it.'

'The gate is wood, though.' Kubulai drank more of the k'miss. The sweet taste made him pucker his lips. 'I think we ought to set fire to it. We can try an assault on the bastion at the eastern end of the wall at the same time. It's the weakest place. If we burn out the gate the Ch'noze will have to post more men to guard it. Maybe they will weaken their strength along the wall enough for us to force our way in.'

Kadan finished his k'miss. He set his cup aside. 'It's not going to be all that easy. It's a steep ride up to the gate.'

'I have men out cutting battering rams,' Kubulai said. 'And we are making ladders. We can scale the wall.'

'The conscripts first, of course.'

Kubulai nodded and showed his teeth. 'I thought I would give Orcadai the attack on the gate.'

A courier was picking his way through the camp towards them. Kubulai stood up so that he could be

339

seen, and the man trotted his st'lyan over and saluted. 'Lord, I have a message from the commander of the scouts. The Ch'noze army is assembling on the plain to the east of N'tan.'

Kadan's head came up. 'How reliable is this?'

'Khan, it's certain. I spoke to a hundred commander who was sent to find them. He rode around their outposts only six days ago.'

Kubulai gestured to an orderly. 'Go and find D'mitri S'zltan.'

'They won't stay where they are,' Kadan said. 'If they want to keep us at a disadvantage, they should come east.'

'Do you suppose they know that?' Kubulai looked round.

'Probably the people who are advising them do.' Kadan frowned. 'Damn the aliens,' he said. 'I hope your father knows what he's doing.'

D'mitri strode down the line of tents and ducked in through the lean-to which Kadan had erected in front of his fire. He said, 'If you have sent for me to tell me about the Ch'noze, I have heard. It's all through the camp.'

Kubulai sat down again. 'Take half a tuman and go west. I want at least a day's warning if the Ch'noze are moving against us.'

'I'll take my honour guard and the thousand of your father's tuman I commanded before Pesth,' D'mitri said. 'That's nearly fifteen hundred men. I don't need half a tuman. Commanding them will only slow me down.'

'If you're caught against the mountains...'

'I'll try not to be, but if I am, I can escape better with fifteen hundred than I can with five thousand.

340

We'll be more mobile.'

A great shout went up from the wall of the city near the main gate. The gate cracked open, and a handful of men rode through. The sun was bright, and Kubulai shaded his eyes with his hand so that he could see. An escort of Ch'noze warriors was riding down the causeway, guidons on their lance heads. One man bore the emblem which signified a truce. The city ramparts were swarming with people watching.

'Somebody should go and find out what they want,' Kadan said.

'I'll go.' Kubulai struggled his feet into his boots. He borrowed the courier's st'lyan and rode out of the camp towards the end of the causeway. The whole Yek camp was watching. Men had come out of their tents, and they were crowded along the arc of the picket line so that they could see. Orcadai was sitting his st'lyan at the bottom of the path which led up to the causeway. 'Where are you going?' he demanded.

Kubulai gestured at the oncoming Ch'noze, and when Orcadai saw them he looked surprised. Kubulai rode up the slope at a walk.

The Ch'noze had drawn up, waiting. There were ten of them, all clad in mail or boiled leather. Their unbound hair was blown out by the wind.

'Do you speak our tongue?' The foremost Ch'noze sidestepped his mount as Kubulai rode up onto the causeway.

Kubulai reined in. 'Well enough. Say whatever you have come to say.'

The leader of the party was a gaunt man in late middle age whose facial tattoos were faded so that they looked like lines on his face. 'I want to speak to Burun Khan.' He walked his equine forward.

'Burun is not here.'

'Alexei Khan, then.'

'He is not here either.'

The Ch'noze had slate-grey eyes. He stared past Kubulai in the direction of the camp. 'Are you a man of rank?'

'I am Khan of K'chin.'

The other men in the escort started to protest that they would be satisfied only with someone in authority. They would not speak to a lesser man. Kubulai drew in on his reins as if he intended to turn and ride away. The leader gestured angrily at his men to silence them. Then he looked back. 'How are you called?'

'My name is Kubulai.'

'Alexei's son.' The Ch'noze nodded. 'Well enough. I have ridden out to warn you to ride away. The whole Ch'noze army is coming to crush you – a hundred thousand men.'

Kubulai laughed softly. 'Even if what you tell me is the truth, it is no deterrent. But as it happens your army is several days west, and there are not that many clansmen in Ch'nozia. In any case we will take T'tai tomorrow or the next day.'

'Not if we have anything to do with it!' A man in the middle of the escort shouted. His comrades nodded angrily. One waved his lance. Kubulai shrugged, amused, and took up his reins again.

'You are wasting my time,' he said. 'I thought you had come out to offer surrender.'

The Ch'noze tried to speak, but his words were drowned out by the roar of anger from his men. When he could be heard again he said, 'Do you have the authority to agree terms?'

Kubulai raised his eyebrows. 'You are in rebellion,' he said, 'and you have broken the Yasa. If you want to give yourselves up, I will consider it.'

'Never!' The man who had shouted before rose in the stirrups.

The leader said, 'Withdraw your army from Ch'nozia and we will make peace. You can see that the clans are united. We want to elect our own ruler. We want to decide our own laws.'

'Indeed.' Kubulai showed his teeth. 'I'm sure we can manage to establish peace here without your assistance. Surrender now and you will live. If you do not, we will sack your city and burn it to the ground. Your people will become slaves.'

The Ch'noze looked appalled by the prospect. Then he shook his head stubbornly. 'We shall never surrender,' he said.

It was as if the words were a signal. The man who had shouted at Kubulai aimed his lance and charged. The leader reined around hard, throwing up his arm to prevent the attack, but the younger man ignored the attempted intervention. He set himself to pierce Kubulai through the chest.

Kubulai spun the st'lyan around. The Ch'noze tried to follow, his lance wavering. It swiped at the air above Kubulai's head.

Several arrows thudded into the Ch'noze. One took him in the chest, another in the throat, and he fell out of the saddle and sprawled on his back on the hard ground. A roar of outrage had started up from the Yek camp. Men along the perimeter were moving forward, weapons out.

Kubulai rode to the edge of the causeway and threw up a hand to stay them. Then he glanced back at the leader. 'If I let my comrades near you, you are all dead men.'

343

'But we are here under an emblem of truce,' the Ch'noze protested. 'Your men killed his father. He was mad for revenge –'

'He was a rebel. I never met a Ch'noze who could be trusted.' Kubulai stared coldly. 'Ride away before I give my men leave to deal with you.' He spun the st'ylan round and galloped down the slope to the camp. The men on the outskirts were cheering as he rode past, and their officers were struggling to keep order. Kubulai slowed the st'lyan, then rode her through the crush to Kadan's tent.

'What was all that about?' Kadan asked. 'What did they want?'

'My blood for one thing.' Kubulai dismounted. He tossed the reins to the courier. 'Terms for another.'

Kadan had a k'miss flask in one hand, and he was holding a half-filled cup in the other. The spirit slopped from it. 'What kind of terms?'

'Nothing acceptable.' Kubulai took the cup out of Kadan's hand and drank from it.

'And are they going to surrender?'

'Of course not.'

'Move up, damn you!' Kubulai lashed at the heads of the men who were crowding towards the ladders with his reins. Smoke was billowing down over the wall of the city, and he could see nothing past the crenellations of the battlements. The shouts of the men drowned his voice. He drew breath, ready to shout again, and tasted the sickly sweetness of the smoke on the air. Something just beyond the wall was on fire – the early fire arrows had started it maybe. 'Move!'

The Yek were on foot, crowded together. They

344

pressed forward. Behind them on a piece of raised ground were other troopers, still mounted. Kubulai reined around and rode up to them. He saw Jehangir at one end of the line. 'Fire faster. Clear the top of the wall. There are still Ch'noze up there.'

'We can't see it, Khan.'

Along the wall close to the gate men cheered – a great roar which tore at the sky. Kubulai stared back in that direction, and then he rounded on Jehangir.

'What do you mean, you can't see it? You know it's there, don't you? Tell your men to shoot faster.'

The wind shifted suddenly. The smoke blew up away from the wall and Kubulai saw that there were now only a few Ch'noze left on top of it. Above the level of the wall the sky was black with arrows.

A courier came racing along the depression at the base of the wall. He saluted Kubulai. 'Khan, the main gate has collapsed and we are forcing our way inside.'

'Good.' Kubulai stood in the stirrups. 'Jehangir, send half of your men to the ladders. Then take the rest and go round to the gate. Hurry up, or there won't be anything left to plunder by the time you get inside.'

Half the troopers abandoned their st'lyan. They went down to the foot of the wall. The ladders were solid with moving men. Kubulai hauled the dun mare's head around, then lashed her with his reins so that she bolted across the snow-covered ground towards the gate. A tower on one side of the entrance was streaming smoke. Charred embers lay on the cobbles, and a section of timber hung at an angle from a hinge. Kubulai forced his way through the hurrying men and rode inside. A wide street at the rear of the bailey was packed with struggling troopers. Smoke rolled across their heads.

'Khan.'

One of Kadan's officers was on the roof above Kubulai's head. He found a handhold and leaned out so that he could be heard. 'The Ch'noze have thrown up hurdles and they have pushed carts into the end of the street. Make everyone push. We can clear it if we -'

A roar from the end of the street announced the removal of the obstruction. Men started to move forward.

'I was outside the wall.' Kubulai gazed up. 'What is happening here?'

'There are fires all through this part of the city.' The officer got to his knees, and stared across the roofs. 'Men are looting in this quarter, even though we aren't in control of it yet.'

Kubulai nodded. He urged his st'lyan forward, and then suddenly it pulled up again.

'Watch your heads!' Someone shouted a warning. A volley of arrows thudded into the fence at Kubulai's side. Then a firearm banged, and he looked up, outraged. The Ch'noze had climbed up onto the flat roofs of the buildings on the left side of the street. Only one man had a gun, but Kubulai marked him. He nocked an arrow and fired, and the Ch'noze who had moved in front of the man with the gun was hit in the chest. He tumbled over the edge of the roof onto the heaving mass of the troopers below. Most of the Ch'noze had shields. They ducked behind them, but other troopers were shooting now. An arrow went through a shield, and the man who was holding it went down. Kubulai looked for the Ch'noze who had used the firearm. Whatever its source, the man who had taught a Ch'noze to break the Yasa merited disembowlment.

A barrier at the head of the street crashed as it was torn aside. Every man with a bow was letting fly at the Ch'noze now, but enemy arrows still rained down, and every so often the single gun banged. A trooper in front of Kubulai gasped and toppled from the saddle. Kubulai yanked another arrow from his case and fired again. The crush was easing. Suddenly something slammed into his thigh just below the skirt of his coat. The men on both sides of him suddenly surged forward. The dun mare broke into a trot and followed them.

He had been shot. The bullet had gone right through his thigh, but it had not penetrated the saddle. Kubulai put his hand down and felt the metal lodged in the leather. His wound hurt. Pain throbbed up from it. He eased his foot from the stirrup and saw that his breeches and the side of the saddle were soaked with dark red blood. Kubulai pressed his hand over the hole to stop the flow. A loose st'lyan trotted up beside the dun, and the two animals ran together to the end of the street. They crowded into one another, trapping Kubulai's leg, and he yelled and swore at the agony in his injured thigh.

The troopers ahead were charging out into what looked like a marketplace. At the far side of it was the wall of the citadel. A Yek guidon flapped from the wall. Orcadai was standing on the cobbles in front of the doorway. His face was streaming blood. 'Our garrison is still inside,' he shouted. 'The Ch'noze couldn't get to them.'

Kubulai waved a hand in acknowledgement, and then he rode on. A woman screamed shrilly from a

347

sidestreet, and he heard a Yek warcry. He reined in. The bleeding seemed to have stopped now, but the leg of his breeches was soaked with gore, and he could feel the wetness of it inside his boot.

There were barricades across the end of the next street. Men were waiting behind them with bows and swords in their hands. Kubulai sidestepped the dun into a gateway. A crowd of troopers charged past. They ran right up to the carts and furniture which were crammed between the houses and hurled themselves at the defenders, overwhelming them. Pain thumped abruptly in Kubulai's leg. He glanced down and saw that the wound was pouring blood again. Quickly he slapped his hand over the entry hole. The gate was opening. Kubulai glanced back over his shoulder. A youth came out into the street, a dagger in his hand. He slashed at the st'lyan's legs.

Kubulai dived off the dun's back. He knocked the youth through the open gateway into the courtyard beyond. The collision brought him down on his injured leg, and he gasped. The youth was scrabbling away across the flagstones, the dagger still clutched in one hand. Kubulai lurched to his feet. He saw that several Ch'noze had got up onto the roof of one of the houses across the street. He snatched at the dun's reins and dragged her into the yard. Then he tore his bowcase from the saddle. The men coming along the street were dodging into doorways to avoid the arrows sleeting down. Kubulai pulled out his bow and nocked an arrow. He let fly at a man who was silhouetted against the skyline. Orcadai ran into the end of the street. He yelled something and pointed at the Ch'noze on the roof. Kubulai nocked another arrow.

348

Suddenly he sensed a movement at his back. He turned swiftly and saw that the youth had crept forward. His hand was coming around, the dagger extended. Kubulai lunged away to the side. The dun screamed and its hooves rattled on the stones. Kubulai kicked out, knocking the youth back so that he banged into the wall. He raised the dagger and started forward again. Kubulai remembered the arrow in his bow and fired. Then he turned to look out into the street. Arrows were whistling across the rooftops. The Ch'noze who were not killed ducked out of sight.

Kubulai looked round the yard. His injured leg gave a single great pulse of pain. A woman with grey hair came out of a doorway. She saw the youth Kubulai had killed, and raised her hands to her face, wailing her grief.

'My son,' she cried out. 'You've killed him.'

Kubulai dragged himself across the courtyard. He pulled his arrow out of the youth's chest. 'I would have let him live,' he said, 'only he tried to come up on me.'

The woman bent and took the dagger out of her son's hand. She slashed at Kubulai, but he knocked her away. He retreated towards the gate, but she did not attempt to follow. Her hands clasped over the hilt of the dagger, and she stabbed herself. 'My son will need me to show him the way through the shades,' she said.

The blade did not go in cleanly. It turned on a rib, and blood spurted from the wound. Kubulai put his bow down and caught her as she fell. He remembered that the Ch'noze believed that there was a pathway to Heaven, and thought that to die so was foolish. 'That isn't the way to do it,' he said.

She stared at the blood. Some of it was on her hands,

349

and she wiped them on her skirts. 'It hurts,' she said.

'What did you expect?' Kubulai asked her.

He laid her on the flagstones, then picked up the dagger and jammed the point into the wooden frame of a bench. After that he staggered across to the gate again. Troopers were racing up the street, yipping triumphantly. When he turned back the woman was dead. He stared at his surroundings. There seemed to be nothing worth plundering. Close to the door there was a window. He went and looked through it. Gold cups lined a shelf. He eyed them, and found that he was hanging onto the window frame. Spots danced in front of his eyes. He felt sick, and swallowed. Suddenly his legs gave way and he fell.

He was lying flat on his back when he woke up. A tall woman with hair the colour of ripe corn was leaning over him, a bowl in her hand. Kubulai swiped at her. The bowl was full of gruel. It splashed across the bedcover. The woman backed away, a patient look on her face. She was Ch'noze. Kubulai looked around the room. 'Where am I?'

'Inside T'tai.' She put the bowl down and washed her hands in a basin which was on a table beside the window.

'T'tai.' Kubulai lay back. 'We didn't burn it all then. How long have I been sick?'

'A day and a half.'

'Hunh.' Kubulai stretched. His thigh felt tight, and he guessed that the wound had closed and was healing.

The door opened and Kadan came into the room. 'Good,' he said. 'You're awake.'

Kubulai stared at him. 'I got shot in the thigh. Lead must be poison.'

'The wound was clean.' Kadan looked from Kubulai to the woman. 'Get him something to eat.' He glanced back at Kubulai. 'You bled more than any man I've ever seen. The stones of the yard where my men found you were covered with it.'

The woman went out of the room. Moments later she returned. She had another bowl in her hands. Kubulai eyed the contents. He said, 'If that's gruel, you can take it away again.'

'It's stew.'

Kadan sat down on the end of the bed. 'I was just starting to get used to being in command,' he said. 'Why didn't you stop when you were hit? If you'd closed the wound, you wouldn't have bled so.'

'I was busy at the time.' Kubulai reached out and took the bowl from the woman's hands. 'I assume the Ch'noze haven't come east yet.'

Kadan lifted one shoulder. 'They're about three days' march away.' He glanced at the bowl and then at the woman. 'If you give him that he will get sick again.'

Kubulai could see that the woman was trying to formulate a reply. After a moment she gave up and shook her head. 'No.'

'It will be up to you to clean the floor if he does,' Kadan said disapprovingly. 'Leave us now.'

She raised her eyebrows. Then she shrugged and went out through the door. Kubulai stared after her. He caught Kadan's eye. 'Does she belong to you?'

'You can have her if you want her.' Kadan wrinkled his nose. 'You're in the western part of the city. The rest of it burned during the sack. If we want to garrison this area again we will have to rebuild.'

It did not make sense to burn down a city which

would have to be used again. Kubulai shook his head. 'We'll build somewhere else. We ought to settle Yek on this land when the rebellion is over.'

Kadan shrugged noncommittally. He stared away out of the window and Kubulai used his talons to fork meat out of the bowl of stew. He chewed slowly. When he was finished he laid the bowl aside. Kadan was still looking out of the window. Then his head came round. 'You ought to rest,' he said.

'You can command until tomorrow.' Kubulai drew his knees up. He did not feel sick, but he supposed that if he had lost a lot of blood he was lucky to be alive. An ordinary wound would have closed straight away. Because he had been careless he had nearly bled to death. It would have been a stupid way to die. He eyed Kadan. 'How big is the Ch'noze army which is moving against us?'

'Fewer than fifty thousand men,' Kadan responded. 'Most of their strength seems to be Gepid and Tatar.'

The sky outside the window was blue. Kubulai craned to see out. 'What is the weather doing?'

'It hasn't snowed again,' Kadan said. 'But it's still cold.' He stood up. 'I could fight this battle. You have been sick.'

'Not that sick.' Kubulai gave Kadan a level stare. 'Send Orcadai to see me.'

Kadan pursed his lips. 'As you wish,' he said. He went over to the door, and then he turned. 'Do you want the woman?'

'What's her name?'

'Oh.' Kadan frowned. 'Chan, I think. Ask her when you see her.' He left the room.

When he woke up again it was dark. The woman was

in the room. Kubulai could smell the scent of her body. He spoke her name and she started up.

'Light the lamps,' Kubulai said.

Her clothing rustled when she moved. She had been sitting in a chair beside the window. The taper she brought glowed like a slow match. She applied it to the wick of the lamp, and it flared. 'I thought you were asleep,' she said.

'I have slept enough. Who are you?'

She produced a nervous smile. 'Chan, the daughter of Fong. My father was the harbour master here.'

'Was? Is he dead?'

She nodded. Her eyes were expressionless. 'You're in my house.'

'Oh?' Kubulai wondered if her father had been killed when the Yek had stormed the city, but he did not ask. 'What family have you?'

The woman was lighting a second lamp. She wheeled on him. 'No family. My father is dead; my mother is dead; my sister is gone – nobody knows where – and I have to take care of you. They tell me I belong to you. Is that true?'

Kubulai had been wary of her, thinking that she was about to try an attack. Now he relaxed. In this mood she would not attempt anything. He smiled, amused that he had been worried about a woman. Her voice was low and heavy when she spoke again.

'You killed them all,' she said. 'Everything burned, people trampled, and the houses looted. Now there is a curfew at sunset, and everyone has to be indoors or they may be killed. The blood ran down the gutters like water. I saw it.'

'Not everybody died.' Kubulai watched her face. 'You are still alive. The rest would be too if the men who led you had surrendered.'

She made a face. 'I'm alive because I was afraid,' she said. 'When your men broke down the door I fainted.' She laughed in self-mockery, and Kubulai flinched at the sound.

He sat up. 'The Ch'noze had protection under our law,' he said. 'Was independence so attractive?'

A frown worked its way onto her face. 'We had the right to be free,' she said.

'Free to do what?' Kubulai demanded. 'We only kept a garrison here to prevent you from slaughtering one another. The freedom the Ch'noze seek is an illusion.'

Her head went back. 'I would expect you to say that,' she said haughtily.

Kubulai grinned at her. 'Stop trying to make me angry. It's against our law to harm a slave.'

'Do brutes have laws?'

'I don't know. The Yasa is good law.'

'I hate you.'

'Just me?' Kubulai laughed. 'Insulting me will achieve nothing. Use your common sense.'

'Don't laugh at me.'

'You are very amusing.' A cup of k'miss had been left on the table at the side of the bed. Kubulai reached for it and drank. Setting it down again he missed the edge of the table. The cup fell, the k'miss splashing across the floor.

'Now look what you have done,' she said. She got a cloth out of a cabinet on the wall and mopped up the liquid. Kubulai lay on his side and watched her. Eventually she stood up. 'Am I your property?' she asked in a low voice.

Kubulai shrugged. 'Mine or Kadan's.'

The woman grimaced. 'He is a monster. You are all

ugly. Flat faces and tilted amber eyes.'

'Hunh.' Kubulai thought about the women he knew, grinning.

'You think it's funny,' she said.

'It is. Our own women think we're ugly.'

'Do they? I'm not surprised.'

'Few men are considered handsome,' Kubulai said. 'I think it depends on one's point of view. To us the Ch'noze aren't very attractive, you know. You are too tall, and your skin is too white. Your nose is the wrong shape – it's too long.'

She looked offended. She gazed at the cloth in her hand, then dropped it in a bowl on the table by the window. 'Am I expected to sleep with you?'

Kubulai stared at her, surprised. Then he realised that she had said it to gain the initiative. He was tempted to say yes to see what she would do. Finally he shook his head. 'We have laws about that too,' he said. 'It's your choice.'

'They won't come to us,' Orcadai said. 'We have beaten them too often.'

Kubulai stood in the stirrups to ease his back. Kadan at his side was trimming the point of one talon with the blade of his d'jaga. His reins lay across his st'lyan's neck. Behind them a full tuman rested their animals.

'Jehangir.' Kubulai waved an arm. He disliked the emptiness of the landscape. They were two days west of T'tai, and they had seen not a hoofprint – no trace of the Ch'noze.

Jehangir trotted up from the head of the escort. Kubulai pointed ahead. 'Take five hundred men and ride advance guard. Push them until you're half a day in front.'

'Yes, Khan.' Jehangir reined around. He galloped his st'lyan back towards the tuman. His voice rang out and men jogged out of the orderly mass of riders to form a separate column alongside. Kubulai turned, running his eye across the men around him.

'Orcadai. Take another five hundred and ride north. Move parallel with the coast, but don't get so close that you will be trapped there if you meet the Ch'noze. Stretch out but stay in contact.'

Orcadai stared, and then he turned in the saddle. 'Kadan?'

Kadan nodded. Kubulai did not look at him. Orcadai drew in on his reins and spun his st'lyan around. He trotted away along the front rank, gesturing to hundred commanders. Kubulai waited until Orcadai's hand moved to indicate a man from the tuman which was normally commanded by D'mitri. Then he shouted, 'None from D'mitri's tuman. Take others.'

Orcadai brought his mare to a standstill. He looked in Kadan's direction. Kubulai brought the ends of his reins down across his st'lyan's shoulders. The dun leapt forward into the space between Kadan and Orcadai.

'Take others, Orcadai,' Kubulai said.

A soft laugh cut across the silence. 'Do as he says, Orcadai,' Kadan said.

Kubulai looked over his shoulder towards a group of thousand commanders. 'Yazan, take five hundred and ride rearguard. Sebu, another five hundred and run a screen between us and the mountains to the south.'

Two burly officers from D'mitri's tuman swung out and started to collect men. Jehangir was already riding away. Orcadai trotted his st'lyan up to Kubulai.

'The customary signals, I suppose.'

'Of course.' Kubulai nodded. 'Or do you need to be reminded what they are?'

Orcadai went crimson. Kubulai prodded the dun mare in the side with the toe of his boot and rode past him. The shadow of the standard-bearer's signal pole arched out across the snow. Commands echoed down the lines, and all at once Kubulai was flanked on both sides by files of Yek troopers. Kadan rode up, his face expressionless. 'You sent D'mitri out to find the Ch'noze,' he said. 'Don't you trust him?'

The snow sparkled under the glare of the sun. Kubulai narrowed his eyes against it, smiling. 'It's the Ch'noze I don't trust,' he said. 'D'mitri is in contact with the main part of their army. They could try to outflank us.'

All the indications from D'mitri's scouts suggested that the Ch'noze were withdrawing ahead of the Yek advance. It was unlike the clansmen to avoid a fight, and Kubulai guessed that their advisers had persuaded them to some kind of strategy designed to take the Yek by surprise.

'You begin to remind me of Burun,' Kadan said.

It was not intended as a compliment, but Kubulai showed his teeth in a grim smile. 'Good,' he said. 'If Orcadai crosses me again, I'll remind you of him even more.'

The Ch'noze continued to move away to the west, and a courier from D'mitri brought a message to the effect that he was following them. Kubulai camped early that day to rest the st'lyan and to let Jehangir get far enough in front. A stream of messengers dashed between the main body and the flanks, and the

357

tumans which were now in a single column in the centre milled unhappily through patches of trees. The snow was still thick on the ground, and Kubulai spent half the night making sure that there was enough grazing in the meadows. Where the snow was thin enough the st'lyan pawed through it to get at the grass. Elsewhere they stripped the bark from the trees and ate what foliage had survived the onset of the colder weather. Kubulai went to sleep satisfied that the animals could forage well. The night was moonless, and a rising wind rustled the tops of the trees where they had camped.

The following day the army camped after nightfall. Now that the camp routine had been fixed the orderlies had the st'lyan turned out to graze and the cooking pots over the fires before Kubulai had walked the stiffness out of his knees. Kadan remained uncommunicative, and both nights he sat at a fire with his officers. The second night Kubulai went looking for him. The fire was in a clearing in the middle of a stand of tall oak trees. Kadan sat on his saddle on one side of it, shovelling half-cooked gruel into his mouth. Kubulai stood just beyond the light of the fire until the men on both sides of Kadan noticed he was there.

One man stood and bowed, and the rest nodded. Kadan lifted his head, and stared coldly.

The Ch'noze captive came up to the fire, his arms full of firewood. His face was slack with fatigue, but when he saw Kubulai his eyes became murderous. Kubulai laughed at both of them and then he turned on his heel and strode back to his own fire.

That night before he slept he walked around the entire camp. A thin crescent of moon had risen over the tops of the trees, and the snow lay blue beneath it.

To the west the long plain was like a silver sheet which seemed to stretch away into infinity. Kubulai stared across it, bracing himself against the weariness he suddenly felt. The wind sighed in his ears. He trudged back to his fire, following the trails broken by the st'lyan as much as he could. Then he rolled himself in his cloak and slept.

He woke shivering. It was far colder than the morning before, but some men were already up. They stamped their feet and slapped their arms against their sides to get warm, and their breath smoked in the air.

Kubulai sat up. A light fall of snow had drifted across his cloak during the night, and it had melted from the heat of his body, then frozen into a crust. He stood up, crackling and shedding ice. The cold struck him in the face like a blow, and he gasped.

'Eat up and get mounted!'

Kadan's voice echoed through the trees. An orderly at Kubulai's fire was heating a pot of stew. Han, the Ch'noze captive, came up leading Kubulai's st'lyan. Kubulai held out his hand and took the lead-rope. The dun was unsettled by the extreme cold. Kubulai thrust the doubled end of the rope into his belt and picked up the bridle and put it under his armpit so that it would warm up. The orderly got up from the fire. He picked up Kubulai's saddle and slung it onto the dun's back.

The st'lyan reared and almost dragged Kubulai off his feet. He staggered, grabbing at a tree for support. The dun plunged, throwing itself back on its haunches. Its hooves thrashed the air above Kubulai's head. He wrapped one arm around the tree and caught the end of the rope, bracing his feet apart. The orderly dashed up. When the dun reared again he caught the

359

near foreleg at the fetlock and threw his weight against the dun's shoulder. The st'lyan crashed down on its side. Kubulai leapt across flailing hindlegs to sit on its head.

Somebody was laughing. Kubulai looked up and saw that Kadan was sitting his chestnut a short distance away. He was tossing a snowball from one hand to the other. Kubulai glanced at the dun's rump. A splash of snow marked it. Kubulai jumped up.

Kadan cocked his arm to hurl the second snowball. He backed his st'lyan up. Kubulai took several running paces and hurled himself at Kadan, knocking him out of the saddle. Kadan rolled on the ground and the chestnut bolted.

'Somebody catch that beast.'

Kubulai gestured towards the departing st'lyan. Kadan was sprawled on his back. He looked stunned.

The dun was on its feet again. The orderly was holding it by the head. Kubulai took the rope and waved the man away. He saddled quickly, then mounted. A trooper had recovered Kadan's chestnut and was leading it back. A dark bruise was already colouring Kadan's cheek. Kubulai rode up past him. 'Did you bump into something, Khan?'

'Yes. But I will be revenged.' Kadan smiled so that his teeth showed.

'Indeed.' Kubulai brought his whip down so that the thongs snapped in front of Kadan's face. He gave the dun its head. It had gone only a few strides before it shied. Kubulai wrestled with the reins. Something struck him between the shoulder blades. He knew it was a snowball, and he galloped the dun out of range.

Han's equine was about ten hands shorter than the

dun. When he rode at Kubulai's side his head was level with the st'lyan's saddle, and Kubulai had to look down to watch the expression on his face.

'Your army is running away,' Kubulai said. 'If your leaders had any courage they would turn and fight.'

The Ch'noze had a long face which was all angles. A flash of something appeared in his eyes, and then it was gone again. 'When they are ready, they will turn and crush you,' he said.

'Oh?' Kubulai gave him a condescending smile. 'And when will that be?'

'Soon.' Han said.

Kubulai wrinkled his nose. 'Maybe the Gepids are fighting the Tatars,' he suggested.

'The clans have agreed peace.' The Ch'noze gave Kubulai a haughty stare. 'They are united against the common enemy.'

It was not a phrase any Ch'noze would have thought up for himself. 'United by what?' Kubulai asked curiously.

A wary look appeared on Han's face. He compressed his lips stubbornly.

Kubulai sighed. 'I think it happened this way,' he said. 'Some foreigners came to the Ch'noze. They convinced the clans that the only way to rid themselves of the Yek was to combine. It's my guess that they went to the Gepids or the Tatars first, because the lesser clans were sent out with the part of the army which came to meet us. Probably the foreigners told the war-leaders that they would give them help to make themselves the rulers of this land, but the Gepids and the Tatars thought they would be clever. They let your clansmen expend their strength fighting us. If you had beaten us, they would have fallen on you while you were still weak from the battle. You didn't beat us, so probably they hope you have killed enough of us so that the odds are in their favour. Either way they don't have to worry about your clan any more. After the war is over the Gepids will attack the Tatars. Maybe the foreigners have promised to help them to win.'

The colour had gone from Han's cheeks. He said, 'How do you know all this?'

'Oh well.' Kubulai gave him an oblique look. 'The first part we were already sure of. The men who came to the Ch'noze are aliens from another world. They don't really want to help you. They only want to cause trouble for us.'

'To what end?' The Ch'noze looked puzzled.

He had not denied any of it, Kubulai thought. He drew in on the dun's reins. A st'lyan's pace was longer than an equine's, and so the rhythms of the two animals' movements were different.

'Eventually they want to make themselves masters of this world,' Kubulai said. 'Whoever is left after the war is over, they will have only one clan to deal with in the future instead of several. At present it's good for us, because once we have beaten the Ch'noze army, we will be able to bring peace to this land.'

Han looked down his nose. 'You're very confident,' he said sourly.

Kubulai laughed softly. 'We have reason to be,' he responded. 'If the clans were really united our task would be difficult. We are fielding fewer men for one thing. But the war-leaders can't resist settling old scores. That's why the Arpid were allowed to run up against us. What proportion of the Ch'noze strength have we destroyed so far – maybe a third? I should think the aliens who are advising your commanders are tearing their hair out. I never knew a Ch'noze who was willing to listen to good advice.'

A courier came down the line. He reined in beside Kadan, shouting. Kadan gestured, and the man rode away.

'You are saying we have been betrayed,' Han said in a low voice. 'You are telling me my father died for nothing.'

Kadan was reining around. Kubulai glanced back over his shoulder at the Ch'noze. 'Your own leaders have betrayed you,' he said. 'But it is the aliens you should blame.' He kicked the dun into a trot and rode up the side of the column to meet Kadan.

'D'mitri says the Ch'noze have separated into two armies,' Kadan reported. 'Most of them are waiting for us at the place where the little river winds across the plain. The rest are moving around to the south. It's just as you suspected. They are going to try to outflank us.'

Kubulai nodded. 'Detach one tuman as we planned. Recall Jehangir and Orcadai, and send to D'mitri to swing round to the south. Tell him to stay in contact with the flank attack. You know what to say.'

Kadan nodded. 'It has all fallen out as you expected,' he said. 'How gratified you must be.'

'Oh well.' Kubulai gave him a flat stare. 'I don't think Jehan gave me the army to satisfy a whim. You know it's been a while since we had to fight any kind of a war.'

'You mean we have grown soft.' Kadan made a face. 'I'm not sure I agree with you. Now tell me why he chose you and not me.'

'That's easy.' Kubulai showed his teeth. 'I have more to prove than the rest of you.'

*

The dun st'lyan snorted, and Kubulai stood in the stirrups to stare ahead. Silver-blue in the moonlight, the river meandered like a garden path between the trees. The bank on the far side was high, and the overhang cast a shadow on the water. Two riders were threading their way through the undergrowth. Kubulai saw that they were Yek, and he settled back into the saddle.

He had forgotten how many men there were in three tumans. All along the level ground to his right the troopers waited. They were not supposed to move, but the groves of young trees were full of movement.

There was no wind and the temperature had risen. Kubulai glanced at Jehangir, who was carrying the staff with the lanterns. All four of them were shuttered.

'Yellow lantern,' Orcadai called from the far end of the line.

Kubulai reined his st'lyan forward. Over the plain to the north-west a single yellow light flickered. He counted the flashes. There were four. No one who was not looking for them would have seen them. He spurred the dun and it bolted, crashing through the brush at the edge of the bank. Men were packed around him. They charged across the river.

The bank on the other side was slick with ice. The dun scrambled up it, and Kubulai found that he was in the middle of the front rank as it hurtled onto the level plain beyond. At the end of the meadow was D'mitri. He had half a tuman, and he was practically surrounded by the Ch'noze.

Kadan's lanterns flashed on the summit of the hill beyond. Kubulai nocked an arrow and shot. It hissed through the air and skipped into the packed mass of the enemy. Kubulai fired again, keeping his arrows low. All around him the bowstrings sang.

'Yip-yip-yip-yip!'

It was the call which had been agreed. Kubulai reined in hard. He stood in the stirrups again, craning to see what was happening. The screams and shouting echoed across the plain. Kadan was on the high ground to the north of the Ch'noze line. From there the whole army could see the lantern signals. A red light flashed. Kubulai spun the dun around and rode through the pack towards Jehangir. The Yek front line crashed into the Ch'noze wing, folding it back on itself. D'mitri's men broke free and rode across the front of the army. The Yek who were not engaged pushing the Ch'noze back cheered. Kubulai broke loose from the pack. He galloped the dun over to join Jehangir.

'Khan, I nearly came looking for you.' Jehangir brandished the lantern pole. 'Green light.'

D'mitri's standard-bearer came up. He seized the staff with the lanterns from Jehangir's hand and jerked one of the cords. The green lantern flashed. The light caught the standard-bearer's face so that he looked like a corpse. Kubulai turned and looked back at the Ch'noze. The Yek were disengaging, their line straightening. They charged again, yelling, and the air between the two armies became black with arrows.

'Look at D'mitri,' Jehangir said.

Kubulai reined around. D'mitri had run his men up onto the higher ground at the far end of the Ch'noze line. They packed the slope, shooting down into the mass of the enemy. The Ch'noze howled, and the whole of the end of their line slewed away.

'Where is Orcadai?'

Jehangir pointed towards the Yek left flank. The tuman which was under Orcadai's command was moving out to encircle the Ch'noze who were opposite. A formation angled to meet the threat, and a series of small explosions rang out.

'Damn them.' Kubulai sat up straight in the saddle. 'They are using firearms.'

The Yek charge petered out. The bark of the guns was regular. 'They are firing volleys,' Jehangir said. 'I wonder who taught them that.'

'Signal Kadan,' Kubulai said. 'And send the reserve tuman up to push them west.' He gazed back towards the left flank. Orcadai's men were withdrawing in good order. They were volleying arrows down on the Ch'noze, but their line was dangerously thin.

Lanterns winked suddenly across the plain. A solid formation of troopers moved up, then wheeled off to come up behind Orcadai's men. They charged through their open ranks and crashed into the Ch'noze flank. Firearms banged at intervals.

'Are we winning?' Jehangir yelled.

'Not yet.' Kubulai stared off towards the high ground where D'mitri had halted his tuman. 'Give D'mitri's sign and two long blues.'

The end of the Ch'noze line was swinging round. Their centre was still a straight line, but both wings were bent back in long curves, one to meet Orcadai's assault, and the other to deal with D'mitri. Blue lanterns glared. 'He hasn't seen them,' Jehangir said.

Kubulai yanked an arrow out of his case and nocked it. 'Keep signalling,' he said to the standard-bearer. He lifted the bow and drew to his cheek. The arrow skipped across the end of the Yek right flank.

Several heads turned, and then somebody shouted. The signal was repeated down the whole front line. A lantern flashed an acknowledgement from the slope. The Ch'noze were only just starting to envelop the base of the hill when D'mitri's men started to stream away.

Guns banged on the left. Kubulai stood in the stirrups and peered through the darkness. Clouds were passing across the face of the moon, and it was hard to see what was happening. The lantern signals were the only splashes of colour. Everything else looked grey or silver in the moonlight.

The Ch'noze had repulsed the Yek charge again. Kubulai looked for the yellow light which would indicate Orcadai's command post, but he could not see it. Another volley of shots rang out. 'We have to get them moving,' Jehangir said.

'Orcadai's sign and a long blue.'

'He won't do it.' Jehangir made a face. He gestured to the standard-bearer.

'He'll do it.' Kubulai stared along the line. The Ch'noze wing which had moved to intercept D'mitri had split off from the rest of the army. The enemy centre was moving forward. 'If we can't push them west, we'll let them chase us east. It will work out the same in the end. Shut all lanterns. Let's go.'

The troopers under Orcadai's command had whirled their st'lyan around, and were riding away. The Ch'noze on the wing which had been curved back to face them moved out, and then the whole formation wheeled into line. Ch'noze voices bellowed triumphantly. The gunfire had ceased.

Kubulai spun the dun round. He rode flat out across the level ground towards the river. The st'lyan launched itself off the bank, and slid on its haunches down into the water. Kubulai clung to its mane. When he was on the other bank he looked back. The Ch'noze were already starting to cross. He dropped his reins and nocked an arrow, twisting round in the saddle to shoot. All along the bank were Yek troopers who were doing the same.

'Yip-yip-yip-yip!'

Jehangir's high call ranged over the Ch'noze shouts and the noise of the fighting. Kubulai shot another arrow, and a Ch'noze equine stumbled and pitched its rider into the river.

Orcadai's men were already racing away. Kubulai gritted his teeth. He lashed the dun with his reins and galloped after them. As soon as he was out in the open he looked back. Orcadai's command was being chased by a force which appeared to be made up of the Ch'noze wing and part of the centre. The men who were coming after Kubulai were close enough to be throwing their lances.

A great roar went up to Kubulai's left. Kubulai had an arrow drawn, and he released it before he looked. The men of D'mitri's command had come around behind the Yek centre. They smashed into the Ch'noze pursuit. Ch'noze voices cried out in alarm.

Kubulai spun his st'lyan around, and he charged with the rest. Yek war cries drowned out every other sound. A solitary gun banged, and the Ch'noze formation disintegrated. Where the Yek passed through it the snowfield was trampled and littered with bodies and discarded weapons. Kubulai reined in, searching for Jehangir.

Kadan's lanterns flashed. Kubulai guided the dun around behind the troopers who were assembling into line. He saw Jehangir and rode over to him. 'That worked well,' Jehangir said. He sounded pleased, as if the plan had been his.

Kubulai nodded. He was panting for breath, and the icy air made his chest hurt.

Files of troopers trotted across the level ground in the direction of the river. Kubulai stared at them. The left flank had been composed of a full tuman, and a second had been sent up to support the attack against the guns. Now only about a tuman and a half remained.

'We lost a lot of men,' Jehangir said.

'I can see that.'

The firearms had provided the Ch'noze with an advantage so long as they had been used in a defensive formation. The moment the Ch'noze had ridden out in pursuit of the Yek the advantage had been lost, for the clansmen had lacked the discipline to move cohesively. It had been every man for himself.

They rode back across the river. The Ch'noze were fighting on a much narrower front now, for they had lost one wing of their army and part of their centre. Kubulai rose in the saddle and stared to the right. D'mitri's tuman was coming around the end of the Yek line, and the slope above the Ch'noze was once more packed with men who were shooting down at the enemy ranks. The whole Ch'noze wing peeled away out of range.

'Send D'mitri's sign and two short greens,' Kubulai said. 'Maybe Kadan feels like fighting.'

'Shouldn't we warn him?'

Kubulai shook his head. 'He'll see what is going to happen.' He reined the dun around and rode along behind the Yek centre to get out of the way of the men from Orcadai's command who were coming back into the line. The Yek front was much wider than the Ch'noze formation now.

Jehangir and the standard-bearer urged their animals up to Kubulai's side. The Yek battle formation now looked like the head and horns of a bull. In the centre there was a solid block of men which had scarcely moved since the start of the engagement. Orcadai's command was the element which Kubulai had pulled back – the pretended retreat which had enticed the Ch'noze wing into a trap. Now Orcadai had regrouped with a full tuman, and he was curving the end of his front line round as if to envelop the Ch'noze. Volleys of arrows rained down on the packed mass of the enemy. A part of what had previously been the Ch'noze centre began to angle out to anticipate a flank attack.

A green lantern flashed from the hill at the other end of the line where D'mitri was positioned. Suddenly his whole tuman charged downslope. They engulfed the Ch'noze wing like an avalanche. There was a crash and a roar which drowned out every other sound, and then the entire Ch'noze flank seemed to dissolve. Men streamed away in disorder.

'They didn't expect that,' Jehangir said happily.

The Ch'noze were not great tacticians, and they had expected the obvious – an attack by the Yek left on their exposed right wing. Now only the centre of their army remained intact. Gunfire banged at intervals from the middle of their front line. Yek troopers roared in anger. Arrows sped across the space between the two armies.

Orcadai rode up through the ranks of his men. He was carrying a weapon which resembled a hackbut – a tube of iron which was bound with metal straps to a long

370

cradle of wood. The wood had not been shaped so that the end would fit against a man's shoulder, but there was a swivel arrangement at the midpoint of the length which Kubulai thought was designed to accept some kind of support or stand. Firing seemed to be achieved by applying a match to a vent or touch-hole.

'This is what they are using,' Orcadai said.

Probably the Ch'noze had not had either the time or the facilities to produce more complicated weapons. The hackbuts could be made with little more than simple forging equipment. Kubulai stared at the thing, and made a face. 'Destroy any you find,' he said.

The firearms were an alien notion. Kubulai guessed that the agents of the Empire who were advising the Ch'noze had thought that their use would tip the balance. In fact the guns had only made the Yek angry, and had increased their determination to win.

Orcadai nodded. He dropped the hackbut on the ground, then sidestepped his st'lyan. 'We should finish it now,' he said. 'When you ordered us to pull back I thought you had lost your mind, but it worked well. I wonder why they didn't wheel their wing and attack our centre.'

'They couldn't resist the opportunity to chase us,' Kubulai said.

The Yek centre had been ready in any case. The hill on which Kadan had been positioned provided a view of the whole plain. He would have moved one of the tumans in the middle of the formation out to form a new wing, and then the Yek who were pretending to retreat would have charged up round them. Either way the Ch'noze would have been destroyed.

'They look more than they really are,' Orcadai said.

371

He stood in the stirrups and gazed across at the Ch'noze. 'I didn't realise it until they charged, but their ranks aren't as tight as ours.'

'I don't suppose it occurred to you that we might need help when you started to withdraw,' Kubulai said. 'Three of us were being chased by about a thousand Ch'noze. They ran us right across the river.'

'I didn't notice,' Orcadai responded sweetly.

'They made us look ridiculous. A command post shouldn't have to worry about being chased.'

The lighter colour of the sky to the east indicated that it was nearly dawn. Kubulai watched Orcadai's face and saw his amusement. Orcadai gestured. 'Who will be left to laugh when all the Ch'noze are dead?'

Kubulai pursed his lips. Eventually he would have to teach Orcadai a lesson. This was not the right time. He said, 'Move your tuman round to encircle them. Watch for signals.'

Orcadai nodded. He spun his st'lyan round and rode away. Kubulai watched the formations start to extend. A flock of birds flew overhead, heading east. He stared after them, and saw that the horizon was beginning to turn yellow from the light of the rising sun.

He cantered down to D'mitri's end of the battle. The Ch'noze were at a standstill, drowning in a downpour of Yek arrows. What had started as a series of lines was becoming a circle around their command. A ring of bodies lay where they had drawn back. Many of them were no longer mounted. Kubulai saw one segment of their strength develop a charge towards the centre of D'mitri's line, but long before the Ch'noze equines were past the litter of bodies the clansmen were dead. The arrows did not slacken. He pulled up beside D'mitri.

'Kadan says no mercy,' D'mitri said.

Kubulai wrinkled his nose. 'They knew the law about guns,' he said.

D'mitri nodded. 'How many did Orcadai lose?'

'About half a tuman, but not all to gunfire. They were steadier than we expected.'

'Someone has been training them,' D'mitri said. 'If there are aliens with their army, they are over there.' He nodded towards the Ch'noze centre.

Kubulai nodded. A body of about a hundred Ch'noze had broken out of the circle. They were all on foot, and were holding their shields locked together so that the Yek arrows were unable to make any impression. About a thousand troopers on st'lyan rode down on them. Like an armoured lizard the band of Ch'noze continued on, and the Yek wheeled away, unable to do much harm.

D'mitri gestured to his standard-bearer. 'Signal the reserve.'

The standard-bearer jerked one of the lantern cords. Kubulai watched the Ch'noze, wondering who had taught them the manoevre. 'I don't think they want to fight,' he said.

'That's too bad.' D'mitri glanced towards all that remained of the Ch'noze centre, and then he reined around. A solid mass of Yek troopers came out from behind the wing. They cantered down on the formation. The Ch'noze stopped and seemed to brace themselves. Whooping, the troopers charged. Most of them had acquired swords, and they tried to chop with them at the Ch'noze shields. The clansmen yielded a little, and a gap opened in the shield ring. Yek war cries rang out, and Kubulai opened his mouth to shout for archers. Before he could make a sound the Ch'noze

373

had locked their shields again, and the Yek were thrown back.

'This is ridiculous,' D'mitri said. He rode over to talk to a thousand commander, and the troopers reorganised themselves and tried again. Three or four men broke through the shield ring. Kubulai saw them above the level of the dismounted Ch'noze, and then they were pulled from their st'lyan and slaughtered.

Kubulai gathered his reins. He caught the attention of an officer who was waiting nearby, and they trotted their st'lyan towards the Ch'noze. The troopers were forming up for another attempt. Kubulai rode as close as he thought wise, nocked an arrow and drew back as far as he could, then loosed. The arrow went through a shield, and a man cried out.

He halted the dun and selected another arrow. This time it struck the metal rim of a shield in the outer ring, bounced, and took a clansman in the middle of the formation in the throat.

The Ch'noze seemed to realise that they were in danger. They attacked the troopers who were encircling them, but the troopers pulled back hastily. Kubulai aimed for the patches of faces he could see above the shields. Some of the Ch'noze were clad in heavy mail, and they were difficult targets. The Yek drew back from the locked shields every time the formation moved forward. Then they moved in again so that the firing could continue.

The shield ring grew smaller and smaller. Every time a man fell, the rest closed ranks. Once they stopped as if they were giving up, but then they came on again. Kubulai gestured to the waiting mass of mounted troopers beyond, and they charged ponderously. They smashed into the shields and bore them down, hacking with their swords. One Ch'noze pulled a trooper out of the saddle. He mounted and tried to ride away, but even before he had reined around he was killed. Arrows slammed into him.

There was nothing left of the tortoise when the charge drew back. Kubulai rode across the ground and stared at the faces of the dead. All of them were Ch'noze - Gepid clansmen, he thought - and none looked strange or alien.

D'mitri rode over. He dismounted, pulled an arrow out of the chest of one of the dead men and inspected the barbs behind the tip. 'Name of God,' he said. 'Do they think they are killing fish?' He threw the shaft away. 'How is the battle going?'

Kubulai looked back down the field. 'Kadan has moved the reserve tuman around,' he said. 'The Ch'noze can't get away.'

'Are there many left?'

'A thousand or so.'

'Hunh.' D'mitri nodded. 'I had forgotten what it was like to wage war like this.'

There would be so few Ch'noze left by the time they were finished that it would be several generations before they would be strong enough to rise again. If we can teach them to live in peace, Kubulai thought, all this will have been worthwhile.

D'mitri got back into the saddle. He gazed across the field. 'If we go and help Kadan, it will be finished sooner,' he said.

'Then let's go and help him.'

'You slaughtered them,' Han said. 'They had no chance.'

The killing had continued until well into the day. A

few thousand of the Ch'noze had escaped when their left wing had collapsed, and Kubulai had sent Kadan out in command of a full-strength tuman to pursue them. Because they had employed firearms in contravention of the Yasa, they were all condemned to die.

Kubulai was walking through the piles of dead on the battlefield. He glanced round at Han. 'They had their chance before it started,' he pointed out. 'This is war. The essence of war is to kill the enemy without getting killed yourself. Fairness does not come into it. If we gave our enemies a chance once we started to fight, then we would be slaughtered. We would be lying here, and not the Ch'noze.'

Yek troopers were hauling dead Ch'noze out of a heap of men who were piled around what had been their command post. Normally they would not have bothered, but if alien agents had been with the Ch'noze army, Kubulai was determined to find a trace of them. Each body which was dragged from the chaos was laid on its back. The faces which were still recognisable were left uncovered. Any dead men who were not obviously Ch'noze were marked by a lance which was planted in the ground. Kubulai saw one sticking up between the feet of a corpse in the next row. He walked over to it, then turned and motioned to Han.

'How about this one?'

The dead man was stocky and fair, with blue eyes. He might have been Ch'noze, but he had no clan markings tattooed on his face.

Han came over. He examined the slack features, and then he shrugged. 'Khan, I don't know. I don't think he's one of the men who spoke to my father.'

'How many times did you see them?'

'Oh. Twice or maybe three times. They were with the Tatars more than they were with us.'

Kubulai grunted. He bent down and inspected the dead man's hands. 'He's certainly not Ch'noze,' he said. He gave Han a sharp look. 'He has no talons.'

Some of the dead were renegade C'zaki, mercenaries who had probably fought for the promise of plunder. Kubulai touched the skin of the corpse's palms. It was soft, and so probably the dead man had not been accustomed to bearing arms. He might have been a scribe in the service of one of the Gepid or Tatar chiefs, but it seemed unlikely. A search of a waist pouch produced nothing of interest. If this was an alien, he had taken care to carry nothing on his person which would betray his origin.

'Khan, I found this.'

One of D'mitri's thousand commanders came up through the rows of dead men. He held out a grey box, and Kubulai recognised it at once as an alien communicator. 'Where was it?'

'In the saddlebag of one of the equines.' The officer pointed towards the fallen Ch'noze standard. 'There.'

It was proof enough. 'Bring this one.' Kubulai indicated the dead man at his feet. 'Also those four.' He pointed at lances he had tagged with strips of cloth. They marked the bodies he had been uncertain about.

D'mitri picked his way through the carnage. 'Have you found them?'

Kubulai shrugged. 'I'm not sure. Send to T'tai for five large casks. We'll pickle the bodies of the ones we're not positive about. Maybe we can get them identified.'

'And then what?' D'mitri looked appalled by the idea.

'I don't know.' Kubulai went past him. Then he

turned. 'I'm going hunting. Follow me as soon as you are ready.'

'I'll catch up with you at N'tan.' D'mitri stretched and sighed. 'I am sore all over. I don't think I'm as young as I used to be.'

Kubulai laughed at him. He collected a small escort of Merkuts, and started along the trail of the fleeing Ch'noze.

Heading west he gathered up the small companies of Yek troopers who had separated away from Kadan's command to follow the diverging trails. They found Ch'noze clansmen hiding in ditches at the edges of fields, in the forests, and in several of the villages, and killed them all. The villagers they did not harm. The men who took refuge in the settlements were often found in the little fields where the Ch'noze buried their dead. Kubulai decided that they attached some kind of significance to such places. Probably they never killed anyone while he was around a grave.

It was nearly evening when he rode up to a village which was surrounded by a low wall. About two hundred men had joined his escort. Beyond the village there was an enclosed meadow in which there were great clumps of the wooden markers the people used to indicate places of burial. Kubulai thought that it was a waste of good land. The meadow was packed with men who had fled from the last battle. Most of the villagers had come out to stand on their wall, but at the entrance to the burial ground a man wearing the ceremonial robe of a headman was waiting. He watched Kubulai as he rode up. Around his feet lay swords and mail coats in heaps.

'Lord, this ground is sacred,' he said in Ch'noze. 'You

risk the anger of Heaven if you venture in.'

'You fill me with dread.' Kubulai showed his teeth. 'Get out of my way.'

'You cannot pass.'

A trooper beside Kubulai thrust with his lance, taking the headman in the chest. He fell without a sound. Kubulai urged the dun through the gate into the meadow. There were Ch'noze everywhere. Some were kneeling, their arms wrapped around the grave markers. Kubulai brought his st'lyan to a halt, uncasing his bow. The Ch'noze who were watching flinched. Passively they waited to be slaughtered. The troopers dismounted, came up to his side, and began to shoot. A corner of Kubulai's mind dwelled on the horror of what he was doing. He aimed each shot carefully, doing his best to ensure that each death was quick, his hands working without reference to what was passing through his mind. At least the people would not have to move the dead far to bury them.

Early the next morning a similar thing happened at a small gathering of houses on the road down to N'tan. Here it was the women who waited to plead for the lives of their menfolk. They begged him for mercy on their knees, and Kubulai stood in the middle of a group of them, allowing the sound of their voices to merge into a formless murmur, waiting for them to finish. At last they seemed to understand that he was not to be deterred from his purpose, and their voices died away. One woman had captured Kubulai's hand, and was clinging to it as if she would stay him. He bent and loosened her fingers. 'It is the law,' he said, then walked away. The troopers were waiting with their arrows nocked. Bowstrings hummed as they started the killing. The women they left unharmed, for they had done no wrong. After it was over, they mounted and journeyed on.

N'tan was much larger than T'tai, and by the time the Yek army rode up to the wall it was decked with flags and banners. The commander of the Yek garrison was a Keraistani with an olive skin and glittering dark eyes. When he emerged from the gate to greet Kubulai, the people lining the wall cheered wildly.

'Lord,' the Keraistani said, 'I am very pleased to see you.'

If the various garrison commanders had been more alert, probably the Ch'noze would not have been able to organise their rebellion. Kubulai stripped off his gauntlets while he considered what to say in reply. The plain beyond the city was packed with men, and already the tents were going up. 'I heard you were besieged.' Kubulai gave the Keraistani a stare.

'We were until three days ago.' The Keraistani nodded. If he was aware of the coldness of Kubulai's manner, it did not show.

It meant that the Ch'noze had pulled all their men back to the army before the battle. Bands were still wandering the hills, and the force D'mitri had scouted during the journey west was probably still trying to outflank the Yek advance. Kubulai pursed his lips. 'How many men have you?'

'Nearly a thousand,' the Keraistani said.

'And yet it did not occur to you to scout the Ch'noze when they rode away,' Kubulai commented.

Wagons were rolling through the gates towards the army assembled on the plain. They were filled with sacks and barrels. The garrison commander gestured nervously. 'Lord, those are provisions for your army.'

He did not attempt to respond to Kubulai's censure.

An alien vessel came up very fast from the south-east. Kubulai looked round, and he saw that Kadan was gathering men. D'mitri was galloping his st'lyan flat out towards the gate. Troopers streamed behind him.

If the aliens had come to rescue their agents, they were too late. It was unlikely that they had come to avenge the Ch'noze, Kubulai thought. It was clear that the aliens cared as little for the Ch'noze as they did for the other races of the world. He eyed the hovering oval ship and wondered what weapons it carried. The alien ambassador had sworn that these smaller vessels were unarmed, but of course that was a lie.

D'mitri reined in so hard that his st'lyan sat down on its rump. 'Are we being attacked?' he asked.

'Not yet.' Kubulai glanced up at the people lining the walls of the city and saw that they had fallen silent.

The alien vessel was descending slowly. Kubulai reined around and rode off the road into the open meadow which extended the length of the wall. He recalled what his father had said about the power of the alien weapons, and a feeling of frustration overcame him. If the offworlders started to fire on the assembled army, they would be unable to retaliate.

'We are like the meat in a trap,' D'mitri said. He urged his bay up to Kubulai's side. 'We are not equipped to fight them if they attack us.'

'At least there will be no doubt that we are at war,' Kubulai observed. Whether they died now or later seemed to make little difference. If the Yek had to fight a war on alien terms, they would be slaughtered.

The ship was by now a hundred drem above the road. Suddenly it shot sideways. It swooped across the meadow. Hot air washed over Kubulai, and his st'lyan screamed and reared.

'They are going to land,' D'mitri said. He sounded relieved.

Kubulai did not reply. The vessel came to rest on the grass. The door in the side opened, and his father jumped out onto the ground. He was followed almost at once by the alien ambassador, and they were joined by several men Kubulai did not recognise. He turned in the saddle. 'Go and bring up the carts which contain the casks with the men we want to identify.'

D'mitri raised his eyebrows. 'Are you sure that's wise?'

'Just do it.'

Alexei was making no attempt to cross the meadow. He stared around, then said something to the aliens who were grouped beside him, and everybody laughed. Kubulai walked the dun forward. His father did not appear to have brought a guard, and he seemed perfectly at ease in offworlder company. The realisation disturbed Kubulai, and he adjusted his expression to hide his feelings.

'Father, good day.'

Some of the people on the wall had seen Alexei among the aliens. They shouted his name and cheered him. Alexei caught hold of the dun's bridle. He looked up at Kubulai, shading his eyes with his free hand. 'Well, child,' he said, 'I'm told you're something of a general. Won't you get down? It hurts my neck to talk to you like this.'

Kubulai kicked his feet free of the stirrups. He slid to the ground. 'You're in strange company.'

382

'Hunh.' His father grinned. 'I knew you'd say that. It's a matter of convenience.'

'They are our enemy,' Kubulai said. He had spoken quickly in Yek, and now he glanced at the aliens to make sure that none of them understood. Then he met his father's eyes again. 'Their agents were advising the Ch'noze army.'

'Not very successfully, it would seem.' Alexei did not look as if he was surprised by the news. 'Have you proof? I heard you took no prisoners.'

'You heard correctly.' Kubulai ignored the note of criticism in his father's tone. He looped his reins over the dun's head and let them trail on the ground. The mare began to crop at the grass. 'They were using firearms during the last battle, and we have been killing them ever since.'

'Then how can you be sure that they had advisers?'

'Well, for a start I have one of the alien communicators in my saddlebag.' Kubulai gestured to the dun's back. 'We picked it up on the battlefield. Do you want to see it?'

'Not here.'

'I thought not.' Kubulai smiled grimly. The moment the aliens were asked to explain the evidence, the pretence would be over. 'You're not ready to fight them yet.'

'Oh.' Alexei looked amused. 'Did I say we were going to?'

Two carts bumped off the road. The drivers were standing on the shafts which ran between the yokes of the oxen, and D'mitri was riding behind. His expression showed his disquiet. Alexei stared. 'What are these?'

'They're a surprise.' Kubulai signalled to the men on

383

the backs of the carts. They rolled the casks to the ends of the platforms, then kicked them out onto the ground. A trooper ran up with tools, and he righted one of the casks and began to work off the top.

The aliens were watching curiously. Kubulai waited until the lids had been prised off the casks, and then he nodded. The men toppled the casks so that their contents spilled out. The brine flowed away like a river, and the pale naked bodies of the dead men sprawled in heaps. The carters straightened their limbs, laying them on their backs. Then they retreated.

D'mitri dismounted. He gave his reins to the trooper. Then he turned to face Alexei. 'Khan, this wasn't my idea.'

'Look at the ambassador,' Kubulai said.

The aliens were craning their heads to look at the dead men. One of the offworlders said something to the ambassador, his voice low, and he pointed at a corpse at one end. The ambassador came past Kubulai. When he was close enough to the dead to see their faces he stopped. He went pale. After a moment he turned to address Alexei. 'Khan, why are we being shown this?'

The question was directed at his father, but Kubulai took it upon himself to answer. He said, 'These are the bodies of men we recovered after a battle with the Ch'noze. They are not clansmen, and so I wanted my father to see them, to get his opinion. If we can identify them we will impose a penalty on their people as punishment, because they were taken in rebellion against us.' He gave the offworlder a flat stare. 'Maybe they are C'zaki.'

The expression on the ambassador's face was impossible to interpret. Slowly he nodded. Then he inclined his head politely to Alexei and rejoined the others.

'I can see that everything men are starting to say about you is true,' Alexei said. 'I would not have been so ruthless.'

It was a kind of compliment, Kubulai supposed. He wrinkled his nose. The aliens were talking quietly in a group. Kubulai watched the ambassador, and then he glanced at the corpses on the grass. 'He recognised one of them,' he said.

'Maybe.' His father unfastened the front of his coat. He smoothed a hand down the facings. 'I think he is aware that you don't believe they are C'zaki.'

'I hope so.'

'In other words you intended it as a warning.' Alexei frowned. 'Don't you think it would have made sense to discuss it with me first?'

'If it has made them think twice about meddling in our affairs, it is justified,' Kubulai responded. He knew he sounded defensive. The dun's reins were lying in the grass at his feet. He bent down and picked them up. 'Are you staying long?'

'I'm going back today. Is your campaign here finished? I have orders for you from the Kha-Khan.'

'The campaigning's finished.' Kubulai drew the reins through his fingers. He stroked the st'lyan's nose, and let the animal lick his hand. 'What orders? I don't understand why you brought the aliens here.'

'Oh.' Alexei opened his eyes wide. 'They brought me. I asked them to. I thought it would be a good idea for them to realise that the Yek don't believe in half-measures when it comes to waging war.'

Kubulai grunted. He guessed that there was more to

385

it than that, but he knew better than to ask for explanation. 'What orders?' he asked again.

'You're to be at Kinsai by the end of the month,' his father said.

'Why?'

'Never mind why. I hear you're fighting with Kadan. Is it serious?'

The sudden change of subject unsettled Kubulai. He dug at the grass with the heel of his boot. 'You hear a lot. Kadan is my business. I'll deal with him my own way.'

'Indeed?' Alexei raised his eyebrows, and then he gave a bark of laughter. 'You have changed since you became Successor.'

Kubulai thought he was being mocked, and he flushed. He turned to walk away, unwilling to argue. Then he stopped and looked back. 'I'm Heir only in name,' he said. 'Don't ever look to me to take Jehan's place.'

'Not until the time comes.'

'Not even then.'

His father and D'mitri both stared. Alexei said, 'You got command of the army because the Kha-Khan wanted you to learn to accept the fact that necessary acts sometimes have terrible consequences.'

'So that I would know how to be ruthless when the necessity arose,' Kubulai said. 'I have been such an apt pupil, you must be pleased.' He stared away, and the memory of the Ch'noze he had ordered killed forced its way back to the forefront of his mind. The faces of the slain were a blur. He could not remember individuals.

'I suppose that's one way of looking at it,' Alexei responded. His tone was patient. He pursed his lips.

'You must not fear the burden of responsibility that goes with the throne. If Jehan did not believe you would be equal to it, you would not have been chosen.'

D'mitri was stirring the grass with his toe. Kubulai glanced at him, wondering what he was thinking. It was not the place to be discussing such a subject. Beside the alien vessel the group around the ambassador were watching the exchange. Because it was in Yek, there was no way for them to know what was being said.

Kubulai had often heard old men speak in reverential tones about the weight of duty which came upon the man who was elected to the Dragon Throne. Authority was balanced by responsibility, it was said. For himself he knew that he did not fear the responsibility of kingship more than any other burden. Rather he mistrusted his own nature, resisting the moment when instinct would tell him that he had satisfied his own will in preference to the needs of the people. No one had ever been able to define for him the point at which nature took over from judgement. Few men seemed to see that a conflict might exist between them, and it was assumed that a ruler was a man selected because he was capable of ignoring personal preference when called upon to decide what was to be done. Kubulai did not believe that he possessed that quality of selflessness, and he could not understand why Jehan and the others thought otherwise.

He became aware that his father was staring, waiting for a response, and he took a breath, searching for the words which would explain how he felt. Finally he said, 'If you think that it is the weight of duty I fear, you are mistaken. It is not the burden of responsibility but of power I seek to avoid. I know myself too well ever to desire the throne.'

PART FIVE

A Matter of Interpretation

'In many ways the rebellions were good for us,' Jehan said. He sat down on the edge of the dais which was in the centre of the small audience chamber. A tray which held cups and jugs of wine had been placed on the polished wood at his side. He lifted a cup, then gestured with his free hand. 'The Khanate was growing complacent,' he continued. 'The revolts in Ch'nozia and the Alan country revealed the flaws in our system of provincial government, and showed us that we have to change our approach to the training of men who are to have independent commands – garrison commanders and the like.'

'It sounds as if you think we ought to thank the aliens for causing the trouble,' Jotan said sarcastically. The Kha-Khan's father was clad in a long coat of midnight-blue silk. He paced the gold-decorated floor, and then turned. 'I only know that in my province the harvest rots ungathered in the fields. Vaslav and Jaroselsk are in ashes, because their inhabitants held out against us. The country where we fought is like a wasteland, and most of the people are starving.'

Suragai shifted his weight quietly from one foot to the other. He was not sure why he had not been dismissed before the start of the discussion. Now he felt a sense of acute embarrassment because he was present to witness the confrontation which was taking place.

Even though he was Jehan's father, in rank Jotan was still only provincial governor of the Alan country, and Suragai was amazed at the lack of respect he showed when he spoke. No one had the right to address the Lord of the Earth so discourteously. It was not proper.

'If the people are starving, we will feed them,' Jehan said calmly. His head went round, and he addressed Alexei. 'If we requisition corn from your granaries at Khitai, can you manage?'

Alexei was sitting on a stool which had been brought to the side of the dais. He nodded. His expression when he looked past the Kha-Khan at Jotan was thoughtful, but he said nothing.

'In that case the grain can go by sea from Losan.' Jehan nodded, satisfied. He gave Jotan a penetrating stare. 'As for the people who have lost their homes, I imagine you have already made arrangements for their shelter.'

Jotan was tall, and he was in his late middle years. As a young man he had been lanky, and his frame had been defined by sinew and muscle. Now he had gained weight he looked softer. A dangerous flush made its way onto his cheeks. 'Of course I have,' he said ponderously. 'My intent in raising the matter was not to complain, or to ask for aid. The aliens have committed acts of war against us and yet we pretend that they are our friends. I question that policy. Were the decision in my hands, all contact with aliens would be forbidden.'

Burun was sitting on a cushion which had been placed on the floor. His head came up. 'The decision is not yours,' he said matter-of-factly.

Suragai perceived an undercurrent to the conversation, but did not understand it. He recalled the rumour – that Jotan had been behind an attempt of some kind to gain power over the throne in the days before Jehan had become Kha-Khan. It was said that only Burun knew the truth of the matter, but now Suragai guessed that Jehan and Alexei were also privy to it. Their expressions as they watched Jotan were reserved, as if they sat in silent judgement, and it was apparent that they did not trust his motive for speaking.

The pattern of intrigue was ever-present in the affairs of the court, and suddenly Suragai saw that it was like a flaw in an otherwise perfect jewel. The knowledge troubled him, and he wondered where in the past the Yek had gone wrong. The Yasa had been designed to ensure that order would prevail in the world. Now that Suragai saw how precarious the balance was between order and chaos he was overcome by a feeling of dismay. Our affairs are no more well ordered than those of the Alan or the Ch'noze, he thought. We deceive ourselves believing otherwise.

There were latticed windows in the wall behind the dais, and through them came the sound of a bell tolling the hour. The noise shattered the silence, and Jehan stirred. He stared at the cup in his hand as if he did not know how it had got there. Then he laid it on the tray. 'You want me to announce that I am declaring war on the aliens,' he said. He did not look at his father as he spoke.

'They are our enemies,' Jotan responded simply.

'Their interests are not ours,' Burun rumbled. 'That at least is true.' He stood, uncoiling himself from the floor in an elastic movement which surprised Suragai every time he saw it. Burun was an old man by comparison with the others in the room, but he never seemed to show his age. Sometimes he complained of rheumatism or stiffness in his joints, but these were disabilities which disappeared magically whenever he was required to shoot or to ride.

'Say rather that the interests of the Empire are not ours,' Jehan observed precisely. He stroked his cheek with a forefinger. 'The aliens are people like us. Some of them are men of good faith.'

It was clear that the correction did not please Jotan. He frowned disagreement. 'We cannot afford to make a distinction.'

'I don't think our situation is all that grave,' Jehan said mildly. 'Declaring war is certainly not the answer.'

Alexei had been watching Jotan steadily the whole time. All at once Suragai realised that Jotan's intent was not concerned with persuading Jehan to break off relations with the Empire; rather he desired to throw doubt upon the loyalty of the aliens who were close to the throne. Suragai remembered his own mistrust of Alexei, and he flushed and looked at his feet in case his reaction should be noticed.

'If we have to fight at all,' Burun said, 'we ought to fight on our terms.'

Jehan looked as if he had heard the observation before. 'A war against the Empire is impracticable,' he said. He stood up.

Suragai guessed that Burun and Alexei and Jehan had agreed what they were going to do about the aliens, but that they did not trust Jotan far enough to tell him. He shifted his weight once more, and Burun's head came round for an instant. 'Patience, Noyon,' he said softly. His dark eyes twinkled, and then he looked away.

Jotan did not seem to have heard. His head was down as though he was pondering how to proceed. Suddenly he straightened. 'You are the Kha-Khan,' he said to Jehan. 'But you are also my son. I never offered you counsel but it was out of concern for your interest, and if you will not heed me now, it is pointless for me to remain here. Have I your leave to depart?'

Suragai knew that he would have flinched or looked away in the face of such a declaration. Jehan only stared without expression, and then waved a hand. 'By all means.'

'In that case I bid you a good day.' The bow Jotan produced was calculated to perfection. Less would have been rude and lacking in respect, but more would have been self-abasing. He turned and strode to the door, opened it, and left the room.

Alexei's expression remained unchanged, but Burun's nose wrinkled as if something had irritated him. A moment passed, and then he went over to the dais and took a cup from the tray. It was the one Jehan had laid aside, and it was filled with wine. Burun drank.

Jehan was gazing towards the door. Abruptly his head came round. 'Give me something to drink.'

They were trying to pretend that nothing out of the ordinary had occurred, Suragai thought. He deduced that events of this kind had happened before, and in the instant of deduction knew that the tales about Jotan were true, and pitied him. It must be terrible to know that one would never be trusted again – that every action was suspect, and that even honest motives were incapable of being accepted. Most awful of all was the fact that Jotan's father and son were united against him, their attitude unforgiving. It made

Suragai wonder how Jotan could live with the shame.

Burun poured wine from a jug into one of the cups. He gave the cup to Jehan without looking at him. 'My son still hates you,' he said to Alexei.

It was as if Alexei was absorbing the information. He stared blankly into the middle distance at first, and then his head came up. 'Did we ever imagine it would turn out different?' he asked.

'I suppose not.' Burun sounded regretful. He drank again, and then put his cup down carefully. He turned and stared at Suragai. 'Noyon, you remind me of your grandfather,' he said.

Suragai could not think why. He flushed, supposing he was being complimented, but could think of nothing to say.

'Burun means you have the quality of silence,' Alexei said, and smiled suddenly. 'I never thought of either you or my father that way, but it's true.'

Burun filled a third cup with wine, and held it out to Alexei. 'I think it's the hardest lesson of all for a boy to learn,' he said. 'Most men who have nothing to say find it hard to remain silent.' He grinned as if he was remembering someone in particular. Then he looked back at Suragai again. 'Tell me what you have heard from Kubulai.'

Suragai was unable to conceal his surprise. It was the last thing he had expected to be asked. 'Khan, he sent me news of his campaign against the Ch'noze.'

'Nothing else?'

The letter had arrived by ordinary courier the previous day. Suragai searched his memory. 'He told me to give his regards to my sister,' he said.

Alexei sat up abruptly. 'Well now,' he said.

Burun gestured impatiently. 'I'm interested in what

he said concerning the aliens.'

It occurred to Suragai that they could have intercepted Kubulai's letter without difficulty, but had not. He hesitated, unsure how to answer.

Jehan sipped at his wine, and then rolled the bowl of the cup absently between the palms of his hands. 'Noyon, speak,' he prompted. 'Whatever Kubulai may have told you, neither you nor he has anything to fear.'

Suragai did not think that he had needed such reassurance. It unsettled him. He said, 'Lord, he spoke only of his belief that the aliens had instigated the Alan and Ch'noze rebellions.'

'Aah.' Burun nodded as if he had just received the answer he sought. He gave Suragai a keen stare. 'He said no more than that?'

'No.' Suragai shook his head. The line of enquiry was quite mystifying. He could divine no reason for it.

Alexei got to his feet. He drank once from the cup he had been given by Burun, and then set it down on the edge of the dais. Burun seemed to become aware of him, and glanced quickly back over his shoulder. 'Would he have told anyone else?'

They were discussing Kubulai, Suragai realised. Alexei was frowning. 'I doubt it,' he said.

Suragai sensed that he was not going to be given any kind of explanation relating to the questions he had been asked. He watched Jehan's face. The Kha-Khan appeared to be lost in thought. Finally he looked up. When he saw Suragai staring, he smiled. 'Noyon, I would explain our interest in Kubulai's letter if it was needful for you to know,' he said.

It was disconcerting for Suragai to discover that his thoughts were so plainly displayed upon his face. He felt himself redden.

The door opened. A N'pani entered the chamber. He prostrated himself, and then got to his knees and offered Jehan a scroll of parchment. Jehan gestured to Burun, who took the letter. He broke the seal with an extended talon. The N'pani prostrated himself again, and then withdrew.

Burun scanned the scroll briskly, then passed it without comment to Jehan. He glanced at Suragai. 'You are recruiting men to work for the aliens,' he said. 'How many have you found so far?'

'Not many.' Suragai gazed past Burun in the direction of the Kha-Khan, but Jehan was immersed in the letter and did not look up.

There was little doubt in Suragai's mind that Burun already knew how many men had been gathered, for his spies were everywhere. So far fifty workers had been sent on to Marakan. More were coming in, but recruitment was slow because of the harvest.

It was apparent that the letter contained good news. The atmosphere in the audience chamber was suddenly easier, and when Jehan passed the scroll to Alexei he smiled.

'Maybe we can help you to find a few more.' Burun gave Suragai a level stare.

The offer was so remarkable that Suragai was unable to conceal his surprise. He guessed that whatever information the letter contained, the need to delay the alien enterprise was now at an end. He returned Burun's stare. 'I'm sure the trade commissioners would be grateful. Do you want to put them at their ease? Whatever you are preparing, surely it is timed for the Kha-Khan's anniversary?'

Alexei put the letter down on the dais. 'I told you he

would work it out,' he said. He sounded amused.

Burun did not turn. He eyed Suragai for a moment, then gestured. 'If they think we are trying to avoid more trouble, they will become careless,' he said.

The Kha-Khan was wearing loose silk trousers. He hitched at them, smoothing the material with one hand. Then he looked up at Suragai. 'Tell me about the alien woman,' he said.

Suragai allowed himself to look offended. 'Lord, I have told her nothing.'

'I don't believe that I have suggested such a thing,' Jehan responded calmly. 'Tell me about her.'

'Oh.' Suragai gathered his thoughts. 'Well, her name is Natalia. She has the rank of lieutenant in the Navy of the Empire. She is young and attractive, and the leader of the trade commission has told her to make friends with me.'

'Is she noble?'

'No.' Suragai shook his head. 'Lord, I have told your grandfather about my conversations with her.'

Burun showed his teeth, then nodded. 'So you have, Noyon.' He gave Suragai a speculative stare, and Suragai shifted uncomfortably.

'She told you that Fedyev ordered her to become your friend,' Alexei said. 'Do you think her honesty was meant to disarm you? She must have known that you would guess that her interest in you was not real.'

It was a question which troubled Suragai every time he considered it. He wrinkled his nose. 'Khan, I'm not sure it matters. She doesn't ask me about anything important, and even though she does not try to avoid giving answers to my questions, I am sure she realises that I don't altogether trust her.'

'You told Burun that she is unhappy about the fact

that she is required to accept orders from a civilian.'
Alexei pursed his lips. 'Is that the attitude of all the
officers?'

'Khan, it seems to be.' Suragai tried to remember if
he had discussed the subject specifically with Constantin, and a vague recollection of part of a conversation surfaced in his mind. 'It is something to do with
honour, I think. The Navy is sworn to enforce their
law. The officers don't trust the traders to act lawfully
where profit is concerned. They don't even trust the
chief men of their government.'

'That accords with what I remember.' Alexei nodded. He glanced sideways at Jehan, and it was as if a
message of some kind passed between them.

'Repeat what you know about the Empire's reasons
for desiring trade with us,' Burun said.

Now that he thought about it, Suragai was sure that
Constantin had been even more concerned than Natalia about the possibility of conflict between trading
requirements and the law. He shrugged. 'The officer
who pilots the alien vessel they have given me so that
I can recruit men says only that there are pressing
reasons,' he said. 'Both he and the woman have told me
not to ask what they are. I think it is to do with their
duty. Maybe the reasons are secret.'

It was only now that he was being subjected to such
careful interrogation that Suragai wondered if what
had been said was possibly of greater importance
than he had previously thought. Alien concerns were
so strange that it was difficult to decide what ought to
be of interest. He had reported what Natalia had said
because she had been told to engage his attention.
Now he recalled incidental details of conversations
with Constantin, and it troubled him because he

could think of no way to decide what was of significance.

'You are right in your supposition that what we have planned is timed to take place during the celebrations to mark the anniversary of my accession,' Jehan said suddenly. He stood up. 'It is a matter of convenience in some respects, because it gives us an excuse to invite all the aliens to Kinsai.'

'Also there are other factors,' Alexei commented drily. He gave Suragai a sharp stare. 'You don't need to know what they are, but you should be aware that it is essential for the ambassador and the traders to be here at the end of the month. We have to be certain about the location of their vessels.'

The trade commission possessed two ships, one of which was on loan to Suragai so that he could recruit men for field work. 'Only the officers pilot their vessels,' Suragai pointed out. 'If they are all at Kinsai, their machines will be here also.'

'As we calculated,' Burun said softly. He was looking in Alexei's direction as he spoke. Alexei nodded expressionlessly.

If occurred to Suragai to wonder if they planned to capture the alien ships. Probably Alexei knew how to pilot them, but even if the vessels were armed as the Yek suspected, it was hard to see what advantage would be provided by their capture. Suragai remembered how Jehan had dismissed the suggestion that it might be possible to wage war on the Empire. Certainly the Yek would need many more than the few ships which were available if they were to succeed.

'Two of the officers are your friends.' Jehan was watching Suragai's face as he spoke. 'Could you kill them if you had to?'

Suragai swallowed. The question was a test of course, but it did not occur to him to lie. He recalled the remote expression which had appeared on Jehan's face as he had watched his father walk from the room. Then he thought about Natalia and Constantin. It would be terrible to be like Jotan. He nodded slowly. 'If I had to.'

'So much for friendship,' Alexei said. He looked disapproving.

'The aliens are my friends,' Suragai said steadily, 'but this is my land.' He met Alexei's censuring gaze without flinching. After a moment Alexei nodded, and then looked away.

The test had been nothing to do with loyalty, Suragai realised, and he supposed that it was some abstract quality of character which had been under examination. An odd kind of respect was discernible in Burun's eyes.

'Sometimes the Yasa is hard to obey,' Jehan said. He spoke so softly that it was not clear if he was addressing anyone in particular.

Suragai had not considered the Yasa when he had given his answer. He only knew that friendship counted in the end for very little. Duty and order were necessary to civilised life.

When I am older I will have doubts like other men, he thought. Only now while I am young are the issues so easy to resolve.

Suragai's mother and sister were occupying apartments in Alexei's house. Behind the house there was a garden which was enclosed by a high wall. Even in the middle of the day there were patches of shadow, and although the air was still the place seemed cool. A

402

stone well overflowed water which ran across the cobbles of a winding pathway and disappeared into a culvert. Suragai supposed the culvert led to the huge water catchment tanks which were dug into the foundations of the city. The well was almost certainly supplied from that source, for there was no such thing as a natural water table on top of the spire of rock on which Kinsai stood. Suragai trailed one hand through the water, and small fish nudged inquisitively at his fingertips. He found a dry place on the wall and sat down.

He had thought that he was alone in the garden. Now he heard the sound of Turakina's voice. He looked round and saw that she was standing in a pool of shadow beyond a nearby tree. A servant was with her, and she was directing the man as he tried to position her chair. The servant was burdened with a wooden box of paints and a board covered with pinned sheets of paper. He managed to open the canvas chair with difficulty, then bowed to Turakina when she took the box and sketch block out of his hands before dismissing him imperiously. Suragai watched the performance, grinning. Ever since he had told his sister that Kubulai had spoken of her in his letter, she had been behaving impossibly. Neither Kubulai nor Turakina had sought the betrothal when it had been suggested at first. Now it seemed that Turakina's interest had been engaged. Suragai supposed it was feminine nature.

He still felt unhappy about the way he had been questioned about the contents of Kubulai's letter. The direction the questions had taken suggested that Kubulai possessed knowledge about the aliens which was shared by no one other than Jehan and his council

- knowledge they had expected him to impart when he wrote to Suragai. Now it occurred to Suragai that Kubulai would come to pay his respects to Turakina when he returned to Kinsai, and he began to consider how to enlist her aid to find out what Kubulai knew. He would not have cared, Suragai thought, save that the Kha-Khan had assumed that he had already been told. Now the thing was like a thorn sticking into his consciousness. He would be satisfied only when he had discovered the detail.

He glanced in Turakina's direction and saw that she was sitting down. She moved, and it became apparent that she had unfastened the front of her gown. Suragai frowned and stared around at the shadows, but he could see no one. The high wall protected the garden from prying eyes.

If she was aware of his presence, Turakina gave no sign. Because she was in the shadow Suragai was unable at first to see what she was sketching. He watched her brush as it moved across the paper. At the end of the stroke she stopped and looked down at herself, holding the fabric of her gown away from her breast. After a moment her brush moved again.

Suragai felt the heat of embarrassment rising up from his collar, and he stood up abruptly. Turakina was painting herself. Probably she would not be doing it if she thought anyone was watching. He turned, intending to go quietly into the house. A movement beyond the place where Turakina sat made him stop. He saw that Turakina's head had gone round. She said something Suragai could not hear, and he followed the direction of her eyes and saw that Constantin was leaning against a tree near the wall. The offworlder was staring at Turakina as if he had never seen her before. His face was pale.

'Get away from me!' This time Turakina's voice rang out. 'You have no business here. Go on, get away from me. I don't want you here.'

Constantin said nothing. He was staring so hard at Turakina that Suragai was sure he must be able to see through the material of her gown. The attitude of aliens to nakedness among women was different, of course. Suddenly Turakina picked up her box of paints and hurled it. The colours struck Constantin across the face, but he stood as if turned to stone.

Suragai went quickly across the grass. Constantin came away from the tree almost as fast. A defensive expression appeared on his face, and Turakina seemed to realise that the offworlder was no longer looking at her. She refastened the facings of her gown hastily, but she did not look round.

'Constantin, you are unwelcome here,' Suragai said. He gave the offworlder a level stare.

'I was waiting for you,' Constantin said. 'I fell asleep, and when I woke up she was already here. I'm sorry…'

'Go into the house and wait for me. You need a wash.'

There seemed to be no point in exhibiting anger. Turakina was staring down at the ground. Suragai put a hand on her shoulder. He gave the offworlder a hard stare, and Constantin flinched, then went off quickly towards the house.

'He didn't touch me,' Turakina said in a small voice.

'You didn't give him time,' Suragai said, and felt her shiver. He pulled Turakina to her feet and spun her round. She had shut her eyes tight. 'What were you thinking of?' Suragai demanded.

'I thought I was alone,' Turakina responded. Her voice tailed off.

405

'That's obvious.' Suragai took a breath, and then he shook his head in exasperation. 'Don't go anywhere alone while the aliens are still among us. Their standards of conduct are different from ours, and they don't know the meaning of civilised behaviour.'

He put his arms round her and realised that she was trembling. Suddenly Suragai knew that Turakina had been frightened by her experience. Tears were streaming down her cheeks, and he held her close and rocked her as if she was still a little girl.

'I'm sorry,' Constantin said. 'I woke up under the tree and she was there.'

Several files of men were moving through the door of the hall Suragai had commandeered as a base for recruitment of the workers intended for Marakan. He waited until they had passed, and then he gave the offworlder a hard stare. 'You were closer to her than I was. How much of her gown was open when you saw her?'

Constantin went crimson.

Suragai could feel the anger building up inside his chest. He knew that the incident had been Turakina's fault, but the problems it caused were a result of the fact that the aliens did not know how to behave. No Yek would have reacted as Constantin had to a woman's nakedness, and a civilised man placed in the offworlder's situation would not have stared. Instead he would have averted his eyes to avoid giving offence. It was Constantin's conduct which had frightened Turakina. Now Suragai was faced with an impossible situation. He said, 'I ought to kill you. Kubulai will kill you if he gets to hear of it.'

There were still faint stains on Constantin's face. His

eyes slid away. 'I'm sorry,' he said dully. 'Maybe I should ask for duties off world.'

'What would that achieve?' Suragai demanded impatiently. He looked in through the hall door. Inside there were about forty men. They were queued up in front of tables at which N'pani clerks were seated. The N'pani were filling in the blank spaces in the labour agreements Suragai had authorised, and as each man stepped forward he was required to sign with his chop. The numbers of men coming forward to volunteer for employment by the aliens had increased quite dramatically since Burun had let it be known that he was in favour of the idea. The men in this batch were mostly Keraistani. Probably a few of them were spies, but they all looked like farm workers. Now Suragai wondered if the aliens would be gratified, or only suspicious.

He stepped back from the door to allow the men leaving to come out into the street. Several of them bowed. It was late in the afternoon, and the sunlight had reddened everything and a haze hung in the air. Part of the paving in front of the hall was in deep shadow. The off worlder was loitering in it, his expression uncertain. Suragai signalled to his orderly to bring up the st'lyan, and then he turned and gave Constantin a stare. Constantin reacted nervously.

'I don't suppose you could help it,' Suragai said. 'But you frightened Turakina badly. It's not the fact that you looked at her which is the source of the offence. It's how you looked, and your failure to know when to leave. Think of it like an invasion of privacy, and then maybe you will understand.'

Something seemed to register in Constantin's eyes. He said, 'The Manchu have a custom which relates to that sort of thing. It's considered impolite to stare at anyone, no matter what they are doing. Their code of manners is determined by the fact that there are so many of them, and the walls of their houses are often no more than screens, so privacy is very important. I never thought of the same kind of custom applying here.'

Suragai knew about the Manchu. One of the men who had come to the world with his grandfather was of that race, and so the privacy custom was well known. It was why Suragai had used it as an example, because he had reasoned that an alien would understand.

'Now that you know about it, you will be able to avoid giving offence again,' he said. He took the reins of his st'lyan from the orderly's hands and mounted. Then he looked down at Constantin again. 'I expect it was a shattering experience to be rejected by a woman – particularly since the women on other worlds probably regard you as special. You're not taking it at all well, but if I were a gambler I would bet you four good st'lyan that the next time you see my sister you'll look at her just the way you did today. Mount up if you're coming. We have things to do.'

Suragai's grandfather's house was build upon a natural plateau which rose above the curtain wall of the city. The morning room was supported out from it on stilts, and reached into nothing so that to stand at the foremost edge of the platform was to seem to be poised above an abyss. Kinsai was constructed on top of a plug of volcanic rock which rose sheer for almost five hundred drem out of an almost perfectly flat and featureless plain. In the late afternoon, with the red sun setting and the dust from the caravans crossing the plain hanging on the air, the whole edifice looked like a great monolith rising out of the depths of a brooding red sea.

'Is this a courtesy call?' Suragai the elder asked, 'or do you have a purpose in coming to see me?'

They were standing at the front of the platform on which the morning room was constructed. It was his grandfather's favourite place for receiving guests, and now Suragai wondered why he had caused his house to be built in such a style. To stare out over such a view was disconcerting to say the least. It made him feel small and insignificant.

'I came to talk to you about the trade commissioner's message,' he said.

'I thought you would.' His grandfather nodded. 'You wonder what it means, and how it affects my loyalty to Jehan.'

Suragai had not thought to pose an enquiry so explicitly, but he saw no point in denying what was on his mind. He nodded his head, meeting his grandfather's eyes steadily.

The man who had once been Sergei Rostov was tall and broad-shouldered. Now that he was in late middle age his hair was silver. It was dressed Yek style – the front part of the scalp had been shaved, and the remainder was drawn into a queue which had been folded forward and bound with black cords. He was wearing the formal coat of midnight blue which denoted the rank of officer of the court, and beneath it was the high-collared tunic worn only by Gentlemen of the Household. He stirred, peering down into the haze which covered the plain. 'You know I was once a servant of the Empire,' he said. 'It has been nearly forty years as people around the universe reckon time, but probably the trade commissioner's message means that my wife – the wife I had before I came to this world – is still alive.'

It should not have come as a surprise, Suragai thought. He watched his grandfather's face carefully for expression, but saw none. 'Then will you go to her?' he asked. 'Maybe you could bring her here.'

His grandfather laughed softly. 'The lady I was married to in those days is a niece of the Emperor. I don't think she would care to live here.'

Probably he meant that she would not care to share her husband with two other women. It had surprised Suragai to learn that the Empire regarded polygamy with disfavour. It was by no means universal in the Khanate, of course – a man took to wife the women by whom he had children, or those who were willing to live as part of an arranged household – but the fact that men and women on other worlds appeared to be so incapable of controlling their emotions that they permitted jealousy and discord to destroy the harmony of a relationship was simply a confirmation that they were indeed uncivilised.

Suragai remembered that his mother had once told him that his offworlder grandfather regarded the life he had led before he had come to the Khanate as a thing separate from his present existence. He knew that his curiosity had been fed by his mistrust – because he did not comprehend alien motivations – and suddenly he felt ashamed to have doubted that his grandfather would remain loyal to the Kha-Khan.

'What does Fedyev's message mean?' he asked. 'What will you do? If you want me to, I will carry an answer.'

The older Suragai shook his head. 'When he comes to Kinsai I will talk to him,' he said. 'I believe he thinks that the knowledge that I have a wife in the care of the Empire can be used to force me to serve his interests. If that is the case, then he does not know me. Even when I was the Emperor's man, I would have refused to swerve from my sworn duty.'

A horn rang out on the city wall. The parapet which ran behind the wall was wide enough for two carts to be driven side by side along its length. It crossed the face of Suragai's grandfather's house at a level ten drem or so below the supports for the legs on which the morning-room floor was braced. Suragai glanced idly down, and saw that a company of troopers of the guard – Merkuts by their appearance – were marching along from the direction of the gate, picking up the sentries who had completed their tours of duty, dropping off the night watch. The column of men passed out of sight beneath his feet.

'This question of loyalty troubles you,' the older man said. He did not look round as he spoke. 'On this world a man of your race swears one oath of service and keeps it all his life, or he is considered forsworn. But consider the case of the C'zak or the Ch'kasian who serves in the army. Once maybe he swore fealty to a chief or a warlord. Now he serves the Kha-Khan. Is he the less loyal because he was not born in Jehan's service?'

In theory he was not. Suragai had heard the terms of this argument before, and knew that the Yasa was quite specific. It did not alter his personal belief that the only safe tie was blood, and that non-humans were never to be entirely trusted. He flushed. 'Grandfather, I meant no offence,' he said.

'Noyon, I know precisely what you intended,'

411

Suragai's grandfather responded. Abruptly he turned. The movement was full of such contained violence that Suragai jumped. He waited until the older man had stepped back inside the room, then he followed. Open lattice screens lined the side walls of the chamber, and through them the gardens which had been laid out below the house could be seen.

'It is the presence of the aliens that troubles me,' Suragai said. He watched his grandfather's face for a reaction. 'I cannot understand why we are still treating with them now that they have demonstrated that they are our enemy.'

The older man pursed his lips. 'The reasons are complicated,' he said at last. 'Probably you have heard some men suggest that we ought to be afraid of the power of the alien weapons. It's true that the Empire could destroy this world if it chose to, but then the poppy would also be destroyed. We are continuing to talk to the ambassador and the traders because we don't know yet how far they are ready to go to overcome us. If we sever our relationship with them, we will be forcing them to select an alternative course to the one they are following now, and it may be an approach we have no means of dealing with. They aren't about to go away because we tell them to. They have to decide for themselves that it is too costly to remain.'

It was the first time anyone had explained the issues so that they were capable of being understood. Suragai made a face. 'You're saying that we may have to accept their presence,' he said.

'I'm saying that until we discover what means they are prepared to use to ensure that they control what happens here, we have to deal gently,' his grandfather said.

412

The calls of the posted sentries echoed up from the rampart below the morning room. Every time a man used the countersign it was picked up and transmitted along the wall. Suragai found the sound reassuring, for it meant that the city was protected, and that order was being maintained. 'The Kha-Khan wanted to know if I could kill any of my alien friends if I had to,' he said.

'Oh?' The older man's head came round sharply. 'What did you say?'

'I said that I could.' Suragai hesitated, and then he flexed his hand and gestured. His extended talons glittered. 'My mother is half an alien, and my father is Alan by birth, but –'

'– but still you are Altun.' His grandfather nodded. 'Now I understand why you came to see me.'

It had been the only way Suragai could think of to tell this man of alien background that even blood would count for nothing if it came to war. He avoided his grandfather's eyes, grateful that he was not required to say more. Another call rang out from the wall below, and the countersign was repeated and carried away as if by the wind.

'I will return in ten days,' Constantin said. He pulled himself up into the entrance of the alien vessel. Inside the hull was packed with men, most of them Keraistani with apprehensive expressions on their faces.

Suragai eyed the men he had recruited to work in Marakan. He had no doubt that a few of them were Burun's agents, but there seemed to be no way to identify them even if it mattered. 'Tell the commissioner what I said.' He glanced up.

'I will.' Constantin nodded.

The message Suragai had concocted simply stated that Fedyev's message had been delivered, and that Suragai Khan had said that he would discuss the matter when the traders came to Kinsai. Suragai thought it ensured that the trade commissioners would attend the celebration of Jehan's anniversary no matter what other distractions presented themselves.

'Shall I give Natalia your regards?' Constantin asked. He smiled.

Suragai wrinkled his nose. It was the kind of message a man would send his betrothed – the kind Kubulai had sent to Turakina – but he supposed the alien was incapable of appreciating that. 'Tell her what you like,' he said.

To accommodate Kubulai and to honour his new status as a general of the army, Jehan had provided him with a large house which was near Kinsai's south watchtower. A guard commanded by one of Kubulai's captains – a Merkut called Jehangir – had moved all the new occupant's gear into it days before Kubulai himself arrived. The house had two storeys and an enclosed garden, and it was staffed by a retinue of slaves which seemed to expand every time Suragai looked. A lot of them were women.

'How pleasant it is to see you again,' Kubulai said, sliding into a chair. He draped one leg across the arm, then gestured to a manservant who was waiting with wine. There was a new scar on his chest just below the neckline of his shirt, and more muscle than before decorated his frame. 'I would have enjoyed your company had you not been engaged nursemaiding aliens,' Kubulai said. 'No one else plays chess half so well.'

'I'm flattered you missed me,' Suragai responded drily. He waited while the slave served the wine, and then sat down. The man was a Ch'noze, and his facial tattoos indicated that he was a member of the Arpid clan.

'Han, thank you,' Kubulai said. He waved to dismiss the slave, then swirled the wine in his cup and drank. After a moment he eyed Suragai. 'I'm fighting Kadan,' he said. 'I want you to help me deal with him.'

'Oh?' Suragai looked down at his wine. It was dark red, and a sweet smell rose from it. He sipped at it, hiding what he was thinking. He had already heard accounts of what had happened between Kubulai and Kadan during the campaign. 'I'm not sure I want to be involved.'

'You are involved,' Kubulai said brusquely. 'Remember the race? He would have killed all three of us.'

Suragai clenched his teeth. The new authority in Kubulai's voice unsettled him. 'I think I'd like to know who started it,' he said.

'He did, of course.' Kubulai looked surprised. 'He's my uncle. Why should I desire his dishonour?'

Their relationship was not that precise, Suragai thought, but did not say it. He watched Kubulai's face and decided that he was telling the truth. A feud between Kadan and Kubulai made no sense, except that Kadan was jealous because Kubulai had been named Successor.

'I never did anything to hurt him,' Kubulai said. 'He is responsible for everything that has happened between us. He tried to set Orcadai against me while we were fighting the Ch'noze. Now I have to deal with him, to show him that he cannot use me this way.'

Kadan fresh from a campaign would be hard to kill,

Suragai thought. 'Let me mediate it,' he said.

Kubulai snorted. The door behind him flew open and a tall woman with fair hair came into the room. She stopped in her tracks when she saw Suragai. Kubulai turned round in his chair. 'What is it?' he demanded.

The woman gave him a shy smile. 'Your bath is ready.'

'Oh.' Kubulai did not return the smile. He glanced once in Suragai's direction, looking embarrassed. 'I'll come in a while. Keep the water hot.'

'Of course,' the woman said. She went out through the door without looking at Suragai again. Kubulai turned back. He drank some more wine, then put his cup down.

'She's new,' Suragai said politely. 'Where did you get her?' He was amused because Kubulai was incapable of concealing the fact that he was sleeping with one of his slaves.

Kubulai produced a level stare. 'At T'tai,' he said. 'She nursed me when I was wounded.'

'She looks as if she might be good at it,' Suragai agreed blandly.

A gleam of annoyance entered Kubulai's eyes. 'She is,' he said pugnaciously. He glared at Suragai. Suragai grinned back. After a moment Kubulai ran one hand up over his scalp, and then he shook his head. 'Damn you,' he said. 'You are mocking me.'

'I'm trying not to,' Suragai said. He adjusted his features. 'What are you going to do about Kadan?'

'I haven't decided yet.' Kubulai frowned. He got up out of his chair and paced over to the window, then stood staring out into the street.

If Kubulai wanted to fight Kadan according to the

law, he needed the Kha-Khan's permission. Suragai was not sure how Jehan would react to a request from Kubulai - a general who was also his nephew - for leave to offer kanly against Kadan - not only the Kha-Khan's admiral but also his cousin. Probably it would not come to that.

Suddenly Kubulai swung round. He said, 'I will help you with the aliens if you will aid me against Kadan.'

It meant that Kubulai was almost bound to reveal whatever it was he knew - the secret Jehan had expected would be disclosed in the letter Suragai had received. Suragai nodded. 'Very well.'

Kubulai looked as if he was surprised that Suragai had conceded so easily. He produced a suspicious stare. 'No matter how I decide to deal with Kadan, you will help me,' he said. 'You agree?'

'I just said so.' Suragai stood up. He gave Kubulai a level stare. 'Your bath is waiting.'

'I thought you were trying not to mock me,' Kubulai said. He went past Suragai towards the door. When he reached it he looked back. 'About the woman,' he said. 'Do you think Turakina will mind?'

'Only if you get her with child before you are married,' Suragai said, and laughed at Kubulai's startled expression.

No one had seen Kadan return to Kinsai, but the windows of his house were open and there were guards outside. They saluted Suragai when he went up to the door, and then stood aside. Inside the hall the boxes and furniture were lying just as they had been unloaded from the carts which had brought them. The door to a room on the right of the hall was lying open, and inside Kadan was stretched in solitary abandon on a couch. A fire set in a tray of sand flickered beside the door, and a pot of gruel was steaming over it, but there was nobody else in the chamber. Kadan was snoring in a drunken stupor. He stank.

Suragai sat down on his heels beside the couch. He shook Kadan by the shoulder, but Kadan only stirred and mumbled, licking his lips, and then was still again.

A woman came through the door. She stooped down beside the fire and stirred the pot. Suragai waited until she looked up, and then said, 'Does he ever eat?'

'When he wakes up.' The woman nodded. She put the spoon back in the pot.

'And how often does that happen?'

'Once or twice a day.'

The floor of the room was carpeted with cheap cloth, but it was clean. Suragai straightened. He stirred the cloth with the toe of his boot.

'When he has had too much to drink he gets sick,' the woman said. She came over to the side of the couch and looked down at Kadan. 'When that happens I take up the cloth and burn it.'

Suragai pursed his lips. 'Don't let him have any more wine,' he said. He felt appalled by Kadan's condition. He recalled that he had seen T'zin, the brother of Nogai the fourth Kha-Khan, like this once, and now he knew why the similarity between the two men had stirred in his mind. 'Give him water or ch'ban,' he said. 'Make him take some meat when he wakes up.'

'He'll beat me.'

'No.' Suragai shook his head. 'Do you know who I am? This is my uncle. Tell him it is my order.'

418

'Yes, Noyon.'

Suragai went outside. He rode back through the streets to Alexei's house. Already the buildings were being decked out for the procession to mark the anniversary of Jehan's accession to the throne, and wooden arches were being raised across the main thoroughfares. A shower of rain came down out of nowhere. Drops of rain pattered on Suragai's shoulders, and his st'lyan kept its head down round its knees. Steam rose from places where water lay on cobbles which had been heated by the sun.

Alexei was dismounting outside his house when Suragai rode up. An escort of Merkuts milled around in the yard. 'I looked for you earlier,' Alexei said. 'Somebody told me you went to see Kadan. How did you find him?'

'I found him drunk,' Suragai said sourly. He threw his reins to an orderly.

'Indeed?' Alexei made a face. 'He's only been back in Kinsai a few days. It usually takes longer than that. He only drinks heavily when he has nothing better to do. He must be unhappy about something.'

Suragai was not sure how he was expected to react. He said, 'I think it has something to do with his feud with your son. I'm going to mediate it. It makes no sense for them to fight.'

'I agree.' Alexei looked amused. 'I heard you had agreed to support Kubulai against Kadan, but I knew it could not be true.'

If Alexei had heard it, probably it was all over Kinsai. Suragai stared at him. 'I told Kubulai I would help him to deal with my uncle if it came to that,' he said. 'I didn't promise not to try to bring them to a truce.'

Alexei laughed. 'It's a neat distinction,' he said. 'Did you come to see me? Let's go inside.'

The smell of meat cooking in the kitchens at the back of Alexei's house made Suragai's mouth water. He followed Alexei through the door. The central hallway of the house had a ceiling which was also the roof. Rafters of pale sanded wood supported the timbers, and the rain which was still falling resounded off the tiles above. Around the hall there were galleries off which the passageways to the upper rooms ran. A woman looked over the rail as Suragai shed his damp coat. Her face appeared at the corner of his vision like an indistinct pale oval, and by the time he had turned was gone again.

'You've been asking questions about the aliens,' Alexei said. He clapped Suragai on the shoulder. 'I can't blame you for your curiosity. I was the same at your age.'

The confusion of relationships often caught Suragai by surprise. He remembered that the older Suragai was Alexei's father. Because they were both alien it was sometimes hard to place them within the bloodlines of the Altun. They belonged in truth nowhere. 'My grandfather told you,' Suragai said.

'He mentioned you had spoken to him,' Alexei said mildly.

It meant that Alexei probably knew about Suragai's attitude to the question of the conflict of loyalties in the matter of the aliens. Suragai waited for Alexei to comment, but he said nothing. Instead he walked across the hallway and pushed open the double doors to the family chamber. The room beyond was empty. Alexei turned and gestured Suragai inside. A table on one side of the room was arranged with cups and flasks of wine and k'miss. Alexei filled two cups with wine and gave one of them to Suragai. 'Ask your questions,' he said.

Suragai was at a loss to know how to begin. He tried the wine and found that it was sweet, fit more for women than for men. Carefully he set his cup down on the table. 'I don't understand anything the aliens are doing,' he said at last. 'The trade mission is important to the Empire, they say, and yet they have only a few men engaged on it. It's not how we would behave.'

'That's true.' Alexei nodded. He had not touched his wine. 'I think it depends on how much time they have had to prepare, and to what extent they are keeping the discovery of the poppy a secret. If they use too many resources, somebody will be bound to notice. The men of the trade commission are from a cartel known as the Nicoleyev. If they want to keep the discovery of the poppy a secret – maybe so that they can drive up the price – it would make sense for them to use only a few men at first.'

Commercial concerns were so completely alien to Suragai that he felt that there was no point in attempting to understand them. He frowned to show how he felt about the subject. 'To attempt conquest for the sake of profit makes no sense,' he said.

'Oh.' Alexei laughed. 'I think the Nicoleyev and the other cartels would disagree with you. Your values are different from theirs. If you had been brought up in the Empire, probably you would see it as they do.'

Suragai doubted it, but he could think of no way to say so without offering offence. 'The aliens honour you,' he said flatly. He gave Alexei an inquisitive stare.

'They pretend to do me honour,' Alexei responded.

He did not seem to be offended by the implication which lay at the back of Suragai's observation. 'Were I not a khan, and Jehan's counsellor, they would revere me as a member of the family of the Emperor. Because of my situation they are unsure where my loyalties lie, as you are.'

Suragai flushed. 'The Kha-Khan trusts you,' he said.

'But you are not Jehan,' Alexei said, and he showed his teeth. 'Noyon, it is the ambiguity of my position which makes me valuable to the Khanate. The ambassador and the traders have to believe that I have retained something of their system of values, and so they will seek to enlist me to their cause. When they do, they will reveal the truth of their intentions, and the reasons which drive them. It is information we must have before we act.'

It came to Suragai that he was being told all this for a purpose. 'Khan, I'm honoured by your confidence,' he said. 'What is my part in all this?'

'I can't tell you that,' Alexei replied, and he raised his cup and drank.

Kadan tipped his head back so that his neck rested on the rolled edge of the couch. 'Name of God, I feel rotten,' he said.

Suragai spooned several chunks of meat into a bowl and offered it to him. Kadan tried to push it away. He shook his head. Suragai put the bowl down on the floor at the side of the couch. 'You have to eat,' he said.

'I can't think why.'

'You're the Kha-Khan's officer. He needs you.'

'Oh?' Kadan's eyes opened. 'What's happening? Is it the aliens?'

'Not yet.' Suragai watched Kadan steadily. Even if Kadan knew what was intended, he would never admit it.

'I'm only one of many,' Kadan said. He closed his eyes again. 'One worthless half-breed among so many proper men.' He moved a hand up to cover his face. 'I'm … I feel terrible.'

'You shouldn't drink so much.'

'I need to drink. Give me something.'

'No.'

'Damn you.' Kadan tried to sit up. 'I'm not a slave. You can't treat me like this.'

'The Kha-Khan needs you,' Suragai said patiently. It was the only thing he could think of to say which would prevent Kadan from falling into a stupor again.

Kadan lurched to his feet. He stumbled across to the door of the chamber and made his way out into the hall. Suragai followed him. Kadan got as far as the outside door. He got it open, and then he fell, sprawling over the threshold to be sick. The red sunlight shone down angrily. Out in the street the people who were passing turned to watch Kadan. Kubulai cantered up on a bay st'lyan. He reined in, his face flushed. 'Get him back inside,' he shouted at Suragai. 'He's your uncle. Will you let everyone see him like this?'

'Why not?'

Kubulai's eyes blazed. Suragai put his hands in his belt and glared back at him. 'Don't give me orders,' he said. 'You're trying to win me onto your side, remember.'

'Hunh.' Kubulai looked at Kadan again. 'He's done now. Take him inside.'

Suragai went over to Kadan and dragged him back

423

inside the house. Kubulai galloped his st'lyan away in a clatter of hooves. When he had gone Suragai grinned and closed the door. Kubulai was torn in two by the problem of balancing Kadan's loss of face against the duty of his feud. There was no honour to be gained in obtaining the submission of a drunkard.

Kadan said, 'Give me something to drink.'

'No.'

'Suragai, I shall die.'

'I don't think so.'

'Who was that at the door? Were they laughing at me?'

'No.'

'It was Kubulai. Where did he go?'

'Up the street.'

Kadan got to his feet. He supported himself against the wall until he was back in the room again, and then lay down on the couch, his breathing ragged. Suragai sat down beside the fire. After a while Kadan seemed to sleep. His shoulders moved, and he murmured something. The meat in the bowl at the side of the couch was cold, and Suragai poured it back into the pot on the fire so that it would heat, then sat once more, complacent at the depth of his patience, to wait for Kadan's awakening.

The Ch'noze Kubulai had captured before T'tai was working in the yard. When he saw Suragai he bowed awkwardly. 'The Khan is at the palace,' he said in fractured Yek.

'Thank you.' Suragai nodded. 'I'll wait for him.'

He dismounted. His st'lyan was a piebald – a young mare he was riding to accustom her to the noise and confusion of the city streets. As soon as Suragai let go

424

of the reins the mare clattered across the paving towards the well which stood in the corner of the yard. The Ch'noze jumped up, and ran and caught the trailing reins.

'Oh no,' he said in his own tongue. He dragged the piebald's head around, away from the well. 'You're too hot to drink yet.'

The st'lyan whickered. It butted at the Ch'noze, and then nosed at his hand, licking it to get the salt. The Ch'noze laughed. He led the piebald back across the yard to Suragai.

Suragai took the reins and tied them to the hitching post beside the gate. A company of Yek troopers came down the street, and when their officer saw Suragai he saluted. Suragai nodded an acknowledgement. When he turned he saw that the Ch'noze was watching the files of men and st'lyan. There was an odd, brooding look on his face.

'I hope you don't stare like that all the time,' Suragai said. 'I know men who would not need much more excuse to strike you.'

The slave's lips compressed, and then he shrugged. 'I don't know how to be a slave,' he said. 'It's against my nature.'

'I see.' Suragai grinned. 'You're an Arpid, aren't you? Better a slave than dead. What is your name?'

'Han.'

'You've learned some Yek.'

'Yes. I can't speak much.'

'Your accent is terrible. Speak Ch'noze.' Suragai sat down on the bench where the man had been working. 'How were you captured? Was it in battle? Your master didn't tell me.'

'I was asleep.' The Ch'noze hesitated, and then sat

425

down. The table between them was littered with gear and items of harness. The slave eyed Suragai warily. He said, 'I was supposed to be on guard, but we had been running for a day and a half, and I was tired. When I awoke there were men all around me. Your soldiers killed everyone else, but they left me alive.'

'And so now you hate us.' Suragai wrinkled his nose. 'Do you talk back to the khan like this?'

'He doesn't seem to mind.'

'That's because he's strange.' Suragai grinned. 'Get me something to drink.'

The Ch'noze got up and went into the house. While he was gone Suragai watered his st'lyan. He filled a wooden bucket from the well and carried it to the hitching place. At first he cupped water in his hands so that the mare could lap at it. Then when he judged that she was cool he let her drink her fill. He dropped the bucket beside the wall and sat down again at the bench. The Arpid came out into the yard with a flask and a cup. He poured k'miss into the cup and gave it to Suragai.

'Thank you.' Suragai drank. The slave sat down. He picked up a leather girth and started to rub it with a cloth. Suragai watched him. The Ch'noze seemed to sense that he was being scrutinised, and he looked up. A spark of resentment smouldered in his eyes.

Suragai gave him a level stare. 'What rank are you?'

'My father was war-leader of our clan. I think he was killed in the battle on the 'Sit.'

'In that case you're probably the chief of the Arpid now. I expect the khan will release you now that there is peace.'

'So that I can do what?' The Ch'noze looked angry. 'My people are slaughtered and I am dishonoured. A

Yek would not have let himself be taken. A Yek would not submit to slavery.'

'Oh.' Suragai grinned at him. 'We're different.' He drank some more of the k'miss. 'I'll talk to the khan about you. Maybe he doesn't realise how you feel, and it seems to me that he has slaves enough. Don't try to escape. We kill slaves who run away, and you would certainly be caught.'

'I saw Kadan,' Kubulai said. 'He was sober for a change.'

'Good.' Suragai sidestepped his st'lyan around a wagon which was parked across the middle of the street. Planks had been placed across the sides of the wagon, and men were standing on them so that they could reach the cable which had been strung from the buildings on both sides. A half-pinned banner which was painted with Jehan's arms dangled down inside the cart.

Kubulai edged his bay up so that he was riding at Suragai's side. 'You were supposed to help me to deal with him,' he said.

'There wasn't anything you could have done while he was dead drunk,' Suragai pointed out. 'If you think about it, I've done you a favour.'

'Indeed.' Kubulai looked down his nose. 'I wish I thought you did it for me. He's worse than ever now.'

Because Kadan was sober he was full of invention. Only six days remained until the anniversary of the Kha-Khan's accession to the throne, and those which were past had been filled with incident. An archery contest which had taken place before dawn in the concourse in front of the Golden Yurt had woken the city, because the contestants had used arrows with

427

whistles tied to the flights. Angry troopers emerging from the adjacent barracks had been doused with ink released from bladders which had been suspended from the crosspiece of the gate, and it was probably not a coincidence that the guard the previous night had been nominally under Kubulai's command.

'He is embarrassing me,' Kubulai said severely.

'You are not the only target,' Suragai countered.

That was certainly true. Kadan had enrolled most of the otherwise unemployed Gentlemen of the Kha-Khan's Household as willing participants in his schemes, and a number of other khans had fallen victim to their at times brutal sense of humour.

'There is to be a competition for the lances this afternoon.' Kubulai looked worried. 'I'm marshal, and the alien ambassador is to be present. I'm certain Kadan has something planned for that.'

'Then maybe it would be a good idea to find out what it is,' Suragai suggested. 'You could turn it upon him.'

A thoughtful expression appeared on Kubulai's face. 'Yes.' He nodded, and then gave Suragai a sharp stare. 'You're determined we're not going to fight,' he said.

'Against Kadan, ridicule will be much more effective,' Suragai said.

Every Yek trooper was trained in the use of the lance, and excellence was expected in this as in every other military art. A cavalry lance was a drem-and-a-half-long ash pole which was topped with a blade of tempered steel. The usual competitions involved tent-pegging – where a man was required to ride a course of ten pegs at the gallop, spearing the peg ends as he rode – and quintain.

A quintain was a wooden figure which was mounted on a swivel post. Traditionally it was designed with extended arms, one of which held a shield which was the target, while the other was loaded with a sand-filled bag. A poor hit, because of the pivoting arrangement, gave a passing rider a crippling clout on the back of the head. It was a popular spectator sport.

The news that nearly every prominent member of Jehan's court had agreed to compete had caused the city to empty. The tilting-ground was down on the plain – a stretch of level ground about half a verst in length which was shaded along one side by stands of broad-leafed trees. The area beneath these was packed with people. An awning had been erected on poles on the grass on the opposite side of the field, and to it eventually came the Kha-Khan and his guest, the alien ambassador.

A crowd of contestants had gathered at the bottom of the tilting-ground, and they saluted respectfully. Then they resumed their discussion about the conditions, while Kubulai rode up towards the awning to get Jehan's permission to start.

Suragai was standing to one side. The earlier part of the afternoon had been taken up with a contest between the ordinary troopers of the tuman from which was drawn the current garrison of Kinsai. A course of tent pegs had been used, and now these were being lifted by groups of orderlies.

'That's not a quintain,' someone said.

The conversation taking place behind Suragai had so far been rather less technical than he had anticipated. A gentleman of the Kha-Khan's Household had spent some time discoursing loudly about a new pair of boots, and where the members of his audience had employed their wit at all, it had been at the expense of the serious contestants who were now assembled closer to the trees.

Suragai glanced briefly towards the place where the quintain usually stood. The traditional figure had been replaced with a barrel on which were painted eyes, nose, and mouth, along with a line to mark the midriff and thus the point of high and low scoring.

'You've noticed,' Kadan said.

The sound of his uncle's voice made Suragai turn. What Kadan had planned for the occasion he did not know, but Kubulai had been down to the tilting-ground about midday, and had come back smiling. If he was the person responsible for the quintain's replacement, it was thus far beyond Suragai to discern the point of the jest.

'It will be harder to hit,' a noyon of the Arcut said. 'Mark how the face of the barrel curves. There will be a few split heads today.'

In fact only one arm now extended away from the pivot, and the bag at the end of it appeared to be only partly full of sand. Suragai wondered if the weight of the barrel had prevented the use of anything bulkier. He stared past the courtiers at Kadan, and saw that he was gazing up the field, a speculative look in his eyes. When he saw Suragai watching, he smiled. He came through the crowd.

'Nephew,' he said, 'are you taking part in this?'

'I'll watch a while,' Suragai temporised.

Kubulai rode back down the course. He reined in when he reached the place where Suragai was standing, and then he stared down. 'Khan, good day,' he said. He gave Kadan a level stare.

'Is it?' Kadan showed his teeth. 'I hear you are in charge of this nonsense. Is this the best entertainment you can offer?'

Most of the men around Kadan fell silent, and Suragai saw that some who were at the back of the crowd were straining to hear what was being said.

'I'm surprised you bothered to attend if that is how you feel,' Kubulai observed evenly. He let his reins fall loose on his st'lyan's neck. The st'lyan was a bay with brilliant black points. When it tossed its head, the gold chasing on its horn caught the sunlight.

'I couldn't bear to stay away,' Kadan said. 'I hope you are competing. I could do with a laugh.'

The few remaining fragments of conversation died abruptly. Kubulai rested a hand on one thigh, and then he leaned forward out of the saddle. 'I think I can hear the drink talking,' he said. 'You wouldn't dare to mock me if you were sober.'

A dangerous flush appeared on Kadan's cheeks. It was as if he considered a retort, then rejected it. Suddenly his countenance cleared, and he laughed harshly. 'Drunk or sober, I can still beat you,' he said. 'I would offer to match you, but probably you think I have embarrassed you enough.'

Kubulai sat back in the saddle. He glanced round at the course, and then gestured one-handed. 'Somebody get me a lance.'

Alexei was at the head of a group of officers who forced their way through to the front of the crowd. 'Aren't we ready to start yet?' he demanded.

'We have some business to settle first, your half-brother and I,' Kubulai said tightly. He had his eye fixed on Kadan as he spoke. Kadan folded his arms,

431

looking pleased with himself. An officer of the Kha-Khan's guard made his way up to the front of the press with a lance. He passed it up to Kubulai, who tested the shaft between his hands. The lance was made from very light-coloured wood. Kubulai swung it in a circle, and the steel head flashed as it reflected the light.

'Who rides first?' Kubulai looked back at Kadan.

'You are already mounted,' Kadan pointed out. He was still smiling broadly.

Kubulai looked as if he intended to argue, and then suddenly he shrugged and gathered up his reins. He wheeled his st'lyan around and urged the animal away towards the target, breaking into a gallop when he was ten or fifteen drem from the mark. His lance seemed to waver at the last moment. The point nocked the wood with a thud which resounded across the field, and there was a derisive cheer from the spectators as Kubulai ducked to avoid the swing of the pivot.

Suragai glanced quickly at Kadan and saw him frown, disappointed. Whatever he had intended, it had been to do with the quintain, and apparently the plan had failed.

Alexei was watching as Kubulai rode around in a wide circle. 'He must be sick,' he said. 'That's the worst I've ever seen him perform at this.'

The officers lining the end of the course catcalled at Kubulai as he rode past them. Kubulai gestured rudely. He pulled up in front of Kadan and threw the lance at him. 'We've heard your talk,' he said. 'Now back it up.'

Kadan's st'lyan was a chestnut with a mane which had fine gold hairs running through it. Kadan reined the beast into a curvet, and then he charged off down the length of the tilting-ground towards the quintain. He aimed the lance straight and true, and it impaled the painted nose of the target. The thud of the impact was followed by a hiss and a puff of steam. Water flooded out of the gash the lance had made in the wood, soaking Kadan as he rode past below. The people watching among the trees howled with delight.

Kubulai had stayed in the saddle to watch. Now he dismounted, laughing. 'Kadan had the barrel filled to the brim with water,' he said. 'That was why he wanted me to ride first.'

Suragai stared up the course. The stream of water from the wound in the stave had diminished to a trickle. 'I don't understand how you stayed dry.' He turned to look at Kubulai. 'You hit the barrel. I heard you.'

'I aimed low,' Kubulai said. 'When I discovered what Kadan had done I had the barrel emptied. Then I put in a copper above the centre point and filled it up again.'

'That was why he looked so disappointed when you rode back.' Suragai recalled the expression on Kadan's face. 'He thought it had run dry.'

At least a few of the loitering gentlemen had been privy to Kadan's intent, and now that the jokester had fallen victim to his own ingenuity their amusement was unbridled. Kadan came down the field to whoops and jeers which far exceeded those which had been directed at his opponent. Kadan's hair and tunic were dripping, and the look on his face indicated that he knew who had bested him. Reining in before Kubulai he looked down. 'Khan, for that I

433

shall want my revenge,' he said.

'Oh?' Kubulai looked innocent, and then he gave Kadan an amused stare. 'In that case you will have to try another sport. So far as this one is concerned, I think we have all been sufficiently entertained.'

One of the officers of Kubulai's personal guard was hovering beside the gate to meet the cavalcade which wound back up from the tilting-ground to the city after the competition was over. As soon as he saw Kubulai he came forward, saluting. 'Khan, I thought you might have come sooner. The dispatches from Ch'nozia are not marked urgent, but I knew you would want to read them.'

Kubulai reined in. Suragai sidestepped his st'lyan out of the way of the people who were coming up the road behind, and gathered his reins to prevent the piebald from tossing its head.

'I didn't see the courier,' Kubulai said. 'How did you expect me to know that dispatches had arrived?'

'The slave should have told you.'

'Slave?' Kubulai sat back in the saddle. 'What slave?'

'The Ch'noze,' the officer said. 'I sent him to find you.' He gestured with both hands. 'I didn't have anyone else to spare. All my men were down watching the tilting.'

'You sent him after me.'

'Yes. Surely he found you?'

'No.' Kubulai shook his head, and then glanced round in Suragai's direction. 'Did you see him?'

'Not I.' Suddenly Suragai remembered the conversation in the yard in front of Kubulai's house. The expression on the slave's face came into his mind. This is my fault, he thought. He caught the officer's eye.

'Did you give him a st'lyan to ride?'

'Yes.' The officer looked apologetically at Kubulai. 'Khan, he has the roan with the white feet.'

'Name of God,' Kubulai said. He stood in the stirrups, then waved to a hundred commander who was coming up the road with a party of men. 'Arugai, bring your men and follow me. One of my slaves has run off. We'll need torches.'

Suragai said, 'Don't be too hard on him.'

Kubulai looked stern. 'You know the law. He has to die.'

They rode back down onto the plain. It was already dusk, and the air was hot and heavy. Kubulai levered the top off his arrow case and touched the flights of the arrows inside, counting them. Then he put a hand on the bow case which hung from his saddlebow.

Suragai glanced towards the setting sun. He guessed that the Ch'noze would not want to risk riding along the roads, and so probably he would keep to the fields and the grassland. It meant that they would be able to follow his trail once they found it, even in the dark. He urged the piebald up to Kubulai's side. 'Which way do you think he will go?'

'North-west,' Kubulai said. 'He'll go home.'

The troopers were spreading out across the plain which lay beyond the road. They leaned out of their saddles to see the ground. 'I told him you would probably release him now that the war is over,' Suragai said. 'You must have treated him badly to make him do this.'

'I did nothing. He's a Ch'noze. They don't think the way we do.'

Suragai laid a hand on Kubulai's arm. 'Don't hurt him. He doesn't understand what it means to be a slave.'

Kubulai pursed his lips. 'I was too soft with him,' he said.

They started north and west. Ahead of them the plain rolled on dead flat towards the D'neistr River. After the sun went down there was bright moonlight, and every detail of the landscape was distinct.

The st'lyan covered the ground at a fast trot. The Ch'noze would not have wasted time as soon as he got away from the road, but probably he had been forced to hide from caravans and casual passers-by until then. His facial tattoos would have given him away, and anyone who saw him would have known that he was a slave.

A trooper swerved across behind them. He held out a torch, and Suragai took it and thrust it through the straps behind his saddle. No one else had lit a torch yet – there was no need here, and no one wanted to ruin his night vision.

At the river they paused while the troopers searched through the trees along the bank. Suragai felt sure the slave had crossed by now. He rode slowly down onto the soft soil beside the water's edge, looking for hoofprints. A man at the far end of the line called out. Kubulai reined around towards him, and they all crossed together, following the trail which ran clear across the ground.

This was C'zakia. Suragai recognised the low hills on the skyline ahead. The piebald's head came up suddenly, as if it sensed something in the distance. Suragai stood in the stirrups and stared. The movement was all but lost in the grey between the sky and the plain.

Somebody else was pointing ahead. A st'lyan broke into a canter, and Kubulai shouted, ordering the trooper to rein back to a trot.

Han was far ahead. If he made it to the hills it would take time to dig him out. Probably they would need more men. All the other troopers had seen the movement in the darkness in front now, and they drew together into orderly files.

The moonlight made Suragai's eyes ache, and everything beneath it was either black or silver except in the distance where it was grey. The steady rhythm of the st'lyan's movements took Suragai's concentration away from the task of pursuit, and he became aware of the hollow feeling in his stomach. A length away Kubulai's features were gaunt, and the bones in his face looked like rocks sticking up beneath the skin. Suragai called to him, and he veered over.

'How should I punish him?'

Suragai frowned. 'It doesn't matter what I think. The Yasa is perfectly clear. You have to kill him.'

'I'm not sure it's right.'

'It could be what he hopes for. He talked to me about honour. You know how the Ch'noze are. He thought he had dishonoured himself by submitting to slavery.'

Kubulai made a face. 'In that case I wonder why he delayed so long.'

'Some Ch'noze believe that when they die their spirits become birds, and are taken up into the sky. They aren't afraid of dying.'

'But I told him I would return him to his homeland,' Kubulai said. 'He would have been the leader of his clan. It's beyond comprehension.'

'We wouldn't submit to slavery.'

'That's different,' Kubulai said.

Suragai eyed him, amused. 'That's what I told him,' he said. 'Sometimes it surprises us when other races

437

take the same approach to honour that we do.'

Kubulai frowned. 'You're turning into a philosopher.' He stood in the stirrups and stared ahead. 'He has stopped,' he said. 'Do you suppose he has a weapon?'

'Possibly.'

The Ch'noze appeared to have dismounted. Suddenly he got back up on the white-footed roan and rode off again. Suragai peered at his outline against the horizon. 'Even if he had no weapon when he ran off, he has acquired one now.'

'A stick maybe.'

'He's young and strong. Would you take on any Ch'noze in hand-to-hand combat?'

'No.' Kubulai made a face. 'Not unless I had to.'

They kept riding. The Ch'noze had surrendered his lead when he had stopped, but he seemed to be making no attempt to push the roan to a faster pace. Apparently he was satisfied to maintain the gap which separated him from his pursuers.

'Did you ever hear tell of Burun's father-in-law?' Kubulai asked.

'Vortai. Yes.'

'It's said that he only ever allowed his slaves to ride st'lyan that were lame or wind-broken.'

'Name of God.' Suragai produced a snort of amusement. 'I hope he never wanted anything in haste.'

'All the same, we would have caught up with Han by now if that roan was unsound.'

'I'm not sure I like the idea of keeping poor stock for slaves to ride.' Suragai wrinkled his nose. 'I remember that roan. It has a weakness in the off-fore. I wouldn't be surprised if it goes lame eventually.'

He studied the outline ahead and saw that the slave

was much closer. The roan was not going to have a chance to go lame. Suragai prodded the piebald in the side with his toe, and it moved up into a faster pace.

'That's a nice mare,' Kubulai said admiringly.

'She's skittish yet in a crowd – no good for fighting – but she'll keep up forever on ground like this.'

'It's the breeding.' Kubulai nodded. 'Do you recall my father's dun stallion – the one he kept at stud? All the st'lyan he runs now are direct descendants from that one animal. They all have endurance. I should never have let my father give him to Jehan.'

'Well, a request from the Kha-Khan …' Suragai paused.

'Request, nothing. My father told Jehan the dun would never father white foals, but Jehan said he'd dye the coats if he had to. He has a whole herd of them now – dun and bay, with never a white hair between them. Han's nearly in range.'

'I can see him.' Suragai reined across. He held up a hand to stop the oncoming troopers. 'Don't kill him yet. I think the Khan wants to persuade him to surrender.'

The troopers moved into line abreast. The Ch'noze was looking back, and now he reined around and halted his mare. In his hand he held a long pole – a branch from which he had stripped the bark and twigs. In the poor light it might have been mistaken for a lance. Suragai saw something glitter at the tip, and he pursed his lips. Probably the slave had secured his d'jaga to the end of the pole. Maybe that was why he had stopped.

Kubulai rode forward slowly. He uncased his bow and nocked an arrow. Suragai rode up quietly behind him.

'Han,' Kubulai shouted, 'give yourself up and I will not punish you.'

The Ch'noze did not answer. He was sitting up straight in the saddle. His fair hair looked like a silver cap in the moonlight.

'Surrender,' Kubulai called again. He walked the bay forward.

The slave brought the pole down and locked it between his bent arm and his side like a lance. He kicked the roan into a gallop and charged them. Kubulai waited until the Ch'noze was so close that he could not possibly miss, and then he raised his bow. He shot the slave in the chest.

The Ch'noze toppled out of the saddle. He hit the ground and lay still. The roan ran on past Suragai, and a trooper wheeled his st'lyan around to catch it.

Kubulai walked his st'lyan up to the Ch'noze. The slave was on his back, his hands clutching at the arrow shaft in his chest.

'Idiot,' Kubulai said. He dismounted.

Suragai allowed his reins to fall slack across his mare's neck. He kicked his feet out of the stirrups and slid to the ground. Kubulai was kneeling down beside the slave. The Ch'noze tried to say something, and then it was as if he smiled. The arrow trembled in his chest, and his head fell limply to the side.

'Is he dead?' Suragai stared down.

'Yes.' Kubulai grasped his arrow by the shaft and extracted it.

The troopers rode up around them. Suragai caught the hundred commander's eye. 'Ride off,' he said. 'We don't need you any more.'

They departed, leaving the roan tethered to a bush.

Kubulai lifted the dead slave and draped him across

the mare's back. He lashed the body so that it would not move, and then they started back towards Kinsai, following the wide trail broken by the troopers.

Kubulai said, 'How are we to govern such as these?'

'Maybe we aren't meant to,' Suragai said.

'Which of you is going to escort me?' Turakina demanded.

Because the betrothal between Turakina and Kubulai had not yet been formalised, it was the custom that they should not be left alone in a room together. Suragai stretched his legs out under the table, and he kicked Kubulai on the ankle. 'You are her suitor, not I,' he said.

'Am I?' Kubulai sat up. 'I thought I was a husband-to-be. Surely that's different.'

Turakina pursed her lips. 'If you won't be serious, I will go,' she said. 'Someone has to be my escort to the procession.'

'Both of us will have duties,' Suragai pointed out. There was no good reason why Turakina should not attend with their mother and Alexei's wife, and Suragai knew that she was only pressing the issue because she was determined to be seen to be adult by the other ladies of the court. He glanced across the table at Kubulai. 'My sister is a shrew,' he said. 'I don't know why you want to marry her.'

'Nobody else would have him,' Turakina said haughtily.

Suragai grinned. 'That's not what I've heard.'

Kubulai did not react. He was inspecting a plate of sweetmeats. After a moment he selected one and popped it into his mouth.

'The whole court is talking about his behaviour.'

Turakina got up out of her chair. She moved around the table behind Kubulai, and Suragai saw the light of wickedness glinting in her eyes. 'In fact no one is talking about anything else,' she said. 'I do not mind myself. He looks well. I like a sober appearance in a man.'

'Sober?' Suragai crowed. 'Kubulai?'

Kubulai looked as if the conserve had stuck in his throat. He spluttered, and then swallowed. He turned round and gave Turakina a stare. 'I always knew I had some fine quality you admired,' he said. 'Now ask me why I have agreed to have you.'

'Who but a wife would love you?' Turakina retorted. She looked down her nose.

Suragai laughed. Kubulai was staring at Turakina as if she had turned into a toad. He pushed his chair back from the table and swung round towards her. Turakina took a hasty step backwards. 'Tell me about the Ch'noze woman,' she said.

Kubulai shot a glance towards Suragai. 'Did you tell her?' he asked.

'Not I.' Suragai guessed Turakina had heard it from one of the evil tongues around the women's court. There were any number of wives and courtesans who would have delighted in detailing Kubulai's domestic arrangements, even though they were quite normal.

'Are you jealous?' Kubulai eyed Turakina warily.

'Have I reason to be?' She surveyed him coolly. 'Khan, if I am to be the mistress of your household, I ought to know what it contains.'

It could be a year or more before they married, Suragai thought. He grinned at Kubulai's discomfiture, for Turakina was already demonstrating that she was competent to deal with any man.

Kubulai stood up. 'Lady, it would please me to escort you to the procession if my duties elsewhere permit,' he said. He bowed formally.

Turakina's gown was a beautiful thing of embroidered russet silk. The facings and the overlay on the skirt were brocaded, and when she moved the weave caught the light of the lamps so that the fabric seemed to glow. As she blushed, the freckles across the bridge of her nose disappeared. 'Khan, thank you,' she said prettily. She maintained the poise of womanhood for a moment longer, then spoiled the effect with a girlish grin. 'In that case my brother will be free to pay escort to the alien woman.'

It was Suragai's turn to be put out of countenance. 'Oh,' he said. 'Will I, indeed? Well now.'

After Kubulai and Turakina had gone out into the garden, Suragai went through the hallway, passing the room where Alexei was entertaining the alien ambassador. The door of the chamber was open, and when Suragai paused at it the conversation ceased abruptly. Suragai bowed to Alexei, and he pulled the door closed. At once the murmur of talk recommenced. The voices reached Suragai, but not the words.

Suragai went upstairs and entered the empty audience chamber which was situated at the side of the gallery. The arched end window was open, and he sat down on the ledge, staring out at the night.

A window in the room below was open, and from here Suragai could hear the alien's voice as clearly as if he sat beside him. A draught of air ruffled the tops of the trees in the garden. Kubulai and Turakina were silhouetted in a patch of moonlight on the grass beyond the trees. Turakina said something in a low

443

voice, and Kubulai laughed. They moved on into the shade.

At first the ambassador appeared to talk of ordinary things: the progress of the trade mission and the grateful appreciation the Empire was prepared to extend for the facilities the embassy had been given. Alexei's status as a close counsellor of the Kha-Khan meant that the ambassador had many questions about the conduct of the court and the manner in which the Khanate was governed. Those to which Alexei responded, he answered with discretion. Suragai listened, one leg drawn up so that he could rest his cheek on his knee, and he thought that it was not Alexei's fault that he had been born alien, or that because of it the other aliens sought him out when they wanted to know something.

Now the ambassador was discussing people Suragai did not know – members of the Imperial court which was on a world called Knossos. Suragai furrowed his brow in an effort to remember the ambassador's name – Rogacheff – no, Borocheff; that was it. The ambassador talked about the Emperor's son, the Prince Feodor, who from what the ambassador said lived in the pocket of a Baron Andreeyev. Whenever Borocheff spoke the baron's name he laughed and slighted him. Suragai began to wish the ambassador would come to the point. Alexei said nothing at all.

At last the ambassador said, 'To be candid, my lord, there are doubts about the prince's suitability to inherit the throne. I am House Nicoleyev, as you know, and my uncle the baron is counselling the Emperor to look to one of the other branches of the royal family for a successor.'

There was a long silence. Suragai leaned out of the

444

window and looked down, but he could only see the shafts of light which were escaping from Alexei's room onto the paving of the arcade.

Alexei said, 'Neither the Andreeyev nor the Nicoleyev are so great that they ought to be permitted to direct the Emperor's choice. In the days when I knew the Empire there were men about the court who would have destroyed both houses for presuming beyond their station.'

'Your own family supports my baron –'

'I doubt that.'

Suragai found that he was shivering, and yet he knew that it was not cold. He was glad that the finality in Alexei's tone would end the conversation, even though the ambassador was only now beginning to reveal his intent. He stood up.

'My lord, it would be in your own interest to listen to me,' Borocheff said sharply. 'By earning the Emperor's favour now you could inherit the throne.'

'Name of God,' Suragai murmured.

Alexei said, 'I am the servant of the Kha-Khan.'

'Alone on this world you had no choice,' the ambassador said smoothly. 'Consider your lineage, however, and reflect that you are once more in touch with the Empire through its servants. For supporting our interests now you could earn a reward which would be out of all proportion to what would be required of you.'

Suragai bit his lips. The comparison the ambassador implied between the Khanate and the Empire was as slighting as his reference to the Andreeyev.

There was no response for a time. Then a chair scraped the floor, and Alexei said, 'Well, maybe. I will talk to you again when I have considered your words. Good night.'

Suragai waited until the ambassador had left before going downstairs again. The door of Alexei's council chamber was open once more, and Alexei was standing in front of the fireplace, a gold cup full of wine in one hand. At the sound of Suragai's footsteps he turned. 'Where have you been?' he asked. 'The ambassador wanted to thank you for your attention to the traders.'

'I was in the garden,' Suragai said. 'You know Kubulai is here to see Turakina.' He could not meet Alexei's stare.

Alexei smiled. 'We will all be relieved when the betrothal has been concluded,' he said.

Suragai nodded. 'What did the ambassador want?'

'Nothing important.' Alexei raised his cup and drank, then he looked round again. 'Don't look so sour. I know you don't like the task you have been given, but it won't be forever, and the Kha-Khan is very pleased with you.'

Suragai could think of nothing to say, and so he nodded again. In spite of what he knew he found Alexei's words comforting. He looked down at the fire, wishing that he had not overheard what had been said, so that he could feel a measure of trust.

In the morning Suragai went with Bhutan to see the Sechem. It was a father's task to take his son to have his talons coloured for the first time, but Kaidu was still in Marakan, and neither Kaidu's brother Hulagu nor Suragai's father D'mitri was available. Accordingly the role had fallen to Suragai. Kadan had not been asked, although he was a closer relation.

'Will it hurt?' Bhutan asked apprehensively.

It was the fourth or fifth time he had posed the same

question. Suragai produced a frown of amusement, then remembered his own trepidation on a similar occasion, and he shook his head and smiled. 'No,' he said. 'Your talon grows from a place which is like the root of a tree. There is no feeling at the base of it, and that is where the dye goes.'

'Oh.' Bhutan looked thoughtful. 'I wish I could have gold talons like yours.'

'You will have talons of silver-blue like those of your father,' Suragai said. 'It's a very unusual colour. You will be only the fifth man in the world to wear it.'

A special family colour had been created for Alexei and for his father when they had come to the Khanate, so that they might distinguish themselves from other men. Their eye shading was tinged with it, and any of their descendants who were not Altun were entitled to it.

The information seemed to appease Bhutan, and he held himself up proudly in the saddle. He reined his mare around an obstruction in the street, and then he came up to Suragai's side again. 'What about my eyes?' he asked. 'Will they be shaded today?'

'Not today,' Suragai said patiently. 'Your father will do that when he comes home.'

'On my Name Day.' Bhutan bounced up and down on his st'lyan's back. 'And then I will have gifts.'

'A sword for one.' Suragai nodded. 'You won't have to steal mine any more.'

Bhutan had the grace to blush. 'I only did that once,' he said.

'So you did.' Suragai laughed. 'And you've grown up a lot since then.'

The College of Sechem was on the street which led

from the grand concourse at the front of the Golden Yurt to the gate of the city. It was a modest building of rose-coloured stone which was constructed as a rectangle around an enclosed yard. To enter, one rode under an archway and through a paved arcade. The hooves of the st'lyan rang on the stones of the paving. Inside the yard it was peaceful. A gowned acolyte was raking the tan which was spread across the cobbles, and when he saw Suragai he bowed politely.

'Seku Sechem is expecting us,' Suragai said.

The acolyte nodded. He pointed to a passage which led off from the centre of the cloister which surrounded the yard, and bowed again. Suragai lifted Bhutan down off his mare, and then he looped the st'lyan's reins through a ring in the wall. A robed figure passed along the cloister, head bowed. Bhutan looked subdued. 'I've never been here before,' he said.

'Not many people have,' Suragai responded mildly.

There were thousands of Sechem in the world, but only here in Kinsai were they gathered in great numbers. The Sechem were responsible for recording and studying all the knowledge of the Khanate, and they were the ultimate arbiters of the law. Some spent their lives specialising in one field of learning – it did not matter that their knowledge might never be applied – but others dealt on a more practical basis. They directed the education of the young, and they were responsible for any aspect of public works which necessitated the appliance of technology. A single Sechem might be accompanied wherever he went by as many as twenty assistants – a few of whom would become Sechem themselves one day. An assistant acted as a walking reference library for his master, and was required to memorise entire portions of recorded science. Some Sechem were physicians – although the races of True People had small need of their ministrations. They had rights of travel and access throughout the Khanate, and the only requirement imposed on them by the Yasa was the duty to impart information whenever it was demanded of them.

At the end of the passage there was a large room with stone walls. A vat of liquid was bubbling gently in the centre of it, and to one side there was a long bench which showed signs of much scrubbing. On it there was a tray of sand in which a small brazier had been placed, and on the brazier was a retort which was full of what appeared to be molten metal. A man wearing a long crimson gown was at the bench. He was very old, and had only a halo of silver hair. He bowed to Suragai, and Suragai inclined his head politely. 'Sechem, I greet you.'

The Sechem seemed to realise that Bhutan was nervous. He smiled, and produced the bow to which only a boy who had passed his tenth Name Day was entitled. 'Good morning, Noyon.'

Bhutan preened. He drew himself up, and then bowed carefully.

'Everything is ready,' the Sechem said.

'Good.' Suragai nodded. 'Bhutan, sit down.'

'Sit here, Noyon, if you will.' Seku indicated the end of the bench.

Bhutan sat down. He eyed the retort on the brazier dubiously. 'Is that for me?' he demanded. 'It looks hot.'

It came to Suragai that it must be terrible always to need the attentions of a physician. Fear of the unknown and lack of understanding about what was to occur would be the worst elements, he supposed. The peoples of the non-human races of the world – the C'zaki, the Ch'kasians, the Alan and others – got sick, of course, and so they required the ministrations of the Sechem. Now Suragai wondered if the experience of being given attention was not in many ways as frightening as the feeling of being ill, and for the first time he sympathised with the men who sought to prolong their lives and ward off sickness and disease by the use of a drug. Because he himself was immune to everyday ailments – all the people of the races of True People were – it was not a problem which had occurred to him before. Bhutan was not sick, but he was about to receive a treatment of a kind, and was afraid. Suragai realised that the mystery which surrounded the act of talon-colouring was very like the artificial secrecy which was permitted to shroud the practice of the healing art. It was wrong for people to be afraid when their concerns could be relieved by knowledge which was possessed by others. The fact that the Sechem knew everything should not give them power, for there ought to be no currency in learning, and even the most arcane knowledge ought to be available to all. It meant that there was a flaw in the Yasa, and Suragai was troubled by the awareness of it. He gestured brusquely to the Sechem. 'Explain it to him.'

'As you wish, Noyon.' The Sechem's face showed no change of expression. He indicated the retort. 'The tint is being heated, certainly, but sometimes things are not what they seem. There is a substance which is liquid even when it is very cold, and this we mix with colours to make the tint for talons. It would poison non-humans, but it does not harm the True People because they are immune. Some heat is needed so that the colours will combine, but it is lost very quickly to the air. Touch the flask if it troubles you, Noyon. I promise you will not be burned.'

Hesitantly Bhutan put out a hand. He brushed the side of the retort with the tip of one finger, then looked up quickly, his expression surprised. 'It's quite cold,' he said.

'And now I think it is ready,' Seku said. He lifted a small cloth-wrapped bundle from the other end of the bench. Returning to Bhutan's side, he sat down. When he unfastened the binding around the bundle he un-rolled the cloth so that the instruments inside were revealed. They shone as if they had been burnished.

The Sechem lifted a thing that looked like a tube with a tapering point. He inserted it into the retort and drew up some of the liquid. 'Noyon, put your right hand on the bench and extend your talons,' he said.

Bhutan eyed the instruments in the Sechem's hand warily. He shot a glance in Suragai's direction, and Suragai nodded. He put a hand on Bhutan's shoulder. Bhutan drew a deep breath, and then flexed his right hand. His talons were practically translucent. He rested his hand on the bench.

'Noyon, you will feel nothing when I inject the tint, but if it troubles you, then close your eyes.'

'I am not afraid,' Bhutan said bravely. He watched steadily as the first talon was treated. As soon as he was sure that it did not hurt, he relaxed. The process was completed swiftly.

When it was over Bhutan examined his fingertips, and extended and retracted his talons several times. 'I can't see a difference,' he observed. He sounded disappointed.

'The change will occur gradually,' Suragai said. He was proud of the way Bhutan had behaved, and knew how hard it must have been to show courage in the circumstances. 'As your talons grow, the colour will appear. When you are older you may have it deepened if you wish.'

'Oh.' Bhutan stood up. He turned towards the door which led to the passage, and then remembered his manners. He gave Seku an abbreviated bow. 'Sechem, I thank you for your service.'

'Noyon, you are most welcome.' Seku smiled. When he inclined his head the sunlight coming through the high window behind him illuminated the threads of fine hair which stood out around his scalp so that they looked as if they were on fire.

They walked together back to the yard. In one of the corners of the cloister there was a workshop. The big double doors at the front of it had been thrown open, and looking inside as he passed Suragai saw that the shape of a dragon had been constructed out of plaster and paper and gum. Now it was being painted. 'What's this?' he asked.

'A contrivance for the procession,' Seku said. An expression had appeared on his face as if he wished that Suragai had not seen what was being fashioned.

Suragai had heard about the dragons of K'chin, but this was nothing like them. Rather it resembled the creatures of the legend. It had a long tail which was being painted with green scales, and tiny wings sprouted from a point around an imaginary spine.

'Does it do anything?' Bhutan was already past the end of the open door. A man working beside the head of the figure turned quickly. When he saw Suragai, he bowed.

'Does it?' Suragai raised an eyebrow at the Sechem.

'It blows fire,' the Sechem said unwillingly.

452

'Oh.' Bhutan bounced, his features animated. 'How I wish I could see that.'

A man in a long blue gown came out of the back of the workshop. He stopped when he saw Suragai and Bhutan, and then he bowed politely. 'Good morning, Noyon.'

'Kobe.' Suragai was unable to hide his surprise. 'I thought you were in N'pan.'

'I was,' the Sechem said. The Kha-Khan's technologist was a tall, thin man of indeterminate years. He had talons, but Suragai had never been quite sure of his race, and had never dared to enquire.

'My cousin would like to see this thing work,' Suragai said.

The two Sechem exchanged glances, and then the blue-robed man shrugged. 'It isn't complete yet, of course, but I believe we can demonstrate it,' he said. He gestured to the man who was working on the dragon's head, and they ran the construction out through the workshop doorway. Suragai bent down to look, and he saw that the whole contraption was mounted on sets of wheels.

The workman ducked beneath the body of the beast. It was uncomfortable to continue to crouch down, and Suragai straightened. After a moment the dragon's lower jaw descended. A sound like the grinding of a set of badly oiled gears emerged from the orifice, and then came a muted thumping from the body.

'The oil has to be pumped up,' the blue-robed Sechem explained. 'Watch now.'

A stream of liquid was being ejected from the dragon's mouth. A muffled curse came from inside the body, and the sound of pumping recommenced.

This time when the oil was forced out it was ignited. A tongue of fire more than a drem in length was emitted. Bhutan applauded happily.

'Amazing,' Suragai said, amused. The oil which had been spilled on the cobbles was catching now. A plume of smoke rose, and he stepped back to avoid the fumes, then looked at the two Sechem. 'Isn't it a little dangerous?'

'Oh well,' Kobe said, 'it isn't designed to be set off in a crowd or in an enclosed space, Noyon. It's going to be placed on the grand concourse near the palace steps. The head is metal, although there is a covering of plaster as you can see. It should be safe enough.'

'I'd like to see it breathe fire again,' Bhutan said. He eyed the head of the dragon hopefully.

'Maybe once more,' Suragai said. 'But after that we ought to go.' He gave the Sechem a look, and Kobe grinned and nodded. He bent down and said something to the man who was inside the body. This time the oil was ignited the moment it was pumped from the nozzle Suragai saw was hidden in the upper jaw. A satisfying column of fire was blown across the yard. The st'lyan tethered along the cloister reared and screamed.

'Thank you.' Suragai inclined his head. He led Bhutan away, boosting him up onto the back of his mare. The workshop doors were already being closed, and both Sechem had disappeared.

Suragai frowned. Mechanical toys were as much the Sechem's province as anything else, he supposed. It didn't make sense for the Kha-Khan's chief technologist to be involved in their making, however. Without a doubt he had better ways of occupying his time.

'After the procession there will be banquets,' Turakina

454

said. She drew a strand of silk through one of the figures near the border of the tapestry she was embroidering. 'I will be seen by everyone.'

'When you are Kubulai's wife, everybody in the world will know who you are,' Suragai pointed out. He leaned past her to look at the picture. 'This is very confused. There is no order in it.'

'I like a busy scene,' Turakina said. 'Simple work is no pleasure to the eye.'

Suragai frowned. 'But look how crowded it is.' He guessed that Turakina had something special to say, and waited for her to find her way to it. 'I know this place,' he said, looking at the tapestry again.

She nodded. 'It's the town below Alexei's castle. The people hold a dance in the square on Midsummer Day.'

'Oh.' Suragai peered at the design. 'Name of God, what are these people doing?'

'Dancing.'

'That isn't what it looks like to me.'

Turakina pursed her lips. 'Country people behave more casually than we do,' she said.

Suragai examined her. 'It's as well you're to be married,' he said at last.

She made a face at him. 'Do you think I don't know how men and women behave?' she asked.

'I would hope you have no personal experience.' Suragai looked down his nose. 'Whatever your maids have told you, believe half of it.'

Turakina frowned. 'You would not be so proper were I not your sister,' she commented.

It seemed to him that the conversation was moving onto dangerous ground. He shifted uneasily, watching her face.

'Women are not at all reserved with one another when they talk,' Turakina said suddenly.

'I can imagine.' Suragai grinned.

'But they speak about men as if they are st'lyan,' she said, and frowned. 'How is a woman to know which men are like that, and which are not? They do not all keep concubines.'

A door banged somewhere in the house, and Suragai heard the sound of footsteps on the stairs. He listened to them for a moment, and then looked at her. 'You are thinking about Kubulai and the Ch'noze woman,' he said. 'Does it still trouble you that he has her? I thought you understood. You were quick enough to offer me your maid.'

'If I knew what she provides him that I will not ...' Turakina paused.

Suragai wrinkled his nose. 'If you asked Kubulai about it he would tell you,' he said. 'I should not speak for him, because all men do not think the same, but to answer you I would say that a man finds much the same in one woman as in another. Only in their nature are they different, and therein lies the contrast between them. Kubulai did not take the Ch'noze woman because he sought something he would not have from you, but rather because she was available and you were not.'

'And after we are married?' she asked.

'After you are married you will be a wife, and the mistress of Kubulai's household,' Suragai said seriously. 'If the Ch'noze contributes harmony to your house you ought to keep her, but in any case she should not suffer dishonour, and your husband's good name should be preserved.'

'It's very complicated,' Turakina said. She snipped at

a thread on the face of the tapestry, and then glanced back over her shoulder. 'The aliens take only one wife,' she said slyly.

'That's different,' Suragai said. 'I don't know why you are bringing them into this.'

'I can see four ships apart from the lander,' D'mitri said. He reined across to Suragai's side. 'Where are the other two?'

Suragai dropped his reins on his st'lyan's neck. 'I asked about them this morning,' he said. 'Both of them were sent to Marakan. They should be here soon.'

'They used to ask our permission to move a vessel from one place to another.' D'mitri sat forward in the saddle. 'Now they seldom trouble themselves. It's going to make things difficult for us.'

The level ground close to the lander was now dotted with tents and prefabricated shelters. Suragai studied the chaos and frowned. He gestured. 'Short of using troops, I can't control them,' he said. 'Is that what Alexei wants?'

His father snorted. 'God, no. But once all the ships are here, we will have to find a way to stop them leaving again. We need them in our sight on Anniversary Day.'

It was a requirement upon which Suragai had already taxed his imagination. He said, 'I'll tell them the days leading up to the anniversary are sacred. They are still wary of offending our customs. I will say that the use of most machines is prohibited. They will understand that.'

D'mitri nodded approval. 'Good.' He gave Suragai a sharp stare. 'Do you know what Alexei intends?'

'No.' Suragai shook his head. 'I thought you did.' He

had said nothing to anyone about the conversation he had overheard between Alexei and the ambassador.

'If I did, I would tell you,' D'mitri said.

'Just as I would tell you, if I knew.'

'Of course.'

They smiled knowingly at one another. D'mitri urged his bay on into the meadow. Even where there were no tents, the grass had been cut down, and it was rotting because it had not been stacked. Suragai grimaced at the waste. The straw could have been used for feed, and he wondered why the captain of the guard company attached to the alien camp had not done something about it. Probably he had never imagined that the aliens would leave it lying about. It made no sense to destroy growing things simply to clear the ground. Everything in the world had a use and a purpose.

An alien vessel came up very fast from the south. It hovered briefly, and then dropped down beside the others. A hatch opened, and people got out.

D'mitri stood in the stirrups. 'That's a different pattern from the others,' he said. 'I don't think I've seen its like before.'

Suragai drew in on his reins. It was hard to distinguish one alien vessel from another, but he was sure his father was right. 'I think it's what they call a barge,' he said. 'Look, there's the ambassador.'

Borocheff was striding across the grass towards the people who were descending from the ship. Other aliens were emerging from tents and shelters. They converged on the landing area.

The new arrivals were strangers. One of them was a woman, and Suragai saw that everyone else was deferring to her. He experienced a gnawing surge of disquiet.

The offworlders had not brought in any additional people for nearly a month. It was a bad omen that they had chosen this particular moment. He rode forward.

The ambassador was in the process of greeting the woman who had arrived with the barge. When he bowed he moved his hands out to his sides in the same gesture of obeisance Suragai had seen used to Alexei. It meant that the woman was of Imperial royal blood. He stared at her. She was tall and stately, with fair hair which was gathered up around her head with a kind of circlet which Suragai guessed must be a clasp.

At the sound of his st'lyan's hooves on the ground the ambassador turned. Suragai reined in. He dismounted by swinging one leg across in front of his saddle and then sliding on his bottom down the st'lyan's side to the ground. '*Shen* Ambassador, good day,' he said.

Borocheff bowed politely, but he looked nervous. 'Noyon, the traders are not here yet,' he said.

'I can see that,' Suragai responded drily. He stared past the ambassador at the woman. 'Lady, good day,' he said, and bowed.

The woman had a gold caste mark similar to Alexei's on one cheek. Suragai thought that her features were too fine for anyone to think her beautiful. Her age he could not guess at. The colour of her hair and the tone of her skin suggested that she was quite young. Then Suragai looked at her eyes. The expression in them was old, and past knowing.

'Exalted one, this is the son of the daughter of your husband,' the ambassador said flatly.

'Indeed?' The woman raised her eyebrows. She subjected Suragai to a cursory examination. 'Then he knows my son,' she said.

D'mitri was already riding up behind. Suragai showed his teeth. 'Lady, you ought to ask me that,' he said softly.

Several of the men in the group standing behind the alien ambassador stirred, looking offended. Borocheff's expression became apprehensive. He said, 'Noyon, this lady is a niece of the Emperor. It was our thought that her presence would do honour to the Kha-Khan on the occasion of the anniversary of his accession.'

Suragai pretended to believe him. 'The attendance of all the aliens has been commanded,' he observed matter-of-factly. 'The Kha-Khan is the Lord of the Earth. All the world exists to do him service, and there shall be no end to it before the sun falls.'

He saw that the response did not sit well with them. The woman looked haughty, and the men muttered to one another and glowered. Suragai guessed that they were put out of countenance because he was not more obsequious to her. Only the ambassador reacted with good grace. 'Noyon, we should have advised you of our intent,' he said. 'But truly we were not sure that a person of such rank would be prepared to visit us.'

It was not to be supposed that the ambassador really thought that Suragai was deceived by his explanation, but Suragai raised his eyebrows as if he did not believe that such attention to the courtesies was in fact necessary. 'You are all the guests of the Khanate,' he said dismissively. 'I will tell the Kha-Khan about the compliment you seek to pay him. I have no doubt that he will understand your intent.'

If Borocheff realised that there was more than one way to interpret Suragai's reply, he gave no sign. He bowed again. Both of the vessels being used by the trade commissioners came up quite suddenly out of the east.

Suragai wondered if he ought to offer to carry a greeting from the woman to her husband. He could not imagine the older Suragai married to her, but the ambassador's aside during the introductions had confirmed the relationship. 'Lady, I think you are also here to see my grandfather,' Suragai said to her.

The expression in her eyes suggested that she thought the purpose of her visit was none of his concern. She eyed him coolly. 'I think he may have forgotten me,' she said at last.

'Not at all,' Suragai responded cheerfully. 'He spoke of you in my hearing only a few days ago.'

She had mentioned Alexei but once, Suragai thought. Probably the aliens could not conceive of a situation where a person of the quality of their royal family would desert his loyalty to his own kind. Because they disparage us, they are blind, he said to himself. He guessed that the woman intended to persuade Suragai Khan to serve the interests of the Empire. He did not know if the ambassador had already attempted it, but if he had, then clearly it was felt that the outcome was in doubt.

The first of the two arriving ships grounded with a blast of hot air. D'mitri's bay reared, and its forehooves raked the air.

'A meeting after so long will be a delicate matter,' the ambassador said, interposing himself. 'Maybe it should not be hastened.'

Suragai wrinkled his nose. A true wife would not countenance any delay in reacquainting herself with her husband, he thought. Maybe alien customs were different. He shrugged. 'I am at your disposal if you need help to arrange it,' he said. He bowed again to the woman, and then walked away, leading his st'lyan.

D'mitri rode up at his side. 'I did not hear all of that,' he said. 'Who are they?'

'The wife of your wife's father and her retainers,' Suragai said in Yek. The distinction was a fine one which Anglic was incapable of conveying.

D'mitri's jaw dropped. 'Does the Khan know she is here?' he asked.

Suragai was amused by his father's reaction. 'I think he is expecting her,' he said. He saw that Natalia was emerging from the ship which had just landed, and tramped on across the grass to meet her.

'You are quite attractive by our standards,' Turakina told Natalia ingenuously. 'If your hair had more red in it you could almost be Altun. You ought to let it grow.'

Suragai watched Natalia's expression warily. She had required no real persuasion to accept the hospitality of his father's house, and during the period of the festival no restrictions appeared to have been placed on the offworlders who had no official status. Natalia seemed to understand that she was being paid a compliment of a kind. 'This length is convenient,' she said. 'Long hair can be rather troublesome in space.'

The house D'mitri was occupying had a wide paved portico which ran from the end of the garden to the back of the building. The pillars were wreathed around with vines, and tendrils hung down from the roof timbers. Suragai sat down on the long seat which ran beneath. 'Now that you are not dressed like a man, it looks strange,' he said. She was wearing a long embroidered skirt and a light blouse. Turakina had found her slippers to wear, and Suragai saw that

Natalia's feet were very small.

Turakina frowned at him. 'You are a sorry courtier,' she said critically.

Suragai laughed at her. He saw that Natalia was blushing furiously. 'It's not something I've had a deal of practice at,' he said.

Natalia took a moment to regain her composure, and then she said, 'I would not trust flattery out of a man's mouth even if I heard it.'

'That's because you are unused to being treated like a woman,' Turakina said. 'I like being a woman. No one treats a man as prettily. My brother says you think men and women ought to be equal.'

'We have disputed it,' Natalia responded drily. 'I have seen too many cultures where women are chattels to think that any other way is right.'

A trailing plant with huge bell-shaped flowers was growing down among the vines. Suragai pulled a length idly with one hand. The scent from the blossoms was chokingly sweet.

'To be a woman in such a situation would be boring of course,' Turakina observed. 'But on this world a woman is assured her place by the Yasa. It would be terrible to be forced to compete with men. There are much better ways to live.'

The expression on Natalia's face suggested that she disagreed, but was restraining herself from saying so. 'A woman ought to be free to do what a man does if she wants to,' she suggested mildly.

Turakina looked down her nose. 'In the Khanate I don't think there is anything to prevent it,' she said. 'But why should she wish to?'

'Maybe because it is in her nature to be more than a wife and mother,' Natalia replied.

'In that case surely she should choose her own path through life, and not try men's footsteps,' Turakina said frostily. 'Whatever she undertakes, it should be as a woman. Do men in the Empire truly believe that women are their equal?'

Natalia made a face. 'There are laws which require them to pretend that they do,' she said.

In the early morning the city was thick with mist. It clung to the buildings, trailing like smoke wherever men rode through it. Only when the sun was properly risen did it start to disperse.

The st'lyan seemed to sense that they were being groomed for an occasion. Long before Suragai walked down to the stables he heard their screams. A groom leading out D'mitri's bay into the yard had to duck aside to avoid flailing hooves. The st'lyan's iron-shod feet struck sparks off the grey flagstones, and its great gilded horn sliced the air. When Suragai's father had mounted he drew in on the reins. The bay arched its neck, prancing sideways. The other st'lyan which were being led out through the stable door reacted nervously. Grooms called to one another in high, agitated voices. The children of the servants sat on top of the wall, watching with round eyes as the chaos was resolved.

An officer of the Kha-Khan's guard rode suddenly in through the archway from the street. He saluted D'mitri and nodded politely to Suragai. 'Lord, you are to read this,' he said. He held out a scroll.

D'mitri scanned the message. He pursed his lips, and then handed back the scroll and nodded. 'Very well.'

The officer reined around, and then trotted his st'lyan back out into the street. D'mitri watched him depart, a thoughtful expression on his face. Then he stared down at Suragai. 'Don't return here after the procession,' he said. 'Don't go to Alexei's house either. After the people have started to disperse, the curfew bell will sound. Once the streets are clear the watch will have orders to detain anyone who does not carry the Kha-Khan's warrant.'

'What should I do then?' Suragai thought that he ought to have realised that such a precaution would be taken. Whatever was to occur that day, it appeared to be important to control movement in and around the city at a specific moment in time.

'We are both ordered to the palace,' his father said. 'Are you escorting the alien woman?'

'Yes. Kubulai is coming here for Turakina, as you know.'

'He may, if he has not been given orders to the contrary,' D'mitri observed. He looked as if he thought it was likely. 'Keep the woman with you. I don't know what is to happen, but I think it is safe to assume that she should not be at liberty when it starts.'

It was inevitable that Suragai would remember the question Jehan had asked. If Natalia's death became necessary, he was not sure what he would do.

'They haven't trusted anyone,' he said.

D'mitri made a face. 'You mean that ordinary men like you and I know nothing,' he said. 'Maybe we don't have the skills or knowledge which are capable of being employed in this. We are dealing with people who travel between the stars as easily as a courier rides from Pesth to Kinsai. Think about a way of making them afraid to attack us or interfere with us again. Tell me how you would achieve it.'

•

465

Everyone else in the house had left by the time Kubulai finally arrived. Turakina and Natalia had been gowned for hours, and while Suragai paced the garden they waited in the portico, their manner disconsolate. Turakina was unhappy because her escort seemed to have forgotten his appointment with her. Natalia's expression suggested that she was put out of countenance because what she had probably understood to be a ritual of courtship had been interrupted by Suragai's sudden air of preoccupation. When the hooves of Kubulai's st'lyan rattled on the paving in the yard at the front of the house, they both jumped up. Turakina's gown was made from rose-coloured silk. It had figured panels on the skirts, and a high collar like a fan which framed her dressed red hair. She started quickly along the portico, then stopped. Watching her, Suragai thought she took a deep breath. She twitched her skirts into place one-handed. The talons of her free hand glittered briefly, the only sign of her nervousness, and then she turned so that it did not appear as if she was interested to see who was coming through the door.

Suragai grinned. Because it had become obvious that there was going to be no time to lodge st'lyan near the procession route, he had exchanged riding boots for footwear more suited to walking the cobbled streets. He was wearing a variation of the fancy high-collared gold coat of the Altun. It had no fastenings down the front, and so he had been able to insert a *jusei*, the curved Manchu great sword, at the correct angle in his waist sash. He touched the hilt with his fingertips, but experienced no sense of reassurance. Then he strode across the grass towards the covered walkway.

If Turakina expected explanation or apology from

Kubulai, it was clear that she was to be disappointed. When he came through the door from the house he was carrying his spurs in one hand. He tossed them down on a bench, and then he surveyed the occupants of the portico. 'At least you are ready,' he said.

'We could not be else,' Turakina responded, a degree of asperity barely concealed in her tone. 'Were you drunk last night, or was it a woman that detained you? It must be hard at times to decide which of us deserves your attention.'

The ghost of a smile appeared on Kubulai's face. 'The demands on my person are not overly taxing,' he said. 'Are we going to stand here discussing my character, or do you want to attend the procession? Come along.'

Suragai gave him a narrow stare. Kubulai was wearing a sword, and the hilt of a *hiranu* was visible above his boot top. Whatever had delayed him, he had ridden in haste and had not taken time to attend to his appearance. A patch of white like a chalk mark stained the hem of his coat, and there was a hint of it on his hands. Even as he spoke he rubbed them together as if he had only just become aware of it.

'Vice is natural to some people,' Turakina said stiffly. 'There are circles in which it does not matter.'

'I wouldn't know about that,' Kubulai replied. His eyes were guilelessly clear. He seemed to realise that Suragai was watching, and he produced a formal inclination of his head. Then he gave Natalia an abbreviated bow. 'Lady, good day.'

Natalia inclined her head politely. The expression on her face suggested that she was unsure what part she was expected to play in the exchange which was taking place.

'I saw sedan chairs outside,' Kubulai said. He looked at Suragai. 'Are we walking?'

'Yes.' Suragai nodded. 'There won't be time to find stabling.' He turned and bowed to Natalia. 'Lady, if you are ready…'

She rested her fingertips on the back of his hand. Turakina looked discontented. It was almost as if she had hoped for an argument. A horn sounded somewhere across the city, and Kubulai's head went round. 'That's the assembly signal,' he said. 'If we hurry we'll just about make it.' He caught hold of Turakina's hand and drew her towards the door. 'Name of God, come on!'

Except that the pomp and pageant marked the twentieth year since Jehan's accession to the Dragon Throne, the occasion was much like any other. As had become his practice over the years, the Kha-Khan had limited by edict the sums his subjects were permitted to expend in his honour. They in their turn had followed the by now quite traditional course of finding by private means what extra they judged was essential to demonstrate their loyalty, duty and affection for their sovereign lord.

Kinsai's always well-decorated main streets had been adorned with special care to match the themes which it had been agreed were to be presented by the guilds and other semi-official bodies. Apart from the companies of carefully turned-out troopers from the Yek and Merkut tumans, there were to be whole sections of the parade in which the burghers and guildsmen were to march, and most of them had acquired new regalia with which to dignify their appearance in public. In addition there were to be groups in traditional costume from every one of the fifteen provinces. A small number of the commons had even dressed themselves in fur and wore masks so that the Marakani would seem to be represented. In short there were to be all the usual conceits, as well as a few which the organisers hoped would be new to the masses of spectators. As a result the side streets around the assembly point were choked with men, women and children, many of whom were unsuitably dressed for their crowded circumstances. All of them were attempting to preserve often contrived finery towards the moment when the marshals would summon them into line. It was no place for the miniature cavalcade of porters and retainers which Kubulai now tried to lead at a fast pace towards the head of the street which stretched between the grand concourse and the city gates. The sedan chairs were bulky, to say the least. Their porters squeezed them past the first element of a line of wagon-mounted floats, and then stopped. It was clear that it would be impossible to force a way through the press without the aid of armed men. In fact their only escort consisted of two taciturn troopers who seemed to belong to Kubulai. Already the noise of horns and gongs was announcing the start of the procession.

'We'll have to go around,' Kubulai said. He sounded only mildly exasperated.

Stagings ran at the level of about the first floor of many of the buildings, but to carry the chairs up the stairs which led to them was without a doubt beyond the ability of the porters. They followed narrow streets between high red-stone buildings. At one point the thoroughfare had been roofed over. Kubulai walked ahead of the porters under the archway. A

469

man on a st'lyan was trying to come from the other direction, but the way was not wide enough.

'Hey, you there, move aside,' the stranger called. 'Let us pass here.'

Kubulai rested a hand on the hilt of his sword. 'Get out of my way,' he said.

The porters were jammed behind him in the entrance to the tunnel. Suragai pushed past them. He pushed at the st'lyan which was blocking their path, and it backed up with a clatter of hooves. Beyond the tunnel in the widening street a man in a gold-faced coat stood to one side, his face plastered over with a nasty smile.

'Khan, I did not see that it was you.'

Kubulai growled something at him. He gestured to the porters, and they struggled past. Behind the stranger a litter waited. In it was a woman in her middle age, her hair tinted red with dye. She stared down her nose at Suragai as he strode past. The man on the st'lyan's back was a Kerait. His face was flushed as if he was annoyed that he had been forced to give way. Kubulai was already tramping past the sedan-chair carriers towards the end of the street.

'Typical young upstarts,' the woman said.

'Be quiet,' the man in the gold-faced coat said in an agitated tone. 'That's Kubulai Khan.'

Ahead of them loomed the bulk of the burghers' hall. The ends of several side streets had been screened with canvas. Kubulai ripped the end of one of the barriers off the beam to which it had been pinned. Beyond it there was a space like a yard across which a wooden platform had been constructed. The people on top of it were gazing out into the main street on the other side. Kubulai signalled to the porters, and they set down the chairs. The platform had been hung with cloth in Jehan's colours. At the front there was a gap between the cloth and the ground which was big enough for a person on foot to pass through.

Turakina and Natalia got out of the chairs. Kubulai summoned the two troopers to him with a gesture. He spoke to them in a low voice, and seemed to be giving them orders. One man nodded. Turakina saw where Kubulai was standing, and she went to join him. At the same moment the people on top of the platform began to cheer, and the sounds of the music which had been muted before suddenly increased in volume. Natalia walked under the platform and through the hangings. Suragai followed her.

The first troop of guardsmen was just passing the platform. On the pavement a group of four or five young men were loitering, obstructing the way to the steps which led up the platform side. When Natalia emerged into the open they turned. Their expressions were full of mischief. A thin youth in a bright-green coat grabbed Natalia's arm as she tried to pass.

'Fresh meat!' he called out. He waved with his free hand to the others, and then slid it around Natalia's waist. 'Look what I have found –'

She wrenched away from him.

'Oh,' he said, 'she has spirit.' He made as if to snatch a kiss.

Natalia slapped him hard. One of the other men gave a shout of laughter. He said, 'Ogodai, if you need help …'

Ogodai seemed to be dazed at first from the blow he had received. The imprint of Natalia's hand stood out like a badge on his cheek, but he did not let go of her arm. 'That's no way to behave,' he said. He shook his

471

head as if to clear it, and then he began to draw Natalia closer.

Suragai took two swift paces. He seized Natalia's assailant by the collar and rammed him into the timber upright of the platform. 'Take your hands from my woman,' he said in Yek.

The man who had been offering Ogodai his help had moved forward. He blanched, and fell back. The green-coated man twisted his head around so that he could see who was holding him. He went white when he saw Suragai's face, and let go of Natalia's arm as if she was burning hot.

'Lord,' he said, 'I beg your pardon. I thought she was a courtesan.'

The other men were edging away. Suragai felt the anger mounting inside his chest. He said, 'Even a public woman has rights. Get away from here. If I ever encounter you again, I'll kill you.'

He released his hold. The man in the green coat backed up four or five steps, and then he turned and ran off down the street. Natalia stared after him, surprised. She turned. 'Were those people your friends?'

'I never saw them before.' Suragai drew a breath, and then made a pleasant face. 'Don't be angry. They made an honest mistake, because you have no talons. If you had waited for me to escort you, it wouldn't have happened.'

Kubulai and Turakina were coming through the hangings now. Natalia moved to one side so that they could pass. She gave Suragai a hard stare. 'I thought women were protected by the Yasa.'

Suragai flushed. 'They are,' he said. 'But even on this world there are people who think they can ignore the law.'

The procession was still passing over an hour later. The place at which Kubulai had found his way out onto the street was not very far from the concourse. Where the street ended there was a wide expanse of paving broken only by the bridges which crossed the artificial watercourse which ran between banks of stone the whole way around the approaches to the Golden Yurt. A framework like the supports for two great tents had been erected at the junction of the concourse and the street. The structure was of much finer quality than the platforms and stands which had been raised to accommodate the populace. It was floored with sanded timbers and hung with awnings and banners. Beneath its shade Suragai could see Jehan and the principal members of his council. With them were groups of guards and attendants, and to one side were seated the most important aliens – the ambassador, the trade commissioners, and the woman who was related by blood to the Emperor.

'There's my mother,' Kubulai said, and pointed.

'I see her.' Suragai had been counting alien heads. Now he glanced towards the end of the enclosure where most of the women of the court had been seated. Among them he could see his own mother and both of his grandfather's wives. They were grouped around the mother of Kubulai who, because she was the Kha-Khan's sister, took precedence.

Both of his grandfather's wives were looking towards the offworlders. Suragai supposed that they had been told the alien woman's identity, although so far as he was aware she and his grandfather were yet to meet. It seemed like a strange way to behave. Quickly he scanned the faces of the people around

Jehan for his grandfather's bulk. There was no sign of him.

'You were counting the aliens,' Kubulai said. 'Don't worry. They have all been accounted for.'

A line of floats carrying an orchestra of musicians moved past. Kubulai had spoken in Yek, but now Suragai glanced in Natalia's direction to see if she had heard. Her eyes were on the procession.

'Don't ask me to tell you what is going to happen,' Kubulai said. 'Even if I knew it all, I would not speak of it.'

Rows of Suristani on stocky equines rode along the street behind the musicians. About half of the Suristani were women, and Suragai wondered if Natalia had noticed. He eyed her, and then looked back at Kubulai again. 'If we kill the aliens, there will be war,' he said.

Kubulai's eyebrows rose. 'Killing them would not achieve anything. Is that what you think we intend?'

It was on the tip of Suragai's tongue to say that he was so confused that nothing made sense any more, but he did not. He gave Kubulai a troubled stare, then gestured at Natalia. 'She is my father's guest,' he said. 'It will be a breach of the Yasa if she comes to harm.' She had her head turned away, and there was no way for her to know that he was speaking about her.

A grim smile appeared on Kubulai's face. 'The aliens haven't behaved as guests,' he said. 'But don't concern yourself. At the very worst she will be detained.'

At last the procession was coming to an end. It was followed at a careful distance by a line of marshals riding matching st'lyan. They saluted the Kha-Khan as they passed. Behind them came a group of street-sweepers who accompanied a cart drawn by a dun p'tar. They moved slowly, lifting the dung which had been deposited by the equines and st'lyan in the parade, and because most of the spectators were only just beginning to disperse they received an ironic cheer. One of them bowed to the crowd in a rude parody of the salutation the burghers had performed when they had paused in front of the Kha-Khan's box, and Suragai laughed.

He glanced towards the enclosure at the end of the street. Some of the occupants had already left their seats, and the rest were moving. A crowd of courtiers was grouped on the concourse, and a few were starting across the flat expanse of the concourse towards the steps of the palace. Jehan, however, remained. Maybe he had stopped to speak to Alexei, who was at his side. He had risen to his feet, but now suddenly he turned and looked back out at the street again. The street-sweeper had passed the platform from which Suragai watched, and he was repeating his pantomime towards the backs of the departing crowd opposite. It was as if he sensed that someone in the enclosure was looking. His head went round, and he froze. He was almost in front of the box, and only the width of the street separated the lowest and the highest in the land.

Suragai was not sure, but he thought a flash of grim amusement crossed Jehan's features. He gave the street-sweeper a stare of enquiry. The man hesitated, and then he bowed again, carefully this time. At the moment when he was at the deepest point of the bow he glanced up at the box, and the hopeful expression on his face made him look like a precocious child wondering if he was about to be punished. Jehan's aquiline features creased in what might have been a smile, and then very slowly he inclined his head. No one else either in the enclosure or out on the street seemed to have noticed the exchange. Suragai saw that Turakina and Natalia were busy adjusting their gowns, so that they had not seen where his attention was directed, and Kubulai's head was turned away. Jehan moved out of sight into the shadows at the rear of the enclosure. The street-sweeper stared after him for a moment. Then a man working some distance away raised his head and shouted. At once the sweeper turned and trotted back towards the dung cart.

The curfew bell began to sound while they were approaching the palace steps. Turakina had reacted with no surprise to the news that the nobility of the Khanate were to be given audience, and if Natalia wondered why she had not been forewarned, it did not show in her expression. The concourse was by now lined with rows of the Kha-Khan's personal guard, and men were ranked up the sides of the stairs in front of the arched doorway which provided the access to the Golden Yurt's domed central hall. Suragai realised that many of the men in guard uniforms were in fact Yek or Merkuts from Kubulai's and his father's tumans, and he wondered if anyone else had remarked on it. Along the flagstones at the side of the first flight of steps six plaster dragons lay abandoned. They were exactly like the one Suragai had seen at the College of Sechem, and he supposed that it had been decided that they were after all too dangerous for use during the parade. It was apparent that a great deal of time and effort had been wasted on the project, and he wondered briefly who had authorised it.

Inside the hall there were many more armed men.

As the people arrived they were directed politely but firmly in one of several different directions. Suragai saw that those who were allowed to carry on up the great staircase were all either khans or senior members of the court. There were very few women among them. No explanations were being offered about the decision on who was to proceed and who was not, and Suragai saw a protesting Kerait noyon being edged off to the side by two very large guardsmen.

'We go this way,' Kubulai said. He drew Suragai and Natalia by the arm towards a side chamber, and Turakina followed. The room was guarded by sentries who saluted Kubulai when they saw him. As soon as they had passed inside, the doors were closed.

Constantin was sitting on a chair at the end of the chamber. He was being engaged in conversation by a man Suragai recognised as one of Kubulai's officers. When he saw Kubulai the officer bowed, and then withdrew. Constantin did not look as if he suspected anything. He stood up and bowed to Kubulai and Suragai. Then he smiled at Turakina and Natalia.

Kubulai waited until the two aliens had moved together so that they could talk. Suragai saw that Turakina had drawn a little to the side, as if she had been told what was to happen. He touched the hilt of his sword.

'You are going to be taken into the Kha-Khan's presence,' Kubulai said. He looked at Constantin and Natalia as he spoke. 'Before that I have to ask if you are carrying any weapon. You must also surrender the communicators I know you both wear.'

They stared at him, and then Constantin said, 'Khan, I protest. We are the members of an embassy, and guests of the Kha-Khan.'

'I think that is a matter of interpretation,' Kubulai said drily. 'Now you can comply with my demand, or I can have you searched. Which is it to be?'

Constantin barely glanced in Suragai's direction. His lips compressed, and he detached an oblong of some dull metal from the breast of his tunic and held it out. 'I am unarmed,' he said.

Kubulai gestured to one of the troopers beside the door. The man came forward, and took the communicator out of Constantin's hand. He put it down on a table which was against the wall, then returned to his post. 'And now you, my lady,' Kubulai said to Natalia.

Natalia raised her eyebrows. 'Do I look as if I am armed?' she demanded. She extended her arms out from her sides. 'Search me if you care to.'

'Oh.' Kubulai showed his teeth. 'I would, if it was necessary.' He glanced past her at Turakina. 'Is she wearing it?'

Turakina nodded. 'The decoration on her gown,' she said. 'She will go nowhere without it.'

The communicator looked like a sunburst of gems set in gold filigree. Natalia gave Turakina a reproachful stare, and then unpinned the brooch from her gown. Turakina took it from her.

'I should have you both searched,' Kubulai said, 'but I will not. Only remember if you will that my men have orders to kill or at least incapacitate you if you make any move which they interpret as dangerous. Speak only when you are spoken to, and keep your hands from your garments at all times.' He signalled to a trooper who was guarding a door to another chamber. The man opened the door and put his head through it. He said something to someone Suragai

478

could not see. A moment later Alexei came through the door into the room. Constantin bowed reflexively to him, his hands moving out to form the obeisance which recognised the Imperial rank, but Natalia did not react at all.

Alexei was wearing a court dress of midnight blue. The front of his coat was open, and his hand rested on the hilt of a sword. He waited expressionlessly until Constantin had completed his salutation. Then he said, 'So far as I am aware, neither of you has been involved in any of the acts of aggression carried out by the Empire. Accept therefore my apologies for the manner in which you have been treated. I promise you that it was necessary.'

The offworlders did not look particularly appeased. Constantin stirred. 'Khan, are we prisoners here?'

'It is true that your freedom of movement is being temporarily restricted,' Alexei admitted. He gestured with one hand. 'It's not a restriction we intend to maintain for long. Later this afternoon you will once more be permitted to go where you please. Your communicators will also be returned to you.'

'And in the meantime?' Natalia asked. She had not looked at Suragai since entering the room. Now her eyes passed across him as if he was not there.

'As you have been told,' Alexei said, 'you are about to be taken into the Kha-Khan's presence. It's my opinion that it is not absolutely necessary for you to be there. On the other hand you are officers of the Imperial Navy, and you have a reputation for honesty and attention to the law which the Kha-Khan believes we should respect.' He put a hand in the skirt pocket of his coat and withdrew something. 'Both of you will recognise this, I believe.'

The object was a grey box about the size of the palm of Alexei's hand. Constantin stared at it, and then shrugged. 'It's a communicator. A civilian model.'

'It was found in the possession of a man who was acting as a military adviser to the Ch'noze rebels,' Kubulai said. He gave Constantin a cold stare. 'You may have heard some talk about an incident which occurred after we defeated their army. I let the ambassador see the bodies of several men we recovered from the field. They were not Ch'noze.'

Constantin frowned. 'I heard only that you pickled the bodies of some dead men you thought were mercenaries.'

'That was the story I gave out.' Kubulai nodded. 'I did not think it was the right time to accuse the Empire of aiding the rebels.'

This was the information that the Kha-Khan had expected Kubulai to put in his letter, Suragai realised. At first he was annoyed that Kubulai had not seen fit to confide what he knew. Then he reflected that he would have found it hard to hide his knowledge in any dealings with the aliens. Even if he had not put an accusation into words, they would have been aware from his manner that he felt more than ordinary mistrust.

'If the men are dead, there is no proof that they were sent by the Empire,' Constantin pointed out. 'If it is the reason we are being detained, then again I protest.'

Alexei did not look as if he was surprised by the response. He said, 'I hoped I might convince you to take our side in what is to occur. If I had substantial proof, I would bring it before you, but all I have is the unsupported word of individuals. I know that you believe that this is a trade mission, but it is a fact that the Nicoleyev are attempting to create conditions on this world which will necessitate armed intervention.'

Constantin's head went back. He said, 'My lord, you admit yourself that you have no proof. I will transmit a complaint to my commanding officer in space if that is what you wish, but I am sure you know that I have to remain impartial.'

If Alexei was disappointed, he did not let it show. He pursed his lips. 'In that case maybe you will answer a question,' he said. 'Why is trade with us so important to the Empire? This used to be a quarantine world, and you have set aside your own strictest prohibition to make contact with us.'

Natalia was staring down at the floor. She raised her head quickly. 'My lord, times change,' she responded.

A hint of amusement twitched the corner of Alexei's mouth. 'Why so they do,' he said. He gestured abruptly to the guard on the door to the next chamber. The trooper opened the door, and a small man came quickly into the room. He bowed to Alexei.

Suragai stared. He had heard about this man, but had never seen him. His skin was golden yellow, and his features were oddly lengthened as if they had been melted and reshaped. He wore a simple gown and slippers, but carried a sword which was decorated with gold.

Constantin reacted sharply. He said something in a language Suragai did not know. Natalia opened her mouth, then closed it again. She said, 'My lord, that was very clever. We did not know there were Manchu here.'

Alexei glanced at her without responding. He bowed carefully to the small man, and then turned back to look at the aliens again. 'This man was my father's officer,' he said. 'He is as you have observed a Manchu. From the reaction you produced when he entered the room, I gather that the Manchu and the Empire are now at war.'

Constantin looked down his nose. 'The Manchu worlds are in revolt,' he said sourly.

'And as a result there is a scarcity of the *longiverus* poppy.' Alexei nodded thoughtfully. 'It explains everything. I apologise for tricking you into providing the answer to my question. We had noticed that although the numbers of your people on our world had increased, and included every other racial type, the Manchu were not represented. It seemed like a curious omission.'

The Manchu had not moved. Suragai eyed him, remembering that his name was Yuan, and that once he had been an officer of high rank in the Imperial Navy. It seemed hardly possible.

'*Sei-sen*, thank you for coming,' Alexei said. He bowed again to the small man.

It was impossible to tell if the Manchu's expression changed. He made an odd palm-up gesture with one hand, and then turned and went back into the other room. The man on guard at the door bowed respectfully as he passed, and then closed the door.

Alexei turned. 'If we have forced you to betray a trust, I am sorry,' he said to Constantin. 'I imagine you were put on oath not to reveal what you knew about the Manchu. Probably you were told that if we learned of it, we would force up the price we were demanding for the poppy resin. In fact we have no desire to trade in it at all. I told the ambassador once that the poppy causes harm to those who use it. You are not familiar with our law, but the Yasa forbids us from carrying on any enterprise which we know to be harmful to mankind.'

Constantin did not answer. Natalia stirred. 'My lord, you have us at a disadvantage,' she said simply. 'If you hope to convince us that you are acting for the best, we ought not to be prisoners.'

Kubulai grinned at the sally. Alexei looked as if he was considering what Natalia had said, and he smiled frostily at her. 'When this is ended you might consider staying here,' he said. 'There would be a place for you among us.'

'We are convened to sit in judgement on the Empire,' Jehan said.

The place to which everyone had been escorted was the part of the uppermost level of the Golden Yurt which was usually reserved for the cremations of the Great Khans. The oval ceremonial bowl was supported on a dais of beaten gold. This had been shrouded in canvas, and to one side a tented awning had been erected, outside which were gathered a large number of Sechem. A portico provided access from the rooftop courtyard to the upper vestibule of the palace, and under it stood the khans and senior members of the court. The aliens were in front of them in a group, and at Jehan's words the ambassador's head came up sharply.

'Lord,' he said, 'I protest this.'

Suragai was not sure why he and Kubulai were standing separated from the others, but it meant that he had a perfect view of everything. Jehan gave the ambassador a cool stare. 'That does not surprise me,' he said. 'You were not warned why you were being

483

brought here because we did not wish you to forestall us. For the same reason your communicators have been taken from you. After we have done with you, they will be returned.'

The trade commissioners' expressions indicated relief that they were not about to be slaughtered. Only the woman related to the Emperor did not react. Instead she stared past Jehan at the three men who were grouped behind him. Suragai saw that one of them was his grandfather.

'You came here pretending to be our friends,' Jehan said. He looked straight at Ambassador Borocheff as he spoke. 'And had we believed you we would have placed ourselves at your mercy. Even though my officers were suspicious of your intent and took precautions, your agents were able to incite rebellion among the subject peoples. You yourself tried to induce one of my counsellors to betray the Khanate. These are not the acts of friends.'

Alexei's face was impassive. The ambassador was staring at the paving between his feet. Abruptly he looked up. 'Lord,' he said, 'let the man who says I did this come forward, and let any witness be brought. I say you have no proof.'

'Oh.' Suragai cleared his throat so that everybody looked round at him. 'I heard it. I wasn't meant to, but the ambassador talked about the prince who is heir to the throne of the Empire – Feodor, his name is – and he said that if Alexei betrayed us, he might supplant him in the Emperor's favour.'

Even Alexei looked surprised. Jehan stared hard at Suragai, and it was as if he had reached a decision about something. He nodded, satisfied.

'I think that is proof enough,' he said to Borocheff.

'As to the other matter, we have, as you know, preserved bodies of certain men in brine. I am told that were they to be examined by men who are concerned with such things, they could be identified. Of course it is possible that representatives of the Empire might not wish to admit the truth. For that reason it has been my concern to ensure the presence here of officers of the Imperial Navy. I am told that their abiding concern is with the enforcement of Imperial law.'

Everyone who knew who they were stared at Constantin and Natalia. The ambassador's face went pale, and he had obvious difficulty recovering himself. After a moment he managed a dismissive shrug. 'Lord,' he said, 'if the men who are here to trade have broken the law, or if they have engaged in unfriendly acts against you, we will deal with them. So far as my conversation with the noble Alexei is concerned, I do not remember asking him to betray you – although it may have sounded that way to inexperienced ears.' Borocheff directed a glance at Suragai which was filled with a kind of paternal regret. Then he looked back at the Kha-Khan again. 'Rather it was my suggestion that the exertion of some interest in my mission would receive recognition. I am sorry if that approach has offended you or him. If I have been overzealous in attempting to smooth the path of contact between us, it is a demonstration of my concern – of the concern of the Empire – to maintain a working relationship.'

The ambassador's smile and tone were calculated to suggest that nothing more than a misunderstanding had occurred. He did not look at the traders he had implied might now be culpable.

'Indeed,' Jehan said drily. 'I am aware that you are

485

anxious to remove any obstruction which may come to exist to prevent the continuance of trade. No doubt the reason for your concern was at the root of the efforts of your agents to bring about a situation in which the use of force would have been permissible to safeguard your source of supply.'

The reasonable smile pasted across Borocheff's face had resisted everything else, but now it faltered. He said, 'Lord, no reason exists beyond our earnest desire to trade in peace with our neighbours.'

The sun glared like a huge aura at Jehan's back. He stared at the aliens for a moment, saying nothing, and then he gestured with one hand as if he was tired of talking. Alexei stepped up to his side. 'The Manchu worlds are in revolt,' he said flatly. 'It means that the supply of *longiverus* poppy has dwindled to almost nothing. It is only to be found on worlds like ours which have a red-shifted sun, and the Manchu were the principal growers.'

'Which explains your concern.' Jehan surveyed the alien faces grimly. 'You did not dare attack us openly, because we would have fought to the end, and the poppy fields might have been destroyed. You were even reluctant to use the power of your weapons for fear that the land on which the poppy grows would become scorched earth. We found it hard to understand why you chose such covert means to conquer us. Now we realise that you did not think that there was any other way.'

Even though the khans understood Anglic, the point of the exposition seemed to be lost on them. They were restless now, muttering to one another and glaring at the aliens.

Jehan said, 'You hoped that a civil war would tear

486

the Khanate apart. I am told that had this occurred, then by your law it would have been permissible to bring in men and weapons to protect those of you who had established yourselves here.' He glanced towards Constantin. 'Is that not so?' Reluctantly Constantin nodded.

'Protecting you would have involved protecting the poppy fields, of course,' Alexei observed. 'The result would have been a permanent armed presence in Marakan. After that, who knows what you would have been able to achieve.'

It was clear that the aliens were dismayed at the extent of the Kha-Khan's knowledge. Suragai saw hatred in the eyes of the men when they looked at Alexei, and he guessed that they thought they had been betrayed.

Suddenly Fedyev laughed harshly. 'What can they do?' he said to the ambassador. 'So what if they force us to leave? They have not the means to prevent us from returning. Can they wage war on us? I think not.'

The alien woman seemed to move a little to the side as if she wished to distance herself from the men. At Jehan's back stood Burun, and when the woman moved he said something in a low voice to Suragai's grandfather, who was beside him. Suragai saw his grandfather nod in agreement.

'We thought that would be your reaction,' Jehan said calmly. 'And to that end we have prepared a demonstration of our ability to deal with attack.'

The older Suragai had already turned. He gave a word of command to the guards who were standing in front of the tented awning on the other side of the cremation bowl. The troopers unhooked the ropes which supported the covering, and they pulled it to

487

the side. In the space which had been created there were machines Suragai did not recognise. The Sechem crowded around them.

Pitching his voice so that it carried towards the portico where the khans stood, Jehan said. 'We have known for many years that you maintained weapons in our sky. Their purpose was to prevent us venturing out into the Empire in the event that we developed the ability, for you considered that our species would be like a plague upon the purity of your kind.'

The reaction from the khans was a growl of anger. The traders looked nervously back towards the portico, but the ambassador did not move. He was staring at the equipment around which the Sechem had gathered.

Jehan gestured. 'The purpose of a few of these machines will be familiar to you,' he said prosaically. 'Most we found in the places in Marakan which were once occupied by the people of the empire which existed before yours. They are capable of taking power from the sun, and so it has not been necessary to alter them. They are like the telescopes we use to focus the heliographs with which we send messages across the continent, but they are more powerful. With them we have watched one of your vessels as it travelled through the sky above us. We have also established the positions of the weapons I spoke of.'

A Sechem turned, and Suragai saw that it was Kobe. 'Lord, it is nearly time,' he said.

Jehan nodded. Then he looked at Kubulai. 'Give the alien officer his communicator.'

Kubulai produced the grey oblong which Constantin had surrendered. The offworlder took it hesitantly.

488

'The weapons platforms are in geostationary orbit around this world,' Alexei said in a conversational tone. 'One of them is a little to the south of our city of X'nadu.'

The Sechem were now busy with a machine which looked like two metal clamshells mounted on a frame. Suragai stared at it, remembering that he had seen something similar once on a vessel berthed in X'nadu harbour.

'Did you work it out?' Kubulai murmured at Suragai's side. 'We brought everything here inside the dragons.'

Jehan eyed the ambassador. 'I think you have been shown the jewel we call a sunstone,' he said.

Borocheff nodded slowly.

'In that case you know that a sunstone can be cut so that when light is directed into it, what comes out is a narrow beam which produces great heat.' Jehan nodded at the clamshells. 'This is not one of the machines we found, and it is similar to one we used before I became Kha-Khan to heat the boiler of our first steamship. Instead of one stone there are many. The cutting has been calculated so that the light which is reflected is very concentrated. This one is aimed at a particular place in the sky, but we are capable of designing others which will follow where a telescope is directed.'

The Sechem at the clamshells suddenly moved back. Suragai saw that Kobe was bending down to look into a machine which occupied a space near the parapet. When he straightened again, Kobe waved a hand. A young man wearing the robes of an acolyte touched something on the frame which held the clamshells, and they parted. A dazzling beam of red light shot across the sky. Suragai closed his eyes against the brilliance. When he opened them again the clamshells had been closed.

Constantin swore softly in Anglic. He spoke into his communicator. A voice answered. 'The orbital platforms,' Constantin said. 'I think you just lost one.'

There was a delay before the voice responded again. The pitch was much higher this time, and Suragai was unable to make out more than the odd word. Constantin was staring at Jehan. The communicator crackled angrily, and the offworlder lifted it and spoke a single word. 'Wait.'

The khans in the portico were rubbing their eyes. Suragai found that he could still see the red glare which had emerged from the mouth of the clamshell. He closed his eyes tight, then opened them again, trying to rid the retina of the afterimage.

'We can prove that it wasn't chance or an accident if you wish,' Alexei told Constantin cheerfully. 'One of the other platforms is due to pass south of Losan quite soon. If we heliograph them now, they will receive the message in time to shoot it down.'

The news that more than one machine existed seemed to register in Constantin's eyes. He directed a stare of enquiry in the ambassador's direction. Borocheff's face had gone grey. Wordlessly he shook his head.

Jehan said, 'Because you did not see technology, you thought we were primitive. What we have shown you here is only a small proportion of the defences we will range against you. These we moved in secret, fearing that we would be observed from the sky. Now I tell you that we will place machines like these in positions you will never suspect. From this day

490

forward we intend to watch the sky above our world. Approach us at your peril.'

'Approach us and we will destroy the poppy fields,' Alexei said.

Jehan nodded. 'Maybe we will destroy them anyway.'

It occurred to Suragai to wonder why Jehan had wanted the khans to be present. Then he realised that to deal with the aliens it had been necessary to ignore the Yasa. A khan who failed to speak out now would be seen to have condoned the action which had been taken.

The aliens looked stunned by what they had witnessed, and the ambassador was staring at Jehan as though he had just grown an extra head. After a time he licked his lips. 'Lord,' he appealed, 'surely trade can continue now that you have the means to deal with us without fear. I give you my word that no act of the Empire's will ever be directed against the Khanate. We will render hostages from our most prominent families; only sell us the poppy, we beg you. You cannot imagine what we are prepared to give you in return.'

On the other side of the ceremonial bowl the Sechem were dismantling the machinery, and men were carrying it away. Suragai guessed that it would be hidden – probably it would be out of Kinsai inside the hour, concealed in a cart or in a litter, because as soon as the aliens were released it would be vulnerable to attack.

And it will always be this way, Suragai thought. Yesterday the earth was our only concern. Now we must always look at the sky.

Suragai saw his grandfather going across to speak to

491

Kobe. Jehan glanced round, his attention drawn by the movement at his shoulder, and then he looked back at the ambassador. 'I think you take me for a fool,' he said coldly. 'You swore that you were honest once before. I cannot allow you to lie and lie and then, because you wish me to, believe what you say.' He motioned at the captain of the guard. 'Get them out of here.'

The men went, protesting. The woman stood until the older Suragai had turned, and then she addressed Jehan. 'Lord,' she said, 'I ask you to let me greet my husband.'

Jehan gestured dismissively. 'As you wish, lady.' He strode past her into the portico, and at once the khans and members of his court clustered around him, deafening him with their praise.

Kubulai drew Constantin away, and he was joined by Alexei and Burun. Suragai hesitated, and then glanced at Natalia. She had been silent the whole time, and looked subdued. He searched for something to say to her, but it was as if a wall had been raised between them. When she looked in his direction her eyes were empty of expression.

His grandfather came round the side of the dais on which the bowl was mounted. He saw Suragai, and waved to him. 'Noyon, come here. I want a witness,' he said.

The words did not make sense to Suragai at first. He glanced at the alien woman. Her features were frozen. After a moment she seemed to gather herself. She gave Suragai a single glance, then lifted the skirts of her gown with one hand and came past him so that he was behind her, looking at his grandfather.

'Well, husband,' she said. 'I am pleased to see you.'

'Am I still your husband?' The older Suragai looked amused. 'I would have thought they declared me dead long since.'

Nearly all the machines had been removed now. Two men struggled past, a box supported on a stretcher between them. The woman appeared to use the diversion as an excuse to collect her thoughts. Finally she looked up. 'I could have married again,' she said. 'I did not.'

'I did.'

'So I have been told. Your wives were pointed out to me. You married well.'

It was not intended as a compliment, Suragai realised. He shivered at something he heard in the woman's tone. The older Suragai laughed grimly. 'Stay here if it pleases you,' he said. 'According to the Yasa, I am responsible for your welfare.'

She did not appear to take the offer seriously. Her shoulders moved in a kind of shrug, and then she gestured one-handed. 'Or you could come back to Knossos,' she said. 'Much has changed while you have been away.'

'Oh?' The older Suragai wrinkled his nose. 'I think you are telling me that you are in your uncle's favour. I was never at ease around the court, if you remember.'

'And yet you are at ease here,' the woman said.

'That's different.'

Suragai edged to the side so that he could see the woman's face. She looked perplexed, and he guessed that she had not expected to be greeted so formally. 'You loved me once,' she said at last.

A corner of his grandfather's mouth twisted in a wry half-smile. 'So I did,' he said. 'Until you tried to have me killed.'

It was as if every other sound around them faded away. Suragai watched the woman's face, and saw the shock in her eyes. 'I?' She produced a breath of a laugh as she spoke.

'It was a long time before I worked it out,' the older Suragai said. 'My existence threatened no one. Then I realised that so long as I was alive you could not hope to move Alexei closer to the succession. You must have regretted marrying a commoner.'

'You gave me a son,' she answered remotely.

'And had I died as you intended, you would have been seen as the widow of a hero. How close would Alexei be to the throne now?'

'Close. You heard what Borocheff proposed.'

Alexei came quietly up at Suragai's side. He looked at his father. 'What is she offering you?' he asked.

'Nothing yet. I have been explaining to her why I don't trust her.'

'Oh.' Alexei laughed. 'I wouldn't trust her either, if she had tried to kill me.'

The woman went pale. 'This is nonsense,' she said desperately.

'Is it?' Alexei looked down his nose at her. 'Like my father, it took me years to work it out. You used your connection with House Andreeyev to achieve it. They put my father into an escape pod on the *Simonova* and shot him into space above this planet. It was only chance that he wasn't killed. I came after him, which probably no one anticipated, and we survived because the men who came to finish the job encountered a Yek patrol.'

Suragai was not sure why he was still listening. The need for his presence had long since evaporated, he was sure, but he felt as if he was glued to the spot. He had wondered before why his grandfather had avoided the woman. Now he saw the expressions on the faces of both men, and knew that they despised her.

The woman had managed a measure of poise until Alexei had spoken. Now her self-possession slipped. She stared at him. 'That would mean that I also tried to have you killed,' she said. 'You cannot think that.'

Alexei looked as if he was staring into the middle distance. Abruptly his head came up. 'I think probably it was a mistake,' he said. 'The men who made the attempt could not have known that you were employing them. I don't suppose it ever occurred to you that I might get in the way.'

It was hard for Suragai to understand why she did not simply walk away. Whatever her intent in approaching them, she could not fail to realise that they were united against her.

'What, no denials?' Alexei stared at her, and showed his teeth. 'You're not trying very hard to convince us.'

A flush appeared on the woman's cheeks. 'I always thought they had killed you,' she said in a low voice. 'Finding you alive…' She broke off, and her hand gestured.

'Finding me alive made you examine again the plans you had made to get me closer to the succession,' Alexei told her coldly. 'You could not know it, but it was living here that made me realise your intent. There was a man on this world once whose mother schemed to get him the throne.'

'Nogai,' Suragai said, and it was not until the word was out of his mouth that he knew that he had spoken aloud.

Alexei glanced around. 'That's right.'

Suragai saw that his grandfather was staring at the

woman as if he had never seen her before. 'Irina, I did love you once,' he said. 'And for that reason you are free to go. I don't know what you hoped to achieve by coming here. I suppose they told you that this world was barely civilised, and you thought it would be no great task to persuade us.'

Kubulai came round the side of the dais with Constantin at his side. The offworlder bowed to the woman. 'Exalted One, if you are ready, we ought to leave,' he said.

The woman glanced first at Alexei, and then at the man who had been her husband. Silently she nodded. When Constantin went past her she turned to follow him. All at once she stopped. 'Come with me,' she appealed to Alexei. 'You showed these people how to beat us. I don't believe they learned it by themselves. Come with me and help your own kind. There is nothing the Emperor would not give the man who brings Longivex in quantity to the Empire.'

An expression of infinite sadness came briefly onto Alexei's face, and after a moment he shook his head. 'These are my kind now,' he said.

When she had departed there was a moment when it seemed as if no one knew quite what to say next. Then the older Suragai slapped Alexei on the shoulder. 'Women's intrigues,' he said, and laughed bravely.

Alexei produced a reluctant smile, and then finally nodded. 'Yes,' he agreed. 'Women's intrigues.' They went off together towards the portico, and Kubulai followed them, holding Turakina by the hand.

Suragai stared past the ceremonial bowl at the sun. He felt dissatisfied by what had occurred, and recognised that it was the knowledge that the aliens were going unpunished for their crimes which he found offensive. When he looked round he saw that Natalia was still standing where he had left her. He met her eyes, and then said the first thing that came into his mind. 'What are you going to do now?'

The bell marking the end of the curfew rang out from the barracks tower on the far side of the concourse. The signal was picked up by the station on the wall, and then by the one beside the gate. The clamour was confused for a moment, and then the pealing resolved itself into a discernible pattern. Natalia looked down at her hands. 'I'm not sure,' she said, and then suddenly raised her head. 'It isn't the end of it, you know. If you think that, you are a fool.'

Someone on the other side of the dais laughed drily. Suragai peered around the bowl, and saw that Burun was sitting in the small shade under the parapet. 'Of course it isn't the end of it,' Burun said. 'One day we will grow tired of watching the sky – tired of waiting to be attacked – and then maybe we will decide that the earth is not enough, and venture out among the stars.' He stood up and walked round so that he was standing between them.

'Maybe the Empire will return before you are ready,' Natalia suggested. She stared at Burun. 'You are the Kha-Khan's grandfather.'

'That's right.' Burun grinned at her. 'And I am *his* great-grandfather.' He indicated Suragai. 'Are you going to stay?'

Natalia frowned. 'No one has asked me,' she said. 'If I do, then I want to be more than a wife and a mother.'

'Oh.' Burun chuckled. 'I think most women want that.'

Suragai watched the expression on Natalia's face.

When she looked at him he saw a return of the interest he had seen when he had courted her. 'Stay with us,' he said.

She examined him. 'Maybe,' she said.

Burun laughed softly. 'That means yes.'

Suragai went up to her and took her hand. He led her towards the portico, and then a thought struck him, and he stopped and looked back at Burun. 'What will we do if the aliens come before we are ready?'

'We'll think of something,' Burun said. The corner of his mouth twitched. 'Who knows what will happen next year? The sun might fall on us, or we might fall on the Empire.'

Suragai glanced quickly at Natalia, but the implications of the response did not appear to trouble her. Maybe she does not understand, he thought. Now that we rule the earth there is nothing left but the stars. Even if it is not in the Yasa, it is our destiny.

THE EARTH IS THE LORD'S

Book One of the Sunfall Trilogy

William James

Tarvaras – a barren, harsh land, scorched by an unforgiving sun. A land dominated by the Yek, a quarrelsome race, bred for war. And the Yek are about to wage war again, on the Alan, one of the few peoples not subject to their rule.

Admiral Rostov of the Imperial Navy, on a routine survey mission, suddenly finds himself marooned on this strange world, the prisoner of Burun Khan, one of the Yek warlords. Rostov quickly realizes that he has little choice: become a slave, or be trained as a soldier of the Yek and learn their language, laws and ways.

AN ORBIT BOOK

THE OTHER SIDE
OF HEAVEN

Book Two of the Sunfall Trilogy

William James

The great Kha-Khan is dead; his nominated successor,
the unstable seventeen-year-old Artai, awaits confirmation
of his elevation; and the court broods and plots in the
golden-roofed Yek capital.

Burun, the mighty warlord and power behind the Dragon
Throne, intrigues and plans on behalf of his grandson.
And Burun's spymaster, the offworlder known to the Yek
as Suragai, has plans for his son who he hopes will find a
way off Tarvaras, the planet on which they have both
been marooned.

The futures and destinies of the two young men become
entangled in a voyage of discovery to the unexplored
lands of the west, an expedition that could make or break
them both.

AN ORBIT BOOK

THE ENCYCLOPEDIA
OF SCIENCE FICTION

John Clute and *Peter Nicholls*

When the first edition of *The Encyclopedia of Science Fiction* was published in 1979, it was immediately hailed as a classic work of reference. Frank Herbert described it as 'the most valuable science fiction source book ever written' and Isaac Asimov said 'It will become the Bible for all science fiction fans.'

This new edition has taken years to prepare and is much more than a simple updating. The world of science fiction in the 1990s is much more complex than it was back in the late 1970s. The advent of game worlds, shared worlds, graphic novels, film and TV spin-offs, technothrillers, survivalist fiction, SF horror novels and fantasy novels with SF centres has necessitated a radical revision, and this has allowed the inclusion of related subjects, such as magic realism. Accordingly, the book has expanded dramatically in order to cope with the complexities and changes. It now contains well over 4,300 entries – a staggering 1,500 more than the original – and, at 1.3 million words, it is nearly half a million words longer than the first edition.

This is the indispensable reference work not only for every reader who loves, uses and wishes to know more about science fiction, but for every reader of imaginative fiction at the end of this century.

AN ORBIT BOOK

☐ The Earth is the Lord's	William James	£5.99
☐ The Other Side of Heaven	William James	£5.99
☐ The Encyclopedia of	John Clute and	
Science Fiction	Peter Nicholls	£45.00

Orbit now offers an exciting range of quality titles by both established and new authors. All of the books in this series are available from:

   Little, Brown and Company (UK) Limited,
   P.O. Box 11,
   Falmouth,
   Cornwall TR10 9EN.

Alternatively you may fax your order to the above address. Fax No. 0326 376423.

Payments can be made as follows: cheque, postal order (payable to Little, Brown and Company) or by credit cards, Visa/Access. Do not send cash or currency. UK customers and B.F.P.O. please allow £1.00 for postage and packing for the first book, plus 50p for the second book, plus 30p for each additional book up to a maximum charge of £3.00 (7 books plus).

Overseas customers including Ireland, please allow £2.00 for the first book plus £1.00 for the second book, plus 50p for each additional book.

NAME (Block Letters) ....

....

ADDRESS ....

....

....

☐ I enclose my remittance for _____

☐ I wish to pay by Access/Visa Card

Number ⬚⬚⬚⬚⬚⬚⬚⬚⬚⬚⬚⬚⬚⬚⬚⬚

Card Expiry Date ⬚⬚⬚⬚